THAT NIGHT
on the
BRIDGE

MARIYAM ZIKRUR REHMAN

"Only If I would have known,

Only If.... I would have known,

That I'll fall in love with you all over again,

Only to let you go,

One last time.

Only If I would have known...

Only If I would have known!"

BLUEROSE PUBLISHERS
India | U.K.

Copyright © Mariyam Zikrur Rehman 2024

All rights reserved by author. No part of this publication may be reproduced, stored in a retrieval system or transmitted in any form or by any means, electronic, mechanical, photocopying, recording or otherwise, without the prior permission of the author. Although every precaution has been taken to verify the accuracy of the information contained herein, the publisher assumes no responsibility for any errors or omissions. No liability is assumed for damages that may result from the use of information contained within.

BlueRose Publishers takes no responsibility for any damages, losses, or liabilities that may arise from the use or misuse of the information, products, or services provided in this publication.

For permissions requests or inquiries regarding this publication, please contact:

BLUEROSE PUBLISHERS
www.BlueRoseONE.com
info@bluerosepublishers.com
+91 8882 898 898
+4407342408967

ISBN: 978-93-6452-599-2

First Edition: October 2024

Love? It's a simple four-letter word, isn't it? Just four letters, that can mean everything and nothing at all. Love! Is it Dopamine and Oxytocin in our brain? Or perhaps something divine. Only if he would have known...... He wouldn't have fallen for her all over again, only to let her go.

CHAPTER 1

In the heart of an expansive jungle, where the trees stood tall like ancient sentinels, the night was coming alive with the primal sounds of wildlife. Frogs croaked rhythmically in the underbrush; their chorus occasionally punctuated by the distant roar of a jaguar. High above, the dense canopy rustled softly as a gentle breeze wove its way through the leaves, carrying the cool, moist air of the river nearby.

Nestled in a clearing beside this meandering river, a small campsite glowed warmly under the light of a robust bonfire. The flames danced and flickered, casting long shadows that mingled with the darkness of the surrounding forest. Here, three men—Juan, Rudi, and Malcom—sat on folding chairs, their faces illuminated by the firelight as they savored the peace of the wilderness after a taxing week.

Juan, a lieutenant in the local police force, let out a long, tired sigh, the weight of his responsibilities temporarily lifted by the serenity of their retreat. "Every time I think the week's going to be easy, it ends up being a marathon of cases and crises," he lamented, taking a sip of his beer.

Rudi, the local sheriff, laughed in agreement, his laughter echoing slightly in the open air. "Tell me about it. I've been running around so much, dealing with paperwork and budget meetings. I'm starting to forget what my own bed feels like."

Malcom, a seasoned SWAT officer, nodded sympathetically. "At least you guys aren't training newbies. Imagine trying to teach common sense to a bunch of eager beavers who think they know it all because they've watched a few action movies."

Their light-hearted grumbling was a familiar routine, a way to unwind as they shared the camaraderie that only those who serve in law enforcement could fully understand. But as the evening progressed and the sky turned a deeper shade of twilight, their casual conversation was abruptly cut short.

"Oi, look there's something in the water," Malcom interrupted, his tone shifting from amusement to concern as he stood abruptly, his chair clattering to the ground.

The others followed his gaze to the dark, rippling surface of the river, where something unusual caught their attention. Without hesitation, they slipped out of their seats and moved towards the water's edge.

"It looks like a body," Malcom said as they waded into the chilly water, the urgency of the moment propelling them forward.

"Let's not touch it; we might tamper with evidence," Juan cautioned, his professional instincts taking over. "Rudi, you see this?"

Rudi, ever the pragmatist despite his complaints, responded as he joined them in the river. "I swear, we can't even have a quiet weekend without stumbling into a scene from a crime thriller."

Looking around for the necessary tools to handle the situation properly, Juan asked, "Anyone bring gloves?"

"Do I look like I carry gloves everywhere?" Malcom shot back; his frustration evident in the sarcastic edge of his voice.

"I don't know— Maybe?" Juan muttered, deciding to at least turn the body toward them with utmost care. As he did so, the serene expression on the woman's face struck him profoundly, a stark contrast to their grim discovery.

"It's a woman, early twenties—" Malcom leaned close trying to assess the situation, when suddenly, the woman coughed, startling everyone.

"She's alive! She's alive!" Malcom exclaimed, a mix of relief and renewed urgency flooding his voice as the situation took an unexpected turn, transforming their quiet night by the river into an urgent rescue mission in the wild heart of the jungle.

The quiet of the forest was shattered by the urgency in Malcom's voice as he scrambled backward in the water, shock etched on his face. Juan's quick reflexes took over, and he waded into the river, his hands steadying the woman as she coughed, her body convulsing with the effort to expel the water from her lungs.

"She's alive!" Juan repeated, his voice a mix of relief and astonishment. He carefully cradled the woman, supporting her head as she struggled to breathe, her eyes fluttering open to reveal a disoriented gaze.

Rudi sprinted to the water's edge, his sheriff's training propelling him forward. "Get her to the shore, gently now," he instructed, his tone authoritative yet laced with concern.

Together, Juan and Malcom carried the woman out of the cold embrace of the river, laying her on the pebbled shore. Juan tilted her head to the side, helping clear her airway, while Rudi rummaged through their emergency supplies for a blanket.

As the woman's breathing steadied, Juan examined her for injuries, his hands working with professional precision. "No visible wounds, but she's hypothermic," he said, wrapping her in the blanket Rudi handed him.

Malcom, having regained his composure, knelt beside her, trying to offer some warmth with his own body heat. "Who are you?" he asked, but the woman could only shiver in response, her eyes filled with confusion and fear.

Rudi had already dialed emergency services, his voice calm as he relayed their location and the situation. "Hang on, help is on the way," he reassured her, his hand finding hers, offering a silent promise of safety.

Juan watched her, a protective instinct flaring within him. "We've got you," he murmured. "You're safe now."

Her eyes locked with Juan's for a moment, and something unspoken passed between them—a gratitude, a recognition that, even in her weakened state, she was being cared for.

I curled in chest of someone who had brown eyes and tousled hair, I don't know why it felt calm...but it was not the only thing I didn't knew, I didn't know anything, anything at all.

The flickering flames of the campfire cast a warm glow over the scene, contrasting starkly with the chill that had settled over the riverbank. The woman, still wrapped tightly in the blanket, seemed to find solace in the heat radiating from the nearby fire, her body gradually ceasing its violent shivering.

Juan, sitting close to her, watched over her with a mixture of concern and curiosity. His law enforcement instincts mingled with a personal concern that was unusual for him—he was typically the one to maintain a professional distance. But something about this woman's vulnerable state tugged at his heartstrings.

Malcom and Rudi stood a few steps away, speaking in hushed tones. "We need to find out who she is, but first, she needs a hospital," Rudi said, his voice low but firm.

"Yeah, but look at her, man. She's out of it. Scared, probably doesn't even know where she is," Malcom replied, casting a worried glance back at the woman.

Juan overheard and nodded. "Let's keep her warm and calm until the paramedics arrive. Can you guys set up a bit more of a windbreak with the tarps? It might help."

Rudi immediately set to work, directing Malcom to help him. They maneuvered their camping gear to create a makeshift shelter around the woman, enhancing the protection provided by the fire's warmth.

Meanwhile, Juan gently tried to communicate with her, his voice soft and reassuring. "You're safe here with us. Help is on the way, okay? Can you tell me your name?"

The woman blinked slowly, her eyes meeting Juan's again. She opened her mouth, hesitated, and then spoke with a voice so faint it was barely above a whisper. "I... I don't remember."

"It's okay, you're probably in shock. What's the last thing you remember?" Juan continued, trying to keep her engaged.

Her brow furrowed as she strained to think, her gaze drifting to the flames. "Water... cold, dark water," she murmured, shuddering at the memory.

Juan placed a reassuring hand on her shoulder. "You don't need to try too hard. It will come back when you're ready."

By the time the emergency services arrived, led by the beam of flashlights cutting through the dark, the woman was more alert but still visibly confused. The paramedics, with practiced efficiency, assessed her condition, praising the makeshift camp setup.

"We'll take it from here, gentlemen," one of the paramedics, a woman with a kind face, said as they prepared to transport the woman to the hospital. "You did good keeping her stable."

As they loaded her onto the stretcher, Juan felt an inexplicable reluctance to let her go. He handed her into the care of the paramedics, his hand lingering in hers for a moment longer than necessary. "You'll be alright," he reassured her, trying to imprint a sense of safety in her unsettled mind.

"Thank you," she whispered, her grip tightening briefly around his fingers.

As the ambulance drove away, the three men stood in silence, watching the red lights fade into the night. The suddenness of the ordeal left them with a lingering unease, the night's tranquility shattered by the reminder of how quickly fate could turn.

Malcom broke the silence first. "That was wild, huh? Think she'll be, okay?"

Rudi nodded; his eyes still fixed on the path the ambulance had taken. "She's tough, made it through whatever happened to her. But man, what a night."

Juan remained quiet, his thoughts with the mysterious woman. He couldn't shake the feeling that there was more to her story, something that might eventually come back to involve them again. He resolved to follow up at the hospital later, to ensure she was indeed alright and maybe help unravel the mystery of her identity.

The trio resettled by the campfire, the warmth of the flames doing little to dispel the chill that had settled in their bones. Conversation turned to lighter topics, an attempt to restore some normalcy, but their glances to the dark river were frequent, each man lost in his thoughts about the stranger who had briefly entered their lives and the tumultuous events of the night.

Unbeknownst to them, their actions that night had set in motion a chain of events that would entwine their destinies more closely with the mysterious woman's than they could have imagined. As the stars twinkled overhead, silent witnesses to the unfolding drama, the quiet of the forest seemed to promise more secrets waiting to be uncovered, carried on the whispering winds that rustled through the trees.

"Let's follow her to the hospital," Juan said, his decision met with nods from Malcom and Rudi.

They gathered their belongings quickly, extinguishing the fire and packing up their camp with a newfound urgency.

Driving behind the ambulance, the silent understanding among them was clear—they were involved now, linked to the mysterious woman's fate by their actions this night. Each man was lost in his thoughts, pondering the strange twist their weekend getaway had taken.

At the hospital, they waited in the emergency room lobby, the fluorescent lights casting a sterile glow over their anxious faces. When a doctor finally approached them, they stood in unison, eager for any news.

"She's stable, but we're keeping her overnight for observation," the doctor explained. "She appears to be suffering from hypothermia and some minor injuries from being in the water. We're also evaluating her for amnesia."

"Can we see her?" Juan asked, the protective instinct still strong.

"Briefly, yes. But let her rest; she's been through a traumatic event," the doctor cautioned, leading them to her room.

Inside, the woman lay on the hospital bed, her expression one of deep contemplation as she stared at the ceiling. Her eyes turned towards the door as Juan, Malcom, and Rudi entered, a faint smile touching her lips.

"Hi," she said quietly, her voice still frail but filled with a warmth that seemed to light up the sterile room.

"Hey," Juan replied, stepping forward. "How are you feeling?"

"Confused," she admitted, "but warmer."

They chuckled softly, easing the tension in the room. Each man introduced himself properly, giving her not just their names but reassurances of their continued support.

As they talked, the woman's gaze lingered on Juan, something unspoken yet profound passing between them—a connection, perhaps, or a prelude to a deeper understanding that would unfold in time.

As the night deepened, a tranquil silence enveloped the hospital, cradling its occupants in a quiet embrace. Within these walls, under the soft hum of fluorescent lights, a new bond was being woven—born of circumstance and nurtured by the innate human need to care and be cared for. For the woman with no memory, the faces that now surrounded her bed began to pierce the darkness that had smothered her life, offering faint glimmers of light in her obscure world.

Doctor Mustafa entered the room with a quiet efficiency, his presence immediately soothing. He smiled gently at the woman as he approached, his eyes quickly scanning the monitors by her bedside to check her vitals. "How are you feeling tonight?" he inquired, his voice soft yet clear.

After adjusting the flow of the IV drip, he took a moment to assess her responsiveness before diving into deeper questions. "I know this might be difficult, but do you remember anything? Perhaps a family member, a friend, or any familiar faces?"

The woman shook her head initially, her expression clouded with confusion and frustration. Yet, at the mention of a 'friend,' something flickered in her eyes. She nodded hesitantly, murmuring, "Friend," with a hint of certainty.

"Good, very good," Doctor Mustafa encouraged, his tone lifting with hope. "Can you tell me who your friend is?"

She seemed puzzled for a moment, then lifted her hand slowly and pointed. The doctor's gaze followed her gesture, landing on Juan who was standing by her side. Juan looked over his shoulder, checking behind him before turning back to the group, his expression a mix of confusion and surprise.

"What?" Malcom inquired, glancing between Juan and the woman.

"He's not your friend, my dear, we just met tonight," Doctor Mustafa gently corrected, but the woman persisted, pointing at Juan again, more deliberately this time.

Juan's eyebrows arched in surprise, and a tentative smile crept across his face as he met her gaze. "Um, I think there might be some confusion," Juan responded softly, his voice warm yet filled with uncertainty. "We just met tonight, after my friends and I found you by the river."

The room fell silent for a moment, the weight of the woman's confusion and the mysterious bond she felt towards Juan hanging in the air. Doctor Mustafa nodded understandingly, preparing to delve deeper into this unexpected clue, while everyone else exchanged curious glances, wondering how deep the currents of memory might run for their mysterious new acquaintance.

The woman looked confused for a moment, her brow furrowing as she tried to piece together her fragmented memories. "I... I'm sorry, I don't know why I thought..." Her voice trailed off, and she looked genuinely distressed at her mistake.

"It's okay," Juan reassured her, his voice soothing. "It's completely understandable given what you've been through. Maybe I just remind you of someone else?"

Dr. Mustafa, observing the interaction, nodded thoughtfully. "It's not uncommon for patients with traumatic amnesia to misplace memories or transfer familiar feelings onto new faces. It's a part of the brain trying to make sense of what it can't fully remember."

Rudi leaned in slightly, trying to lighten the mood. "Looks like you made quite the impression, Juan."

Juan gave a half-smile, but his concern was palpable. He turned back to the woman. "Regardless of memory, we're all here to help you. You're not alone in this."

The woman nodded, a slight flush of embarrassment coloring her cheeks. "Thank you," she murmured, her gaze lingering on Juan a moment longer before shifting to include all three men.

As the hushed conversation around her identity continued, the room's door opened once more, admitting two detectives who carried with them the air of urgency typical of their profession. They nodded to Doctor Mustafa and approached the bedside with a palpable sense of purpose. One of them, a tall woman with sharp features, held a small evidence bag in her hands.

"Good evening," she began, her voice firm yet not unkind. "We have a couple of items that were found with you. We're hoping they might help jog your memory."

She carefully placed two necklaces on the small tray beside the bed. The first was a simple chain with a pendant spelling out 'Rehman' in delicate, curling script. The second was more ornate, featuring a beautifully cut emerald set in a drop pendant, which shimmered under the fluorescent lighting.

"These were in your possession when you were found," the second detective, a stocky man with a gentle demeanor, explained. He watched her face intently for any sign of recognition. "Do you remember anything about these items?"

The woman reached out slowly, her fingers trembling as they touched the 'Rehman' pendant first. She held it gently, turning it over in her hands, but her expression remained puzzled, distant. Then her hand moved to the emerald necklace, and her fingers clenched around it instinctively, as if recognizing its importance.

"Does this mean something to you?" Doctor Mustafa asked softly, observing her reaction closely.

She nodded slowly, her eyes locked on the emerald pendant, but her voice was still uncertain. "Friend," she repeated, the word slipping out as though she was testing it, trying to connect it with the images flooding her mind.

Juan stepped closer; his curiosity piqued. "Do you remember who gave them to you? Or where you got them?"

Her gaze shifted from the necklace to Juan, and then to the detectives and back to the doctor. She shook her head, frustration wrinkling her brow. "No... just... friend."

The detectives exchanged a glance, their expressions a mixture of frustration and empathy. "We'll need to take these back for further analysis," the female detective said, repackaging the necklaces with careful hands. "But rest assured, we're doing everything we can to uncover your identity and understand what happened."

Doctor Mustafa nodded; his eyes thoughtful. "It's all right," he reassured her. "You're safe here, and these might just be the key to unlocking your past. We'll take it one step at a time."

As the detectives and the doctor continued to discuss the next steps, the woman lay back against her pillows, the word 'friend' echoing in her mind like a beacon, guiding her through the fog of her forgotten life. With each passing moment, the faces around her not only represented her present safety but also potential links to a past that was just beginning to reveal itself.

After a few minutes, Dr. Mustafa suggested it was time for her to rest. "We'll continue our assessments in the morning," he explained. "It's important to let your body and mind recover."

Eventually, her eyelids began to droop, fatigue pulling at her despite the adrenaline of the night's events and the warmth of the new company. Juan noticed and suggested, "Maybe you should try to get some sleep. We'll be here when you wake up."

"Would you stay? At least until I fall asleep?" she asked, a slight tremble in her voice that hinted at the fear of being alone with her fragmented thoughts.

Juan nodded, pulling up a chair closer to the bed. "Of course, I'll stay right here."

Malcom and Rudi decided to step out to give her some space, whispering their goodnights and promising to check in early the next morning.

As the woman drifted off to sleep, her last conscious thought was of the reassuring presence of her newfound friend by her side, a sentinel in the unknown landscape of her life. Juan watched her, the rhythmic rise and fall of her breathing a silent music in the quiet room. He pondered the strange twist of fate that had brought them together, a twist that felt increasingly like the beginning of something unexpected and profound.

As the night deepened and the hospital's fluorescent lights hummed softly in the background, Juan remained seated by the woman's bedside, his thoughts wandering. He watched her sleep, her features relaxed, the earlier tension eased by slumber. Every now and then, he glanced at the machines monitoring her vitals, reassured by the steady beeps that indicated her condition was stable.

Outside, the hospital was quiet, the usual nighttime activities muted, as if the world were holding its breath. Juan's mind replayed the evening's events—the unexpected rescue, the woman's fragile state, and her inexplicable recognition of him. He couldn't shake the feeling that this was the beginning of something significant, a pivotal moment not just in her life but in his as well.

His reverie was interrupted when a nurse entered quietly to check on the patient. She offered Juan a warm smile. "You're staying late," she observed, making a note on the chart.

"Yeah, she asked me to stay until she fell asleep," Juan explained, his voice low. "She seemed pretty shaken up."

"That's kind of you. Amnesia cases can be tough. They sometimes hold on to new people like lifelines," the nurse said, adjusting the IV drip slightly. "You're doing a good thing here."

Juan nodded, unsure of what to say. The idea of being someone's lifeline was more than he had bargained for when he decided to follow the ambulance to the hospital. Yet, there he was, drawn into the mystery and humanity of this woman's plight.

After the nurse left, the room settled back into silence. Juan's eyes occasionally drifted to the woman's face, searching for signs of distress or discomfort in her sleep.

Seeing none, he allowed himself a moment to relax, leaning back in the uncomfortable hospital chair.

His thoughts drifted to his friends, Malcom and Rudi, and their initial reluctance about getting involved. They had quickly come around, their inherent goodness overriding any hesitation. Now, here they were, embroiled in a stranger's crisis, their weekend plans turned upside down.

As dawn approached, the first hints of light began to filter through the hospital window, casting a soft glow across the room. The woman stirred slightly, her eyes fluttering open. She looked confused for a moment, then her gaze focused on Juan, and her expression softened.

"Did you stay all night?" she asked, her voice husky from sleep.

Juan smiled gently. "I did. You asked me to stay, remember?"

A blush crept up her cheeks as she nodded. "I remember. Thank you," she said, shifting slightly in the bed. "I... I still don't remember much else, though. It's all just bits and pieces."

"That's okay," Juan reassured her. "It might take some time. The important thing is you're safe now."

She nodded, looking around the room as if seeing it for the first time in the light of day. "What happens now?" she asked, a trace of vulnerability in her question.

"Now, we wait for the doctors and detectives to do their job and make sure you're okay," Juan answered. "And I'll be here if you need anything."

Her eyes met his, gratitude evident in her gaze. "I don't even know your name," she realized aloud.

"It's Juan," he reintroduced himself with a friendly nod. "Juan Heinrich Ramirez."

"Juan," she repeated, as if testing the name on her lips. "Thank you, Juan, for everything."

As they talked, the door opened slightly, and Malcom peeked in, his expression brightening when he saw she was awake. "Hey, looks like our patient is up. How are you feeling?"

"Better, thank you," she replied, managing a small smile.

Rudi followed, carrying a tray with coffee and some pastries. "We figured everyone could use a good breakfast after last night," he said, setting the tray down on a small table.

The normalcy of the gesture, the simple kindness, seemed to comfort her. The room filled with a new energy, a gentle camaraderie as they all took a moment to enjoy the simple breakfast together.

As they ate, the woman's eyes kept returning to Juan, a silent acknowledgment of his steadfast presence through the night. Something unspoken but profoundly felt was forming between them, a bond forged by circumstance but rooted in something deeper.

The dimly lit room hummed with a soft tension, gently eased by the playful banter between the group gathered around the hospital bed. The red-haired man caught the woman's inquiring gaze and met it with his own, his blue eyes shimmering under the fluorescent lights like ocean waves.

"What is your name?" she asked, her voice tinged with the strain of her own uncertainty.

"Rudi, Rudolf Liam Merci," he introduced himself with a flourish, then pointed at the man next to him. "And this is Malcom Grump," he joked, sparking a chuckle from the woman.

Malcom sent Rudi a playful glare for the presidential quip. "Ignore him, he's got a strange sense of humor. I'm actually

Malcom Wyatt," he said, extending a hand, which the woman shook with a tentative smile.

"It's nice to meet you all, really. I just wish it were under better circumstances," she sighed, her voice tinged with a mix of amusement and melancholy. "I don't even know my own name."

"We can fix that," Juan chimed in, picking up a pastry from a nearby tray. "You already have a surname from your locket, Rehman, right?"

"So, Rehman it is," Rudi added, his voice light.

"Ummm—Juanita Rehman," Malcom proposed with a mischievous grin, causing the woman to burst into laughter.

"Rudolfi!" Rudi shot back playfully.

"Let's settle down—Grace suits you, Miss Grace Rehman," Juan suggested, a gentle smile playing on his lips as Rudi looked on, eyebrows raised, surprised at Juan's earnestness.

"Grace is a bit common, though," Rudi mused, tapping his chin. "She looks spirited. What about something with a twist?"

"Graxe then, Graxe with her X factor, even in amnesia," Juan said, his smile broadening, warmth radiating from him like the cozy glow of a hearth.

"I still like Juanita," Malcom interjected, earning a roll of the eyes from Juan.

"Rudolfi! Are you all nuts? Rudolfi Rehman," Rudi exclaimed with dramatic flair, only for Malcom to playfully slap his cheek, turning his head to the side. Rudi quickly snapped back, his expression a mix of amusement and mock indignation.

"Juanita!" Malcom insisted, narrowing his eyes in feigned seriousness.

Amid the lighthearted discussion and the volley of suggested names, the woman—now affectionately dubbed Graxe—couldn't suppress a laugh, a sound that felt surprisingly light and genuine given her circumstances. Her laughter seemed to dispel some of the lingering tension surrounding her mysterious condition.

"Graxe, then," she declared, still chuckling. "It's unique, I'll give you that."

Juan nodded, pleased with the consensus. "Graxe it is. But only until you remember your real name, or we find out what it truly is."

The room settled into a comfortable rhythm as they conversed, each man contributing in his own way to make Graxe feel at ease. Malcom leaned back, relaxed yet attentive, while Rudi's humor kept the mood buoyant. Juan, though, appeared more contemplative, often gazing thoughtfully at Graxe, as if trying to decipher the enigma she presented.

A knock at the door interrupted their makeshift breakfast gathering. A nurse stepped in first, followed by a doctor carrying a clipboard. The doctor, a woman with kind eyes behind thin-framed glasses, surveyed the room with a smile as she noticed the lively group gathered around the bed. "Good morning," she greeted, her voice warm. "I see our patient is in good spirits. How are we feeling this morning, Miss Rehman?"

"Better, thank you," Graxe replied, though the name still felt like an ill-fitting coat, unfamiliar and strange on her lips.

The doctor nodded, flipping through the pages on her clipboard. "Well, I have some good news regarding your condition. Your tests have come back clear, and physically, you're making a good recovery. The hypothermia is no longer a concern, and your minor injuries are healing well. However," she continued, her tone shifting slightly, "the head trauma is something we need to keep an eye on. The concussion you sustained, specifically at the occipital lobe at the back of your head, appears to have caused some retrograde amnesia."

Graxe's expression faltered at the mention of her memory loss, a reminder of the vast gaps in her mind and the mystery surrounding her own identity. She touched the bandage at the back of her head, feeling the tenderness beneath it. Sensing her unease, Juan gave her hand a gentle, reassuring squeeze.

The doctor noticed the interaction and softened her tone. "The injury has led to some swelling in the brain, which has likely impacted your ability to recall past events. In many cases of traumatic brain injury like yours, the memory loss can be temporary, but we'll need to monitor your recovery closely. We'll arrange for a neuropsychologist to speak with you; sometimes, engaging in cognitive therapy or discussing familiar experiences can help trigger lost memories."

"Thank you, Doctor," Graxe said, managing a small smile despite the lingering anxiety etched on her face.

The doctor smiled back, offering a bit of optimism. "We're here to support you every step of the way. If you feel any dizziness, headaches, or if anything comes to mind, please let us know immediately. And remember, patience is key. The brain is a remarkable thing; sometimes it just needs a bit of time."

With a final nod, the doctor and nurse left the room, promising to check in later. The atmosphere shifted slightly, the reality of Graxe's condition settling in among them.

Rudi stretched, pushing his chair back as he stood. "Well, I guess it's about time we head out and let you get some more rest. We'll be around, though, if you need anything," he assured her, his usual playful demeanor replaced with a genuine concern.

She nodded, the warmth of his words seeping into her bones, giving her a small spark of hope in the midst of the fog clouding her mind. However, a sudden pang of loneliness at the thought of them leaving tugged at her heart.

"Thank you, for everything. I don't know what I would have done if you hadn't found me."

"It was nothing," Malcom said, waving off her gratitude. "Just being at the right place at the right time."

"But we mean it," Juan added. "If you need anything, we're just a call away."

After saying their goodbyes, Juan, Rudi, and Malcom left the hospital, each man quiet as they walked to their car, lost in their thoughts about the unexpected turn their weekend had taken.

Back in her hospital room, Graxe reclined against her pillows, the quiet feeling almost oppressive after the warmth and chatter of her visitors. She turned her head towards the window, staring at the sky, a patchwork of clouds against a stretch of blue, hinting at a day of change. In the days that followed, Graxe's routine settled into a steady rhythm—doctors' visits, therapy sessions, and endless hours of gazing out the window, lost in the blur of her thoughts. The amnesia felt like an impenetrable wall, each attempt to remember her past hitting that barrier and crumbling into frustration.

A week after her rescue, Juan returned for another visit. He found her sitting up in bed, a small stack of books balanced on her lap, courtesy of the hospital staff who hoped to keep her mind occupied.

"Hey, Graxe," Juan greeted her, a warm smile lighting up his face as he saw her expression brighten slightly.

"Juan," she replied, her voice carrying a genuine note of happiness. "I didn't expect to see you again so soon."

Juan pulled up a chair beside her bed and settled in. "I wanted to check on you, see how you're doing. Any new memories coming back?"

Graxe shook her head, a hint of frustration crossing her face. "Nothing yet. It's like there's a fog in my mind that just won't lift."

"Give it time," Juan said gently. "These things can take a while. But I brought you something that might help."

He handed her a small journal and a pen. "Try writing down whatever comes to mind, even if it doesn't make sense. Sometimes getting it out on paper can help clear the fog."

Graxe accepted the journal, a small glimmer of hope appearing in her eyes. "Thank you, Juan. I'll try anything at this point."

As they talked, Juan noticed subtle changes in her demeanor—she was more confident now, yet still wrapped in the uncertainty of her situation. There was a vulnerability to her that made him want to protect her, to help her piece together the fragments of her life.

After a few moments of comfortable silence, Graxe's expression grew more serious. "Juan, have there been any updates about the case? About who I am?" she asked, her voice tinged with both anticipation and anxiety. "I'm supposed to be discharged soon, and I feel like I'm still stuck in the dark."

Juan's face softened with empathy, and he leaned forward slightly. "The detectives are still investigating. They've been looking into the two pendants you were found with—the one with 'Rehman' inscribed on it and the emerald pendant. They're trying to trace them back to see if they lead to anyone who knows you."

Graxe's hand instinctively moved to her throat, where the pendants had been when she was found. "And? Did they find anything?"

Juan hesitated for a moment. "Well, they haven't found much about the 'Rehman' pendant yet—it seems to be a common design, nothing unique that stands out. But the emerald pendant... it's a bit more distinctive. It's quite old, possibly an heirloom. They're checking with local jewelers and even looking into missing persons reports that might mention it."

Graxe frowned, absorbing the information. "So, there's still no concrete lead on who I might be?"

"Not yet," Juan admitted. "But don't lose hope. Sometimes, these things take time. And now that you're being discharged, maybe getting out of this sterile environment will help trigger something."

Graxe's gaze drifted back to the window, her voice soft with uncertainty as she asked, "But... where will I go? What is home for me now?" She stared out at the patchwork sky, a mixture of clouds and blue that seemed to mirror the confusion swirling within her.

"Listen, Graxe," Juan began, his voice soft but deliberate, pausing as he carefully chose his next words. "When you leave here, you don't have to do it alone. My friends and I, we talked about it, and if you need a place to stay while you figure things out..." He hesitated, searching her face for a sign. "I have a home. I live alone, and there are plenty of spare rooms."

Graxe looked up, surprise and a touch of gratitude crossing her features. "You'd do that for me?" she asked, her voice almost incredulous.

"Of course," Juan replied without hesitation, his eyes steady and sincere. "We're in this together now. Whatever comes, you've got us."

The weight of his offer settled between them, solid and real—a symbol of the unexpected bond that was forming, born from a chance encounter on the banks of a river and growing into something deeper. For a moment, the room seemed to brighten as Graxe's lips curved into a genuine smile—the first true smile Juan had seen from her since they met. It was small but radiant, lighting up her face and filling the room with a newfound warmth.

"Thank you, Juan," she said, her voice steady and heartfelt. "For the journal, for the offer... for just being here."

Juan nodded, his smile matching hers, a quiet understanding passing between them. "Always," he murmured.

Outside, life continued with its usual rhythms, oblivious to the fragile but meaningful connections being forged within the quiet walls of a hospital room. But inside, something had shifted—something small yet profound. Graxe opened the journal Juan had given her and let the pen hover over the first blank page. Then, she began to write, each word a tentative step towards unearthing the fragments of her forgotten past and shaping a future that, while still shrouded in uncertainty, seemed a little less daunting now. She wasn't alone in this journey; she had found kindness, and perhaps, in time, she would find herself too.

And so, with the ink flowing across the page, a new chapter of her life began—one filled with questions and the hope of answers, but also with the comfort of new friendships and the promise of starting over.

As Graxe continued to write, the room around her seemed to fade away, replaced by the blank canvas of her thoughts. The pen felt awkward in her hand at first, the words coming slow and unsure. But as she let herself relax, she began to jot down anything that came to mind—a stray thought, a flicker of an image, a feeling she couldn't quite place. It was a strange kind of freedom, pouring out her confusion and fear onto the empty pages, giving them a form she could see and touch.

Meanwhile, Juan watched her from his chair, his heart swelling with quiet admiration. Here was someone who had lost everything—her past, her identity, her sense of who she was—yet she was still pushing forward, trying to reclaim something of herself from the shadows of her own mind. It was a strength he didn't often see, and it stirred something deep within him.

"What are you writing?" He smiled softly, leaning over her should to check, the scribbles, then smiled, realizing, it was its random scribbling, but a beautiful poem. A poem that echoed her silence..., a hauntingly beautiful silence... she felt inside.

"To the skies I stared and questions I asked,

Why me? Why I am so different and apart?

From the world's image of normal that fits,

Why I am different from them every bit.

I stared at stars, urging them to reveal,

Why was it so difficult to be me?"

"You have a gift, Graxe." Juan spoke softly, rubbing her back, as both stared at the blue ink, sharing a moment of serene silence passing between them.

After a while, Graxe looked up, her eyes meeting his. "It feels strange," she admitted, her voice soft. "Writing down things that don't make sense, not exactly ... but also comforting, in a way. Like maybe if I keep writing, I'll find a thread that leads somewhere."

Juan nodded, his smile encouraging. "That's the idea. Sometimes, it's the small things that bring us back. A word, a smell, a feeling. You never know what might trigger a memory."

Graxe glanced down at the journal again, turning a blank page over with a gentle, deliberate motion. "I want to remember," she said quietly. "Even if it's painful. Even if it's confusing. I want to know who I am."

"You will," Juan assured her, his voice filled with quiet confidence. "We'll help you. And until then, you've got a place with me."

There was a knock on the door, and a nurse appeared, her face bright with a professional smile. "Sorry to interrupt," she said softly, "but it's time to finalize your discharge papers, Miss Rehman. I'll need a few signatures, and then you'll be free to go."

Graxe nodded, setting the journal aside. She felt a mix of anticipation and nervousness bubbling up inside her. She had been waiting for this moment—a chance to step out into the world again—but now that it was here, it felt a bit overwhelming. The unknown stretched before her like an endless horizon, both daunting and full of possibilities.

Juan stood and placed a reassuring hand on her shoulder. "We'll take it one step at a time, okay? No pressure. Just one day at a time."

She took a deep breath and nodded. "One day at a time," she echoed, her voice steadier now.

After signing the necessary forms and receiving final instructions from the nurse, Graxe was officially discharged. As she stood up from the bed, she felt a strange sense of liberation mixed with fear. She clutched the journal close to her chest like a talisman.

Juan led her through the sterile corridors of the hospital, out into the fresh air of the parking lot. The sun was setting, casting long, golden rays that bathed the world in a soft, warm glow. Graxe took a deep breath, feeling the crisp air fill her lungs. It was like tasting freedom for the first time.

"Ready?" Juan asked as he opened the passenger door of his car.

She looked at him, and for the first time since waking up with no memory, she felt something other than fear or confusion. She felt... hope. "Ready," she said, sliding into the seat.

As they drove away from the hospital, Graxe looked out the window at the world passing by—a world she was a stranger to yet also a part of. She watched the buildings and trees blur into one another, her thoughts quiet, her heart beating a little faster with each mile. She didn't know where this journey would take her or who she would find herself to be at the end of it. But she knew she wasn't alone. She had Juan, she had her newfound friends, and most importantly, she had herself—a blank slate, a new beginning.

The drive was quiet, filled with the hum of the engine and the sound of the world rushing by. Graxe watched the landscape change from the urban grid of the city to the open stretches of country roads lined with tall trees, their leaves whispering secrets in the wind. She clutched the journal in her lap, her fingers tracing the edges as if it were her lifeline to a past she couldn't remember and a future she was just beginning to shape.

As they turned onto a long, private road flanked by tall, ancient oaks, Juan glanced at her from the driver's seat, a gentle smile tugging at his lips. "We're almost there."

Graxe nodded, her heart beginning to pound in her chest. She hadn't thought much about where Juan lived, but she was about to find out.

The car finally emerged from the thick tree line, and she saw it: Ramirez Mansion. It was breathtaking, with a semi-circular driveway paved with smooth pebbles that crunched under the tires as they pulled up. In the center of the driveway, a large stone fountain bubbled softly, a testament to old-world charm against the backdrop of a more modern design.

The mansion itself was an imposing structure of European architecture, its white stone facade stretching upward with tall windows and a grand double door framed by intricate carvings. Ivy climbed up the walls, adding a touch of nature to the stately home. The golden light of the setting sun bathed the mansion in a warm glow, reflecting off the glass and casting long shadows that danced across the driveway. Nearby, a lazy river meandered gently through the estate, its waters catching the last rays of daylight.

Juan parked the car and turned to her, his expression soft and reassuring. "Welcome to Ramirez Mansion, Graxe. This is home—at least, for as long as you need it to be."

Graxe's breath caught in her throat as she stepped out of the car, her eyes wide with wonder. "This... this is where you live?"

Juan chuckled; a bit sheepish. "Yeah, I know it looks a bit much, but it's just me here most of the time. Plenty of space, and, like I said, plenty of spare rooms."

As they walked towards the grand entrance, Graxe took in every detail—the manicured gardens, the sound of water trickling from the fountain, the scent of freshly cut grass mixing with the crisp evening air. She felt a sense of calm settling over her, a contrast to the sterile environment of the hospital. Here, it felt like there was room to breathe, room to think.

Juan opened the heavy double doors, revealing a spacious foyer with high ceilings and a sweeping staircase that curved gracefully to the second floor. The interior was a blend of classic European elegance and modern design—crystal chandeliers hanging above polished marble floors, sleek furnishings set against walls adorned with tasteful artwork.

Graxe stepped inside, her footsteps echoing softly in the vastness of the space. She couldn't help but marvel at the beauty of it all, the way the light filtered through large windows and bathed the room in a golden hue. "It's... incredible," she whispered, feeling a mix of awe and disbelief.

Juan smiled, pleased that she seemed to like it. "Come on, I'll show you to your room. You can settle in, and later we can have dinner. No pressure. Just take your time to get comfortable."

He led her up the staircase, their steps echoing in unison. As they reached the second floor, he guided her down a long corridor, passing by rooms with tall wooden doors until he stopped at one near the end. "Here we are," he said, opening the door to reveal a spacious bedroom with a large window overlooking the grounds, including a view of the lazy river winding through the estate.

The room was cozy yet elegant, with a king-sized bed draped in soft linens, a writing desk tucked into a corner, and a reading nook by the window. Sunlight poured in, casting warm patterns on the floor, making it feel welcoming and serene.

Graxe stepped inside, her eyes sweeping over the room. She turned back to Juan, her voice filled with quiet gratitude. "Thank you, Juan. For everything. I don't know what I'd do without you."

Juan's smile was genuine, his eyes meeting hers with a sincerity that touched her deeply. "You don't have to thank me, Graxe. We're in this together. And who knows? Maybe this place will help you find some answers—or at least give you a bit of peace."

She nodded, a sense of calm washing over her. "Maybe it will," she said softly. She watched as Juan closed the door gently behind him, leaving her to explore her new surroundings.

For a moment, Graxe stood still, taking in the quiet of the room. She set the journal down on the desk, running her fingers over its cover. She walked over to the window and looked out, watching the sky deepen from gold to a soft purple, the first stars beginning to appear.

This was the beginning of something new. A new chapter, filled with uncertainty but also with possibility. As she stood there, the breeze from the open window caressed her face, and for the first time in what felt like forever, she felt a spark of hope.

The road ahead was unknown, filled with questions and the shadows of a past she couldn't yet grasp. But it was her road to walk, and she wasn't walking it alone. With a deep breath, Graxe turned back to the room, ready to face whatever came next.

The chapter of her life at the hospital had closed. Here, in the warmth and safety of Ramirez Mansion, a new one had begun. And somewhere in the spaces between memory and forgetting, between the past and the present, Graxe would find her way—one day, one step, at a time.

CHAPTER 2

On the crisp night of July, I stood Inside the grand halls of the Ramirez mansion, the aroma of simmering tomatoes and fresh basil filled the air, mingling with the faint scent of old wood and polished marble. The kitchen was alive with the bubbling sounds of a pot on the stove, the rhythmic chop of a knife on a cutting board, and the quiet hum of a life built on unexpected beginnings. Warm sunlight streamed through the tall, arched windows, casting long, golden shadows that danced across the tiled floor.

Eight months had passed, since I was discovered in the river, and life was finally piecing back together. I stood at the stove, stirring a pot of rich tomato sauce, the recipe I had nearly perfected with Juan's playful assistance over the past few months. The scent of garlic and herbs mingled in the air, bringing a sense of warmth and comfort that wrapped around me like a favorite blanket. I called out, "Jui!" and almost immediately, Juan sauntered in with that effortless grace he always carried, a playful smile tugging at his lips. He slid his arms around my waist from behind, pressing a quick kiss to my temple.

"What are we cooking today, Amor?" he asked, the familiar cadence of his voice tinged with the lazy chew of gum.

I tilted my head up at him, feigning irritation. "Bhot marungi, how many times have I told you not to chew gum? What if it gets stuck in my hair?" I puffed my cheeks out in mock annoyance, and he chuckled, his laughter a deep, rumbling sound that always made my heart skip a beat.

"Drama," he murmured, leaning in to kiss my cheek, and I shot him a mock glare.

"You're feeling brave today, aren't you, Lt?" I teased, watching as he rolled his eyes, then reached for a napkin to spit out the gum.

"Anything else, Señora?" he asked, his voice low as he brushed a kiss along my nape, sending a shiver down my spine. I turned in his arms, tapping his nose playfully.

"How about you do the dishes today?" I suggested with a pout and my best attempt at puppy eyes. "Terra is on leave—Mr. Amnesiac."

Juan chuckled, his eyes sparkling with mischief. "Ah, trying to put me to work, huh? Is that how you treat your personal hero?" His tone was light, teasing, and I couldn't help but laugh, playfully pushing him away.

"Hero or not, you're not getting out of chores, especially when Terra's away. Even heroes do dishes," I declared, turning back to the stove to give the sauce one last stir.

With a dramatic sigh, Juan pulled up his sleeves, stepping up to the sink. "Alright, alright, you win, Señora. But only because I can't resist those puppy eyes."

We fell into an easy rhythm, moving around the kitchen in a dance we'd come to know well. The past eight months had been a journey of discovery—not just of this place or of Juan, but of myself. A place where I had once been a stranger now felt like home.

Dinner was a simple affair—spaghetti tangled in a sauce we'd both come to perfect through a mix of trial, error, and a lot of laughter. As we set the table together, the setting sun bathed the dining room in a warm, golden glow. I watched the way the light played across Juan's face, highlighting the warmth in his eyes as he looked at me.

"So, how was your day at the precinct, Lt. Ramirez?" I asked, twirling the pasta onto my fork, my gaze fixed on his.

His face lit up as he began to recount his day—the challenges, the small victories, and the camaraderie of his role as a lieutenant in the NYPD. I listened intently, fascinated by the passion in his voice, the way his eyes sparkled with every story he shared.

When the meal was done, Juan kept his word and began clearing the table, loading the dishwasher with a determination that made me smile. I leaned against the counter, watching him, feeling a sense of peace settle over me.

"You know," I began softly, my voice barely above a whisper, "I never thought I'd find myself in this place—not just here in this mansion, but here with you, feeling like I belong."

Juan paused, turning to face me. His expression softened, and he crossed the room to take my hands in his. "Graxe, from the moment we found you, there was something about you that felt...right. Like you were meant to be here with us. And every day since has only made me more certain of that."

His words wrapped around my heart, and I leaned into him, resting my head against his chest. The steady beat of his heart beneath my cheek was a comforting rhythm. "I may not remember my past, but I'm so grateful for my present, for you, and for this new life," I said, my voice thick with emotion.

Juan hugged me closer, his embrace a protective cocoon. "And I'm grateful for you, every day. No matter what the future holds, we'll face it together."

I smiled, pulling back just enough to look up at him. "Okay, Mr. Ramirez, enough. We have dishes to wash and a kitchen to clean," I teased, playfully smacking his chest.

He grinned, a mischievous glint in his eyes as he leaned in, his voice dropping to a low whisper. "You're boring, Mrs. Ramirez. I was thinking about..."

Before I could respond, he turned me in his arms, pressing me against the counter. I felt his arousal against my thigh, and I bit my lower lip, my breath hitching at the intensity in his eyes.

His gaze darkened with desire, his voice a husky whisper against my ear. "I was thinking about how we could spend the rest of the evening."

A shiver ran down my spine, his words igniting a familiar warmth within me. I pushed him back slightly, giving him a teasing look. "Are you suggesting we skip the cleaning for now?"

Juan's laugh was low and seductive. "Well, I am the lieutenant here. I think I can make some executive decisions."

His hands found my waist, pulling me flush against him, his body heat radiating through the thin fabric of my dress. His scent—an intoxicating mix of cologne and the freshness of the outdoors—filled my senses, making my head spin. The reminder of our solitude only heightened the tension between us, the air thick with unspoken desire. His lips found mine, the kiss deep and full of promise, as if he were pouring all his emotions into that one moment. His hands roamed my back, pulling me impossibly closer.

When he finally broke the kiss, his gaze held mine, intense and full of intent. "Let's take this somewhere more comfortable," he suggested, his voice a mix of command and longing.

Without waiting for my response, he scooped me up in his arms, carrying me out of the kitchen. I laughed, a light, free sound that echoed through the halls, my arms wrapping around his neck. The dishes and half-cleaned counters were quickly forgotten, insignificant compared to the desire that simmered between us.

He carried me through the mansion's quiet corridors, each step taking us further away from the routines of the day and deeper into our private world. When we reached the master bedroom, he gently set me down, his hands never leaving my body.

The room was dimly lit, the last rays of the sun casting long, shadowy fingers across the floor. Juan's hands cupped my face, his touch tender. "I love you, Graxe," he whispered, the sincerity in his voice wrapping around me like a warm embrace.

"I love you too, Juan," I replied, my heart swelling with emotion. He leaned in to kiss me again, this time slower, softer—a contrast to the fiery passion of moments before.

As we undressed each other, the discarded clothes seemed to symbolize shedding the layers of the outside world, leaving only the raw truth of our connection. Our kisses became more urgent, our touches more insistent, each one an affirmation of the bond we shared.

The bed welcomed us, the cool sheets a stark contrast to the heat between us. Juan's touch was both familiar and electrifying, each caress stoking the flames of desire that had ignited the moment we met. Our bodies moved together in a dance that felt timeless, each kiss, each touch, a reaffirmation of our love and the life we were building together.

Later, lying in Juan's arms, I felt a profound sense of peace I hadn't known in so long. His steady heartbeat beneath my ear was a comforting rhythm, a reminder that in this vast, unpredictable world, we had found each other.

As the night stretched on, Juan and I lay tangled together, our breaths gradually slowing to a peaceful rhythm. The warmth of his body against mine was a reassuring anchor, pulling me deeper into a sense of belonging I had almost forgotten existed. Here, in this quiet sanctuary, the world outside seemed distant, irrelevant—a mere whisper compared to the symphony of our entwined heartbeats.

I closed my eyes, savoring the tranquility. Yet, somewhere in the back of my mind, a lingering thought refused to settle. It was as if a thread connected this moment of contentment to something unfinished, a past not entirely forgotten but not fully remembered either.

Juan's arms around me tightened slightly, as if sensing my fleeting unease. "What's on your mind, Amor?" he murmured, his lips brushing my hair.

I hesitated, unsure how to express the vague, unshaped worry that danced on the edge of my consciousness. "Nothing," I whispered back, deciding to let the peace of the moment wash over me. "Just...thinking about how grateful I am for this, for us."

He kissed the top of my head, his breath warm and steady. "Me too, Graxe. Me too."

Unbeknownst to up. In a different mansion, thousands of miles away. A room was bathed in the cold blue glow of a computer screen and there sat a man, a man who was on the verge of breakdown. James Cross was still searching. His eyes, shadowed with exhaustion, scanned page after page, his heart heavy with the weight of loss. For him, the world had narrowed down to a single purpose—a relentless quest for closure, for answers, for Mariyam. No matter how far the world moved on, for James, the search was an unending loop, a mission he couldn't—and wouldn't—abandon.

"Why would she jump?" He had asked himself a thousand time, yet no justified answer ever came out of him. His brain already knew what his heart was failing to accept. His wife... was gone. Yet, here he sat, slumped, in his chair. Hoping, pleading to anyone (living or dead), that would listen.

"Please... please... Come back to me, Mariyam! Please come back to me." He closed his eyes shut, tears streaming down his face, as his shoulders shook with suppressed sobs.

---.

Inside our mansion, the night air was thick with the scent of jasmine, wafting up from the garden below. Inside the mansion, nestled under the soft glow of moonlight streaming through the bedroom window, I snuggled closer to Juan's chest, tracing lazy patterns on his skin with my fingertips.

"Do your parents still hate me?" I asked softly, my voice a mix of curiosity and lingering insecurity.

Juan's chest rumbled with a low chuckle. "Who cares? They're stupid. You married me, not them," he said, his tone casual yet dismissive. I swatted his chest lightly.

"I care," I insisted, my lips forming a small pout. "And stupid, huh? How would you feel if our son came home with a woman he found on a riverbank—no past, no name, no religion?"

I continued drawing little circles on his chest, my fingers dancing over his skin. Juan caught my hand and brought it to his lips, planting a soft kiss on my knuckles. "I'd feel very proud," he murmured, pulling me closer and nibbling on my lips playfully.

I rolled my eyes, a smile tugging at my lips. "Proud? Really?"

"Absolutely," he replied, his tone filled with teasing sincerity. "And just so you know, my sister Anayeli's daughter, Tabitha, thinks you're a mermaid because of some tv show she watched— 'Folclore Del Oceano.' I think it was called." His laughter was rich and deep, vibrating through his chest.

"Tabitha? That little munchkin? She's not even six!" I burst into laughter, the image of her wide-eyed, imaginative face coming to mind.

"Oh, she's convinced," Juan continued, his grin widening. "She's plotting to push you into the pool someday for the grand reveal."

I shook my head, still laughing. "And what do you say, Mr. Ramirez? Should we give her a show? A grand reveal?" I gestured towards the balcony, a silent invitation to take a dive into the pool below.

Juan's eyes twinkled with mischief as he looked at me. "If we're lucky, she's already spying from her window," he said with a grin.

Without another word, he scooped me up in his arms, his playful energy infectious. "Then let's not disappoint our little detective, shall we?" he teased, carrying me toward the balcony. The night was warm, and a gentle breeze brushed against our skin, carrying the floral scent from the garden below. Above us, the moon hung like a delicate crescent, its silver light painting the mansion and pool in a serene glow.

As we stepped onto the balcony, I could see the pool shimmering below, the surface reflecting the moonlight like liquid silver. Juan set me down at the railing, and we both leaned over, scanning for any sign of our tiny spy.

And there she was—Tabitha, with her little face pressed against a window across the courtyard. Her eyes were wide with excitement, caught in the thrill of her secret operation. When she saw us looking back, she ducked down, only to pop up again with a sheepish grin and a tiny wave.

Juan laughed, his hands framing my face gently. "Ready for your grand reveal, my beautiful mermaid?"

I nodded, feeling a rush of excitement bubble up inside me. "Let's make it a show to remember."

Juan took my hand, and on a shared breath, we both leapt from the balcony. The air rushed around us, and then we were plunging into the cool, welcoming embrace of the water below. The pool enveloped us, and for a moment, everything was a blur of bubbles and movement before we resurfaced, laughing and gasping for air.

Above us, we heard Tabitha's delighted squeals echo across the courtyard. "I knew it! I knew it!" she shouted, her little hands clapping together in glee.

Juan and I swam to the edge of the pool, our faces animated with mock surprise. "You caught us, Tabitha! Whatever shall we do now?" Juan called up; his voice filled with mock concern.

Tabitha bounced with excitement, her small frame practically vibrating. "You have to show me your mermaid tricks now!" she demanded; her voice high-pitched with anticipation.

"Only if you promise to keep our secret," I replied, playing along, my own laughter bubbling up. Juan pulled me out of the pool, grabbing a towel and wrapping it around my shoulders. He kissed the top of my head, his voice dropping to a whisper. "You make even the silliest moments magical, my love."

We continued our playful act, diving back into the water and flipping our 'fins' like mermaids, drawing more of Tabitha's delighted laughter. The night air was filled with her giggles. "I promise! I promise!" she cried, nodding vigorously, her eyes wide with wonder. "But you're a mermaid, and mermaids are supposed to sing! Could you sing for me?" Her voice was eager, brimming with the innocence and admiration unique to her young age. I sighed and glanced over at Juan, who couldn't help but smile.

"Well, Tabby, I'm not your typical mermaid," I explained softly, drawing her in close. "I can hum a poem for you instead!" I offered, and she nodded, her eyes wide with excitement.

"To be or not to be,

To see or not to see…"

I started, but soon enough, Anayeli, Juan's sister, appeared on the patio, her expression a mix of amusement and exasperation, cutting our fun short.

"What on earth are you two up to now?" she asked, hands on her hips, but there was a smile tugging at her lips.

"We're just showing Tabitha some mermaid tricks!" Juan said, his voice full of innocent cheer.

Anayeli shook her head, laughing softly. "Only you two could turn a simple swim into an evening spectacle." She looked up at her daughter. "Come on, Tabitha, let's leave the mermaids to their swim. It's way past your bedtime."

"But, Mom!" Tabitha whined; her face scrunched in protest.

"Tomorrow, you can help me make breakfast for our guest mermaid. How about that?" Anayeli offered; her tone gentle but firm.

Tabitha's face lit up with the promise of more mermaid adventures. "Okay, Mom!" she agreed, giving us one last wave before she followed her mother inside.

Juan and I exchanged a look, a shared smile of pure contentment. "Well, Mrs. Ramirez," he said, wrapping his arms around me again, "looks like we've got a breakfast date with our biggest fan."

I laughed, leaning into him, feeling the warmth of his body against mine. "I wouldn't miss it for the world."

The night continued to wrap around us like a comforting blanket, the stars twinkling above, as we enjoyed the simple joy of just being together.

Once they were gone, Juan and I lingered in the pool, floating on our backs and staring up at the stars. The water was soothing, and the serenity of the night wrapped around us like a soft blanket.

"You know," Juan started, his voice thoughtful, "when I think about how we met, how all of this came to be... it feels like destiny."

I turned to look at him, moved by his words. "It does, doesn't it? A strange, wonderful destiny."

He swam closer, wrapping his arms around me. "Graxe, with every day that passes, I'm more and more grateful for that night by the river. You've brought so much light into my life."

"And you've given me a home, a family," I replied, my voice thick with emotion. "I couldn't ask for more."

We kissed, a gentle, lingering connection that spoke volumes more than words ever could. As we eventually climbed out of the pool and headed back into the mansion, hand in hand, the future seemed bright with endless possibilities. Whatever challenges might come, whatever mysteries lay unsolved in my past, I knew I faced them not alone, but with Juan by my side, my partner in every sense.

Back inside, as we dried off and changed, the comfort of our shared life enveloped me like the plush towels we wrapped ourselves in. The laughter, the love, the shared moments of joy and silliness—it all wove together into a tapestry of a life I never expected but now couldn't imagine being without.

As we settled into bed, the quiet of the night settling around us, Juan pulled me close, his warmth a tangible promise of his presence. I reached over to the bedside table to turn off the lamp, but my hand stilled as my eyes fell on our wedding picture in its delicate silver frame. I picked it up, holding it close as memories from that day flooded back, vivid and bittersweet. The joy of that moment was unforgettable, but it hadn't come without its share of shadows.

I remembered that day so clearly, the day Juan's parents visited unexpectedly. It had been only a few months after he found me by the river, and our relationship was still finding its footing. I was in the kitchen, my hair a mess, wearing one of Juan's oversized shirts as I tried to make sense of a new recipe I had found. I peeked out cautiously, wiping my hands on a dishcloth. There they stood—his father, tall and stern, his face etched with disapproval, and his mother, her lips pursed into a thin line as she scanned the entryway. Juan greeted them warmly, but I could sense the tension immediately. It was as if the air had thickened with unspoken words and disapproval.

They had not come to visit before. I could tell by the way their eyes moved around the place, taking in every detail, that they were measuring it against the idea they had of their son's life. They saw me then, standing in the doorway of the kitchen, and the room went quiet. His mother's eyes narrowed slightly, and I felt exposed, like I was intruding in a place I didn't belong.

Juan came down the stairs, his face lighting up with a smile that faltered just a little when he saw the tension in the air.

"Mom, Dad," he said, stepping forward to hug them, "this is Graxe."

She didn't say anything to me, just turned to Juan and said, "We need to talk. Now."

Juan glanced at me, his expression caught between frustration and apology. He nodded and led them into the sitting room, the door closing softly behind them. I didn't mean to eavesdrop, but their voices carried, filled with tension and something almost hostile.

"Juan, this is ridiculous," his mother's voice came, low and simmering. "How can you let this...woman stay here? You found her on the riverbank with no memory, no background. You know nothing about her!"

My heart clenched, and I pressed my back against the wall, trying to steady my breath. I knew his parents were wary of me, but hearing it out loud like this still cut deep.

"She could be dangerous," his father added, his voice low but firm. "How do you even know she is who she says she is? You found her by a river, for God's sake! And now you want to keep her here? For how long will she burden you, Juan? Until it's too late for you to make a proper life for yourself?"

"She's not a burden, Papá," Juan replied, his voice steady but strained. "Graxe has become part of my life—our life. She's not some charity case; she's, my partner. I love her."

His mother's voice was sharp, cutting through the air like a knife. "Love? You're thinking with your heart, not your head. We came here to talk to you about your future—your real future. We've been speaking to the Martinez family, and their daughter—"

Juan cut her off, his tone rising with frustration. "Stop. If you're here to talk about arranging a marriage for me, I'm not interested. I've chosen who I want."

I felt a pang in my chest, a mix of fear and sadness, as I realized what this was really about. They wanted me gone, out of their son's life. They saw me as an obstacle to his future, a burden that he needed to shed. I bit my lip, fighting back tears, my heart breaking in ways I hadn't expected.

I didn't wait to hear more. I turned and rushed back to our room, my mind racing. Maybe they were right. Maybe I was a burden to him, a complication he didn't need. What if he was better off without me? I glanced around the room that had become my sanctuary, my safe haven, and I felt a sudden urge to leave before I could cause him any more trouble.

My hands were trembling as I pulled out a small suitcase and began packing my clothes, tears blurring my vision. I could hear my own heartbeat thundering in my ears, a painful rhythm that matched the breaking of my heart. I had to make this easier for him, to let him be free of this weight. I could leave, disappear, just like I had appeared that night by the river.

I was zipping up my suitcase when I heard the door to our room creak open. I turned to see Juan standing there, his face a mixture of confusion, anger, and something else—hurt.

"Graxe, what are you doing?" His voice was tight, like he was holding back a storm of emotions.

I tried to keep my voice steady, but it came out choked. "I heard them, Juan. I heard everything. They think I'm a burden. They want me gone. And maybe they're right. I don't want to make things harder for you. I should leave—"

Before I could finish, he crossed the room in two quick strides and grabbed my shoulders, his grip firm but gentle. "No," he said fiercely. "No, you don't get to decide that for me. They don't get to decide that for me. I don't care what they think. I choose you, Graxe. I choose us."

Tears spilled over my cheeks, and I shook my head. "But Juan, they're your family. I don't want to come between you—"

"They're my family, yes," he interrupted, his eyes blazing with determination, "but you're my family too. The moment I pulled you from that river, I knew there was something special about you. I don't care about your past or what anyone thinks. You're here with me, and that's what matters."

I looked up at him, my vision blurry with tears, but his face was clear, his expression resolute. "You're my home, Graxe. Wherever you are, that's where I want to be."

His words washed over me, warm and unwavering, and I felt something inside me break free. The suitcase slipped from my hands as I collapsed into his arms, sobbing against his chest. He held me tightly, his hands stroking my hair, whispering reassurances over and over.

"We'll face it together, always," he murmured, his voice steady. "I promise."

From that day on, I never doubted his love, his commitment. Our wedding came soon after, and though his parents never fully accepted me, they came to tolerate our union, if only for Juan's sake. But as I looked at our picture now, nestled safely in its frame, I realized how far we'd come since that day.

I set the picture back down, a soft smile tugging at my lips. I turned to switch off the lamp and snuggled back into Juan's warmth. Whatever challenges lay ahead, whatever shadows still lingered from my past, I knew one thing for certain—our love was stronger than any fear, any doubt. And that was more than enough.

"What are you smiling about?" Juan murmured, his voice low and soft in the dark room.

"Nothing," I replied, shaking my head as I snuggled closer into the warmth of his embrace. The feel of his arms around me, the steady beat of his heart against my ear—it all felt like a reaffirmation of the promises we'd made to each other. But his question had pulled me from my reverie, stirring a memory that was both frantic and filled with a surprising amount of joy. "Just wondering how you managed to organize the priest, decorations, rings, chapel, and whatever guests we had in what, 60 minutes that day?"

Juan chuckled, the sound vibrating through his chest. "Ah, that was quite the operation, wasn't it? Rudi and Malcolm were a big part of it. They might be tough guys on the outside, but they have a knack for pulling off the impossible when it matters."

Juan laughed, a deep rumble that I felt against my cheek where it rested on his chest. "Hey, sometimes you have to take charge, right? Besides, I saw the look in your eyes. You were ready to leap, and I was right there with you."

I pulled back slightly, lifting my head to look at him, my grin widening. "Are you sure you're Mexican and not some Bollywood hero? Because the way you took my hand and walked us right out of that mansion, right in front of your parents, was straight out of a movie. And wait a minute! You didn't even propose, and I didn't even accept. So, you just assumed I'd marry you?" I chuckled, my laughter bubbling up from deep within.

Juan's eyes sparkled with amusement. "What can I say? I'm a man of action." He smirked, his fingers brushing a stray lock of hair behind my ear. "Besides, I figured if I got you out of there fast enough, you wouldn't have time to say no."

I laughed harder, playfully smacking his chest. "So that's what that was! A tactical maneuver?"

"Exactly," he replied, grinning. "I've learned from the best action movies—act first, ask questions later."

Shaking my head, I snuggled back against him. "You're unbelievable, you know that?"

"Maybe," he whispered, his voice taking on a softer, more tender tone, "but I knew what I wanted, Graxe. I wasn't about to let you slip away just because some people couldn't see what I saw. I knew right then and there that I wanted to marry you, with or without anyone's blessing."

I felt my heart swell at his words, a familiar warmth spreading through my chest. "You've always been brave like that," I said softly. "I didn't even know how much I needed that kind of courage until you came into my life."

He smiled, pressing a gentle kiss to my forehead. "I guess we make a pretty good team, then. Your strength, my impulsiveness. It's a good balance."

"Oh, so now I'm the strong one?" I teased, raising an eyebrow. "A few minutes ago, you were the hero."

"We can be each other's heroes," he said, his tone more serious now. "We already are."

The sincerity in his words made me fall silent for a moment, my fingers tracing the lines of his jaw. "Do you remember how you looked at me when we got to the chapel?" I asked, my voice a soft whisper in the dark.

He nodded, his eyes softening as he recalled the moment. "I looked at you like I was seeing my future. Because I was."

I smiled, feeling a tear slip down my cheek. "And I looked at you like I was finally finding my way home."

He brushed the tear away with his thumb, his touch gentle and comforting. "Because you were."

We lay there in the quiet for a moment, the weight of everything we'd been through together settling around us like a warm, protective blanket. The past, with all its trials and tribulations, felt distant now—just stepping stones that had led us to this point.

"You know," I said after a while, my voice filled with a mix of amusement and nostalgia, "there was a moment, right before the priest asked if anyone had any objections, when I half expected your parents to burst in and drag us both out of there."

Juan chuckled softly. "Rudi and Malcolm were on lookout duty. I think they were prepared to barricade the doors if necessary."

"Always the strategist, huh?" I laughed, imagining the two of them playing bouncers at our wedding. "You really thought of everything."

"For you? Always." He grinned, pulling me closer.

As I nestled deeper into his embrace, I realized that this was all I had ever wanted—a love that was bold and unwavering, a partner who saw me for exactly who I was and still chose me every single day. And in that moment, with the night wrapped around us and Juan's heartbeat steady under my ear, I knew we could face whatever the future held.

"Goodnight, my not-so-Mexican, almost-Bollywood hero," I whispered, a smile on my lips.

"Goodnight, my brave, beautiful Graxe," he murmured back. "I love you."

"I love you too," I replied, feeling the truth of it in every fiber of my being.

And with that, I closed my eyes, knowing that no matter what challenges lay ahead, we would face them together, side by side—just like we always had.

The morning light streamed through the kitchen window, casting a warm, golden glow across the room. The smell of sizzling bacon filled the air, mingling with the fresh, citrusy scent of oranges I had just squeezed. I stood at the stove, my movements precise and familiar, as I carefully flipped the eggs in the pan, making sure the yolks stayed intact. The quiet hum of the refrigerator and the occasional clatter of a pan were the only sounds, blending harmoniously with the soft morning stillness.

Outside, the day was coming alive. I could hear the distant chatter of birds and the low rumble of a car passing by. The sunlight slowly crept across the wooden floor, bringing a sense of peace to the moment. I placed the eggs on a plate, added crisp slices of bacon, a few pieces of freshly cut avocado, and poured a tall glass of orange juice. With the breakfast tray in hand, I turned and walked toward the dining table, each step deliberates, enjoying the calmness of the morning.

As I set the tray down in front of Juan, who was already seated at the table, he looked up from his newspaper and smiled, his eyes warm with affection. "Gracias, Mrs. Ramirez," he said softly, his voice thick with that melodic accent I had come to adore.

"My pleasure, Mr. Ramirez," I replied with a smile of my own. His lips curled into a grin, and he leaned forward, gently taking my hand and placing a soft kiss on my knuckles. His touch was warm, and I felt a small flutter in my chest, a familiar comfort in his gesture.

"Mi Esposa, te amo," he murmured, his thumb brushing over my hand as he spoke. His face broke into a mischievous smile as he pinched my cheek playfully.

I rolled my eyes at his antics, but the amusement tugged at my lips. "Te amo más, mi esposo. Te amo mucho," I countered, leaning into his playful mood. He narrowed his eyes, a spark of delight dancing in them.

"Huh—someone's picking up my Spanish, huh?" he teased, his grin widening.

I shook my head with a chuckle. "Yo no hablas español. Yo hablo inglés, Señor, Mucho gusto," I said, my attempt at Spanish making his laughter ring out across the kitchen. His laughter was deep and infectious, filling the room with warmth as he pulled me closer, his hands steady on my waist.

Before I could protest, he pressed his lips against mine, and we kissed, deep and unrestrained. His lips were soft but demanding, and before I knew it, he passed a small bite of his egg from his mouth to mine. For others, it might seem morbid, but for us, it was an intimate and playful routine—a daily ritual that felt oddly comforting.

"You know, that's how mama birds feed their babies," I chuckled, chewing on the bite he'd given me.

Juan's chest puffed with pride; his eyes alight with mischief. "I am your mama bird, my chick," he joked, his tone laden with double meaning, and we both burst into laughter again.

Once breakfast was finished, Juan stood up, holding his tie in his hand, looking at me with a sheepish smile. I shook my head, amused by this familiar scene. "Seriously, Lt. Ramirez," I teased, "do your colleagues know that the formidable 29-year-old lieutenant doesn't know how to tie his own tie?"

He shrugged, a playful grin on his face, as he bent down slightly so I could reach him. I tiptoed to match his height, smoothing his collar and tightening the knot of his tie. My hands moved to polish his medals, adjust his holster, and smooth his shirt. With a final pat on his chest and a quick fix of his hair, I placed his cap on his head, completing the look.

"You look handsome," I said softly, and Juan's cheeks flushed pink, his blush making him even more endearing. He pulled me in for another kiss, and this time, we shared a piece of gum between us.

"Amor, do you know James Cross?" Juan asked suddenly, his tone casual.

I blinked, caught off guard by the name. I shook my head slowly. "What? I don't know him. Who is he?"

Juan's mouth dropped open, his expression one of mock horror. "Mi amor, mi Vida—the James Cross! The famous hero!" He waved his hands dramatically, exaggerating his disbelief.

I laughed, smacking his arm lightly. "Okay, okay, who is he then?"

"He's an actor, and he has a premiere today. Guess who's in charge of the security detail?" He waggled his eyebrows, his grin stretching from ear to ear.

"You?" I guessed, already knowing the answer.

He nodded enthusiastically. "Yes! At Times Square, from six till ten-thirty. Me, Rudi, Malcom, Linda—Diaz, we're all on duty. Do you want to come? You can get autographs and pictures! I can pick you up at five," he suggested, his eyes sparkling with excitement.

I wrinkled my nose, genuinely confused. "Why? I don't even know him. Is he famous?"

Juan paused, a look of disbelief flashing across his face before he erupted into laughter. "Graxe, he's not just famous; he's one of the biggest movie stars in the world! 'Beyond' is a massive action movie series, and he does most of his own stunts. It's kind of a big deal."

His enthusiasm was infectious, and though I was still trying to grasp the significance, a small spark of curiosity ignited in me. "Okay, it does sound like a once-in-a-lifetime experience. I'll come."

"Perfect!" Juan clapped his hands together, his delight evident. "It'll be fun. Plus, it might trigger some memories, or at least give you new ones to cherish."

The day passed quickly, filled with the soft hum of the city outside and the soothing rhythm of my brush as I painted. It was a hobby I had taken up to fill my days, a way to quiet my mind. Yet, as I painted, my thoughts kept drifting to the evening ahead—the crowds, the flashing cameras, and the promise of something unfamiliar. It was daunting, but Juan's excitement was enough to pull me in.

By five, I had dressed carefully, choosing a simple but elegant dress that Juan had helped me pick out. When he arrived to pick me up, his eyes lit up with a mix of love, admiration, and something deeper that I couldn't quite place.

"You look stunning, amor," he said, spinning me around gently, his smile wide and approving.

"Thank you, mi amor," I replied, feeling a flutter of nerves mixed with excitement. Then, hesitating slightly, I added, "However, can we take a 30-minute stop at Dr. Mustafa's? I completely forgot about my appointment until the last minute." I pleaded, looking up at Juan with a hopeful expression.

Juan sighed, his enthusiasm dimming just a little. "You're still going to those appointments? It's almost a year now, amor," he said gently, his tone filled with a mix of concern and frustration.

I looked down, my fingers absently playing with the pendant around my neck—the one with "Rehman" engraved in delicate cursive. It was a small, tangible link to the life I couldn't remember. "I want to know who I am," I confessed softly, my voice barely above a whisper. "It's not that I'm not happy here, I love you, but... Who was I before you found me in that river, Jui? What is my real name? Do I have a mom? A dad? What do they look like? Do I have siblings? A brother or a sister?"

Juan's face softened, his dark eyes reflecting the conflict he felt. He reached out, cupping my cheek gently, his thumb stroking the skin just below my eye. "Graxe," he began, his voice tender yet firm, "I understand your need to know, I do. But sometimes the past is best left where it is—in the past. You have a new life now, a new family. I'm your family."

I leaned into his touch, closing my eyes briefly. His warmth, his presence—it was my anchor, my safe haven amidst the storm of uncertainty that sometimes raged inside me. But that storm never truly settled. I wanted answers. I needed them, like oxygen.

Opening my eyes, I met his gaze, my resolve evident. "I know you are, Jui. And I'm grateful. You saved me when I had nothing—when I was no one. But this isn't about leaving behind what we have. It's about understanding where I come from so I can fully embrace where I am now." My voice trembled with emotion, each word laced with a mixture of desperation and hope.

He sighed deeply, the frustration in his eyes giving way to reluctant acceptance. "Alright, thirty minutes, but no more," he relented, giving a small nod. "We don't want to be late to see this so-called James Cross, do we?" His attempt to lighten the mood brought a weak smile to my lips.

"Thank you, Juan," I whispered, squeezing his hand gratefully.

The drive to Dr. Mustafa's office was a quiet one. The bustling noise of New York City surrounded us, but inside the car, there was only the soft hum of the engine and the unspoken words hanging in the air. I glanced over at Juan from time to time, his jaw set in a hard line, his knuckles tight on the steering wheel. I knew he hated these appointments, hated what they represented—a past I couldn't remember and a life that he felt was slipping away every time I reached for it.

Dr. Mustafa's office was tucked away in a quiet building off a less busy street, a contrast to the frenetic energy outside. We walked in, and I immediately felt the familiar wave of calm wash over me. The room was warm, filled with soft lighting and the scent of lavender. Dr. Mustafa, a kind-eyed man in his late forties, stood up from his desk as we entered.

"Graxe, it's good to see you," he greeted warmly, his gaze shifting briefly to Juan, who gave a curt nod in response. "And Lieutenant Ramirez, always a pleasure."

"Likewise," Juan replied, his tone polite but strained.

I sat down on the familiar couch, the leather creaking slightly beneath me. Juan settled beside me, his hand on my knee, his thumb rubbing small circles in an effort to calm his nerves—or perhaps mine.

Dr. Mustafa took his seat across from us, his expression neutral but attentive. "How have you been feeling, Graxe?"

I took a deep breath, my fingers once again fiddling with the pendant around my neck. "Restless," I admitted. "There's still so much I don't know, and it feels like every time I get close to a memory, it slips away."

Dr. Mustafa nodded, his expression understanding. "That's often how the mind protects itself. But sometimes, confronting those barriers is the only way through." He leaned back, his eyes studying me carefully. "Any new memories, dreams, or thoughts that stand out?"

I hesitated, glancing at Juan, who gave a small nod of encouragement. "There's been... a name. A name that keeps coming back to me in bits and pieces. I don't know if it's mine or someone else's, but it feels important. 'Rehman,'" I said, the word tasting foreign and yet strangely familiar on my tongue. "It's engraved on this pendant," I added, touching the necklace around my neck.

Dr. Mustafa leaned forward slightly, his eyes narrowing thoughtfully. "And when do you see or hear this name? In dreams, or just during the day?"

"Both," I replied. "It's like a whisper, sometimes in my own voice, sometimes in another's. I see flashes of... a boy. Maybe two. But it's always hazy, like looking through frosted glass."

Juan shifted beside me, his grip on my knee tightening slightly. "Is there any way to find out what this name means, doctor?" he asked, his voice carefully measured.

Dr. Mustafa nodded slowly. "We can certainly look into it. Sometimes names can be significant triggers for repressed memories. It's a good sign that you're starting to recall more concrete details, Graxe. But remember, these things take time. Your mind is working through trauma at its own pace."

Juan's jaw tightened, but he said nothing. I could feel his impatience simmering just beneath the surface, a tension that had been building for months. He wanted me to move on, to forget the past I couldn't remember and embrace the life we had now. But for me, the unknowns were like tiny splinters buried deep in my mind, nagging at me, demanding to be unearthed.

We finished the session with Dr. Mustafa advising me to continue journaling my dreams and thoughts. As we left his office, I felt a mix of hope and frustration bubbling inside me. The more I discovered, the more I realized how little I truly knew.

The car ride to Times Square was tense. Juan was unusually quiet, his eyes fixed on the road ahead, and his usual light-hearted demeanor replaced by a brooding silence. I could sense his worry, the way his fingers tapped nervously against the steering wheel.

"Juan," I began softly, turning to face him, "I'm sorry if this upsets you. I know it's not easy, but I need to find these answers."

He sighed, his grip on the wheel loosening just a little. "I just don't want you to lose what we have now, Graxe. What if digging into this past only brings more pain?"

I reached out, placing my hand over his. "Maybe it will. But I believe that knowing who I was will help me understand who I am now. It doesn't mean I love you any less. You've been my anchor, Jui."

He nodded, but I could see the fear still lingering in his eyes—the fear of losing me to a life neither of us understood.

As we approached Times Square, the mood shifted. The energy of the city wrapped around us like a vibrant, pulsating rhythm. The flashing lights, the buzz of anticipation from the crowd, and the sight of the red carpet laid out ahead brought a new sense of urgency to the evening.

The bustling chaos of Times Square enveloped us as soon as we stepped out of the car. The air was electric, buzzing with excitement and chatter from the crowd that had gathered for the premiere. Bright lights flashed from the massive billboards overhead, illuminating the throngs of people lining the streets, waiting eagerly to catch a glimpse of their favorite stars. A crimson carpet stretched out before us, flanked by velvet ropes and swarming with reporters, photographers, and fans.

Juan held my hand firmly, guiding me through the sea of bodies with the ease of someone who was used to navigating through such chaos. His grip was reassuring, a steadying presence amidst the frenzy of the crowd. He was in his element here—focused, vigilant, his eyes scanning the surroundings for any signs of trouble. I watched him shift seamlessly into his professional mode, the tension from earlier replaced by a calm determination.

"This is exactly how I described it, isn't it?" Juan said with a grin, leaning close so I could hear him over the noise. "Chaotic, dazzling, and absolutely overwhelming."

I nodded, a small smile tugging at my lips despite the flutter of nerves in my stomach. "You weren't kidding. It's like another world out here."

We moved closer to the cordoned-off area where a line of limousines was pulling up one by one, delivering their precious cargo to the red carpet. I could see flashes of bright dresses, tailored suits, and the glittering smiles of celebrities as they stepped out, waving to their fans and posing for the cameras. The atmosphere was a whirlwind of excitement and anticipation.

Suddenly, the crowd erupted into a deafening cheer. I followed their gaze and saw him—James Cross. He stepped out of a sleek black car, his presence commanding and magnetic. Tall and broad-shouldered, he moved with the easy confidence of someone used to being the center of attention. His hair was tousled just right, his smile effortlessly charming as he waved to the fans who called his name.

"There he is," Juan said, leaning close again. "James Cross, the man of the hour."

I watched him, my curiosity piqued. James Cross was undeniably captivating. He had a presence that filled the space around him, and the crowd seemed to feed off his energy, their cheers growing louder as he approached the red carpet. Yet, as I looked at him, a strange sensation settled over me—a sense of familiarity that I couldn't quite place. It was as if I had seen him before, somewhere beyond the glossy pages of magazines or the flashing screens.

"Want to try to meet him?" Juan's voice cut through my thoughts. His eyes were bright with excitement, eager to share this experience with me.

I hesitated for a moment, then nodded. "Why not? Could be fun," I said, my voice more confident than I felt.

Juan grinned and led me closer to the edge of the crowd. As we maneuvered our way through, James continued to charm his way down the red carpet, stopping occasionally to sign autographs and take selfies with fans. He was just a few feet away now, his eyes scanning the crowd as he smiled for the cameras. And then, suddenly, his gaze landed on me.

For a moment, everything seemed to slow down. The noise of the crowd, the flashing lights, the chaos—all of it faded into the background as James Cross stared at me. His expression changed, the easy smile slipping from his face. His eyes widened, a flicker of shock and disbelief crossing his features. It was like he had seen a ghost.

"How are you—" he started; his voice barely audible over the din of the crowd. He took a step forward, his hand lifting as if to reach out to me.

I tilted my head, confused by his reaction. "Mr. Cross?" I said, my voice uncertain, but before his hand could touch me, someone else intervened.

A young man with wavy raven-black hair and the same striking blue-green eyes as James stepped forward, pulling him back firmly but gently. James stumbled a little, caught off guard, but the young man—his son, Aamon—steadied him, his expression calm but serious.

"I'm sorry for the trouble, sir," Juan interjected smoothly, stepping between us and James. "It's just, my wife is a big fan."

I glanced up at Juan, confusion knitting my brow. He gave me a subtle shake of his head and a roll of his eyes that clearly meant, "Ignore it." I nodded, leaning into him, trusting his judgment even as my mind buzzed with questions.

Behind us, I could still feel James Cross's eyes on me, burning with an intensity that sent a shiver down my spine. As his team ushered him away, his gaze remained fixed on me, a look of profound recognition etched on his face.

"What was that, Jui?" I whispered to Juan as we began to move away from the red carpet, blending back into the crowd.

"Who knows? These people are a bit crazy," he said lightly, miming a loose screw with his finger to his temple. His humor was an attempt to ease the tension, and it worked—we both burst into laughter, the sound a welcome release from the odd encounter.

As we walked away from the premiere's chaos, the bright lights and noise faded into the background. We weaved through the bustling streets of Times Square, finding a quieter spot as the night began to settle around us. The city was still alive with energy, but it felt more distant now, less overwhelming.

Once we were a safe distance away, Juan turned to me, his expression a mix of concern and curiosity. "Graxe, are you okay? That was a bit... intense back there."

I nodded, though the image of James Cross's startled face lingered in my mind, unsettling in its intensity. "I'm fine, Juan. It was just surprising to see someone react like that. Do you think he mistook me for someone else?"

"Maybe," Juan mused, his brow furrowed in thought. "Celebrities meet so many people; maybe you just remind him of someone. But let's not let it spoil our night, okay?"

I smiled, reassured by his rational explanation, and squeezed his hand. "Of course not. Let's enjoy our evening."

Juan smiled back, and we decided to end our night with a walk through the Central Park, enjoying the cooler air and the relative peace away from the crowds. As we strolled along the winding paths, our earlier encounter with James Cross began to fade into the background, replaced by the quiet rustle of leaves and the distant hum of the city.

Yet, as we walked, I couldn't shake the feeling of that intense recognition in James's eyes, the way he had looked at me like I was someone he had known intimately. It was like a puzzle piece in my life that didn't quite fit, a thread that begged to be unraveled. But for now, I chose to stay in the present—with Juan, my anchor, my safe harbor in a world still filled with so many unknowns.

The night air was cool and refreshing, the sky above us a deep, inky blue speckled with stars. Juan's arm was around my shoulders, holding me close as we walked, our footsteps soft against the gravel path. We talked about everything and nothing—the future, our plans, the life we were building together. For tonight, that was enough.

But as we strolled deeper into the park, beneath the canopy of trees and away from the prying eyes of the city, the question lingered like a whisper in my mind: Who was I before all this? And why did James Cross look at me like he had seen a ghost?

——

Meanwhile, back at the premiere, the incident with Graxe had left James Cross visibly shaken. As his team ushered him inside and away from the cameras, his mind raced, replaying the moment over and over. The resemblance was uncanny, and for a brief second, he had thought he was looking into the eyes of Mariyam, his lost love.

"Aamon, did you see her? Did you see how much she looked like—" James started, his voice choked with emotion.

Aamon, who had been by his father's side, supporting him, nodded solemnly. "I saw, Dad. It's uncanny. But it couldn't be her, right? We've been searching for months with no sign."

James paced a small circle, his hands running through his hair in frustration. "I don't know, son. But how many people can look that much like her? And her reaction, she seemed just as shocked to see me."

"Maybe it's worth looking into," Aamon suggested, always the rational one. "We can ask the security team for footage, see if we can learn anything about her."

James nodded, a new determination setting in. "Do it. Find out everything you can. I need to know if it's really her."

The rest of the evening passed in a blur for James. Despite the success of the premiere and the accolades for his performance, his mind was elsewhere, caught in the web of possibilities that the chance encounter had spun.

Back at their mansion, Juan and I were oblivious to the storm we had inadvertently stirred. We arrived home, still wrapped in the comfort of each other's company. As Juan locked the door behind us, he turned to me with a smile.

"Tonight, was an adventure, huh?" he chuckled, pulling me into his arms.

"Every day with you is an adventure, Juan," I replied, my voice muffled against his chest.

He kissed the top of my head gently. "And I wouldn't have it any other way."

As we headed upstairs to our room, the challenges of the day felt miles away. We were together, and in that truth, we found strength and solace.

But outside the safety of our shared sanctuary, the wheels of fate continued to turn. James Cross, driven by a glimmer of hope and the haunting memory of a face from the past, was setting in motion a series of events that would eventually lead him back to us. Unbeknownst to us all, our lives were about to intersect once again, in ways none of us could have predicted.

Determined, James made a few calls to his contacts in the NYPD, trying to gather information about the event's security detail and specifically about Lieutenant Juan Ramirez and the woman he had called his wife.

As the night grew deeper, the questions loomed larger, casting long shadows over the glitz and glamour of the premiere. For James Cross, the search for truth had taken on a new, urgent direction, driven by a glimpse of someone who might just be the key to resolving the haunting mysteries of his past.

Back at the mansion, as I finally drifted into sleep, the glamour and chaos of Hollywood seemed like a distant dream, a glittering mirage far removed from the quiet, comforting darkness of the room I shared with Juan. Yet, as I lay there, the tendrils of my forgotten past curled around me, weaving through my dreams, whispering of secrets still hidden, of connections waiting to be uncovered.

Meanwhile, in a dimly lit penthouse on the other side of the city, James Cross sat on the edge of his bed, his mind racing. His heart hadn't stopped pounding since the premiere. That face—it couldn't have been a mistake. The eyes, the way she tilted her head—everything about her screamed of familiarity, of a past he thought he had buried. Unable to shake the feeling, he picked up his phone and dialed a number.

"Morris," he spoke urgently into the phone, his voice rough with anxiety. "I need you to find out everything about that lieutenant who was handling security at the premiere tonight. Lieutenant Ramirez."

There was a long pause on the other end, and then a sigh. "James, it's late. And you know what he said—she's, his wife. You've got to let it go. She's not who you think she is," Morris replied, his voice weary but firm. "James, Mariyam is gone. We buried her, didn't we? You've moved on. We all have."

James's head snapped up, his jaw tightening, his eyes flashing with something dark and unyielding. "An empty casket, Morris! We buried an empty casket. Her body was never found." His voice grew more intense, more desperate. "What if—what if it wasn't a mistake? What if she's alive?"

"What if what, James?" Morris challenged, his voice a mixture of frustration and concern. He had seen James go through this torment before, the endless cycle of grief and obsession, and he feared where it might lead this time.

James's breath came out in a harsh exhale, his eyes narrowing. "What if that woman—his 'wife'—is Mariyam? What if she doesn't remember? What if she's been lost this whole time, hiding in plain sight?"

Morris fell silent on the other end of the line, the gravity of James's words hanging heavy in the space between them. He knew the weight of this obsession for James—the endless nights spent searching, the relentless pursuit of answers that had only ever led to more questions.

"James..." Morris began carefully, choosing his words with precision. "If she is alive, if she doesn't remember... digging into this could unravel her life, maybe even endanger her. And you... you could end up breaking yourself all over again."

"I don't care," James said, his voice like steel, unyielding. "I've spent too many nights staring into the darkness, wondering if I missed something. If there's even a sliver of a chance that she's out there, I need to know. I need to be sure."

There was a long pause, and then Morris sighed deeply, resigning himself to James's determination. "Alright. I'll see what I can find on this Lieutenant Ramirez. But James... be prepared for what you might uncover. You might not like it."

"Just do it, Morris," James said, his voice steady but laced with a kind of desperation. "I need to know who she is. I need to know if she's Mariyam."

Morris, well accustomed to James's intensity, nodded briskly. "I'll get on it right away, James. I'll contact the NYPD and pull up everything they've got on Lieutenant Ramirez."

"Good," James replied, his jaw set. The image of Graxe, her shock upon seeing him, was imprinted in his mind, refusing to fade. "And get me the security footage from the premiere, especially the cameras that caught our interaction. I need to see it again."

Morris quickly made the necessary calls, organizing the retrieval of the footage and beginning a deep dive into Juan Ramirez's life. As he worked, James paced his living room, his mind racing with possibilities. Could it truly be Mariyam? After all this time, could fate have brought her back to him in such an unexpected way?

Morris nodded, though James couldn't see it, and hung up the phone. Alone in the quiet of his penthouse, James sat back, his mind swirling with possibilities, each one more unsettling than the last. He could still see her face, that haunting familiarity, the way her eyes had met his with a hint of recognition.

His fingers drummed anxiously on the edge of the bedside table. If she truly was Mariyam, then she was out there somewhere, living another life, with another name, with another man. The thought sent a sharp pang through him—a mix of hope, anger, and something else, something he hadn't allowed himself to feel in a long time.

He had to know. He had to find her. And he had to be sure.

Unbeknownst to him, In the Ramirez Estate, the night unfolded in silence, but my dreams were anything but quiet. They were filled with shadowy figures and fragmented memories—flashes of a bridge, cold water rushing around me, a voice calling out a name I couldn't quite grasp. The darkness seemed to pull me deeper, swirling with faces I couldn't recognize but felt tethered to, voices that seemed to echo from some hidden part of my mind.

I saw two boys, their faces blurred, one slightly older with bright eyes and a mischievous grin, the other younger, more reserved, looking up to his brother. They were running through a field, laughter carrying in the wind, and a name floated in the air around them— "Rehman."

I woke with a start, my breath shallow, the name lingering on my lips like a ghost. Juan stirred beside me, his arm instinctively tightening around my waist, pulling me closer. I could feel the steady beat of his heart against my back, grounding me in the present.

But even in his arms, I felt a growing restlessness—a pull toward a past that refused to let go, a past that, somehow, seemed to be catching up with me, I laid awake thinking about the dream, until sleep lulled me in land of slumber again.

The next morning, I awoke to find Juan watching me closely, his expression contemplative. "Morning," he greeted softly, his hand reaching out to brush a loose strand of hair away from my face.

"Morning," I replied with a sleepy smile. "What's going on in that head of yours?"

He hesitated, then sighed. "It's about last night... at the premiere. The way James Cross looked at you, it's been bothering me. And the way you reacted, Graxe... it felt like you knew him, more than just recognizing a celebrity."

I sat up and gently cupped his face, feeling the stubble on his jaw beneath my fingers. "Really, Juan? I didn't even know his name until you told me. You should know, these Hollywood types are all crazy."

Juan chuckled but didn't let it go. "Yeah, but what if, I mean, you guys knew each other... from before, you know?"

I snorted, shaking my head. "Right, James Cross knew me, and they still didn't find me even though I was just unconscious 10 kilometers away from the Hudson Bridge. That chopper guy must have been blind." We both burst into laughter, and Juan pulled me into a tight hug, his warmth pressing against me.

Meanwhile, in the quiet of his private home theater, James sat hunched over, his eyes glued to the footage Morris had managed to secure from the premiere. His heart pounded as he replayed the moment again and again—the instant their eyes met, the shock, the undeniable recognition on both their faces. He paused the video, zoomed in on Graxe's face, and a chill ran down his spine.

"It's her. It has to be," James whispered to himself, his voice barely audible over the hum of the projector. He grabbed his phone and dialed Morris. "Set up a meeting. I need to speak with this Lieutenant Juan Ramirez immediately."

The pieces were falling into place, the paths of the past and present hurtling toward each other at a dangerous speed. Unbeknownst to Juan and me, our quiet exploration into my lost memories was about to clash head-on with James

Cross's relentless search for the truth, setting the stage for revelations that could change everything.

—

James stared at Morris expectantly, his face tense with impatience. "What more did you find out?" he demanded, pacing back and forth.

Morris, who had spent the early hours digging into Juan Ramirez's background, looked up from his notes. "He's a lieutenant, originally from Mexico, and part of the Lower Manhattan unit. He's practically brothers with the county's sheriff, Rudolf Liam Merci. They're a united front; they won't spill easily. Plus, there's a SWAT officer, Malcom Wyatt—another close friend. And get this—he got married about four months ago. Quite happy, from what I gather, and living in the Ramirez Mansion. He's not just some regular lieutenant, James. He comes from one of the wealthiest families in Mexico and is listed in Forbes' 50 Richest Men of New York, right alongside Sheriff Merci."

James absorbed the information, piecing together the complex web of connections and power surrounding Juan Ramirez. The revelation of Juan's status and his close ties to New York's elite only deepened the intrigue and made James more cautious. He realized he wasn't just dealing with an ordinary man; Juan was someone with significant influence and resources.

"Arrange a discreet meeting, Morris," James instructed, his mind working rapidly through possible scenarios. "I need to approach this carefully. He's not someone we can confront without considering the consequences."

"Understood, James," Morris replied, already contemplating the best way to approach a man of Juan's caliber without arousing suspicion. "It might take some time to set up something subtle."

"Do what you need to," James said, his tone edged with impatience but also a grudging acknowledgment of the complexity of the situation.

Back at the mansion, Juan and I were enjoying a quiet morning, the tension from the previous night now a faint memory in the light of day. The calm, however, was short-lived. As we finished breakfast, Juan's phone rang, breaking the peace. He glanced at the caller ID, frowning slightly when he saw it was from his precinct.

"Excuse me, Graxe, I need to take this," he said, getting up from the table and stepping away to answer the call.

I watched him from the kitchen, noting the tension that built in his shoulders as he spoke. His back was to me, but I could tell from his posture that whatever was being discussed was serious. When he finally returned, his face had shifted into a more somber expression, a stark contrast to the lighthearted mood we'd shared earlier.

"That was Captain Hernandez," Juan said, his brow furrowed. "There's been a request for a meeting through official channels. Someone wants to discuss the security arrangements from last night's event, specifically about... our encounter with James Cross."

I felt a flicker of unease settle in my stomach. "Do you think it's something we should be worried about?"

Juan shook his head slowly, his gaze distant. "I'm not sure yet, Graxe. But it's unusual to have this kind of follow-up after a routine security detail. I'll need to go in and see what this is about."

I nodded, trusting his instincts. "I trust you'll handle it well, Juan."

He gave me a reassuring smile, though it didn't quite reach his eyes. "I'll call you as soon as I know more," he promised, leaning down to kiss my forehead before heading out.

As Juan left for the precinct, the mansion felt unusually large and empty, a strange heaviness settling over the space. The uncertainty of the situation made the house seem almost alive with tension, every creak of the floorboards and whisper of the wind through the trees outside echoing the unease growing inside me.

I moved to the window, watching as Juan's car disappeared down the long driveway, my mind spinning with possibilities. What could this meeting be about? Why was James Cross so fixated on our brief encounter? And why did I feel like a storm was brewing, one that was about to upend everything we thought we knew?

At the precinct, Juan arrived to find Captain Hernandez waiting for him in his office. "Lieutenant Ramirez," the captain greeted, his tone formal but laced with curiosity. "We've received an unusual request from the Cross estate."

Juan's brow furrowed. "Regarding what, exactly?"

Captain Hernandez sighed, sliding a document across his desk. "They want a meeting to discuss the security arrangements from last night. Specifically, they want to talk about your interaction with James Cross."

Juan scanned the paper, his expression tightening. "Did they give a reason?"

"Not directly, but the implication is clear—they have questions about what happened on the red carpet. And they're being quite insistent."

Juan nodded slowly, his mind working through the implications. "I'll go. Better to address it directly and see what they're after."

Captain Hernandez nodded. "Be careful, Ramirez. This feels like it's more than just a routine inquiry."

As Juan prepared to meet with James Cross, the wheels were already in motion, setting the stage for a collision of past and present that neither he nor I could see coming.

And somewhere in the hidden depths of my mind, memories stirred like echoes in a dark, forgotten cavern, ready to emerge and reshape the lives we thought we knew.

James adjusted his cufflink, his gaze steady as he glanced around the dimly lit conference room. He'd chosen his attire carefully—a sharp, tailored suit that exuded authority and confidence. Every detail mattered today. The secluded conference room, nestled in one of the lesser-known buildings owned by one of his subsidiaries, had been chosen with equal care. The walls, adorned with modern minimalist art, and the soft hum of the air conditioning created an atmosphere of both quiet elegance and tension. James had made sure this meeting would remain off the radar, giving clear instructions to Morris to ensure privacy.

He took a deep breath, rolling his shoulders slightly to release the tension building in them. He had played many roles on screen, but this one—this delicate balancing act between discovery and discretion—required a different kind of performance. His mind raced with the possibilities of how this could unfold. Would Juan cooperate? Or would his protective instincts prove to be an impenetrable wall?

He stood by the window, staring out over the city with a mixture of anticipation and apprehension. He'd run through this conversation in his mind a hundred times, but now that the moment was approaching, uncertainty gnawed at him. Was he making the right move? Would this confrontation bring him the answers he so desperately sought, or would it push them further away?

The door creaked open, and James turned to see Lieutenant Juan Heinrich Ramirez enter. The man exuded a calm confidence—his posture relaxed yet alert. With his light skin, chiseled jawline, and piercing blue eyes, he might have been mistaken for a modern-day conquistador. Juan's reputation as a decorated officer with a no-nonsense demeanor preceded him, and James couldn't afford to take any missteps.

"Lieutenant Ramirez," James greeted, extending his hand with a polite smile. "Thank you for agreeing to meet me on such short notice."

Juan's handshake was firm, his eyes steady as he sized up the man before him. "Mr. Cross," he replied coolly. "I have to admit, I'm curious. Your request seemed urgent. What's this about?"

They took their seats at the sleek, minimalist conference table. The room felt cold, the air thick with tension. James took a deep breath, deciding it was best to ease into the conversation. He couldn't risk alienating Juan before getting the information he needed.

"I appreciate you coming," James began, his tone measured. "I know this might seem unusual, but I wanted to talk about Graxe. I couldn't help but notice certain... things last night at the premiere."

Juan's brow furrowed slightly, though he maintained his composed demeanor. "Graxe? My wife? What about her?"

James nodded; his expression serious but not confrontational. "She seemed familiar. Very familiar. It's not something I could shake off. You see, there's someone from my past, someone I've been searching for..."

Juan's eyes narrowed slightly, his instincts kicking in. He'd dealt with countless interrogations in his career, and he knew how to read between the lines. "Mr. Cross," he interrupted, his voice firm but not hostile, "if you have something to say, say it plainly. Why is my wife of such interest to you?"

James met his gaze, recognizing the challenge in Juan's tone. This was a man fiercely protective of his own, a man who wouldn't easily give up information. James needed to tread carefully.

"Lieutenant," James continued, leaning forward slightly, "I'm not here to cause trouble. But I believe your wife may be someone very important to me—someone I thought I lost a long time ago."

Juan's face shifted subtly—his jaw set, and his eyes became harder. The easy-going demeanor was replaced by the controlled stoicism of a man used to high-stakes situations. He had heard enough.

"Graxe Juan Ramirez," he said firmly, as if declaring a fact in a court of law. "She is my wife, Mr. Cross. I don't know what you're implying, but she is exactly where she belongs."

James raised an eyebrow, picking up on the Lieutenant's defensiveness. "I'm sure she is, Lieutenant. But if you don't mind me asking... What was her maiden name?"

Juan's eyes narrowed. "Why do you care?"

James leaned back, trying to appear casual. "Just for my peace of mind. You know how these things are... sometimes it's hard to move on without closure."

Juan could feel the conversation tightening around him. He was well-trained in these kinds of verbal sparrings, but this wasn't a battlefield he was familiar with. For a moment, he considered his options.

"Graxe Rehman," he answered, his voice steady.

James's brow furrowed slightly; his interest clearly piqued. "Graxe Rehman... Huh. Intriguing name."

Juan smirked, sensing the shift in James's demeanor. "She's quite the intriguing woman, yes."

James studied Juan, considering his next move. He needed to press forward without alarming him too much. His gaze drifted to Juan's hands—calm, composed, a soldier's hands. His own fingers drummed lightly on the table's edge.

"And her mother's name?" James asked, almost casually.

For the first time, Juan hesitated. He hadn't expected this question, and he could feel the cracks forming in his carefully crafted calm.

"Ahem... Layla Goodman," he replied after a moment. "Her father was Rehman. It was an inter-religion marriage, hence the name Rehman."

James's eyes sharpened. "Layla Goodman... does she have a history I should know about? Any distinguishing features? Perhaps a scar or an unusual piece of jewelry?"

Juan's facade nearly broke. He clenched his jaw, the controlled calm slipping into something more defensive. He remembered the emerald locket clutched in Graxe's hand when he first found her, and stitches on her right arm.

Juan's brow furrowed as he maintained eye contact with James, a hint of defiance in his gaze. "I don't know what you're implying, Mr. Cross," he said carefully, his voice steady but edged with tension. "Graxe and I have known each other since we were children. We were always close, and when the time was right, we got married. There's nothing more to it."

James felt the shift in the air. Juan's sudden defensiveness was telling; it was the reaction of a man guarding a truth, not revealing one. He needed to press further, but he had to be careful not to push Juan too hard. With a measured breath, he reached into his jacket pocket and pulled out a photograph. He slid it across the table toward Juan.

"Maybe this will help clarify things," James said calmly. "This is a photo of the woman I lost. Look closely, Lieutenant."

Juan hesitated, his eyes flicking down to the photograph. He picked it up reluctantly, his expression unreadable. The picture showed a woman standing on a bridge, her face partially turned away, but her features—the shape of her face, the way her hair fell across her shoulder—were unmistakable. Graxe.

A muscle in Juan's jaw twitched. "I don't see what this has to do with my wife," he replied, setting the photo back down with a bit more force than necessary. "She's not the woman in this picture, Mr. Cross."

James leaned back; his eyes still fixed on Juan. "You're certain about that? Because the resemblance is uncanny. And I have reason to believe she might have been involved in something... something that connects her to me."

Juan's eyes were hard as steel now. "I'm done with this conversation," he said sharply, rising from his seat. "Graxe is my wife, and that's all there is to it. I suggest you stay away from her, Mr. Cross. For both your sakes."

Without waiting for a response, Juan turned on his heel and headed for the door. His abrupt departure left James sitting in the dim conference room, the air still heavy with unspoken tension. He watched the door close behind the Lieutenant, a mixture of frustration and determination settling over him. Juan's reaction had confirmed more than it denied—there was something there, something real. But James knew he'd have to find another way in, a softer approach that wouldn't send Juan running.

As Juan drove away from the building, his hands gripped the steering wheel tight. His mind was racing, replaying every word, every question James had asked. He'd need to talk to Rudi and Malcom, and he'd need to do it soon. James's insinuations were troubling. If James had any inkling of the truth—that he'd found Graxe unconscious in that river, with no memory of who she was, and had given her that name himself—things could unravel quickly.

He remembered the day he had pulled her out of the cold water, the cuts and bruises marring her skin, the distant look in her eyes. She hadn't even known her own name. She was a mystery—a lost soul with no past, and he had given her a future. They named her Graxe, and when no one came forward to claim her, he had decided to take her in. They grew close, and eventually, they fell in love. He had married her, knowing she might never fully remember where she came from.

But now, with James Cross in the picture, that fragile balance was under threat. He needed to protect her, and himself, from whatever storm was brewing.

***

Back in the conference room, James stared at the closed door for a long moment, his mind racing. Juan had left in a hurry—too much of a hurry. There was more to this story, and he was going to find out what it was. For now, he needed to regroup, perhaps reach out to some contacts of his own. This wasn't over. Not by a long shot.

He picked up his phone and dialed a number. "Morris," he said, his voice steady but laced with determination. "I need you to dig deeper. Find out everything you can about Juan Heinrich Ramirez and his wife. I want to know who she really is."

James's mind was ablaze as he put down the phone. The echoes of the conversation with Juan reverberated in his mind, each word Juan spoke, each gesture he made, adding layers to the enigma that was Graxe—or the woman he believed could be linked to his past. The setting sun cast long shadows across the room, mirroring the growing darkness in his thoughts. The stakes were higher than ever.

As the city lights began to twinkle on, James remained seated, his figure a silhouette against the glowing backdrop. The game had indeed just begun. He was not just up against a man; he was challenging a story, a constructed reality that Juan and Graxe had lived in for years. But he had his own role to play, one he couldn't step back from.

Outside, the city hummed with the evening rush, oblivious to the brewing storm in the quiet conference room. James felt the weight of the impending confrontation, knowing it would not be just a clash of wills but of truths, each one carefully hidden and protected over years.

With a deep breath, James stood, his resolve steeling. This quest was more than a mere search; it was a mission to unearth truths potent enough to reshape lives. As the door clicked shut behind him, the atmosphere thickened with anticipation and the promise of revelations yet to unfold.

The chessboard was set, not merely for a game of strategy but a profound battle of destinies. Here, one king fortified his defenses around a queen whose past was shrouded in mystery, while another king sought to uncover and reclaim what he believed was rightfully his. This wasn't just a game of chess—it was a complex dance of fates intertwined, with each move carrying the weight of potential upheaval.

CHAPTER 3

The days passed in a fragile peace, and I let the tension from the past few days slip away like sand through my fingers. I was curled up on the couch, my head tilted like I often do when I'm confused, as Juan took my hand and gently kissed the stitches that ran along my arm.

"Amor," he said softly, his eyes holding a mixture of worry and resolve.

"What is it, Jui?" I asked, sensing the weight in his voice. "You know I hate it when you're sad." I shifted closer, resting my head against his back, feeling his muscles tense beneath my touch.

He hesitated for a moment before speaking. "Amor, we're going to Mexico, okay? Mamá y Papá are calling."

I looked up, my eyes widening with surprise. "Really? I mean... they never really accepted us?" My voice was cautious, searching his face for answers.

He shook his head with a smile—a smile that looked perfect but felt off, like a mask hiding something. "They've come around, mi Vida," he said smoothly, his tone deceptively light. "They want to see us."

"What about your precinct, Amor?" I asked, still skeptical, but Juan chuckled, instead, pulling me closer to his chest.

"Rudi gave me some time off! Turns out I had 124 days of earned leave, and I finally used 90. What do you say, mi amor? Honeymoon?" he suggested, his eyes twinkling.

I squealed in excitement, momentarily forgetting my doubts. "Yay! We can go to Mexico, then the Maldives, then Svalbard... no, first Turkey, then, umm, Japan, and then Medina, Paris, Greece, Spain, and finally Svalbard!" I clapped my hands, and Juan clutched his chest in mock pain.

"What happened?" I asked, suddenly concerned.

"My wallet hurts," he groaned dramatically, and I realized his mockery, and kicked him off the sofa, making him laugh.

And as usual, Rudi arrived just in time to witness the commotion, Malcom trailing behind with beer cans for the guys and my mango smoothie. "Servants are here, mi Rey y Reina," Malcom teased, bowing playfully.

Juan chuckled as Rudi wrapped an arm around me. "How's my little beetle?" Rudi asked, pulling me into a warm hug.

"I'm good, redhead, finally happy," I replied, feeling genuinely lighter for the first time in days. "Thank you for approving his leave."

Rudi smiled, a glint of something unspoken in his eyes. "That's my job." He said pulling me in a warm hug. He looked at me, then at Juan over my shoulder. Juan gave a discreet nod, and I remained blissfully unaware of the silent communication between them.

They had to get me away from here, away from James and the questions that could unravel everything. His father wasn't sick. There was no sudden acceptance from his parents. But there was a very real danger, one that required quick thinking and action. For now, I believed we were headed on a spontaneous honeymoon, blissfully unaware that this was more a flight than a vacation.

In their quiet conspiracy, they'd decided to keep me far from the past that threatened to collide with my present—a present they'd vowed to protect, no matter the cost.

"You look happy today?" I asked, Rudolf. My voice teasing and soft and He shrugged, breaking in a sly grin.

"Well, I have my reasons. "Rudi's eyebrows waggled playfully, his expression teasing yet serious beneath the surface. "Also, I couldn't help but notice—you always wear long sleeve clothes to hide this fish skeleton," he said, gesturing to the faint outlines beneath my sleeves. His words were light, but there was a thread of something more, something calculated, woven in.

I shot him a mock glare, crossing my arms over my chest. "Don't even get me started. I've tried everything. It feels hideous," I muttered, frustration seeping into my tone. "They're probably surgical marks from... my life before I ended up in that river." My words were meant to be sarcastic, but they carried a bitter truth. I had no idea who or what I was before that day. All I remembered was these last few months—almost a year now—spent with these people who rescued me, loved me, took me in. And Juan—especially Juan. He had become my anchor in this sea of uncertainty.

Rudi leaned forward, his eyes glinting with a sudden idea. "And that's exactly why I am happy? Maybe it's your lucky day."

I raised an eyebrow, intrigued despite myself. "What do you mean?"

Rudi glanced at Juan, then back at me, his smile widening. "I have a friend—Carlson Herrera. He's this top-notch plastic surgeon. Just set up his clinic in Lower Manhattan after being in Germany for years, working with some big names. You wouldn't believe the transformations he's capable of. Luckily, He invited me for the house warming drink last night and all I could think of was, how much he can help with that fish skeleton of yours and how our beetle will finally have one less thing to worry about." His nodded vaguely towards my hand, his voice enthusiastic, almost too enthusiastic, and I could see Malcom nodding along, his own expression supportive.

Juan's hand tightened around mine, his thumb brushing over my knuckles soothingly. "Sí, amor. Carlson is really good. A true magician with his hands," he said, his voice warm and encouraging. "He could help you... make those marks disappear, if you want."

I hesitated, considering their words. The idea of getting rid of the scars—those mysterious, ugly reminders of a past I couldn't remember—was tempting. "Really?" I asked, my tone softening as I looked between them. "But I won't give up skin from anywhere else... Remember the last time I was in a hospital? They talked about scraping skin from my thighs—ugh!" I shivered at the memory, wrinkling my nose in disgust.

Juan chuckled at my reaction; his eyes filled with fondness. "Don't worry, amor. I'll make sure they don't touch your precious thighs," he reassured me, planting a gentle kiss on my forehead.

"Exactly!" Rudi chimed in. "And guess what? Carlson has a slot open tomorrow! It's like fate or something. You can get it done before we leave for Mexico."

"Tomorrow?" I echoed; the surprise evident in my voice. "That soon?"

"Yes, mi amor," Juan said, leaning in to kiss my lips, his touch soft and reassuring. "And right after, we'll catch our flight to Mexico. I promise, you'll feel brand new—just in time for our honeymoon."

I chewed on my bottom lip, glancing between Juan, Rudi, and Malcom, their faces all wearing expressions of eager encouragement. A part of me warmed at their excitement, but another part—the part that had always kept me on guard—felt a twinge of unease. It seemed rushed, like they were too keen on the idea.

"We have a flight to catch, though," I said slowly, searching their faces for any hint of why they were pushing this so hard. "I don't want to risk missing it. Maybe we can get it done after we come back from Mexico? It's not like my scars are going anywhere."

Juan's smile faltered, just for a moment—a flicker so brief it was almost imperceptible. But I caught it. He quickly covered it up with a laugh, rubbing my arm as he spoke. "Amor, it's not that big of a procedure. Carlson said it's just a few hours, and you'll be good as new. We can still catch our flight. And wouldn't you rather enjoy Mexico without worrying about hiding your arms all the time?"

I hesitated. His logic made sense, but there was something in the way he said it—like he was trying to convince himself as much as he was convincing me. "I don't know, Jui," I replied, my voice quieter now. "It just seems... sudden. Like why now? I've lived with these scars for almost a year. What's one more week?"

Malcom chimed in, his voice smooth and persuasive. "Think of it this way, Graxe—if you get it done now, you'll have all the more reason to relax and celebrate on the beach. No more worries, just sun, and freedom. You deserve that, don't you?"

I looked at him, then at Rudi, who nodded in agreement. "It's a good idea, beetle," Rudi added, his tone gentle but firm. "We want you to feel your best, and this is a way to leave everything from that river behind. Start fresh, you know?"

Their words swirled around me like a comforting fog, but beneath the surface, I felt an itch of doubt. I knew they cared for me; they'd done so much to protect me, to keep me safe. But why did it feel like there was something they weren't saying? Why did it feel like they were in such a hurry to erase those scars?

"I guess..." I started, trying to align my thoughts. "I guess it could be good to not have to hide anymore. But... are you sure this is the right time? I don't want to be in pain or uncomfortable on our honeymoon."

Juan leaned in, his forehead resting against mine, his voice soft and reassuring. "Mi amor, I promise, it'll be quick and painless. You won't even remember it happened by the time we land in Mexico. And I want you to feel nothing but joy when we're there, okay?"

There was so much love in his eyes, so much sincerity, that my resolve began to weaken. "Okay," I whispered, almost to myself. "If you think it's best."

His face broke into a relieved smile, and he kissed me again, lingering longer this time as if sealing a pact. "It's going to be perfect, Graxe. You'll see."

Rudi clapped his hands, breaking the moment. "Then it's settled! I'll call Carlson and confirm for tomorrow morning. It'll be quick, in and out, and then you two lovebirds can be on your way to Mexico."

I nodded, though something still felt strange about the whole thing. But I didn't want to overthink it. Maybe they were right. Maybe this was a good chance to let go of a painful reminder. Maybe, just maybe, I could finally start to feel like I belonged in my own skin again.

The next morning came too soon. I stood in front of the mirror, staring at my reflection, my fingers tracing the raised lines of the scars that snaked up my arm. Juan was in the shower, humming softly to himself, his usual calm demeanor back in place.

I took a deep breath, trying to shake off the unease that still clung to me. "It's just a few hours," I whispered to my reflection. "And then it'll be over."

But somewhere deep inside, I couldn't shake the feeling that this wasn't just about the scars—that maybe, it was about something far more hidden, something I wasn't meant to see.

As I turned away from the mirror, Juan stepped out of the bathroom, smiling like he always did—so warm, so full of love. "Ready, mi amor?" he asked, his voice light.

I nodded, trying to push away the doubts, the whispers of my instincts. "Ready."

And as we left for the clinic, I took his hand, holding onto the man I loved, even as the world around me felt like it was shifting, like the ground beneath my feet wasn't quite as solid as it used to be.

Upon arrival, we were greeted by Dr. Herrera, a charming man with a gentle demeanor and a reassuring smile. "Welcome, Mrs. Ramirez," he said warmly as he led us into his state-of-the-art clinic. "It's an honor to help you today."

As Juan explained the nature of the surgery—minor cosmetic adjustments to remove the scar tissue from my stitches—I felt a flutter of anticipation. This procedure, while small, felt like shedding another layer of the unknown that shrouded my past.

The operation was brief and went smoothly, Dr. Herrera's skilled hands making quick work of the task. As I recovered in the post-op room, Juan held my hand, his presence a comforting constant. "How do you feel, amor?" he asked, brushing a strand of hair from my face.

"A little groggy, but good," I murmured, squeezing his hand in return. "Thank you, for being here."

Juan smiled, his eyes crinkling at the edges. "Always, Graxe. Always."

Later that afternoon, after a final check-up with Dr. Herrera, we were cleared to leave. "Take it easy for the next few days," Dr. Herrera advised as he handed me a small mirror. "And enjoy your new look."

I examined my reflection, the stitches now a thing of the past, leaving behind barely noticeable lines. The physical reminder of my unknown past was gone, but the emotional and mental journey was just beginning.

That evening, as we packed for our trip to Mexico, the atmosphere in the mansion was one of mixed emotions. Excitement for the journey ahead mingled with the nerves of the unknown. Rudi and Malcom came over to help, turning the task into a lighthearted affair.

"Make sure you bring some sunscreen, Graxe. The Mexican sun doesn't play around," Rudi joked as he tossed a bottle into my suitcase.

"And don't forget your swimsuit. We expect lots of beach photos," Malcom added, winking at me as he packed another of my dresses.

The camaraderie and laughter filled the room, easing the tension and building excitement for our upcoming adventure. Once packed, we gathered in the living room, enjoying a final evening together before Juan and I departed.

"You guys make sure to keep everything running while we're gone," Juan said, half-jokingly to Rudi and Malcom.

"Don't worry, we'll handle everything. Just focus on taking care of Graxe and yourself," Rudi responded, clapping Juan on the back.

The night grew late, and after heartfelt goodbyes and promises to stay in touch, we were off to the airport, the city was asleep as we drove through the empty streets. The airport was bustling, a stark contrast to the quiet streets, and we navigated through security and to our gate with practiced ease.

As we waited to board our flight, I leaned against Juan, feeling a mix of excitement and nervousness. "Mexico," I whispered, looking up at him. "It sounds like a dream."

"It will be, amor," Juan replied, kissing the top of my head. "A dream we'll live together."

The flight was long but comfortable, and as we flew over the ocean, I watched the expanse of blue stretch out below us, feeling like we were flying into a vast, open future. When we finally landed in Mexico, the warmth of the air enveloped us like a welcoming embrace.

When we finally landed in Mexico, the warm, humid air enveloped us like a welcoming embrace. The scent of salt and earth filled my lungs, and for a moment, I closed my eyes and just breathed it in, letting the newness wash over me.

As we moved through customs and collected our bags, I couldn't help but feel a strange mix of emotions—anticipation, hope, and that familiar undercurrent of unease. This was meant to be a fresh start, a way to leave behind the shadows of my lost memories. Yet, I couldn't help but wonder if I was leaving behind more than just scars.

As we stepped out into the vibrant streets of Mexico, Juan slipped his hand into mine, squeezing it gently. "Welcome to your new adventure, mi amor," he said softly, his voice filled with promise.

I smiled up at him, pushing away the lingering doubts. "Our new adventure," I corrected, leaning into him.

For now, I wanted to believe that. I wanted to believe in the warmth of his hand, the promise of a dream lived together. But somewhere deep down, a voice whispered that this was only the beginning—and that some dreams are woven with threads of truth that could unravel at any moment.

"So, are we going to your parent's house?" I asked Juan unsure, because his parents never accepted us openly, just grew comfortable around us.

Juan's eyes twinkled with a mix of amusement and something deeper, something more calculating that was always just beneath the surface. "Not yet, mi amor," he replied smoothly. "First, we'll be staying at a beautiful villa by the beach—just the two of us. A real honeymoon before any family drama."

I nodded slowly, accepting his answer, though the unease in my chest remained. I had come to trust Juan with everything, with my life, but even in trust, shadows could lurk. I wanted to believe this was all for me, all about us, but the nagging feeling that something was amiss wouldn't let go.

The drive from the airport was filled with bright colors and vibrant life. Mexico was alive in a way that felt almost electric—children running in the streets, vendors selling their goods, and music pouring out from every corner. I found myself leaning out of the window, letting the wind whip through my hair, momentarily caught up in the world around me. For a moment, I allowed myself to believe that everything was perfect, that we were just a couple in love, away from the worries of life.

Juan's hand rested on my thigh, his thumb drawing lazy circles over my skin. "Look at you," he said, his voice soft and filled with admiration. "You look like you belong here, like a free spirit."

I turned to him with a smile, wanting to believe him, wanting to sink into the warmth of his words. "I feel free," I admitted, and it wasn't entirely a lie. "But I also feel like there's something you're not telling me, Juan."

He glanced at me, his smile never faltering, but there was a flash in his eyes—of worry, or perhaps guilt. "Mi amor," he said gently, squeezing my thigh, "I just want us to enjoy this. To forget about everything else, even if just for a little while."

The villa came into view, nestled between the palm trees, overlooking the turquoise waters of the Caribbean. It was breathtaking—a private paradise just for us. I couldn't help but gasp as we pulled up the driveway, the white walls gleaming in the afternoon sun, surrounded by gardens bursting with flowers.

"Wow," I whispered, stepping out of the car. "This is... incredible."

Juan came up behind me, wrapping his arms around my waist and pulling me close. "Only the best for you," he murmured against my ear, his breath warm on my skin. "We have the whole place to ourselves. No interruptions, just you and me."

I leaned back into him, letting myself get lost in the moment. "It's perfect," I said, my voice barely a breath.

The villa was everything Juan had promised and more. Inside, the rooms were spacious, filled with natural light and decorated with a blend of modern luxury and traditional Mexican artistry. A large infinity pool overlooked the ocean, and a private stretch of beach lay just beyond it. It was like a dream.

We spent the afternoon exploring our new temporary home, laughing and teasing each other, momentarily forgetting the tension that had followed us here. We swam in the pool, splashing like children, and Juan pulled me under the water, pressing his lips against mine in a slow, passionate kiss that made my heart race.

Later, as the sun began to set, we sat on the terrace, watching the sky turn shades of pink and orange. I rested my head on Juan's shoulder, feeling the warmth of his body against mine, feeling, for a moment, that maybe this was where I was meant to be.

But as the stars began to appear, one by one, that unease crept back in. "Juan," I began softly, "what if... what if I never remember who I was before? What if I never get those memories back?"

He was silent for a moment, his hand stilling on my back. "Then we'll make new ones," he replied finally, his voice steady and sure. "Together."

I wanted to believe him. I wanted to believe that my past didn't matter, that all that mattered was this—here, now, with him. But the way he held me just a little too tightly, the way his eyes stayed just a little too focused on the horizon, made me wonder if he was hiding something from me. If there was more to this trip, more to this "honeymoon," than he was letting on.

"What do you mean, they disappeared?" James Cross's voice boomed through the room, filled with fury and desperation. His eyes bore into Morris, who stood before him with a mixture of anxiety and caution.

"They're not at the mansion, James," Morris responded, wincing slightly at the intensity of James's anger. "Our detective has been stationed outside for the last six days. He's only seen the doorman, Eduardo, and the housekeeper, the Afro lady, Terra, come and go. And yes, his sister Anayeli and her daughter were there too, but Juan and Graxe... they've vanished."

James's jaw clenched, his frustration growing. "What about his precinct?" he demanded; the desperation evident in his voice.

"He's on leave," Morris explained. "I spoke to the Sheriff, but he wasn't forthcoming. He only gave vague responses that Juan wouldn't be back anytime soon."

James's fists tightened at his sides, knuckles turning white as he struggled to piece together the mystery that was slipping away from him like grains of sand. The sudden disappearance of Juan and Graxe added a new layer of complexity to an already tangled web of secrets and suspicions. Every new development only fueled James's resolve to uncover the truth.

"Find them, Morris," James commanded, his voice simmering with a dangerous edge. "I don't care what it takes."

Morris nodded; his brow furrowed with concern. "I'll do everything I can, James. But they've vanished without a trace. It's like they've disappeared off the face of the earth."

"That's not possible!" James snapped. "Call in every favor we're owed, Morris. I don't care what you have to do. I am James Cross, goddammit!" His frustration boiled over, his voice filling the room with a tense, electric charge.

"James—" Morris began cautiously, taking a step forward. "She's not Mariyam. We could be disrupting a peaceful household. They seem happy together—Mariyam jumped from the Hudson—how could she—?"

"I don't care who she is or who they are!" James's voice was a raw, jagged edge, cutting through Morris's cautious words. "Mariyam or not, I need to find her. I need to know the truth, Morris. And I won't rest until I do."

Morris sighed, understanding the depths of James's obsession but also recognizing the precariousness of their situation. "I'll keep searching, James. But we need to tread carefully. We can't afford any missteps, especially if they're innocent. Why wouldn't she recognize you if she were truly—well, you know."

James resumed his pacing, his mind racing with a thousand different thoughts, none of them offering clarity. His obsession with finding Graxe—or perhaps Mariyam—was driving him to the brink of madness. "I don't know, Morris. Something doesn't add up. There's more to this story than meets the eye. I can feel it."

Morris watched him carefully, his concern deepening. "James, I understand your need for closure, but we can't rush this. We need to approach it with caution, especially if there's a chance, she's not who you think she is."

James stopped pacing, his gaze locking onto Morris's with a ferocity that spoke of determination bordering on desperation. "I know, Morris. But I can't shake the feeling that she's the key to unlocking everything. I need to find her, no matter what."

Morris nodded solemnly, understanding the gravity of James's resolve. "I'll continue the search, James. I'll dig deeper, find more information. But we need to be prepared for any outcome."

As the night stretched on, James's thoughts continued to churn with uncertainty and determination. He knew the path ahead would be fraught with challenges, but he was willing to risk everything to uncover the truth—even if it meant confronting the darkest parts of his past.

Meanwhile, thousands of miles away, in the quiet sanctuary of Mexico, the atmosphere was vastly different. I found myself laughing with Juan, the two of us enjoying the peace and warmth of the Mexican sun.

"Amor, what do you like the most about Mexico?" Juan asked, his eyes gleaming with that familiar, loving warmth.

I lifted my plate, my mouth full of delicious food. "Quesadillas, tacos, nachos—fuck you, New York. We're settling here!" I said with puffed cheeks, like a squirrel hoarding nut.

Juan burst out laughing at my enthusiasm, his laughter echoing through the serene courtyard of the hacienda. "I see someone's fallen in love with Mexican cuisine," he teased, reaching over to steal a nacho from my plate.

I quickly swatted his hand away, feigning offense. "Hey, those are mine! Get your own!" I shot back, grinning as I popped another nacho into my mouth.

Juan's laughter was infectious, filling the air with a lightness that had become so rare in recent weeks. "Okay, okay, I'll get my own," he conceded, his eyes sparkling with playful amusement.

As we sat together, savoring the vibrant flavors of Mexico and the simplicity of each other's company, a sense of peace settled over me. For a brief moment, the tension and uncertainty that had plagued us seemed to evaporate, replaced by the warmth of the sun and the ease of our laughter. Being here with Juan felt like finding a home I never knew I needed.

"Amor, do you ever think about the future?" Juan asked, his tone shifting to something more tender as he gazed at me, searching for a genuine response.

I paused, considering his question, then replied with a cheeky grin, "Sí, Señor, I am very worried—where will I find falafel now?"

Juan laughed heartily at my playful response, his eyes twinkling with affection. "Don't worry, amor, I'll make sure you have all the falafel you want, even here in Mexico."

I smiled, my heart swelling with gratitude for his unwavering support. "You always know how to make everything better," I said, reaching across the table to squeeze his hand.

He held my hand tight, his expression suddenly shadowed by a fleeting darkness. "I love you, Graxe. Everything I do is for us," he said, his voice steady but carrying a weight that tugged at my heart.

I paused, sensing the depth behind his words, then nodded. "I know, Juan. And maybe, just maybe, we can actually settle here—but," I leaned in closer, a mischievous glint in my eye, "I am not naming my kids Pedro."

Juan leaned back, a soft blush creeping up his cheeks. "Fine, what about Alejandro or José?" he teased.

I chuckled, shaking my head. "Yeah, right! Like you are Juan. I swear, if I yell 'Juan' in a market, at least fifteen to twenty guys will turn back."

"Hey! That's not true," Juan mock-gasped, looking offended.

To prove my point, I clapped my hands together to dust off the crumbs and shouted, "Juan!" into the middle of the bustling restaurant.

The restaurant fell silent for a moment as several heads turned in our direction, confirming my playful theory. Juan's eyes widened in mock indignation. "See, I told you!" I exclaimed with a triumphant grin, earning a chuckle from Juan and a few puzzled looks from nearby diners.

Juan shook his head, laughing at my antics. "Okay, okay, you win this round, Graxe. But just wait until we're back in New York. I'll find a way to get you back for that."

I raised an eyebrow playfully. "Oh, I'm shaking in my boots, Señor Ramirez," I retorted, my voice dripping with exaggerated flair.

We continued to banter, the playful exchange lifting the weight of our recent worries, if only for a moment. But beneath the surface, the uncertainty still lingered—a reminder of the challenges we faced and the unknown that lay ahead.

As we finished our meal and prepared to leave the restaurant, Juan took my hand, his touch warm and reassuring. "Whatever happens, Graxe, we'll face it together. You and me against the world, remember?"

I looked up at him, my heart filled with a mix of gratitude and love. "Always, Juan. Always."

With that, we stepped out into the warm Mexican night, the glow of the streetlights casting long shadows on the cobblestone streets. Hand in hand, we walked into the unknown, ready to confront whatever the future held, together.

Back in New York, James Cross was consumed by thoughts of Graxe, the woman who had upended his life with her resemblance to his lost wife, Mariyam. The possibility that she could be Mariyam haunted him, a relentless itch that no amount of reassurance from Morris could soothe. As days turned into a blur, James's obsession deepened, fueled by unanswered questions that gnawed at his sanity like a relentless beast. He plunged further into his investigation, his mind racing through every lead, every possibility, every shadow that might hold a clue.

Yet, the more he searched, the colder the trail became. It was as if Graxe and Juan had vanished into thin air. The thought drove him mad. Frustration clawed at his resolve, but he refused to give up. Somewhere out there, Graxe—or Mariyam, or whoever she truly was—held the key to a truth buried deep within his past, a truth he was willing to tear the world apart to find.

"I'm calling a press conference," James declared suddenly, breaking the tense silence of the room. His voice was sharp, determined, and laced with an edge that made Morris's eyes widen in alarm.

"Have you lost your mind?" Morris shot back; disbelief etched on his face. "What will you say? 'I'm stalking a couple because I believe the wife could be my wife—and now I want everyone to look for them because they decided to take a little vacation!'" His words dripped with sarcasm, but beneath them lay a genuine concern.

James's jaw clenched; his face taut with the weight of his obsession. The realization that his actions could spiral out of control, dragging innocent people into chaos, struck him like a punch to the gut. But his desperation overshadowed the logical part of his mind. He couldn't let this slip through his fingers—not again.

Morris studied him closely, his expression filled with concern. "James, you can't do this. You'll only make things worse. Think about the implications—the damage it could cause."

But James was beyond reason, driven to the brink by his need for answers. "I have to do this, Morris. I can't let her slip away again. I need to find her, no matter the cost."

Morris sighed heavily, running a hand through his hair in frustration. "Fine! Look, we don't have to go public with this. I can circulate her picture through our intermediaries, our contacts around the globe, discreetly. But this is the last time, James. Get it together. The world doesn't wait for anyone—not even James Cross."

James's eyes blazed with a manic determination, a hint of madness flickering behind them. "You underestimate me, Morris. This world spins when I will it."

A chill ran down Morris's spine as he stared into James's eyes. He could see the defiance, the sheer stubbornness that bordered on insanity. Once James set his mind on something, there was no stopping him.

"James, please," Morris implored, his voice tinged with desperation. "Think about what you're doing. You're risking everything for a chance that might not even exist. You could ruin their lives, your life, everything you've worked for."

But James's resolve remained unyielding, his gaze unwavering. "I can't let her slip away again, Morris. I won't rest until I find her, until I uncover the truth. No matter what it takes."

Morris knew that arguing further would be useless. James was a man possessed, driven by a ghost from his past. "Fine, I'll do it," Morris relented, his tone heavy with resignation. "But if this goes south, James, it's on you. Remember that."

James nodded, his expression grim and resolute. "I understand, Morris. And I'll take full responsibility for whatever happens."

With a sigh, Morris set about putting James's plan into action. He discreetly reached out to their network of contacts, circulating Graxe's image and description. He could feel a sense of dread settle over him, a heavy weight that pressed down on his shoulders. He couldn't shake the feeling that they were crossing a line that could lead to unforeseen consequences.

As Morris left the room to make the calls, James sank into his chair, his mind a whirlwind of conflicting emotions. On one hand, his need to find Graxe, to understand the mystery of his past, burned within him like an unquenchable fire. But on the other, he couldn't ignore the gnawing fear of causing irreparable harm—of shattering the lives of two people who seemed happy together, who might be entirely innocent.

The room was dimly lit, and the ticking of the clock was the only sound breaking the silence as James wrestled with his inner turmoil. He knew he couldn't let go of his search for Graxe; he couldn't abandon the hope that somewhere, somehow, she held the answers he so desperately sought. But the doubts, the what-ifs, and the shadows of his own actions loomed over him like a specter.

Lost in thought, James didn't hear the soft click of the door opening behind him. Morris re-entered, his expression grave as he took a seat opposite James.

"James, we need to talk," Morris said, his voice heavy with an ominous tone.

James looked up; his eyes weary but sharp with determination. "What is it, Morris?"

Morris took a deep breath, carefully choosing his next words. "I've received some updates from our contacts. But first—" He paused, then leaned forward. "We need to confirm if she is really Mariyam. Tell me about her identification marks."

James nodded, his eyes narrowing as he recalled every detail. "She has stitches on her right hand—she broke her arm once, and the doctor had to place an iron rod. There's scar tissue on her left leg, a mole on her nose, another on her right cheek, and then... on her left bosom, and below it, on her back near the... umm, what do we call it, love handles, yeah. And there's one on her right inner thigh. She has a few injury marks on her legs. Oh, and a nose piercing, too."

As he recounted the marks, his voice softened, and his eyes glazed over with a mixture of pain and longing. He reached into a drawer and pulled out pictures of Graxe, pointing to one with intensity. "Look, she has a mole on her nose, too. You know, I used to tell her that's a compass mark, where God drew her face." He wiped a tear away, his voice breaking slightly. "And the nose piercing, too."

Morris glanced at the picture; his skepticism evident. "That's pretty common, James."

"Are you stupid? A mole right in the middle of the nose is common?" James snapped, his frustration mounting.

Morris sighed, sensing that James's desperation was clouding his judgment. "I get it, James. But we need to be cautious. We can't jump to conclusions based on a few similarities."

James's hands clenched into fists, his nails digging into his palms as his frustration boiled over. "I need to know, Morris. I need to find her. She's the key to unlocking everything."

Morris nodded slowly, his expression still grave. "Alright. I found her social media, and they were spotted at JFK Airport on February 7th, 2024, eight days ago, at Terminal 2. We've requested the passenger list, but Zrak Airlines declined our request."

"How could they decline me?" James seethed; his face contorted in disbelief. He shook his head, his fury building. "I'm James Cross, for God's sake. I won't be denied."

As his anger surged, the air in the room seemed to grow heavier, charged with the intensity of his obsession. James was a man on the edge, teetering between determination and madness, his world spinning in a frenzy of desperation.

Meanwhile, in the tranquil haven of Juan's hacienda in Mexico, the world felt far removed from the storm brewing in New York. Surrounded by the warmth of family and the vibrant beauty of our surroundings, Juan and I were blissfully unaware of the chaos unraveling in James's mind. Here, amidst the rustling palm trees and the soft whispers of the ocean, life was simple, filled with laughter and love.

James Cross leaned forward, his attention sharpening like a knife at the mention of the airport sighting. "We need to find out where they were headed. Can we get any surveillance footage from the airport? Anything that might give us a clue?"

Morris nodded; his face serious. "I'm working on it. I've got someone on the inside who might be able to pull some strings and get us the footage discreetly. But it's going to take some time."

James's impatience was palpable, his voice tight with frustration. "Time is something we don't have, Morris. Every moment counts."

Morris understood the urgency but knew that rushing could lead to mistakes. "I know, James. I'm doing everything I can. In the meantime, we should consider all our options. Maybe there's another way to track them down without raising suspicion."

James began pacing the room, his mind racing through the possibilities. "What about their financials? Credit card transactions, bank statements? Anything that might show us where they've gone?"

"We're looking into that too," Morris replied. "But given Juan's status and resources, they're likely using more discreet means of payment to avoid being tracked."

Frustrated, James stopped his pacing, his eyes narrowing as he turned back to Morris. "Keep me updated on any progress. I'm going to make some calls myself, see if I can shake something loose."

As James worked the phones, tapping into his extensive network and leveraging his influence, Morris continued his efforts to dig deeper through less conventional channels. The situation had grown more complicated than either had anticipated, demanding a careful blend of urgency and discretion.

Meanwhile, in Mexico, Juan and I were living in a world untouched by the storm brewing back in New York. The hacienda was a haven of peace, where the days drifted by in a gentle rhythm of walks through lush gardens, family meals filled with laughter, and quiet moments shared under the shade of blooming trees. The troubles of the world beyond the hacienda walls felt distant, allowing us to bask in the serenity of our secluded life.

As the sun set over the hacienda, casting the sky in vibrant hues of orange and pink, Juan and I sat together on the veranda, our fingers intertwined. The world seemed to pause, giving us a moment of perfect stillness, a brief respite from the unknown future that lay ahead.

"I can't believe how lucky we are to have this," I said softly, my gaze fixed on the sky painted with the last light of day. "To have each other, to have this place."

Juan squeezed my hand, his touch warm and reassuring. "We've been through so much, Graxe. But we've found our way back to each other, to a place of peace and happiness. That's what truly matters."

I smiled, feeling a deep well of gratitude for the man beside me, for his unwavering love and support. "I love you, Juan. More than words can express."

Juan leaned in, his lips brushing gently against my forehead. "And I love you, Graxe. Always."

In that moment, surrounded by the beauty of nature and the warmth of our love, a sense of serenity washed over me. Whatever challenges lay ahead, whatever mysteries awaited us, I knew that as long as we were together, we could face them with courage and determination.

Back in New York, Morris finally received a breakthrough. His contact at the airport had come through, providing surveillance footage of Juan and me at JFK. He quickly forwarded the video to James, who watched it with laser-focused intensity, searching for any clue that might reveal where we were headed.

The footage showed us at the check-in counter, but the destination wasn't visible. James's frustration mounted, the partial answer only serving to deepen the mystery.

"Damn it, we need more," James muttered under his breath, replaying the footage again, his eyes scanning every detail. He watched our interactions closely, analyzing the way we moved, the way we spoke to each other, looking for anything that might provide a lead.

Suddenly, James froze the video, zooming in on a moment where I handed Juan a document—possibly our boarding passes. "Morris, can we enhance this? See if we can make out the details on that document?"

"I'll see what I can do," Morris replied, already working on enhancing the image.

As Morris focused on the enhancement, James leaned back, his mind a chaotic mix of hope and desperation. He was close—he could feel it. The answers he needed, the truth about who I was, seemed just within his grasp. His need to find me, to uncover the reality of my identity, drove him forward like a relentless force that wouldn't be denied.

For now, all James could do was wait, his nerves stretched thin as the hands of fate turned slowly, the pieces of the puzzle edging closer together. The search for Graxe—whether she was Mariyam or not—had grown into something far more than a quest for answers; it had become a test of his will, his patience, and the depths of his obsession.

"Morris, any updates?" James asked, his voice taut with anticipation.

"Not yet," Morris replied, shaking his head, his eyes never leaving the screen.

As James waited, his mind drifted back to memories of his time with Graxe—the fleeting moments, the unanswered questions, the unspoken truths. He knew that finding her, uncovering the truth of her identity, was the key to unlocking the mysteries of his past, of Mariyam, of everything he had lost.

And so, with a renewed sense of purpose, James continued his quest, his gaze fixed on the horizon, where the answers he sought awaited, hidden in the shadows of uncertainty and possibility.

Back in Mexico, as the first stars began to twinkle in the night sky, their soft light a reminder of the vastness of the universe and the infinite possibilities that lay ahead, Juan and I leaned into each other, ready to face whatever the future held, united in love and unwavering in our resolve.

As the night deepened, wrapping us in its embrace, we knew that no matter where our journey took us, no matter what challenges lay ahead, we would always have each other, our bond a guiding light in the darkness.

"Check what flights were leaving from JFK that evening, operating with Zrak Air," James said, his impatience bleeding into his voice.

Morris sighed. "They could be anywhere in the world—India, Italy, China, Japan, Greece, Mexico—"

James's eyes flashed with sudden realization. "Mexico! Mexico! Yes! Juan is from Mexico—where else would they go? Get me every contact in Mexico on a Zoom call now!" He turned sharply to Morris.

Morris, standing up, tried to reason with him. "James, we're disturbing a perfectly happy couple—"

"Do what I say!" James hissed; his eyes wild with obsession.

"You're crazy!" Morris shouted, his patience snapping for the first time. "Fine, Oaxaca! They're in Oaxaca. She updated her story—" His voice softened, trying to reach the man he knew James to be. "James, they are happy together. Can't you see that?"

James's eyes widened at Morris's outburst, a mixture of shock and betrayal flooding his expression. The revelation that Juan and I were in Oaxaca sent a jolt of adrenaline through him, fueling his determination to find us, to uncover the truth that had eluded him for so long.

"Oaxaca," James repeated, his voice trembling with a blend of excitement and apprehension. "You son of a— You had this information all this time?" He turned on Morris, his eyes narrowing with a sense of betrayal.

Morris hesitated; his face conflicted as he considered the consequences of James's actions. "James, are you sure about this? Look at them—" He pushed his phone into James's face, showing a picture of Juan and me, smiling and close. "They seem so happy together, so much in love."

James's face hardened as he looked at the image, a storm of emotions brewing within him. "Oaxaca," he repeated, his voice a low, dangerous growl. "We're going to Oaxaca."

There was no turning back now.

The rhythmic hum of the chopper blades filled the air, drowning out any lingering doubts as James and Morris settled into their seats. With each passing mile, anticipation coursed through James's veins. His mind was set on uncovering the truth that had evaded him for so long. As they touched down in Oaxaca, the vibrant colors of the city spread out beneath them like a painter's canvas. The bustling streets, alive with sounds and smells, were a stark contrast to the quiet serenity of the hacienda where Juan and Graxe had been hiding.

James's focus remained razor-sharp, his thoughts circling around Graxe—his wife Mariyam—who was now someone else entirely. Stephanie, their trusted ally, was waiting for them at a café tucked away on a cobbled street. Her face, a mix of concern and determination, greeted them as they approached.

"James, Morris, I'm glad you made it," Stephanie whispered, her eyes darting around the crowded café.

"We need your help, Stephanie," James said, his voice urgent, almost pleading. "We've tracked Graxe and Juan to

Oaxaca. I need you to find them, to approach Graxe and find out everything you can. Look for the stitches on her right hand."

Stephanie nodded, her eyes narrowing with resolve. "I'm on it, James. But we need to be careful. Juan is no fool."

James's jaw tightened at the reminder of the dangers ahead, but his resolve remained unshaken. "I know. But we can't let fear hold us back. We need to find the truth, no matter what it takes."

With a shared nod, the trio set off into the labyrinthine streets of Oaxaca. The sun hung low in the sky, casting long shadows that danced over the ancient stone buildings. The scent of street food mingled with the distant notes of a mariachi band, but James's mind was elsewhere, focused, unwavering.

Stephanie led them to a quiet café nestled in a corner of the city, where she had heard Juan and Graxe were often seen. As they entered, the bell above the door jingled softly, and James's heart pounded with anticipation. There, seated at a small table bathed in the warm afternoon sun, was Juan, his arm wrapped around Graxe's shoulders as they laughed over steaming cups of coffee.

Stephanie exchanged a meaningful glance with James and Morris before approaching their table, her demeanor calm and composed as she executed their plan.

"Oh my God, girl! Your nails are stunning!" Stephanie exclaimed, her voice bright with feigned enthusiasm as she grabbed Graxe's hand.

Graxe paused, instinctively pulling her hand back. "Ayyyyy, let me see! Where did you get those done?" Stephanie persisted, tugging at Graxe's hand again. Juan chuckled softly, watching the exchange unfold with an amused smirk.

The woman's energy was contagious, and Graxe couldn't help but smile back. She glanced at Juan, who was clearly trying to suppress his laughter. "They are quite something, aren't they?" she said, allowing Stephanie to inspect her nails.

"Wow, they're gorgeous!" Stephanie admired. "I have to show my stylist!"

Graxe beamed, pride evident in her smile. "Thank you! I actually did them myself."

"No way!" Stephanie gasped; her eyes wide with feigned admiration. "You're so talented!"

Stephanie held Graxe's right hand, inspecting it closely. No bandages, no visible marks. The stitches were gone. Stephanie's expression shifted subtly, her eyes sharpening with determination. "I'm sorry, I just had to see how they looked from the back," she said, stepping back and grinning.

James, watching from a discreet distance with Morris, clenched his fists. "Damn it," he muttered. "She doesn't have any stitches. How could this be?"

Morris sighed. "She's not Mariyam, James. She just looks like her. Let it go."

Meanwhile, in the café, Juan caught Stephanie's eye. He raised his coffee mug, his gaze mocking. Stephanie's face flushed slightly, her confidence wavering for a split second as she retreated to where James and Morris were waiting.

"Juan knows we're here," Stephanie muttered, frustration evident in her tone. "He gave me a look... like he knew exactly what we were up to."

James's expression darkened. "He's smart, Morris. Calculated. We underestimated him."

"This is turning into a game of cat and mouse," Morris replied, rubbing the bridge of his nose. "And we're not the cats here."

James leaned against the wall, staring at the bustling street outside. "We need a new approach. This direct confrontation isn't working. Stephanie, go spill a drink on her. Check if she has a mole on her left... right there," he gestured vaguely toward Stephanie's chest.

Stephanie sighed, exchanging a look with Morris. "James, for God's sake, she's not Mariyam."

But James was insistent. "Just do it."

With a resigned nod, Stephanie picked up a piña colada and walked over to the table, 'accidentally' spilling it on Graxe. As she 'tripped,' she pulled at Graxe's top, causing it to unbutton slightly, revealing a small mole on her chest.

"What the hell?" Graxe exclaimed, standing up and covering herself. Juan's eyes flashed with anger as he glared at Stephanie.

"Lo siento, lo siento Mucho," Stephanie stammered, her face flushed with embarrassment as she backed away.

Juan's gaze shifted to the mole and his expression turned grim. "Amor, we have to go," he said quietly, dropping a thousand-dollar bill on the table and guiding Graxe out of the café.

But it was too late. Stephanie's hidden camera pen had captured the mole perfectly.

As we hurried out of the café, I couldn't help but feel a growing sense of unease. "What's going on, Juan? Why are we leaving so suddenly?" I asked, glancing back over my shoulder. It felt almost as if we were fleeing from something—or someone.

Juan didn't answer immediately. He focused on starting the car, his movements quick and precise. Once the engine roared to life, he turned to me with a mischievous glint in his eyes. I managed a small, uncertain smile, but before I could say anything, he leaned over, brushing his lips against my chest, right over the spot where my mole was visible. His lips lingered for a moment before he playfully sucked at my skin, leaving a dark purple mark that perfectly concealed the mole.

"Hey! Naughty!" I laughed, smacking his head lightly. He bit down again, more playfully this time, and I couldn't help but let out a soft moan. Juan pulled back, a smug grin on his face as he deftly buttoned my shirt back up.

"Honeymoon phase two, Mrs. Ramirez?" he teased, his eyes twinkling with mischief. "I heard someone mention Svalbard when we left New York. Under the northern lights—more cold, longer nights…" He grinned wider as my cheeks flushed a deep shade of pink.

"Stop it," I muttered, rolling my eyes, though I couldn't suppress a smile. Juan took my hand and brought it to his lips, planting a soft kiss on my fingers.

But the lightheartedness faded as my thoughts returned to the sudden departure. "Juan… are we running from something?" I asked quietly, my voice tinged with the unease that had settled in my chest.

For a moment, there was only the sound of the car's engine and the distant bustle of Oaxaca's streets. Juan's expression softened, and he kept his gaze on the road, but I could sense the tension beneath his calm exterior.

"Not exactly running, Amor," he finally said, his tone steady but laced with caution. "Just making sure we stay ahead of any surprises."

The weight of his words hung in the air, adding a new layer of uncertainty to my thoughts. As we drove deeper into the labyrinth of Oaxaca, I couldn't shake the feeling that something more was at play, something that went beyond the playful moments we shared.

"Is this about James Cross? You've been different ever since we ran into him," I pressed, noticing how Juan's grip on the steering wheel tightened, his knuckles turning white.

"No, Amor," he said, turning to me with a forced smile. "I've just been busy. And now's the time for us to... travel?"

"You mentioned your father isn't well. When are we visiting him?" I asked, watching as Juan's smile faltered, his composed mask beginning to slip, his web of lies starting to unravel.

He was just a man trying to protect his family, his wife—from whoever this James Cross was or claimed to be. He would go to any length, cross any line he'd never imagined he would—all because he loved me, because he loved me so deeply.

"We'll see them today, before we leave, Amor. And then, to Svalbard? The northern lights are on your bucket list, aren't they? I want to fulfill all of your dreams." He smiled warmly, and I returned the smile, feeling the warmth of his love envelop me.

"Should I book the flights, then?" I asked, looking up at him as I rested my head on his shoulder. He shook his head, a playful gleam in his eyes.

"Grow up, Mrs. Ramirez—JRG is coming." He said, and my eyes lit up.

"It's back from maintenance!" he added, and I squealed with excitement. Our jet, which I had requested to be painted matte black with the JRG monicker, was finally coming back after nearly four months.

"Can I fly it?" I asked, and Juan shot me a sidelong glance before pulling out his phone.

"Let me just check with my lawyer to make sure my life insurance is active," he joked, and we both burst into laughter.
As our laughter faded, a comfortable silence settled over us. I kept my head on Juan's shoulder, feeling the steady rhythm of his breathing beneath me. Yet, even with the warmth of his presence, a sliver of doubt lingered in my mind, curling around my thoughts like smoke.

I studied Juan's profile as he drove. His jaw was set, his eyes focused on the road ahead, but there was a shadow in them—something that hadn't been there before. I reached out, tracing my fingers lightly along his arm.

"Juan, if there's something you're not telling me..." I started, choosing my words carefully. "I need to know. I want to be able to trust you completely."

He glanced at me, his expression softening for a moment. "You can trust me, Amor. Always." He brought my hand to his lips again, his touch lingering as if to reassure me. "But sometimes, protecting you means not telling you everything. You understand that, right?"

I nodded slowly, though his words did little to ease the tension in my chest. I knew he meant well, but there was a part of me that couldn't help but feel the weight of his secrecy. As much as I loved him, I couldn't shake the feeling that something bigger was happening—something I was being kept in the dark about.

After meeting Juan's parents, we quickly packed our things and headed to the private airstrip. The meeting had been brief, filled with polite smiles and warm embraces, but the tension under the surface was palpable. His father seemed tired, frail even, but his eyes carried the same sharpness as Juan's. It was clear there was more going on beneath the pleasantries, but I didn't press. Not yet.

With our suitcases packed and ready, we made our way to the JRG jet, its sleek silhouette gleaming under the warm Mexican sun. The sight of it stirred a sense of nostalgia within me—the familiarity of its luxurious interior a stark contrast to the turmoil that had brought us here.

Once inside, we settled into our seats, the hum of the engine a soothing background noise. Juan clasped my hand, his thumb gently stroking my knuckles. "You okay, amor?"

I nodded, leaning into him. "I'm fine. Just... processing everything."

Juan squeezed my hand, his gaze filled with understanding. "I know it's a lot, but we'll get through this, one step at a time."

As the jet taxied down the runway and lifted into the sky, the sprawling city of Oaxaca grew smaller beneath us, the chaos of its streets fading into the distance. The journey ahead stretched out like a vast, uncharted expanse, its challenges and uncertainties hidden beyond the horizon.

Hours later, we landed in Longyearbyen, Svalbard, the desolate beauty of the Arctic Archipelago spreading out before us. The icy landscape, its stark whiteness stretching to the horizon, was a world away from the vibrant chaos of Mexico, offering a stark reminder of the contrasts in our journey.

We disembarked, the frigid air biting at our cheeks as we stepped onto the tarmac. The sun hung low in the sky, its pale light casting long shadows over the snow-covered ground.

"Welcome to Svalbard," Juan said, his arm slipping around my waist, pulling me close. "Ready for some arctic adventure, amor?"

I nodded, feeling a thrill at the unfamiliar surroundings. "Let's explore this new world, Juan. Together."

We made our way to a cozy cabin nestled at the edge of Longyearbyen, its warm glow a welcoming contrast to the icy wilderness outside. Inside, a crackling fire blazed in the hearth, its warmth filling the room as we settled in.

Juan pulled me onto the couch beside him, his arm draped around my shoulders. "So, what do you think? Arctic honeymoon, just you and me?"

I smiled, leaning into him. "It's perfect, Juan. Just what we needed."

We spent the evening curled up together, the warmth of the fire and the comfort of each other's presence soothing the turmoil that had driven us here. The world outside, with its uncertainties and challenges, seemed distant, a faint echo of a life we had left behind.

But as the night deepened, and the darkness outside swallowed the icy landscape, the knowledge that James Cross's relentless search for me still loomed at the back of my mind, a reminder of the unresolved mysteries that lay ahead.

In the cozy warmth of the cabin, we drifted into sleep, our bodies entwined, ready to face whatever the dawn would bring. The icy winds howled outside, their mournful cries a testament to the stark beauty of Svalbard, a reminder that even in the harshest of environments, life perseveres.

Meanwhile, in New York, James's quest to find us continued, his relentless search driving him to explore every avenue, every lead. The pieces of the puzzle slowly fell into place, their sharp edges promising to reveal the truth that had eluded him for so long.

But for now, in the cold embrace of Svalbard, Juan and I remained together, our bond a beacon of warmth and love, guiding us through the icy landscape, ready to face the challenges ahead, one step at a time.

"James, I have some information." Stephanie burst into James's suite at The Elision Crown Hotel, her breath ragged. "What is it?" James asked, his tone tense. Stephanie, still trying to catch her breath, managed to speak. "It's... about... Graxe."

Morris, standing nearby, rolled his eyes and let out an exasperated growl. "Don't fuel his delusions! His wife died! She committed suicide a year ago! Move past it!" Morris shouted; frustration evident in his voice.

Stephanie shook her head, determined. "He might be digging in the right place, Morris." She looked up, still breathing heavily. "He has a sister—Anayeli. I made friends with her. And she has a daughter, Tabitha, who calls Graxe 'Mermaid.' So, I asked her why."

She took a seat on the edge of the bed, her words tumbling out in a rush. "Tabitha said she came from the ocean, and Uncle Juan married her, like from * Folclores oceánicos. *. And not only that, there are no records of Graxe Rehman before 2023. All her social media was created last year, after March. Then Juan Ramirez got married in September 2023, a court marriage. His parents were upset, and she didn't have anyone—only his friends attended. And then there was a small article in the newspaper on January 12, 2023, five days after Mariyam jumped. A group of campers found a girl near the forested shore of the Hudson. There was a notice—a girl who had lost all her memories. If anyone could identify her, they were asked to come forward. But when the girl was discharged from the hospital, that file disappeared from the records. Rudolf and Juan are from the same precinct where the case was registered. They are a united front; they won't spill. And there's this third ace in the deck, Malcom Wyatt, SWAT and a God-level hacker. Check your phones—are you hacked? Any suspicious activity? Also, Graxe involuntarily adds Hindi when having heartfelt conversations, hinting at her heritage."

James's expression shifted from frustration to a focused intensity as he listened to Stephanie's report. The pieces of the puzzle were slowly starting to fit together, painting a picture that was both complex and unsettling. The implications of what Stephanie suggested were profound; the possibility that Graxe could indeed be Mariyam, somehow alive and without her memories, was a theory that demanded exploration.

Morris, however, remained skeptical and visibly agitated. He paced the room, shaking his head in disbelief. "This is preposterous, Stephanie! You're chasing shadows, feeding into James's obsession. We need concrete evidence, not just coincidences and children's stories!"

James raised his hand, silencing Morris. "No, Morris. She's onto something. We've been looking at this all wrong. This isn't just about finding Mariyam—or Graxe. It's about uncovering a possible cover-up, something bigger than we anticipated."

"I am out of this madness!" Morris stood up; his patience worn thin. "Stop fueling his delusions. He's already losing it," he snapped, but James turned his attention back to Stephanie. "You did well. This information about her sudden appearance, the timing... it's too coincidental. And the clean slate on her social media? It's as if she was meant to appear out of nowhere."

Stephanie nodded, encouraged by James's validation. "Exactly. And about the hacking—I've noticed some irregularities in our communications. Emails I didn't send, calls dropped, files accessed without my intervention. Malcom Wyatt could be behind this, given his reputation."

"Maybe she had other accounts, deactivated after coming into a relationship! Girls do that!" Morris argued. "You are ruining a perfectly happy couple for what? Delusions? Some bullshit circumstantial evidence?"

James turned sharply toward Morris, his eyes hard with resolve. "It's more than circumstantial, Morris. If Graxe really has no past before last year, then how do you explain it? It's our duty to find out the truth, especially if something sinister is behind it."

"Sinister? Really? From what I see, he worships the ground she walks on." Morris was defiant, his skepticism palpable.

Morris's doubts hung in the air, but James's determination overshadowed the tension in the room. He stood up, walking over to the window, staring out at the bustling streets below. "Morris, you've known me for a long time. You know I wouldn't pursue this if I didn't believe there was something worth discovering. Can't you trust my judgment just this once?"

Morris sighed, his frustration waning under the weight of James's earnest plea. "James, it's not about trust. It's about reality. What if you're wrong? What if you're tearing apart someone's life for a ghost?"

James turned back from the window; his gaze steadfast. "And what if I'm right? What if she is Mariyam and something terrible has happened to her? What if she needs our help and we do nothing?"

"Fine, let's entertain this. If she is Mariyam, then what? Even if she is, she doesn't remember you. She's happy with him. What would we do? Drag her back from the only life she knows, the only family she has?" Morris pressed.

"What about my life? My kids?" James roared; his voice filled with anguish.

"James—they've moved on. They've grieved once. Maybe you should too. We see what we want to see. Let's entertain this, okay? He found her? Saved her? Then posted an ad, too? But no one came forward? She got discharged—so probably he or they, all three of them, gave her a safe place to live. Maybe gave her a phone, thus the accounts. Gave her a beautiful name, and then maybe they both fell in love? He married her against his family. Now he is protecting her with everything he has. I don't see the wrong in that. Although I don't think she's her, she didn't have any stitches like you said." Morris held James by the shoulders.

"You want my kids to feel motherless even when their mother is right here? When there is a possibility, she doesn't even know she has kids!" James hissed, his voice trembling with a mixture of desperation and anger.

"It's not about them, James. You've made it about yourself," Morris sighed, his tone softening, but firm.

James's face contorted with a mixture of anguish and frustration as Morris laid out the scenario. Every word seemed to cut deeper into his resolve, challenging the foundation of his year-long search. The room fell silent, heavy with the weight of unspoken fears and what-ifs.

"You're asking me to abandon hope," James finally said, his voice low and strained. "To turn my back on the possibility that she might still be out there, that she might need me."

Morris's eyes softened as he looked at James. "I'm asking you to consider what this obsession is costing you, James. What it's costing your sons. Aaron and Aamon deserve a father who isn't consumed by a ghost of what might be. I get it. I really do. But you have to see the damage you're doing—to yourself, to everyone around you."

James's expression faltered, the strength in his eyes dimming for a moment. The truth of Morris's words stung more than he wanted to admit. He had lost count of the sleepless nights, the strained phone calls with his children, the friendships slowly fraying as he continued his relentless pursuit.

But he couldn't just let it go. Not when there was even the slightest chance Mariyam was alive. His Mariyam. His wife.

Stephanie spoke up softly, her voice steady but filled with empathy. "James, maybe Morris is right, but maybe he isn't. We don't have to abandon this, but perhaps we need to approach it differently. Focus on finding the truth, not just what you want it to be. If there is any chance Graxe is Mariyam, we owe it to her to uncover it. But we also owe it to her to consider the possibility that her life now, the one she's living with Juan, might be where she belongs."

James sighed deeply, rubbing a hand over his face. "I don't know if I can do that, Steph. I don't know if I can be that selfless."

"You can," Stephanie replied gently. "You've always been stronger than you think."

James nodded, but his mind was still a whirl of conflicting thoughts. He knew he had to find answers, but the path forward had never felt so uncertain. He looked out over the city again, his mind drifting to his children—how would they feel if he brought their mother back only for her not to recognize them, not to want them? Would he be saving them, or hurting them all over again?

Morris sighed, a resigned look crossing his face. "Alright, James. If we're doing this, we need to be smart about it. No more reckless moves. No more dragging everyone into the chaos. We focus on finding the truth. We do this the right way."

James nodded slowly. "Agreed. No more reckless moves." He looked back at Stephanie, determination hardening his features once more. "Let's keep digging, but discreetly. We need to get closer to Juan, Rudi, and Malcom. Find out exactly what they're hiding. If they've covered something up, we'll expose it."

Stephanie smiled, though her eyes remained serious. "I'm already on it. But we have to be careful. If Malcom's really involved and he's as good as they say, he'll know we're sniffing around."

"Let him know," James said, his voice carrying a dangerous edge. "I'm done hiding. It's time we find out the truth—whatever that truth may be."

As the weight of their new resolve settled in, Stephanie and Morris exchanged glances, a silent agreement forming. This was it. One last push for answers. The search for Graxe—or Mariyam—would continue, but with caution and clarity, a steady pursuit rather than a desperate chase.

The night deepened outside the window, the city lights twinkling below like a million possibilities waiting to be uncovered. And somewhere in the cold reaches of Svalbard, in a warm cabin glowing against the snow-covered wilderness, the woman they sought lay asleep, her mind free of the storm of questions that swirled in James's world.

For now.

But dawn was coming, and with it, the beginning of the end of this tangled web of secrets, lies, and the elusive truth that could either set them all free—or bind them forever.

*They were two men, each caught in a different kind of love. One was tethered to the memories of a woman who had been his everything—his wife, the mother of his children, the center of his world. His love was a fierce, unyielding force, driven by the belief that she could be found, that she could be brought back to the life they had built together. The other had fallen for the woman she had become—a new identity forged from the ashes of her past, a love born from the moments they had shared and the life they had created together in the here and now. His love was protective, steadfast, and willing to shield her from anything that could threaten the fragile happiness they had found. And so, they stood as opposites on the same battlefield, each willing to risk everything for the chance to claim her heart. Two men, driven by love, destined for conflict, bound by a fate that neither could control, but both were determined to face. *

CHAPTER 4

Beneath the vast canopy of stars, away from the world in that remote cabin in the Arctic wilderness, surrounded by the raw beauty of nature and the relentless fury of the storm, we found solace in each other's arms. Our love felt like it transcended all boundaries and defied every odd stacked against us.

Inside the cabin, the fire crackled and popped in the hearth, casting a warm, golden glow across the wooden walls and simple furnishings. The air was filled with the scent of burning pine and the soft warmth that came from the flickering flames. Outside, the storm continued its relentless assault; the wind howled through the barren trees, a symphony of the wilderness's untamed fury. But within the cozy sanctuary of the cabin, it was just us—lost in a world of quiet intimacy and comfort.

Juan's lips brushed softly along my neck, sending a ripple of warmth through my veins. I leaned into his touch, feeling the steady thrum of his heartbeat against mine. His hands moved over me with a gentle certainty that spoke of both tenderness and strength, his embrace both protective and passionate.

He pressed me close against him, his body radiating warmth in contrast to the chill that seeped through the cabin walls. The rough-hewn wood behind me was cool, a stark contrast to the heat between us, but I welcomed the sensation, feeling the depth of our connection in every breath, every whispered word.

The sound of the storm outside became a distant murmur, overshadowed by the rhythm of our breaths, the steady beat of our hearts. Every caress was deliberate, every movement careful and slow, building on the trust and love we had forged in this secluded place. In that moment, we were lost in our own world, where nothing beyond these walls mattered.

As the moments passed, our surroundings seemed to blur, and all that remained was the intensity of being together. When the quiet settled in and the fire began to die down, casting softer shadows around us, we found ourselves wrapped in a blanket, Juan pulling me closer to his chest. His warmth was a steady comfort against the cold outside, a reminder that no matter how fierce the storm, there was peace to be found here.

"Are you okay?" he asked softly, his voice a low rumble against the quiet.

I nodded, resting my head against his shoulder. "Yes," I whispered. "More than okay."

For a while, we simply lay there, listening to the soft crackling of the dying fire. The wind outside battered against the windows, but inside, the world felt miles away, safe and distant.

"You know," I murmured after a while, my voice soft against his chest, "I keep thinking about how this all began. How you found me by the riverbank, how we ended up here, away from everything."

Juan's grip tightened slightly, his expression hardening for a moment before he softened again, his eyes reflecting the fire's warm glow. "We ended up here because it's where we need to be, amor. Away from all the chaos, all the noise. We can build our own life here."

I nodded, understanding his need for this isolation, but there was still a tug of unease within me. "But Juan, what if there's more to my story? What if there are answers out there that we're hiding from?"

Juan's brow furrowed slightly, his gaze drifting to the flickering flames. "Amor, sometimes it's better to leave the past where it belongs—in the past. We have each other, and that's what matters right now."

I felt a pang of frustration at his words, but I knew he spoke out of love and concern. "You're right," I said softly, even as the doubts continued to linger in my mind. "I just... I feel like there's something missing. Something important."

Juan turned to me, his eyes filled with a mix of love and worry. "If there is, we'll face it together, amor. But for now, let's not let it steal our peace."

I hesitated for a moment, then asked quietly, "Juan—where is the pendant you said I was wearing when you found me? The one with the 'Rehman' name, and the emerald drop I was clutching in my hand?"

Juan's face tightened momentarily, a shadow passing over his features. "I... I put them somewhere safe," he replied after a brief pause. "I'll look for them later, okay? Don't worry about it, amor."

I nodded, though a flicker of doubt still tugged at me. I didn't want to question him, not when he'd done so much for me, but something about his tone made me wonder. As the night wore on, and the wind continued its song outside, I couldn't shake the feeling that perhaps, somewhere buried in the past I couldn't remember, there were secrets waiting to be uncovered. And as much as I wanted to leave it behind, I knew the answers were out there, waiting for me to find them.

James Cross stood by the expansive floor-to-ceiling windows of his penthouse in New York, the city sprawled out beneath him like a vast, glittering web. The skyline was draped in a thick veil of snow, the flakes falling in a relentless, silent dance that covered the streets below. His penthouse was dark, save for the dim glow of the city lights filtering in through the glass, casting long shadows across the polished hardwood floors and the sleek, modern furnishings.

The room was cold, both in temperature and in atmosphere. The minimalist design of black leather and steel, with its sharp lines and muted colors, echoed the chill that seeped into James's bones. His hands were clasped behind his back, his posture tense as he stared out into the winter night, his reflection a ghostly figure in the glass.

The silence was heavy, broken only by the distant hum of the city below and the occasional creak of the building settling in the cold. A half-empty glass of scotch sat on the side table next to a leather armchair, the amber liquid catching the light as it shifted slightly with each step he took. His eyes were fixed on nothing in particular, his thoughts miles away, lost somewhere in the snowy wilderness where Graxe—where Mariyam—might be hiding.

"So, what now?" James muttered; his gaze fixed on the swirling snow outside. The weight of uncertainty pressed down on him, as heavy and unyielding as the storm.

Morris sighed deeply and slumped into a chair across from James. "James, I think we need to consider the possibility that Graxe may not be Mariyam. It's been a year, and all we have are vague similarities and coincidences," he said carefully, his tone steady but weary.

James's fists clenched at Morris's words, his jaw tightening with a mix of frustration and despair. "No, Morris. I can't accept that. There has to be more. There has to be an answer," he insisted, his voice low but fierce. The thought of giving up felt like a betrayal, not just to himself but to the memory of Mariyam.

Stephanie, seated beside Morris, leaned forward, her expression soft and understanding. "James, we're all worried about you. This search... it's consumed you. We're not sure if it's healthy anymore. We have to think about what this is doing to you—and to your sons."

James's gaze flicked to her, his eyes bloodshot and lined with sleepless nights. "And what about the consequences of doing nothing? What if she really is Mariyam, and we let her slip away again?" His voice cracked with a desperate edge, the weight of his fears pressing down like a vice.

Morris shook his head, his expression pained. "James, we're not saying to give up entirely. But maybe we need to take a step back, reassess things. We've pushed too hard, and it might be time to accept that we can't force an answer out of this."

James's face twisted with frustration, his desperation boiling over. "I can't just let go, Morris. Not until I know the truth," he replied, his voice a mixture of pleading and resolve. "What is the updates Steph?"

"Anayeli wouldn't open the door for me, and Graxe and Juan have gone MIA again," she said quietly, looking down as if bracing for his reaction.

"What do you mean, 'gone MIA'?" James shot to his feet, his patience fraying. "Morris, get me the—"

Before he could finish, Morris was already holding out a stack of papers. "Here's the passenger list for all flights leaving Oaxaca, yesterday, the day before, and today. No records of them on any commercial flights," Morris said, his voice calm but tense.

"So how the hell did they leave? And why didn't she open the door? Tell me exactly what happened," James demanded, turning his sharp gaze to Stephanie.

Stephanie rubbed her temples, feeling the weight of yet another dead end. "I went to Anayeli's early in the morning, just like we planned. I knocked, rang the bell, but no one answered. I waited for hours, James. It was like the house was empty."

James began pacing the room, his mind racing with possibilities. "They couldn't have just vanished into thin air. There must be another way they left. Private transport? Could they have used some sort of private charter that wouldn't appear on regular passenger lists?"

Morris, flipping through the papers again, looked up thoughtfully. "It's possible. Juan has the means. They could have used a private jet or even a yacht. Those wouldn't be listed in the usual databases."

James stopped pacing, his mind honing in on this new angle. "Why didn't we consider that sooner? Check for any activity involving private charters, both air and sea. I want every piece of information available," he ordered, his tone clipped and urgent.

Morris nodded, already dialing numbers, his voice low and tense as he reached out to their network of contacts for any leads on private transport. Meanwhile, Aamon, who had been watching quietly, placed a hand on his father's shoulder, a concerned frown on his face.

"Dad, I know how much this means to you, but you're wearing yourself thin. If this turns into another dead end, we need to think about stepping back," Aamon said gently, his voice steady but concerned.

James looked at his sons, his heart heavy with a mix of pain and determination. "I'll consider it, boys. But not yet. Not until I've exhausted every option," he replied, his voice a little softer now, but no less resolved.

Aamon and Aaron exchanged a look, understanding their father's need for closure, even if it meant following him down a path that seemed to grow darker and more uncertain with every step. As Morris continued making calls, and the snow outside fell heavier, James's resolve hardened. He wasn't ready to let go—not yet. Not until every possibility had been explored, every question answered.

James stood by the floor-to-ceiling windows, a glass of whiskey in his hand, his eyes fixed on the snow-covered city below. His reflection stared back at him, eyes shadowed with sleepless nights and a year-long pursuit that had brought him here, to this moment of unsettling realization. The weight of his obsession hung heavy on his shoulders, pulling him deeper into his thoughts.

Behind him, the sound of papers shuffling broke the silence. Morris, seated at the glass dining table, was flipping through documents with a concentrated frown, while Stephanie sat across from him, her laptop open and casting a faint blue glow on her face. They were both weary, worn down by months of chasing shadows and unraveling dead ends, but determined to keep pushing forward.

"Juan left on his own jet," Morris muttered, his voice breaking the tension that hung in the air like a heavy fog. He glanced up at James, whose back remained turned to the room. "We've confirmed it through one of our contacts. A private jet took off from a secluded airstrip outside Oaxaca last night, under the radar. The flight plan was unregistered, but it's him. There's no doubt."

James's grip tightened around his glass, his knuckles turning white. He took a slow, measured breath, his jaw clenched with the frustration of yet another evasion. "Where is he headed?" he asked, his voice low, a dangerous calm threading through it.

Morris shook his head. "That's the problem. We don't know. The jet went off the radar once it left Mexican airspace. It could be anywhere by now. Svalbard, Alaska, even somewhere in Europe. He has the connections to disappear completely."

Stephanie leaned back in her chair, rubbing her eyes. "This guy is good. Every move is calculated. He knew we were closing in, and he got her out of there fast. If we want to find them, we'll need to think smarter, move quicker. He's playing a different game."

James turned from the window, his eyes sharp and filled with a burning intensity. The dim light of the room caught the hard lines of his face, casting shadows that deepened his expression of resolve. "He won't stay hidden for long. Not with Graxe. She's not just some prize he can keep tucked away. If she really is Mariyam, she's coming back, whether he likes it or not."

Morris nodded, though his eyes were cautious. "James, you've got to be prepared for whatever comes next. If she's with him willingly... you might not get the reunion you're hoping for."

James's expression didn't waver. "If she's with him willingly, it's because she doesn't remember. She doesn't know who she really is. I'm not giving up until I've seen her—until I've looked into her eyes and know for sure."

Stephanie tapped a few keys on her laptop, her eyes scanning the screen with focus. "I've reached out to some contacts who might know more about Juan's flight routes. But it'll take time. And if he's really trying to disappear, he'll have planned for this."

James drained the last of his whiskey, the amber liquid burning down his throat. He set the glass down on the bar with a sharp clink, the sound echoing through the quiet room. "We don't have time, Steph. Every minute we waste is a minute he's getting further away."

The fire crackled behind him, filling the silence with its steady warmth, but James felt none of it. His penthouse, normally a sanctuary from the chaos of his public life, felt like a prison now—a place where the walls closed in with every passing second that he wasn't closer to finding her.

"I'll head to the airfield myself," James said, a new determination sharpening his voice. "Maybe someone there saw something—a refuel, a maintenance crew, anything. I'll find a lead."

Morris looked up, concern evident in his eyes. "James, you can't just rush into this. If Juan's as connected as we think, this could be dangerous. You're not exactly low-profile."

James turned to face Morris fully, his expression unyielding. "I've spent a year playing it safe, following the rules, and getting nowhere. I'm done waiting. I need to find her, and I'm not stopping until I do."

"And then what?" Aamon finally broke the silence, his voice trembling with a mix of anger and pain. He had been silent for so long—nearly a year—trying to bury the reality that his mother was gone. "What are you planning to do, Dad? Hurt her all over again? Like you did before? Cheat on her, break her heart so badly that dying felt like a better option than staying with you?" His voice cracked, his emotions spilling over as he struggled to hold back his tears. He blinked rapidly, fighting to maintain his composure, but the weight of his words hung heavily in the room. Without waiting for a response, Aamon turned and rushed out, the door slamming shut behind him.

The room fell into a heavy silence, the echo of the door slamming shut still reverberating through the walls. James stood frozen, his eyes fixed on the spot where his son had just been, Aamon's words cutting deeper than any wound he'd felt in this year-long search. The accusation, raw and unfiltered, hung in the air like a palpable weight, pressing down on everyone present.

Morris shifted uncomfortably, his gaze dropping back to the papers spread out on the table, while Stephanie remained silent, her eyes following Aamon's retreating form. She could feel the tension crackling like static electricity, the deep-seated pain in every word Aamon had thrown at his father.

James's chest tightened, his breath coming in shallow gasps as he tried to process his son's outburst. The sting of Aamon's accusation—of his failures as a husband, as a father—sank into him, a truth he had tried to bury under his relentless drive to find Mariyam. He had known the toll his obsession had taken on his sons, but hearing it spoken out loud, so bluntly, left him stripped of the resolve he had built around himself.

Finally, he spoke, his voice low and strained. "I'm not trying to hurt her again," he said, more to himself than anyone else in the room. His eyes were still fixed on the door, his mind replaying Aamon's words over and over like a broken record. "I'm trying to make things right."

Morris looked up; his expression cautious but sympathetic. "James, I know you think finding her will fix things, but Aamon has a point. If she doesn't remember—if she's happy with him now—forcing this won't bring back what you lost. You might just be opening old wounds, for all of you."

James's gaze shifted to Morris; his eyes hardened but tinged with a deep weariness. "And what if she's not happy? What if she's just living someone else's life because she doesn't know who she really is? Should I just leave her there, trapped in a lie?"

Stephanie finally spoke, her voice calm but firm. "James, we're not saying to abandon her. But you have to be prepared for the possibility that she might have moved on, even without knowing the full truth. If you go in their guns blazing, you could do more harm than good."

James rubbed his temples, his frustration boiling just beneath the surface. "I don't want to hurt her. I just want her to have a choice. I need to know if she's choosing this life with Juan because she truly wants it, or if she's choosing it because she doesn't remember the one, she had before."

Stephanie leaned forward, her tone softening. "And if she does choose him, James? What then? Are you ready to let go?"

The question hung in the air, each word sinking into James like stones. He had been so focused on finding Mariyam—on the possibility of reclaiming the life they once had—that he hadn't truly considered what he would do if she chose a life without him. The thought gnawed at him, creating a hollow space in his chest that ached with the weight of an answer he wasn't ready to confront.

"I'll cross that bridge when I get to it," he finally muttered, his voice barely above a whisper. "But I need to see her. I need to know."

Another tense silence settled over the room, punctuated only by the faint crackling of the fire and the distant hum of the city below. James turned back to the window, his reflection staring back at him once more, and for the first time, he saw not just determination but a deep-seated fear—a fear of losing her all over again, of losing everything.

Morris stood, smoothing the wrinkles from his shirt. "I'm going to check in with some contacts, see if we can find out more about that jet's flight path. Maybe we can narrow it down to a region, get a better idea of where he's headed." He paused, glancing at James. "And, James... think about what Aamon said. He's hurting, too. He's lost his mother, and he feels like he's losing you."

James didn't respond, his eyes still fixed on the snowy cityscape beyond the glass. He heard the door click shut as Morris and Stephanie left, leaving him alone in the vast, cold space of his penthouse.

The fire continued to burn low, the warmth failing to reach him as he stood there, caught between the past and an uncertain future. He thought of Aamon and Aaron, of the pain he'd seen in their eyes, the anger, the grief. He had been so wrapped up in his own quest for answers that he hadn't truly seen theirs. They were right to be angry. He had let them down. But he couldn't stop. Not yet.

James swallowed the last remnants of his whiskey, the burn no longer giving him any comfort. He set the empty glass down, his hands trembling slightly. Outside, the snow continued to fall, thick and heavy, covering the city in a blanket of white. Somewhere out there, Mariyam—or Graxe—was out of his reach, but not beyond it. Not yet.

He turned away from the window, the room feeling too small, too claustrophobic. The walls seemed to close in on him as he walked to the bar and poured himself another drink. He knew he was on the brink of something—something that could break him or finally bring him peace. But either way, he would not rest until he knew the truth, even if it meant losing everything in the process.

James stood there, glass in hand, his gaze drifting to the foggy window. The snow outside continued its relentless dance, swirling through the night like a cold, indifferent whisper of the universe. His thoughts, however, were far from the storm. His mind was lost in the echoes of a voice he hadn't heard in over a year—Mariyam's voice.

His breath fogged up the glass, and without thinking, he lifted a finger to trace a name there—*Mariyam*. His

Mariyam. He could almost see her reflection beside his, as if she were still there, standing next to him, the two of them wrapped in a world only they understood.

"Where would you go if you wanted to find peace?" he asked the memory of her, his voice barely more than a whisper in the silent room. He closed his eyes, trying to pull the answer from the depths of his mind, from the fragments of conversations they had shared long ago.

And then he remembered. A soft smile tugged at his lips as a moment from the past came rushing back, vivid and warm despite the cold reality of the present. She had been laughing, her eyes bright with that playful light that he had loved so much.

"Tum... tum mujhe itna pareshan karte ho na," she had teased, her laughter filling the room like music. "Dekhna, ek din sab kuch chhod kar bhaag jaungi, baraf ki duniya mein, maybe Longyearbyen—ya phir North Pole!" She had said it so casually, like it was a joke, a fantasy, but he could hear the longing in her voice even then. The yearning for somewhere far away, untouched by the chaos of their lives.

James's eyes snapped open, his heart pounding with sudden clarity. "Longyearbyen," he murmured, his breath misting the glass again. He wrote it there with his finger, the letters forming slowly, as if bringing that distant place into focus would somehow bring her closer to him.

He stared at the name on the window, his pulse quickening. It made sense. It was remote, secluded—exactly the kind of place she might have imagined escaping to when things became too much. And if Juan had been listening to her dreams, he might have taken her there, to that icy world where no one would think to look.

James turned sharply from the window; his mind suddenly alight with a sense of purpose he hadn't felt in months. He grabbed his phone and dialed Morris, his fingers tapping impatiently as he waited for his friend to pick up.

"Morris, it's James," he said as soon as he heard the line connect. "I have a lead. I think I know where they might have gone."

There was a pause on the other end, and then Morris's voice came through, cautious but attentive. "Where?"

"Longyearbyen," James replied, his voice steadier now. "It's a remote settlement in Svalbard. She mentioned it once, back when... back when things were starting to fall apart. Said she wanted to run away there, to a place of snow and solitude. It's the kind of place Juan could take her if he wanted to disappear."

Morris hesitated, considering the possibility. "That's pretty far-fetched, James. But if you're sure—"

"I am," James cut in. "Check for any private flights heading that way, or anywhere close. I'm booking a ticket to Norway. If there's a chance she's there, I'm going after her."

"Alright," Morris said, though James could hear the doubt in his voice. "I'll get on it. Just... be careful, okay? This isn't a game. If you're right, and Juan's there with her, he's not going to be happy to see you."

James nodded; his jaw set with determination. "I don't care. I'm not backing down now."

He ended the call and tossed the phone onto the couch, his mind already racing ahead to what he would do once he got to Longyearbyen. If she was there—if she was truly there—he would find her. And he would finally have the answers that had eluded him for so long.

As he stood there, staring at the name scrawled on the foggy glass, he felt a flicker of something he hadn't felt in a long time—hope. It was fragile, like the ice covering the city outside, but it was there. And that was enough to push him forward.

The night stretched on, and the snow continued to fall, but for the first time in what felt like forever, James saw a path through the storm.

James remained by the window, the cold glass beneath his fingertip slowly warming as his breath continued to mist against it. He stared at the word he had written—*Longyearbyen*—as if willing the letters to pull Mariyam back to him. The thought of finally being close, of finally uncovering the truth, made his heart pound with a mix of anticipation and anxiety. He knew this lead was tenuous, a guess at best, but it was the first flicker of hope he'd had in so long.

As he turned away from the window, he heard his phone buzz on the couch. He snatched it up quickly, expecting Morris's voice on the other end. Instead, it was a text message from him.

"Call me."

James didn't hesitate. He dialed Morris, and within seconds, his friend picked up. "James," Morris's voice came through the line, cautious but clear, "I've started looking into private flights heading towards Svalbard. There are a few that could fit the timeline, but nothing definitive yet."

James's pulse quickened. "Keep digging. I'm not letting this lead slip away. If Juan's trying to hide, he would've chosen somewhere off the beaten path, somewhere Mariyam might have wanted to go."

There was a pause on the line, and James could almost hear Morris's hesitation. "James," Morris began slowly, "what if she's not there? What if this is just another dead end? You've got to prepare yourself for that possibility. You've followed leads before that haven't panned out. You need to think about what comes next."

James exhaled, his breath a deep sigh that seemed to echo in the quiet of his penthouse. He walked back to the window, staring out at the snow-covered cityscape. The fear of another fruitless chase gnawed at him, but he pushed it aside, focusing on the faint glimmer of hope he was holding onto. "If she's not there," he said finally, his voice steady but laced with exhaustion, "then I'll find another lead. I'll keep searching until I have nothing left. I've come this far, Morris. I can't just walk away now."

"But, James," Morris pressed, his tone firmer now, "at what point do you draw the line? What happens if there's no more trail to follow? You've put everything on the line—your career, your family. You need to consider what's left for you if this doesn't go the way you hope."

James's grip on the phone tightened, his knuckles turning white again. "I know what I'm risking," he replied quietly. "But I can't stop. Not until I know for sure. If I find out she's truly happy, if she's chosen this new life of her own will, then maybe I can make peace with that. But not without trying. Not without knowing."

Morris sighed, sensing the resoluteness in James's voice. "Alright," he said after a moment, his voice softening with a trace of concern. "I just want you to be prepared. We'll keep looking into the flights, see if we can narrow it down. And I'll get in touch with some contacts in Norway, see if anyone's noticed anything unusual in Svalbard. But James... if this doesn't work out, we need to have a serious conversation about what comes next."

James nodded to himself, understanding the weight behind Morris's words. "Fair enough. But let's cross that bridge when we get to it."

"Agreed," Morris replied. "I'll keep you posted as soon as I have more information. And, James... take care of yourself. You're no good to anyone if you're running on empty."

"I will," James said, though he wasn't sure if he believed his own words. "Thanks, Morris."

He hung up the phone and tossed it back onto the couch. The penthouse felt colder than before, the fire in the hearth barely making a dent in the creeping chill that seemed to seep into his bones. He turned back to the window, staring out at the city lights that flickered like distant stars against the backdrop of snow.

What if she wasn't there? The thought whispered through his mind, insistent and unnerving. What if this was just another wild goose chase, another empty lead that would leave him further from the truth and more lost than ever?

He shook his head, trying to dispel the doubt. He couldn't think like that. Not now. Not when he was so close. *If she wasn't there*, he told himself, *he would just keep looking*. He had to believe that every step, every lead, was bringing him closer to her, even if the path was winding and unclear.

James's gaze drifted to the foggy window once more, to the name he had traced there with his finger—*Longyearbyen*. It was a fragile hope, but it was all he had. And as he stood there, staring at the letters fading slowly into the mist, he whispered to himself, as much a prayer as a promise:

"Hold on, Mariyam. I'm coming."

With that, he turned away from the window, his mind set, his resolve hardened. There was no turning back now.

The early morning light filtered through the frosted windows of the cabin, casting soft, muted rays onto the wooden floor. Outside, the world was a pristine blanket of white, the snow thick and untouched. Juan was still asleep, his deep breaths even and calm, but I was feeling restless, my limbs thrumming with energy. The thrill of the Arctic landscape was calling to me, and I decided I couldn't wait for him to wake up.

I dressed quickly, pulling on my white fur-lined jacket, boots, and gloves, and slipped out of the cabin, the door creaking softly behind me. The crisp, cold air hit my face, invigorating me, and I smiled as I took my first steps into the snow, my breath coming out in white puffs. The pine forest stretched out ahead, a dense cluster of tall, dark trees standing stark against the white ground, and my eyes caught sight of a small movement—a flash of white among the trees.

A polar bear cub. "Hii..." I whispered excitedly, and before I knew it, I was jogging through the snow toward the tiny creature. The cub glanced back, its small black eyes wide with curiosity, and then darted deeper into the forest. A grin spread across my face, and I found myself running after it, my boots crunching loudly against the snow.

"Mr. Softie, wait!" I called out, my voice echoing through the quiet forest. I kept following the little cub, my heart racing with a childlike thrill, until it finally stopped, glancing back at me with a curious tilt of its head. I bent down, reaching out cautiously, trying to soothe its apparent worry with a gentle touch. "Hey there, little one..." I murmured, my hand hovering just above its soft fur. The cub was so small, almost pint-sized, and I couldn't resist the urge to pat him, imagining he'd enjoy the attention. But as my hand drew closer, a heavy sensation settled in my chest—a feeling of being watched.

I turned slowly, and there it was—the cub's mother. A full-grown polar bear, towering and menacing, her massive body framed against the backdrop of the snow-covered pines. She stood on her hind legs, her fur bristling, her dark eyes locked onto mine with a fierce intensity that sent a chill down my spine. I could feel the raw power radiating from her, an unspoken warning not to get any closer.

I crawled back instinctively, retreating on my hands and knees as the bear's roar echoed through the forest, a sound that seemed to shake the very ground beneath me. "Good bear, good bear," I croaked, my voice trembling as I extended a shaky hand toward her. "Mr. Cuddles, that's right, we're friends, aren't we?" My mind raced, half panicking and half trying to remember anything I'd heard about dealing with bears. Playing dead? No, that wouldn't work with polar bears.

Desperation took hold, and I tried another tactic, raising my hands to mimic "paws" in a feeble attempt to appear larger, hoping it might scare her off. The bear eyed me with what seemed like a mix of confusion and anger, then leaned closer and roared again, the sound rippling through my entire body.

"Okay, okay," I muttered, my breath visible in the frigid air. "Maybe not so good of an idea..." I tried to stand up slowly, thinking maybe I could back away without provoking her further. But then, in a swift, terrifying motion, the bear swiped at me—not with the intent to maul, but to grab. Her massive paw snagged my jacket, and before I could react, she began dragging me and her cub toward the denser side of the forest.

Panic gripped me as I stumbled alongside the bear, desperately trying to wriggle free. "Stupid jacket," I cursed under my breath. "Why would I wear white fur in a place full of snow?" I pulled off my cap, letting my black hair tumble out, hoping the contrast might convince her I wasn't a cub. But the sudden movement only startled her further, and she let out another deafening roar, her eyes flashing with protective fury.

My instincts screamed at me to run, and without thinking, I broke free of her grip and sprinted through the snow, my legs pumping as fast as they could carry me. The sound of the bear's heavy paws thundering behind me pushed me onward, my breath coming in ragged gasps, my heart pounding in my chest.

Suddenly, a pair of hands reached out from behind a tree, pulling me sharply into the shadows. A gloved hand cupped my face, covering my mouth before I could cry out. "Stay silent—shh," a man's voice whispered urgently in my ear. His eyes—an intense mix of green and blue—locked onto mine from behind his snow gear. I nodded, too breathless and terrified to do anything else.

The bear roared again, pausing just beyond our hiding spot. She began to sniff the air, searching, her head swinging slowly from side to side. I could feel the man's heart beating against my back as he pulled me deeper into his jacket, his body tensing like a spring coiled and ready to act.

The snow crunched under the bear's paws as she crept closer, her breath forming misty clouds in the freezing air. I held my breath, praying she wouldn't find us, every second stretching out into an eternity. The man's grip tightened around me, his body shielding mine from the bitter cold and the very real threat of being discovered.

The bear huffed softly, her nose twitching as she took one last deep sniff. For a moment, I thought she had found us, my heart nearly stopping in my chest. But then, with a reluctant grunt, she turned away, lumbering back into the forest with her cub in tow.

I let out a shaky breath, feeling my entire body begin to relax as the immediate danger passed. The man loosened his hold on me, his eyes still scanning the forest for any sign of the bear's return. "Thank you," I whispered, my voice barely audible, as I turned to face him. His snow gear concealed most of his face, but I could see his eyes soften slightly.

"We need to get back to the cabin," he said, his voice low and urgent. "It's not safe here."

I nodded, still catching my breath, my legs trembling from both fear and adrenaline. We began making our way back through the forest, each step a reminder of how close I had come to a very different outcome. The trees seemed to close in around us, their branches heavy with snow, creaking softly in the wind.

As we walked, I kept glancing at the man beside me. There was something about him—his confident movements, the way he held himself—that felt oddly familiar. I couldn't quite place it, but I knew I had to ask. "Who are you?" I finally said, unable to keep the curiosity from my voice.

He paused for a moment, then turned to face me fully. "My name is Erik," he replied. "I'm a ranger here in Svalbard. I was patrolling the area when I saw you heading into the forest."

His eyes, a piercing green-blue like the icy waters of the Arctic, watched me carefully. "You should be more careful," he continued. "The wildlife here isn't always as forgiving as the landscapes might suggest. You, okay?"

I nodded, feeling a mix of embarrassment and gratitude. "I was following a cub... I didn't think—"

Erik's lips quirked into a faint smile. "A cub, huh? It's a common mistake. But a dangerous one. Let's get you back safely."

We walked the rest of the way in silence, the forest gradually settling back into its calm after the disruption. When the outline of my cabin finally came into view through the trees, relief washed over me like a warm wave.

"I'll take my leave now," he said, his tone still reserved but polite.

"Thank you," I replied, watching him disappear back into the forest before heading inside. I found Juan already up, his face etched with worry as he made calls, pacing the length of the cabin. The moment I hugged him from behind, his tense posture softened.

"Amour," he breathed, turning to pull me into a tight embrace. "I was going mad with worry. Where were you? What happened, Amor? Are you okay?"

I gave a sheepish grin. "A bear tried to eat me," I confessed, laughing nervously. "And also... she thought I was her polar bear cub."

Meanwhile, in a cabin a few blocks away, 'Erik'—or rather, James Cross—pulled off his snow mask and set it down on a table, his breath still heavy from the encounter. Morris leaned against a wooden pillar, watching him with a bemused expression.

"So, 'Erik,' done playing the hero?" Morris quipped. "Should we go back now?"

James shot him a look. "I had to. The bear was chasing her," he muttered, rubbing his face with both hands.

Morris shook his head, half-amused, half-concerned. "So, you became Erik, huh? Anyway, did it finally quell your thirst? Is she not Mariyam? No stitches on her hand, right? You checked?"

James looked away, his eyes narrowing slightly as he stared out the window into the endless snow. "Yeah, I checked," he said, his voice tight. "No stitches."

Morris sighed, sensing the conflict still brewing within him. "So, what now, James? Keep playing ranger, or face the fact that maybe, just maybe, this might not be the ending you were looking for?" Morris's voice was gentle but firm, his eyes fixed on James, who remained silent, his thoughts seemingly miles away.

James stared out the window, watching the snowflakes drift lazily to the ground, each one unique and delicate, just like his fading memories of Mariyam. For a moment, he said nothing, the weight of the past year pressing down on him, pulling him deeper into his thoughts. His heart was a battlefield of emotions—a conflict between the relentless drive to find his wife and the gnawing doubt that he was chasing a ghost.

After a long pause, he finally spoke, his voice low and laced with frustration. "I don't know, Morris. I just—seeing her, being so close... I can't help but feel like there's something there. Even if she isn't Mariyam, there's this pull. Something in my gut telling me not to walk away just yet."

Morris shook his head slightly, leaning back against the pillar. "You've got to be sure, James. Playing hero out here in the middle of nowhere, chasing after shadows—it's only going to get you deeper into a mess. If she's not who you think she is, you have to be ready to accept that and move on."

James's jaw clenched, his eyes still on the swirling snow. "I can't just walk away, not without knowing for sure. I need to talk to her. Really talk to her. There's something in her eyes, something familiar..."

Morris sighed deeply. "You're not thinking clearly. You're letting hope cloud your judgment. You said it yourself—no stitches on her hand. That was your big clue, remember? If she had fallen like Mariyam did, she'd have scars. But you saw her. There's nothing."

James's mind replayed the moment in the forest, the memory haunting him like a ghost he couldn't shake. He remembered the rough bark of the tree beneath his hand as he reached for hers, his breath held tight in his chest. He had searched her skin with a frantic urgency, desperate to find the scars that should have been there—the scars he knew so well, the ones that would confirm she was Mariyam. But there had been nothing. No scars, no stitches, just smooth, unblemished skin. It should have been enough to convince him that he was wrong, that Mariyam was truly gone, but his heart stubbornly refused to accept it. His mind and his eyes were at war.

Morris, who had been standing quietly by the window, finally turned to James with an expression of weary resignation. "Maybe you're right, James. Maybe it's time to let this go," he said, his voice low and careful, as if handling a fragile truth.

James stared at him; his eyes hollow. "Let go?" he echoed; his voice rough. It sounded foreign to him, like it belonged to someone else. "How can I let go when she's standing right in front of me?"

Morris nodded, his gaze softening with sympathy. "I know it's hard, James. But sometimes, letting go is the only way to find peace."

Morris moved next to the projector, nursing his whiskey, his eyes drifting to the screen in front of them. The images of Graxe and Juan flickered across the display, capturing moments of joy and tenderness. In one frame, Graxe had her hair fashioned into a makeshift mustache across her face, and Juan leaned in close, his eyes crinkled with laughter. There was a light in their eyes, an unspoken connection that transcended the physical. In another image, they sat across from each other at a restaurant, Juan feeding Graxe a piece of cake, their eyes locked in a moment that seemed to hold the world still.

"They look happy," Morris sighed, his voice carrying a note of wistfulness. James shook his head, but tears were forming in his eyes as he nodded, almost against his will.

"What now?" James asked, his voice breaking. Morris pulled him into a hug, patting his back softly.

"It's okay—" Morris began, his words meant to soothe, but James suddenly shoved him away. His gaze snapped back to the slideshow.

"He said she didn't have any stitches, right?" James's voice rose, almost frantic, as he stood up...

"Yes, she didn't have any stitches, James!" Morris replied, his voice edged with confusion. "We checked—"

But James wasn't listening. He tore through the room, tossing aside papers, searching for the remote like a madman. When he finally found it, he scrolled back through the flood of pictures, his breath coming in sharp gasps. And then he saw it.

"There!" he shouted, his finger jabbing at the screen. "What the hell is this then?"

On the screen was an image of Graxe standing by a lakeside, her hand resting on a railing, her face turned towards the serene backdrop. But James's focus was riveted on her arm—the stark, white lines that ran down her skin, scars that seemed to scream at him from the screen. His face twisted with a mixture of shock and anger.

Morris approached the screen slowly, his eyes widening as he took in the sight. "James," he breathed, his voice tinged with disbelief. "Those look like... surgical scars."

James's grip tightened around the armrest of his chair, his knuckles whitening with the force. "How could they miss this?" he growled, frustration boiling over in his tone. "How could they say she didn't have any stitches?"

Morris shook his head, his brow furrowed with concern. "I don't know, James. But this changes things. If those are surgical scars, then—"

"Then she might be Mariyam," James finished, his voice trembling with a mixture of desperation and a dangerous flicker of hope. His eyes blazed as he pieced it together, his mind racing. "The scars were removed by cosmetic surgery—someone's covering it up. Juan knows. He knows she's her."

Morris's face went pale, the weight of the revelation sinking in. "But why? Why would he—"

"Because he loves her," James cut him off, his voice sharp, filled with a newfound clarity. "He loves her, and he doesn't want to lose her. Not to me. Not to anyone."

The room seemed to hold its breath, the truth hanging heavy in the air between them. James's heart pounded in his chest, his mind whirling. This wasn't over. Not by a long shot.

The room felt like it was closing in around them. James's mind was a maelstrom of thoughts and emotions—rage, confusion, a flicker of hope—and he couldn't shake the image of those scars from his head. They had been right there, hidden in plain sight, and now everything seemed to shift under his feet.

Morris took a slow step back, his hand brushing over his mouth as if trying to physically wipe away the shock. "James, if what you're saying is true, this... this could change everything. But you need to think about what comes next. This isn't just about you anymore."

James rounded on him; his eyes wild, almost feral. "What comes next? What comes next is that I go to Juan and demand the truth," he snapped. "He's been lying to her—lying to everyone. He knew she was Mariyam all along and kept it hidden."

"And what do you think that will accomplish?" Morris asked sharply, his voice a counterpoint to James's rising intensity. "You think he'll just hand her over? This isn't a damn trade negotiation, James. You're dealing with people's lives here—her life."

James's chest heaved as he took in Morris's words, but the fire in his eyes didn't dim. "People's lives?" he echoed bitterly. "My wife's life, Morris. My sons' mother. And he's stolen that from them, from me. I need to know if she remembers anything—if there's a part of her that still knows who she is."

Morris hesitated, looking down for a moment before meeting James's eyes. "And what if she doesn't? What if she's not Mariyam anymore? Even if she remembers something, she might not be the woman you knew. What if she chooses to stay with him?"

James was silent for a moment, the thought slicing through him like a knife. He turned back to the screen, the image of Graxe and Juan still flickering there, frozen in that moment of closeness. His breath shuddered out of him, and for the first time, a crack appeared in his resolve.

"Then at least I'll know," he muttered, almost to himself. "At least I'll know the truth. I can't keep living like this—half believing, half doubting. It's tearing me apart."

Morris watched him carefully, the weight of their conversation hanging in the air like a storm about to break. "All right," he said quietly. "Then let's think this through. If we go to Juan, he'll deny it. He'll say the scars are from something else—anything to keep her. We need something more concrete."

James turned to him, his expression hardening again. "You mean proof."

"Exactly," Morris said, nodding. "We need to talk to the people who performed the surgery, anyone who was involved in her cosmetic surgery. If she's really Mariyam and they tried to cover it up, someone had to help. Someone had to be paid off or coerced."

James nodded, his mind already racing ahead, connecting dots and forming a plan. "Morris, check their circle—see if they have any connections to a plastic surgeon. Someone who could've done this kind of work. It wouldn't have been just anyone; Juan would have wanted someone he could trust."

Morris gave a curt nod, reaching for his phone. "I'll get on it. But if they went through all this trouble to hide her identity, they'd cover their tracks well. It won't be easy."

James clenched his jaw, his eyes narrowing with determination. "We don't need easy. We just need a name."

Morris began tapping away on his phone, his brow furrowed in concentration. The minutes ticked by, the silence in the room thick and heavy, punctuated only by the soft clicks of Morris's phone. James's thoughts churned in the quiet, his mind replaying every interaction, every moment where something had felt off. Graxe—Mariyam—had looked at him with recognition, he was sure of it, but there had always been a distance, a barrier he couldn't breach. Maybe now he knew why.

Morris's voice cut through the silence. "Got something," he said, his tone serious. "There's a name that keeps popping up—Dr. Carlson Herrera. He's a well-known plastic surgeon in the area. High-profile clients, works under the radar. But here's the interesting part—he's close to Rudi."

James's head snapped up at that. "Rudi? Juan's best friend and the sheriff?"

"Exactly," Morris confirmed. "Herrera and Rudi go way back. College buddies. And Herrera's known for doing favors for the right people—quiet jobs that don't make it to any official record. If someone needed to hide something, he'd be the guy."

James's heart pounded with a mix of anger and anticipation. "If Herrera did the surgery, he'd have records, notes, something we could use to prove it was Mariyam."

Morris nodded. "And if those scars were removed, there'd be photos before the procedure. Even if they've been hidden or locked away, Herrera's bound to have a copy."

A cold smile tugged at the corner of James's mouth. "Then we need to talk to Dr. Herrera."

Morris raised an eyebrow. "You think he's just going to hand over confidential records because you ask nicely? The guy's not exactly a lightweight. If he's been in Juan and Rudi's pocket all this time, he'll know how to keep his mouth shut."

James's eyes darkened, a grim resolve settling over his features. "No, he won't talk because I ask nicely. But he'll talk."

Morris studied James for a moment, trying to read the hard lines on his face, the tension in his stance. "What are you planning, James?" he asked, his voice cautious.

James turned to him, his expression sharpening, a new fire burning in his eyes. "We're going back to Manhattan," he declared.

Morris's eyes widened slightly. "Manhattan? And what exactly do you expect to do there?"

James smirked, a plan already forming in his mind. "Dr. Herrera runs his clinic there. I'm going to pay him a visit. I'll use my name, my face—whatever it takes—to get into that office. If Herrera has any record of working on Mariyam, I'll find it."

Morris shook his head slightly, a wry smile tugging at his lips. "You think you can just waltz in and ask for confidential patient files?"

James's smirk turned into a full grin. "Not directly, no. But there's always a way, especially when you're a famous actor. I'll use my charm to coax the truth out of his staff. Play the concerned celebrity, looking for the best surgeon to remove a scar." He lifted his hand, showing the faint scar from a stunt gone wrong years ago. "I'll say I'm skeptical, heard he's the best, and see where that leads. Receptionists love to brag about their high-profile clients, especially when they think it's good for business."

Morris crossed his arms, nodding slowly. "And if you find something? If there's proof?"

James's expression darkened, his voice lowering. "Then I take it to Juan, and we end this charade. I want him to see that I know everything. And I want him to know that the game is over."

Morris couldn't help but admire James's determination, even if he knew the risks were high. "You realize this could go south real fast, right? If Juan or Rudi get wind of this—"

"Then they'll know I'm not backing down," James interrupted, his tone firm. "They've been playing me for a fool, Morris. Not anymore."

Morris nodded, knowing there was no talking James out of this once his mind was made up. "Fine. I'll cover things here. But keep me updated. And be careful, James. You're dealing with people who don't play by the rules."

James nodded, his eyes narrowing with steely resolve. "I will. Thanks, Morris."

A few days later, James stood outside Dr. Carlson Herrera's clinic in Manhattan. The sleek, glass-paneled building exuded luxury, catering to the city's elite. He adjusted his sunglasses, his jaw set with determination. He had come alone, dressed sharply but not too flashy, aiming for a look that combined casual confidence with just enough celebrity allure.

As he entered, he put on his most charming smile. The receptionist, a woman in her mid-thirties with a polished demeanor, looked up and instantly recognized him. Her eyes widened slightly, a smile forming on her lips. "Mr. Cross! Welcome! What a surprise to see you here. How can we help you today?"

James leaned on the counter, his demeanor relaxed but his eyes sharp, calculating. "Well, I've heard a lot about Dr. Herrera," he began, his voice smooth and friendly. "I had a little mishap a while back," he continued, rolling up his sleeve to show the faint scar on his hand. "And I'm considering having it removed. Heard he's the best, but, you know, I'm a bit skeptical. I was wondering if I could see some of his work. Maybe some files of his high-profile clients—just to be sure I'm in good hands."

The receptionist chuckled softly, clearly enjoying the attention from a celebrity. "Oh, I assure you, Dr. Herrera is the best in the business. We've had quite a few notable clients who've been very happy with his work."

James nodded, keeping his smile warm. "I'm sure you have. But, you know, a little reassurance never hurts, right?"

The receptionist glanced around, leaning in conspiratorially. "Well, we do have some before-and-after portfolios. I'm not really supposed to share too much, but..." She hesitated, then winked. "For you, Mr. Cross, I might be able to make an exception."

James's smile widened, but his heart pounded in his chest. "I'd appreciate that," he said, his voice low, almost confidential. "I'm really just looking for the best, and I've heard some of your clients had some pretty amazing transformations."

The receptionist beamed, clearly pleased with his interest. She typed something into her computer, then pulled her chair back to retrieve file from a safe locker.

The receptionist opened the safe locker with a quick glance over her shoulder. She pulled out a thick file, bound in a leather cover, and handed it to James with a conspiratorial smile. "These are very confidential, but—"

Before James could grasp the file, a voice cut through the room like a knife. "No, we cannot."

Dr. Herrera appeared, his face tight with anger, striding swiftly from his office. He snatched the file from the receptionist's hands, his gaze piercing as he looked at James. "Doctor-patient confidentiality," he said, his voice cold and measured, his eyes narrowed with suspicion. Without another word, he turned on his heel and marched back to his office, the file clutched tightly in his hand.

James watched him go; his jaw clenched. He knew he'd pushed his luck too far. He turned back to the receptionist, who was now blushing furiously, embarrassed by the reprimand. He offered her a reassuring smile, but his mind was already racing ahead, calculating his next move.

What James didn't know was that six hour before his arrival, another plane had touched down at JFK Airport, carrying Juan Ramirez. Juan had come straight from Svalbard, aware that James was seeking out Dr. Herrera. He was done hiding. The game was shifting, and Juan was stepping back into it—ready to cross, Cross in his own territory. The time for playing defense was over; now, Juan was ready to attack.

Inside Dr. Herrera's office, he was already on the phone. "They're here," he said curtly. On the other end, Sheriff Rudi listened, nodding to himself. He pushed back from his desk at the precinct and stood up.

"Where to, Sheriff?" Officer Markham asked, sensing the tension.

"Something came up," Rudi replied, rolling up his sleeves. "You and Diaz are in charge until I get back." Without further explanation, he strode out, heading directly to the clinic.

Back in the clinic corridor, James paced back and forth, his frustration mounting. He knew Herrera was hiding something, but he needed more than just suspicion. After a few minutes, he sighed heavily and made his way down the stairs to the parking garage. As he reached his car, he noticed a figure sitting on the hood—a police officer, his face partially obscured under the fluorescent lights.

"Excuse me?" James said, his tone both assertive and cautious.

The officer hopped down, his sheriff's badge glinting in the dim light. "What brings you here, Cross, without security? Don't you need protection?" Rudi leaned in close, his voice low, meant only for James's ears. His breath was hot against James's ear, and his tone was dripping with menace.

James didn't flinch. "Look, I'm not looking for trouble," he said, his jaw tightening. "I just need closure."

Rudi chuckled, leaning in even closer, his eyes glinting with a dangerous light. "Stop whatever you're trying to do, Cross," he hissed. "I don't give a damn who you are. I'll drag you out of here in handcuffs for absolutely no reason. Just imagine how that'll look on the front page of every newspaper, in every article circulating on social media. Videos of you, over and over, getting hauled off by the cops. Imagine the headlines: 'James Cross dragged out of parking garage in handcuffs. Police suspect involvement in tax fraud and underground intermediaries.' Tsk, tsk, tsk."

Rudi leaned back, straightening James's coat and collar with a mockingly polite gesture. "I could even call the paparazzi, you know? We hold press conferences pretty often. First and last warning, Cross—how long do you think it'd take me to slip a little bag of white powder into your pocket?"

James felt his blood boil, but he kept his expression calm, unreadable. Rudi's threats were meant to rattle him, to make him back off. But James Cross wasn't the type to back down. He leaned in, pulling Rudi into a sudden, unexpected hug, his face breaking into a grin as a few reporters—no doubt called by Rudi—snapped photos. "Do you have any idea who the hell I am?" he whispered in Rudi's ear, his voice low and filled with a dangerous edge, all while chuckling for the cameras.

Rudi chuckled back, shaking his head, his grin sharp and wolfish. "You know what, yes, we found Graxe—in the canal, unconscious, amnesiac. We're not bad people; we posted ads for her for four months, but no one came forward. So, we took her in, and now she's, our family. Yes, we found her the very next day after your wife jumped from the Brooklyn Bridge. No, you won't find Graxe's file anywhere in any records... call the President if you have to. That's the closure."

Rudi's eyes darkened, his smile vanishing, replaced by a deadly seriousness. "And listen, you won't even get to say a 'hi.' Now, fuck off."

James stared into Rudi's eyes, his smile fading as well. There it was—the confirmation he'd been seeking, delivered with Rudi's own brand of brutal honesty. Graxe was Mariyam. And they'd been hiding her all along.

"Don't think for a second I'm going to let this go," James whispered back, his voice like steel. "You've got my wife, and you think I'm just going to walk away?"

Rudi pulled back, his grin returning as he patted James on the back for the cameras. "Oh, I'm counting on it," he said, his voice light but laced with threat. "Safe flight. Let me escort you to the airport."

James nodded, his eyes never leaving Rudi's. "This isn't over, Sheriff," he said softly.

Rudi just smiled wider, the gleam in his eyes cold and calculating. "Oh, I'm counting on that too."

James climbed into his car, and Rudi watched him drive away, his expression hardening. The game was escalating, and both men knew there were no rules anymore. It was going to get dirty, and only one of them would come out on top.

The air in Manhattan was thick with tension, as if the city itself held its breath, sensing the collision that was about to unfold. Beneath the glossy veneer of luxury and power, a storm was brewing—one built on lies, secrets, and a love that refused to be buried. James Cross, the actor who had played heroes on the screen, now stood at the center of a real-life drama, far more dangerous than anything he'd ever faced in Hollywood. And facing him, Juan Ramirez and his allies, men who had mastered the art of deception and whose loyalties ran deep.

James drove through the bustling streets, his hands gripping the steering wheel, his mind a whirlwind of thoughts. He had his confirmation. Graxe was Mariyam. The woman he loved, the mother of his children, was alive—and she had no memory of the life they had once shared. She had been hidden, taken in by a man who claimed to care for her, surrounded by people who would do anything to keep the truth buried.

But the truth had a way of rising to the surface, like a body in a river. No matter how deeply it was hidden, how carefully it was weighted down with lies, it would always find its way to the light. And James was determined to be the one to drag it up, no matter the cost.

Back at the clinic, Rudi watched James's car disappear down the ramp, his expression unchanging. He knew the stakes, knew the risks. But he also knew Juan. And he knew they had gone too far to turn back now. James Cross wanted a battle; he was about to get one. A battle not of fists or guns, but of wills and shadows, where every move could be the last, and every misstep could spell ruin.

And somewhere in the middle of it all, unaware of the tempest swirling around her, was Mariyam—now Graxe. A woman caught between two worlds, two lives, and two men who would do anything to claim her as their own. Her fate hung in the balance, teetering on the edge of memory and oblivion, and the choices made in the coming days would determine whether she would remain in the dark or finally remember who she once was.

As the sun dipped below the skyline, casting long shadows across the city, the players prepared for the next move. James would not back down; Juan would not let go. And Rudi, with a foot in both worlds, was the wild card that could tip the scales.

The game was no longer about finding Mariyam—it was about keeping her. And in this game, the rules were meant to be broken. One wrong move, and everything could come crashing down. And James Cross was ready to risk it all to bring his wife back to where she belonged.

The stage was set, and the curtains were rising. The next act was about to begin. And in this story, there would be no heroes—only survivors.

CHAPTER 5

The city never slept, and neither did the minds of those locked in a battle over a woman who could not remember her past. For James Cross, every tick of the clock was a countdown—a countdown to truth or destruction. He drove through Manhattan, his thoughts racing faster than the cars around him. He needed to regroup, plan his next move, and decide how to get to Mariyam, his Mariyam.

Morris sat in the passenger seat, his eyes trained on James, worry lines etched deep across his brow. The two men had known each other for years—through the highs of stardom and the lows of scandal—but this was different. This was uncharted territory, and they were losing ground fast.

James's hands gripped the steering wheel, his knuckles whitening, Morris noticing his demeanor sighed. "James, you need to take a breath," Morris said, his voice calm but edged with worry. "This whole damn thing... it's spiraling out of control."

Morris nodded; his face heavy with sympathy. "I know, James. I know this is hard, but maybe it's time to take a step back, to rethink our approach."

James's gaze flickered to Morris, a mixture of desperation and hopelessness in his eyes. "And what, Morris? Just let it go? Let them win?"

Morris shook his head, his hand reaching out to rest on James's shoulder. "No, James. Not let them win, but maybe we need to—"

Suddenly, the road ahead narrowed, and the glint of flashing blue and red lights cut through the evening haze. A checkpoint loomed up in the distance, police cruisers lining both sides of the street, their lights piercing through the dense Manhattan traffic. As James's eyes narrowed, his heart skipped a beat. There, perched like a hawk surveying its territory, was Lieutenant Juan Ramirez. He was leaning casually against his cruiser, his posture radiating authority, but his eyes—those cold, calculating blue eyes—were locked on James's car.

"Ahhhh, Mr. Cross," Juan snarled, stepping away from his cruiser and moving toward James's car. He leaned down, resting an elbow on the open window, his breath fogging the cool glass. "We have intel regarding a drug deal happening in this part of town. We're checking cars for brown sugar. Random checks, of course," he said with a mock smile. "You know how it is. Anyway, kindly step out." He chewed his gum nonchalantly, but his eyes remained sharp, locked onto James's.

James felt a chill creep down his spine. This wasn't a random check. This was a setup. He'd been expecting a move like this from Juan, but not here, not now. His hand slipped into his back pocket, and he felt it—the small, telltale bulge. His heart sank, a lead weight in his chest. **The packet.**

Morris's face went pale as realization dawned, his eyes widening with alarm. "James..." he whispered, but his voice was lost in the roar of blood pounding in James's ears.

Juan's smirk widened; his blue eyes gleaming with malicious amusement. "Well, Mr. Cross? Are you going to step out, or do we need to drag you out?" he drawled, his voice dripping with faux politeness.

James's jaw tightened, his fingers curling into fists at his sides. The burning rage that simmered in his chest threatened to boil over, but he knew he had to keep his composure. The cameras were still watching, recording every movement, every expression, waiting for him to slip.

With a strained smile, James pushed open the car door, stepping out onto the pavement. The cold wind whipped at his face, cutting through the fabric of his coat like a knife. He forced himself to stand tall, his chin held high, despite the gnawing sense of dread that gnawed at his insides.

Juan's grin widened, his gaze flickering to James's back pocket. "Hands on the car, Cross. Let's see what you've got on you," he ordered, his voice laced with a mix of authority and sadistic pleasure.

James's face twisted into a grimace, his eyes blazing with barely suppressed fury. "I don't know what game you're playing, but—"

"It's not a game, Cross," Juan interrupted, his grin twisting into a predatory smile. "It's an investigation. Now, hands on the car."

James's fists clenched at his sides, his nails digging into his palms. The temptation to lash out, to scream and demand answers, gnawed at him, but he knew he couldn't afford to give in. The eyes of the world were on him, the cameras capturing every twitch, every flicker of emotion.

With a slow, reluctant movement, James turned, placing his hands on the hood of the car. The cold metal sent a shiver down his spine, the weight of the situation pressing down on him like a leaden shroud. The reality was stark: he was cornered, and Juan was enjoying every second of it.

Juan stepped closer, his eyes gleaming with a mixture of triumph and malice. He patted James down, his fingers lingering on the pocket that held the incriminating packet. James could feel the tension coil tighter and tighter, like a spring about to snap.

"Should I pull it out and ruin you forever, Cross," Juan whispered in his ear, his breath hot and taunting, "or will you take the next flight and leave? Leave us the hell alone. All I want is peace for me and my wife."

He paused, letting the words sink in, his voice lowering to a dangerous whisper. "Ten seconds to make your decision, Cross. Either leave, never return, and live like James Cross the actor, or... get convicted for carrying ten grams of a controlled substance. Brown sugar? Crystal meth, to be exact. I'll destroy you, James Arthur Cross."

The words were like a slap to the face, cold and final. James's mind raced. Ten seconds. Ten seconds to decide his fate. Juan's eyes bore into him, filled with a hatred that promised no mercy. The cameras were still rolling; the crowd had begun to gather, their eyes hungry for drama, for scandal.

James knew the choice he had to make. His body trembled with the effort of restraint, his breath coming in ragged bursts. His life, his career, his sons—everything hung in the balance of this moment. If he left, he might never see Mariyam again, might never know what really happened that night on the bridge. But if he stayed...

The cold metal of the car hood burned under his palms, the weight of his decision pressing down like a thousand pounds. He knew Juan was bluffing—partially. If he could just turn this around, if he could find a way out of this, he'd have his answer, but the question remained: could he risk it?

James inhaled deeply, his eyes narrowing with a hardened resolve. "I'm not going anywhere, Ramirez," he said, his voice steady despite the storm raging inside. "Not until I get her back."

A silence fell over them, a tension so thick it could be cut with a knife. Juan's smirk faltered, just a bit, but his grip tightened on James's shoulder. The battle lines were drawn.

Juan's expression shifted, his smirk dimming into something more serious, more calculating. His fingers pressed deeper into James's shoulder, a silent reminder of the power he held in this moment. The flashing lights from the cruisers painted their faces in harsh reds and blues, and for a split second, the world seemed to stop spinning.

"Not until you get her back?" Juan echoed, his voice a soft, mocking whisper that only James could hear. "You really think you're in any position to make demands right now? Look around you, Cross. You're surrounded, outplayed, and frankly, I'm losing my patience."

James felt the weight of the stares from the gathered onlookers—pedestrians who had stopped to gawk at the unfolding drama, police officers who stood just close enough to intervene if things went south, and the ever-watchful eyes of the media cameras, lenses glinting like predatory eyes in the dark. It was a circus, and he was the main attraction.

Juan leaned in closer, his lips curling into a vicious smile. "You're going to ruin yourself for her, aren't you? The woman who doesn't even remember your name. How poetic. How tragic." His hand drifted down to James's back pocket, brushing the outline of the packet. "Five seconds, Cross."

James's heart pounded in his chest, each beat like a drum announcing the impending verdict. His mind raced through every possible move he could make, every word he could say to turn the situation in his favor. He knew he couldn't back down; to do so would be to lose everything—his pride, his career, his chance at redemption. But one wrong move, one wrong word, and it would all be over.

Suddenly, a new thought dawned on him—a desperate gamble, but maybe his only way out. He took a slow, deliberate breath, his gaze locking onto Juan's. "You're right, Ramirez," he said slowly, the tension in his voice almost tangible. "Maybe I am outplayed. Maybe you do have me cornered. But there's one thing you're forgetting."

Juan's eyes narrowed, his amusement flickering into curiosity. "Oh? And what's that?"

James's lips curled into a defiant smile. "I still have the public on my side. And they love a good redemption story." He nodded subtly toward the crowd, his voice growing louder, more confident. "And they also love a scandal involving police overreach."

Juan's face darkened, his smirk evaporating. He glanced around at the onlookers, the murmurs of the crowd beginning to grow as they watched the interaction unfold. The cameras were still rolling, capturing every second of their exchange. James knew he had to keep pushing, to make Juan feel the heat of the spotlight.

"You plant that on me," James continued, his voice rising above the noise, "and it becomes your word against mine. And who do you think they're going to believe? The celebrity who's been fighting to get his wife back or the cop with a vendetta?"

A ripple of uncertainty passed through Juan's expression, his grip on James's shoulder loosening ever so slightly. James could see the gears turning in Juan's head, weighing the risks and rewards of pressing forward or backing off. He had hit a nerve, and he knew it.

"You think you're clever, Cross?" Juan hissed, his voice low, his eyes flashing with a mix of anger and grudging respect. "You think you've found a way out of this?"

James's jaw clenched, his resolve hardening. "I think you've underestimated just how far I'm willing to go to get her back. And I think you've underestimated how much the world loves a good underdog story."

Juan took a step back, his eyes still locked on James's, his face unreadable. The tension between them was electric, a silent standoff that felt like it could explode at any moment. The seconds ticked by, each one stretching into an eternity.

Finally, Juan spoke, his voice quiet but laced with an edge of menace. "You're playing a dangerous game, Cross. But I'm not stupid. I know when a play has gone sideways." He took another step back, his gaze sweeping over the crowd. "This isn't over. Not by a long shot."

James felt a wave of relief wash over him, though he didn't dare show it. He kept his face stoic, his eyes hard and unyielding. "No, it's not," he agreed. "But you should know by now, Ramirez—I don't back down. Not when it comes to her."

Juan nodded slowly, a dark smile spreading across his face. "We'll see about that, Cross. We'll see."

He turned sharply, motioning to his officers to stand down. The tension in the air began to dissipate as the checkpoint was cleared, the crowd slowly breaking apart with murmurs of excitement and speculation. The media's cameras continued to roll, capturing the aftermath, the faces of those involved, and the lingering tension that hung in the air like a storm cloud.

James remained by his car, his hands still pressed against the hood, his body rigid with the adrenaline that still coursed through his veins. He watched Juan retreat to his cruiser, the Lieutenant's posture tense and his expression grim. This was far from over, and they both knew it.

Morris, who had remained silent throughout the entire exchange, finally stepped forward, his face pale and drawn. "James," he said quietly, "what the hell was that?"

James exhaled deeply, finally allowing his body to relax. "That," he said, his voice steady but weary, "was me refusing to be cornered. I'm not going to let him or anyone else push me out of this fight."

Morris shook his head, his concern evident. "You're walking a thin line, my friend. A very thin line."

James nodded; his eyes still locked on Juan as he climbed into his cruiser. "I know. But it's the only line I've got left. And I'm not done yet."

The city's hum returned to its usual rhythm, the urgency of the moment fading into the cacophony of Manhattan's night. But for James Cross, the battle had just begun. He knew he had rattled Juan tonight, but he also knew Juan wouldn't stay rattled for long. The Lieutenant was already planning his next move, and James needed to be ready.

Because this was more than just a fight for Mariyam. It was a fight for the truth. And James Cross had just shown he was willing to risk everything to get it.

He took one last look at the crowd dispersing, the city swallowing them back into its ceaseless pulse, and then turned to Morris. "We need to regroup. Get to Rudi. We're going to need allies for what's coming next."

Morris nodded, his expression shifting from concern to grim determination. "You think Rudi will help?"

James's eyes hardened with resolve. "He doesn't have a choice.".

Later that night, as the world outside slumbered beneath a blanket of darkness, I lay wide awake, my body wrapped tightly in Juan's embrace. The room was quiet, save for the rhythmic sound of our breathing and the soft crackle of a candle burning low on the bedside table. Shadows danced on the walls, flickering with every subtle movement of the flame, casting long, wavering shapes that seemed to shift and sway with my restless thoughts.

"I can't shake this feeling," I murmured into the stillness, my voice barely more than a whisper. "Like something's about to happen. My past—it's like it's catching up to us, haunting us." The weight of my words hung in the cold air, and I felt a tremor run through me as I spoke.

Beside me, Juan stirred, his eyes fluttering open. Without a word, he pulled me closer, his warmth enveloping me as if he could shield me from the invisible threat that loomed in the shadows. Our bodies sought each other instinctively, a silent reassurance amid the uncertainty. His breath mingled with mine, forming a quiet, wordless conversation of shared fears and unspoken promises.

His hand moved gently to the back of my head, fingers threading through my hair in a soothing gesture. "I won't let anything happen to you, Graxe," he whispered, his voice a deep, steady anchor in the stillness. "Not now, not ever. Whatever comes, we'll face it together."

I wanted to believe him, to find comfort in the strength of his words, but a shiver of unease still crept down my spine, one that no warmth could dispel. The void of my lost memories loomed like a dark chasm, an abyss of forgotten faces and fragmented moments that threatened to swallow me whole. Shadows of a life I couldn't remember seemed to linger just out of reach, like a cold fog creeping into the corners of my consciousness.

Sensing my tension, Juan held me tighter. "Whatever's out there, whatever this is," he said softly, his voice a low, calming murmur against the darkness, "we won't let it break us."

I nodded, though my heart still pounded with a sense of unease. Lately, those gaps in my memory felt more like gaping wounds, tearing at the edges of my mind. Flashes of places and faces I didn't recognize would come and go, leaving me feeling like a stranger in my own skin. And tonight, an oppressive weight hung in the air, heavy with the promise of something yet unseen, like the calm before a storm.

Juan shifted, propping himself up on one elbow to look at me more closely, his eyes searching mine with a mix of concern and determination. "We could leave," he suggested quietly. "Pack up, start fresh somewhere far away from all this. I don't care, where, as long as I'm with you."

For a fleeting moment, his idea seemed like a lifeline—an escape from this tangled web of forgotten memories and unknown dangers. But deep down, I knew running wasn't an option. Whatever was lurking in my past, it needed to be faced, not fled from. There were answers I needed—perhaps even a reckoning.

"But we just came back from vacation," I reminded him softly, a faint smile tugging at my lips as I tried to ease the tension between us. I looked into his eyes, searching for his familiar warmth.

Juan's expression softened, a gentle smile curling his lips as he pulled me into a tighter embrace. "For you, I'd resign on the spot," he replied, his voice filled with a tenderness that made me chuckle softly. We drew closer under the blankets, seeking solace in each other's presence.

As my eyelids grew heavy, Juan pulled me even closer, his chest a solid, reassuring presence beneath my cheek. His heartbeat, steady and sure, was a comforting rhythm that guided me toward sleep. Yet, even as I began to drift, a part of me remained alert, wary of the shadows creeping at the edge of my consciousness, of what they might hold.

But as sleep finally overtook me, enveloped in Juan's embrace, a wave of serenity washed over me, soothing the lingering doubts that had plagued my mind. Wrapped in his arms, I felt safe, cherished, and at peace.

The soft glow of the candle's flame flickered on the walls, casting gentle, dancing shadows. I nestled closer to Juan, his heartbeat a lullaby that calmed the storm within me. In that moment, time seemed to slow, the world outside slipping away as we found refuge in the sanctuary of our love.

A few miles away, in the same city.... The city stretched out beneath a blanket of early morning haze, its buildings towering like silent sentinels over the winding streets. In a dimly lit office above a bustling street, James Cross stood by the window, his gaze fixed on the endless flow of people below. His jaw was set in a hard line, tension rippling through his shoulders.

"Call Rudolf," he said, his voice low and steady, though a storm brewed beneath his calm facade. His eyes shifted to Morris, his manager, who stood nearby, fidgeting with his phone.

Morris looked up, surprise flickering across his face. "You want to meet with him? He's the sheriff, James. And Juan's best friend. You think he'll just spill his guts?"

James's eyes narrowed; his expression unwavering. "I know who he is, Morris. He won't spill anything sensitive, but I need to hear his story again. I need to understand what he told me last night, word for word."

Morris hesitated, a deep frown creasing his brow. "Are you sure about this, James? Confronting Rudolf could stir up more trouble than it's worth. You know how these things go."

James's jaw tightened further, his gaze darkening with determination. "This isn't about confrontation. It's about understanding the truth, piecing together what really happened to Graxe. There's something there, something he knows, and I need to hear it again. Maybe we missed something the first time."

With a resigned sigh, Morris nodded. He knew better than to argue when James got that look in his eye. He pulled out his phone and reluctantly dialed Rudolf's number. The call was brief, filled with curt exchanges, and when he hung up, Morris turned back to James.

"He agreed to meet, but you've only got ten minutes. He chose a neutral spot—the coffee shop near the precinct."

James gave a short nod, his mind already working through possible scenarios. "That's all I need."

The drive to the coffee shop was quick—quicker than James would have liked. The city streets blurred past in a haze of morning fog and neon reflections, the weight of what was to come pressing heavily on his chest. Morris drove in silence, occasionally glancing over at James, who sat rigid in the passenger seat, his gaze fixed on some distant point beyond the windshield.

As they pulled up to the curb, the coffee shop loomed before them, an unassuming little place nestled between two towering office buildings. The smell of freshly ground coffee beans and the soft hum of morning chatter drifted out onto the street as they stepped inside

The coffee shop buzzed with the late morning rush, a hum of life and energy mixed with the rich aroma of freshly brewed coffee. Patrons jostled for space in the narrow aisles, some tapping furiously at laptops, others leaning into private conversations. James Cross maneuvered through the crowd; his presence barely noticed amidst the chaos. He spotted Morris already seated at a secluded table near the back, far from prying eyes. As he slid into the seat beside his manager, Rudolf Liam Merci, the local Sheriff, strode in. His posture was rigid, his expression unreadable.

Rudolf's entrance wasn't loud, but it was commanding. Without a word, he moved to their table, pulled out a chair, and sat down, his sharp eyes locking onto James. "You wanted to meet," Rudolf said, his voice steady and clipped. "Make it quick, Cross."

James leaned in; his tone quiet but with a tinge of urgency. "Last night, you told me you'd given me closure. I need to hear it again. Straight from you, everything you know about Graxe."

Rudolf sighed, the sound heavy with fatigue, as if the weight of the story he was about to tell bore down on him. He began slowly, his voice tinged with something close to regret.

"A long time ago, there were three friends," Rudolf started, his tone shifting as he wove the tale. "All of them were burdened with responsibilities, chosen by the crown to hold the beacon of justice. They were good men, strong and true, but even they needed a break from the endless trials of their duties. So, they decided to seek refuge, to find solace in nature. Their minds were set, their bags packed, and off they went, deep into a forest, seeking peace."

He paused, his eyes drifting as if he could see the scene unfolding before him. James didn't dare interrupt, his breath held as he waited for Rudolf to continue.

"They spent a few days in the wilderness, enjoying the solitude, the quiet, the break from the world's demands," Rudolf went on. "But destiny had other plans. One evening, as they sat by a river, enjoying the stillness, they spotted something in the water. At first, they thought it was nothing—just debris, perhaps. But curiosity got the better of them. They dove in, hoping to help or at least find out what it was."

Rudolf's lips curled into a faint smile, though there was no joy in it. "What they found was a mermaid."

James's eyes widened, his mind racing. This wasn't just a story. This was a veiled recounting of what had happened, of what Rudolf knew.

"A mermaid," Rudolf repeated, his voice softer now. "Badly injured, unconscious—but still, one of the most beautiful creatures they had ever seen. They thought she was dead, floating there in the cold water, but she wasn't. She was alive, even after being in the water for so long. She coughed, and they rushed her to the healer. She recovered, but her injuries took something from her—not her voice, as in the fairy tales, but her memories. She had no idea who she was, where she came from. When she finally opened her eyes, she only remembered one face. Maybe because he was the one who had dived in and pulled her out, maybe because she had partially gained consciousness in his arms."

James's heart skipped a beat. He knew who Rudolf was talking about.

"He was the hazel-eyed prince, the bravest of them all," Rudolf continued, his eyes never leaving James's. "He fell for the little mermaid, as anyone would. He helped her, stayed by her side. To her, he became the center of her only world, the only anchor she had in a sea of forgotten memories. The trio of friends became her family. They gave her a new name, a new identity, a blank slate to start over. But they didn't give up on finding out who she really was. They searched town to town, hoping someone would recognize her, but no one came forward. Weeks turned into months, and she was finally discharged from the healer's care. With nowhere else to go, the hazel-eyed prince took her in. She stayed with him, still hoping she'd find out where she came from, but as the months passed, nothing changed. They grew closer, day by day, until one day, he confessed his love. And to his surprise, she accepted."

James clenched his fists under the table, his nails digging into his palms. He knew where this was going, but he couldn't stop listening.

"The whole town was happy for them," Rudolf said, his voice tinged with a sadness that hadn't been there before. "Except for the prince's parents. They didn't approve, didn't trust this mysterious woman who had appeared out of nowhere. But the prince fought for her, married her, gave her the world. He worshipped the ground she walked on. They had their happily ever after. Until…"

"Until?" James's voice was a whisper, the word barely escaping his lips.

"Until the prince made a mistake," Rudolf said, his tone darkening. "He thought the tide would stay the same, that their happiness would last forever. But one day, the ocean returned. He took her to a festival by the sea, and that's when King laid eyes on her."

James's stomach churned. He knew what this meant. He had seen Graxe at the premiere, recognized her as his wife, Mariyam.

"Turns out she wasn't just any mermaid," Rudolf continued, his voice now laced with a bitter edge. "She was the royalty, King's wife, and the King recognized her, knew her scars, marks that only someone intimate would know. He referred to a family heirloom she must have had—a engraved crown." Rudolf smirked, the expression cold and calculating. "Or in this case, a necklace with a name."

James's breath hitched. The 'Rehman' pendant. The one Graxe had been wearing when they found her.

"The prince felt threatened," Rudolf said, his voice lowering. "He saw this as a threat to everything he had built, to the life he had created with his mermaid. So, he reached out to his friends again—the red-haired Robin and a cat burglar. He explained his problem. They knew who she was, King's wife, but that was in the past. Now, she was their mermaid. She didn't even want to know where she came from anymore. But the King was relentless. He kept chasing them, trying to reclaim what he believed was his."

Rudolf leaned forward, his gaze piercing. "But how could the prince let her go? She was his, from the moment she opened her eyes and recognized him. Where was King all this time, huh? So, the trio decided to erase every trace of the mermaid's past. Every record of her being found or treated. Even the scars the King mentioned—they were erased. A mage worked his magic, and puff—the scars were gone. The prince took her to a different city, but the King followed. He wanted her back so badly; he was willing to chase them to the ends of the earth. And then, the prince snapped. He knew he had to return, to face this threat head-on. So, he came back, with his mermaid by his side."

Rudolf's eyes bore into James's, the weight of his words settling like a stone in the pit of James's stomach. "And now the chessboard is set. The King is ready to attack and defend, with his queen by his side. His bishops, knights, rooks, and pawns are all in place. The traps are set on every block. And honestly how long can a king stand with only a single bishop?" He gestured toward Morris, sitting silently at James's side. "Either it's a stalemate, or it's checkmate for King. So, it's your turn to roll the dice. What is it, James? Will King stay for the checkmate, or will he concede gracefully? He doesn't have many moves left."

James's face twisted into a grimace, Rudolf's allegorical narrative cutting through him like a knife. The bustling noise of the coffee shop seemed to recede, the world narrowing to the table before him, where the story of the mermaid and her two kings unfolded in chilling detail.

"You think you can rewrite history?" James spat, his voice trembling with barely controlled rage. "You think she won't remember anything? You sick bastards—how could you?"

Rudolf's gaze hardened; his expression unflinching. "How could I? Victors write the history, Cross. And yes, the mermaid hasn't remembered anything so far. What's going to change now, out of the blue? She's happy with him—I've seen that. Trust me, I wanted to propose to her too, but she's been orbiting around him since the day she opened her eyes. When the doctor asked if she remembered anyone, she pointed at him. Sometimes the hardest thing and the right thing are the same."

Rudolf checked his watch, then looked back at James, his lips curling into a mocking smile. "My ten minutes are up, and you're still in New York. Why does n want to destroy himself? Doesn't he have an ocean to return to, his 'daughters' and concubines?"

Rudolf's gaze shifted to another man sitting at a nearby table, his eyes trained on a laptop screen. "Also, the cat burglar is not as kind as Robin Hood." He pointed at himself, then at the man with the laptop, who looked up and gave James a mocking salute, his green eyes gleaming with mischief, the color of deep emerald.

"Hey, Malcom, how are you? Long time no see," Rudolf called out, his voice dripping with sarcasm. "That's my friend—the cat." The man with the laptop, Malcom Wyatt, pulled his hoodie down, revealing his sharp features. He wasn't called the cat just for his cat-like eyes. He was the cat for his ability to go unnoticed, to slip in and out of places without a trace. A master hacker from SWAT, with a talent for sniffing out secrets.

"I've been busy," Malcom replied, his voice smooth and casual, as if discussing the weather. "Working on something... specific. A particular actor. These big names these days, I mean—drugs, women, scandals. Maybe he wasn't missing his late wife as much as he claimed. Should we dig into tax fraud too? Anyway, enough about me. What's the score, Rudolf? Who's rolling the dice?". Malcom chuckled, shaking his head, his gaze shifting between Rudolf and James.

Rudolf stood, his chair scraping against the floor. "Thats for n to decide." He said, gathering his things.

James's gaze darted between Rudolf and Malcolm, the gravity of the situation sinking in. The allegorical tale Rudolf spun—a twisted game of chess with human hearts and memories as the stakes—had revealed a darker side of the quest for Graxe's past, one entangled with deceit and manipulation.

He swallowed hard; his throat dry. "This isn't just about memories or the truth anymore, is it? It's about control. About keeping her under your thumb, away from any truth that might awaken her past."

Rudolf's expression was unyielding, his voice icy. "It's about protecting what's ours, James. You had your chance, your time. You lost that right the moment she hit the water. Now, she belongs to a different story, one where she's safe, loved, and most importantly, free from the ghosts of her past—including you."

James's jaw tightened, his teeth grinding as the weight of Rudolf's words settled in. The coffee shop seemed to fade around them, the background noise replaced by the echo of his own breath. He had come here looking for closure, perhaps even a path to reclaim what he had lost, but instead, he found himself further ensnared in this web of secrets and power plays.

"You talk about protection, but all I see is a prison built on lies," James said, his voice raw with emotion. "She deserves to know who she really is, not just what you've rewritten for her. You think you're protecting her, but you're just scared. Scared that the truth will break whatever fantasy you've created."

Malcom leaned back in his chair; his emerald eyes gleaming with amusement. "Oh, look at him, the noble knight, riding in on his white horse. James, you keep talking about her like she's some lost princess in a tower. What makes you think she wants to be Ever thought of that?"

James's gaze flicked to Malcom, a smoldering fire behind his eyes. "And what makes you think you have the right to decide that for her? None of you have the right to decide what's best for her. She's not some chess piece to be moved around your board."

Rudolf smirked, leaning forward, his elbows resting on the table. "But that's where you're wrong, Cross. Everyone's a piece in this game, whether they realize it or not. And the sooner you accept that, the sooner you can play your role properly—or fold."

"Fold?" James nearly laughed, a bitter sound escaping his throat. "You're underestimating me, Rudolf. I'm not folding, and I'm certainly not leaving this table."

Rudolf's smile faded, replaced by a cold, calculating stare. "Then make your move, Cross. Just remember, every action has a consequence. The last time you acted on impulse, it cost you your wife. How much more are you willing to lose?"

A tense silence settled over the table, the air thick with unspoken threats and the weight of what lay ahead. James knew he was walking a fine line. If he pushed too hard, too fast, he risked triggering a reaction that could further endanger Graxe—Mariyam. But he couldn't stand idly by, not when there was still a chance to bring her back, to break through the fog of her lost memories.

"Maybe I don't need to move at all," James said finally, his voice steady. "Maybe the best move is to wait, to let your house of cards fall on its own. Because if there's one thing I've learned, it's that the truth has a way of coming out, no matter how deep you bury it."

Rudolf's expression darkened. "And maybe that's a gamble you're not prepared to win."

Malcom chuckled again, clearly enjoying the tension between the two men. "Oh, this is going to be fun. A real clash of titans. But I wouldn't get too comfortable, James. Because while you're sitting here, waiting for that truth to dig itself up, we're making sure that it stays buried. You've got no idea what you're up against."

James's lips curled into a slight smile, one filled with determination rather than humor. "I've faced worse odds, Malcom. And I'm still here."

Rudolf stood, pushing his chair back with a deliberate slowness. "We'll see how long that lasts," he said, his voice low and ominous. "But remember this, Cross—you're not the only one who knows how to play this game. And when the pieces start falling, make sure you're ready to catch them."

With that, Rudolf turned and walked away, Malcom following close behind. James watched them go, his mind racing with everything he'd learned. He had come for answers, and in a twisted way, he'd gotten them. But they weren't the kind that brought peace—they were the kind that ignited a fire.

James reached for his phone, his fingers hovering over the screen for a moment. He knew he couldn't do this alone. He needed allies, people who still believed in the truth, in justice. And he knew exactly where to start.

He dialed a number, his heart pounding as he waited for the call to connect.

"It's me," James said when the voice on the other end answered. "We need to talk. It's about Mariyam... and it's time we fight back."

As he hung up, he felt a strange mix of fear and determination settle in his chest. The game was far from over. And if Rudolf, Malcom, and their twisted circle thought they could rewrite Mariyam's story without facing consequences, they were about to find out just how wrong they were.

Back at the mansion, Juan's phone vibrated with a text from Rudolf: "n still in the waters. Keep the queen safe. I played our part."

Juan's jaw tightened as he read the message. The words struck him like a hammer, a surge of protectiveness rising within his chest. He knew what it meant—danger was still lurking, prowling around them like a predator in the dark. n, the code name for whatever threat was brewing, was still out there. He pocketed his phone, already plotting their next steps, his mind calculating every possible move.

When he turned around, he saw me humming softly, lost in my own world, arranging fresh flowers in a vase by the window. The light from outside cast a soft, warm glow around me, and for a moment, Juan hesitated. He wanted to keep this moment intact—this slice of normalcy, of peace. But the urgency in Rudolf's message couldn't be ignored.

"Graxe, amor," he started, his voice calm but carrying an undertone of urgency that was impossible to miss. "We need to talk about something important later."

I looked up, my hands pausing over the delicate petals. I sensed it immediately—something had changed. The way his voice strained, the way his eyes avoided mine for just a fraction of a second too long. "Is everything alright, Jui?" I asked, my own voice tinged with concern.

Juan forced a smile, the corners of his mouth lifting just enough to offer reassurance. He crossed the room and wrapped his arms around me from behind, his chin resting on my shoulder. "Everything's fine, just some precautions we need to discuss to keep our wonderful life intact."

I nodded slowly, leaning back into his embrace, my head resting against his chest. The steady rhythm of his heartbeat was comforting, but his words left a cold knot of unease in my stomach. Precautions? Against what?

The evening settled in, and the warmth of the house became a stark contrast to the chilly air that seeped in from outside. I busied myself in the kitchen, preparing dinner. The rhythmic sound of chopping vegetables filled the silence, a comforting noise that allowed me to think, to push away the creeping dread.

Juan was unusually quiet as he joined me. He leaned against the counter; his eyes fixed on me but his thoughts clearly elsewhere. I could feel his gaze lingering, heavy with something unspoken. After a moment, he spoke, his voice softer, almost hesitant. "Graxe, if anything ever happened to me, I need you to know where everything is. Financials, documents, everything."

I stopped, the knife hovering in mid-air, and turned to look at him, a frown creasing my forehead. "Why would you say that? Why would you say something like that? How dare you?" My words came out sharper than I intended, edged with a mix of fear and anger. I lifted the knife playfully, brandishing it at him, but beneath the jest, there was a sliver of genuine worry.

Juan chuckled softly, stepping forward to kiss the top of my head. "Nothing will happen to me, as long as you are here, Mi Corazon," he murmured, his voice a soothing balm to my frayed nerves. He pulled me closer, rocking me gently back and forth.

"Mi Bastardo," I muttered affectionately, my fingers reaching up to pat his hair. He looked down at me, his mock glare barely masking the warmth in his eyes, and we both burst into laughter, the tension between us breaking like a wave on the shore.

Meanwhile, across town, in a dimly lit hotel room, James Cross was unraveling. "You are destroying yourself," Morris said firmly, his eyes locked on James's wild, tear-streaked face.

"I'll demand a DNA test," James declared, his voice shaking but determined. His eyes were red and swollen from a sleepless night filled with agonizing thoughts and gut-wrenching realizations.

"They're in law enforcement, James!" Morris snapped, trying to break through the fog of his friend's obsession. "They can forge it. You're not thinking straight! Suing them means stepping into their territory. You'll become the villain in her eyes, trying to snatch her away."

James's gaze was glued to his phone, his fingers swiping furiously through photos and stories. His eyes landed on one particular highlight. His breath caught in his throat, and a sad, broken smile tugged at his lips. "She has a crush on me—she remembers, in her own way," he said softly, showing Morris a story where Graxe had casually mentioned a fondness for one of his old films.

"For the love of God, James," Morris groaned, exasperation lacing his tone. "Half of the world's population had a crush on you at some point in their life. And with the things you're doing now, I'm pretty sure she thinks you're a freak. Juan is the hero in her eyes. Why are you trying to be the villain?"

James's eyes burned with a stubborn fire. "She's my wife, Morris. Mine. And I'm losing her to a lie."

"You're losing her because you're letting your obsession destroy you," Morris countered, his voice rising. "Listen to me, James. You're losing the PR battle before it even begins. You need to step back, think clearly. Stop acting like a madman."

James fell silent, his shoulders sagging under the weight of Morris's words. But his mind, as twisted and frantic as it was, refused to yield. Deep down, in the darkest corners of his heart, he believed—no, he knew—that Mariyam, his Mariyam, still remembered him. And he would do whatever it took to prove it. Even if it meant wading through hell itself.

Back at the mansion, the night was settling in, and I was putting the finishing touches on our dinner. Juan had lit a few candles, their soft glow casting long shadows against the walls. The ambiance was calm, serene, but there was a tension underlying everything, a subtle unease that neither of us could shake.

"Jui," I said, breaking the silence as I set the table, "what was that text about earlier? From Rudi?"

Juan hesitated; his face unreadable for a moment. "It's just... work stuff, amor. You know how he gets with his cryptic messages."

I narrowed my eyes at him, sensing there was more to it. "Work stuff that involves keeping me safe?" I asked, my tone half-joking but probing.

He sighed, running a hand through his hair, a sign that he was debating how much to tell me. "I just want to make sure we're prepared for anything. You've been through enough, and I want you to feel secure, always."

I could hear the sincerity in his voice, the underlying fear masked by his calm demeanor. "You're scaring me, Jui," I said softly, my eyes searching his.

Juan stepped closer, his hands reaching for mine. "I'm sorry, Mi Corazon. I don't mean to. It's just...some people are trying to get back at me." He said and I gasped slightly.

"What people Jui?" I asked and Juan's eyes turned distant.

Across town, James sat in his hotel room, a new fire igniting in his eyes. He knew what he needed to do. He couldn't storm in like a madman, couldn't demand a DNA test or a public spectacle. No, he had to play it smart, to play it quiet. He needed to show her, to remind her of the life they once had.

He picked up his phone, dialing a number he hadn't used in years. "Ezekiel," he said when the line connected. "I need your help. I'm bringing Mariyam back. I need everything you have on Juan Heinrich Ramirez. Every detail, every secret. We're going to show her who the real hero is."

On the other end of the line, Ezekiel hesitated for a moment before responding, his voice cautious. "James, you sure about this? You're stepping into dangerous territory."

"I'm beyond sure," James replied, his voice cold and unyielding. "I've been patient long enough. It's time to take back what's mine."

As the candles flickered and cast dancing shadows on the walls, the tension in the room thickened. Juan's words hung in the air, a silent admission of the dangers that loomed just out of reach. His eyes, once so full of warmth and love, now carried a distant, haunted look—a reflection of the battles he fought silently, the threats he kept hidden to protect the fragile world they had built together.

I felt a shiver run down my spine, the cold fingers of fear tightening their grip around my heart. There was something he wasn't telling me, something dark and dangerous that lurked in the shadows of our life. And for the first time since I had awoken without memories, I realized that the past Juan had tried so hard to shield me from was catching up to us, and it wouldn't be long before it demanded to be reckoned with.

Meanwhile, across town, in the dimly lit confines of a hotel room, James Cross was preparing for a war. The man who once held the world in the palm of his hand, adored and idolized by millions, was now reduced to a shadow of himself—driven by an obsession that had consumed every fiber of his being. The phone call to Ezekiel marked the beginning of his final gambit, a desperate attempt to reclaim the love he had lost, even if it meant destroying everything in the process.

James's resolve hardened as he listened to Ezekiel's cautious voice on the other end of the line. He knew he was venturing into treacherous waters, but the fire in his heart burned too hot to be extinguished. He was no longer the man who could stand idly by while someone else lived the life that should have been his. No longer the man who could bear the thought of Mariyam—his Mariyam—being held by another.

The wheels had been set in motion, and there would be no turning back. James Cross was ready to do whatever it took to bring Mariyam back, to tear down the walls that Juan had built around her, and to remind her of the life they once had. The storm was coming, and it would either reunite them or tear them apart forever.

But as the night deepened and the shadows grew longer, one thing became clear: in this battle for love and memory, there was no wrong or right, no truth nor lie, not everyone were the way they looked. When someone thought they were finally unravelling the truth, least did they know, the characters were yet to emerge, the story yet to unfold. This was no end— rather an intermission.

CHAPTER 6

The first light of dawn crept slowly over the Ramirez mansion, bathing the world in a soft, golden glow that melted away the shadows of the night. The morning mist clung to the sprawling gardens like a whisper, delicate tendrils of fog weaving through the manicured hedges and curling around the wrought-iron gates that stood tall and imposing at the front of the estate. The mansion itself loomed grand and timeless, a relic of another era, its stone façade catching the early light with a stately elegance. From the outside, everything appeared serene—a picture of tranquil beauty—but inside, a different story was beginning to unfold.

I woke up to the muffled sounds of life starting to stir. The birds outside my window had begun their morning symphony, their song harmonizing with the faint rustle of leaves in the breeze. The room was still bathed in a cool, dim light, the thick curtains allowing just enough of the morning sun to seep through. I lay there for a moment, cocooned in the soft warmth of the duvet, trying to hold on to the remnants of sleep. But my mind was restless, plagued by snippets of conversations from the night before, Juan's tense words echoing in my thoughts.

Slowly, I pushed back the covers and swung my legs over the side of the bed, my feet touching the cold, polished wood floor. The room was spacious, almost too spacious, with high ceilings and dark wooden beams that crisscrossed above. The walls were adorned with art—landscapes of distant mountains, seascapes of turbulent oceans—pieces that Juan had collected over the years. The centerpiece of the room was an ornate, four-poster bed with intricate carvings that wrapped around its posts like climbing vines. A large window faced the east, the heavy drapes half-drawn, allowing slivers of sunlight to dance on the thick Persian rug that stretched across the floor.

I stood up, wrapping myself in a thick, cream-colored robe that hung by the bedside. I glanced around the room, taking in the familiar yet imposing surroundings. It was beautiful, yes, but sometimes I felt like a stranger here, lost among the relics of Juan's life—a life that had existed long before me. I walked over to the window, pulling the curtains aside to let in more light. The gardens stretched out before me, a tapestry of color and life that seemed to extend endlessly. The roses were in full bloom, their petals kissed by dew, while the towering oak trees swayed gently in the breeze, their leaves rustling like whispers of secrets untold.

My eyes drifted to the edge of the estate, where the distant hills met the sky, and I couldn't help but feel a twinge of longing—a yearning for something just beyond the horizon, something that I couldn't quite name. I shook off the feeling and turned away, heading towards the en-suite bathroom. The scent of lavender and eucalyptus from last night's bath still lingered in the air, and I found myself breathing it in deeply, letting the calming fragrance settle my nerves.

I splashed my face with cold water, the shock of it grounding me in the present. As I looked up into the mirror, I saw a woman who should have felt safe, content. My hair was tousled, my eyes slightly puffy from a restless sleep, but beneath that, there was something else—a flicker of doubt, a question. Who am I really, and why does it feel like a part of me is still missing?

I brushed the thought away and made my way to the wardrobe, pulling out a soft, cream sweater and a pair of dark jeans—simple, comfortable, familiar. As I dressed, I could hear the distant sounds of the staff beginning their daily routines—the clatter of dishes from the kitchen below, the soft hum of a vacuum somewhere down the hall, and the low murmurs of conversations. Life was waking up all around me.

I stepped out into the hallway, the long corridor stretching out on either side, lined with heavy, antique furniture and paintings that seemed to watch with silent eyes. The polished floorboards creaked softly under my steps, the sound echoing off the high ceilings. The mansion always felt different in the morning—a little less foreboding, a little more alive. I headed towards the staircase, the smell of freshly brewed coffee drawing me like a moth to a flame.

As I descended the grand staircase, the warmth of the early sun filled the foyer, illuminating the rich, dark wood and casting long, intricate shadows from the iron railing. The air was crisp, almost invigorating, carrying with it the mingling aromas of breakfast—freshly baked bread, sizzling bacon, and the sharp tang of citrus. I felt my stomach growl, a reminder that I hadn't eaten much the night before.

When I reached the bottom, I noticed one of the staff—Elena, the housekeeper—moving swiftly through the dining room, her hands deftly arranging the silverware with a precision born from years of experience. She looked up and offered a warm smile. "Good morning, Mrs. Ramirez," she greeted me, her voice gentle, almost motherly.

"Good morning, Elena," I replied, returning her smile, though mine felt thinner, stretched over the tension I was still carrying from last night. "It smells wonderful."

"Chef prepared a special breakfast today," she said, her eyes twinkling. "French toast, your favorite."

I couldn't help but smile a little more genuinely at that. "Thank you, Elena. That sounds perfect."

She nodded and continued with her tasks, and I made my way to the small breakfast nook that overlooked the gardens. It was one of my favorite spots in the mansion, a place where I could sit and watch the world wake up, where the sunlight streamed in through the large bay windows, painting everything in a warm, golden hue. I settled into a chair, feeling the tension in my shoulders begin to ease just a little.

But even as I tried to embrace the morning's quiet peace, my thoughts kept drifting back to Juan's words. "Some people are trying to get back at me." The way he had said it, the look in his eyes—there was more to it than he had let on. I picked up a cup of coffee that had been placed there for me, its steam curling up like a ghost, and took a slow sip, letting the bitter warmth spread through me.

A knock on the front door jolted me from my reverie, my heart leaping into my throat. I turned towards the foyer, my stomach twisting with a mixture of anticipation and unease. Who could it be at this hour?

I set the coffee cup down, the porcelain clinking lightly against the saucer, and rose from my chair. My hand trembled slightly as I reached for the knob, a million thoughts racing through my mind. I opened the door to find a stern-faced police officer standing before me, his uniform crisp and his eyes sharp, assessing.

"Mrs. Ramirez?" he asked, his voice tinged with an unsettling mixture of formality and urgency.

"Yes," I replied, my voice faltering slightly. "How can I help you?"

The officer's gaze flickered behind me, scanning the interior of the mansion, his expression tightening. "I'm here to inform you that Lieutenant Juan Ramirez has been detained for questioning at the precinct. It's a routine investigation, but we need you to come down to the station."

A chill ran down my spine, the officer's words sinking into me like a cold dagger. The thought of Juan being questioned, of him being entangled in some kind of investigation, sent a surge of fear through me.

"What?" I stuttered, my voice trembling. "Why? What's going on?"

The officer's face remained impassive; his gaze unwavering. "I'm not at liberty to discuss the details, Mrs. Ramirez. But I assure you, it's a standard procedure."

A surge of panic gnawed at my insides, the thought of Juan being taken away, of him being ensnared in some kind of legal quagmire, sending my thoughts into a tailspin.

"I need to see him," I said, my voice laced with desperation. "I need to know what's happening."

The officer nodded, his expression softening slightly. "We'll take you to him, Mrs. Ramirez. Please, follow me."

The officer led me to a waiting police cruiser, the drive to the precinct unfolding in tense silence. The city rushed past in a blur, the familiar streets twisting into an ominous labyrinth as my mind raced with questions, my heart pounding in my chest.

When we arrived at the precinct, the officer escorted me inside, his hand gently guiding me down a sterile corridor lined with cold, fluorescent lights. The sound of voices and the hum of machinery echoed off the walls, adding to the oppressive weight that settled over me.

Finally, we reached an office, its door ajar. The officer gestured for me to enter, his face a mask of stoic professionalism.

I stepped inside, my breath catching in my throat at the sight of Juan sitting at a desk, his face lined with a mixture of tension and anger. Across from him sat another officer, her eyes fixed on Juan with a mix of suspicion and impatience.

"Jui," I breathed, my heart clenching at the sight of him.

Juan's head snapped towards me, his expression softening into a look of relief. "Graxe," he murmured, his voice tinged with weariness.

The female officer's gaze flickered to me, her brows furrowing. "Mrs. Ramirez, please take a seat."

I hesitated, my gaze lingering on Juan, before slowly sitting down beside him. The room felt stifling, the air thick with tension, the weight of unanswered questions pressing down on me.

"What's going on?" I asked, my voice strained.

The female officer's face remained impassive, her eyes narrowing as she glanced at Juan. "We received a tip that Lieutenant Ramirez might be involved in a matter that requires further investigation. For now, we're simply asking questions, gathering information."

A surge of anger flared within me; the thought of Juan being dragged into some kind of investigation igniting a fierce protectiveness. "What kind of information?" I demanded; my voice tinged with desperation.

The officer's gaze flickered back to me, her lips pressing into a thin line. "I'm not at liberty to discuss the details, Mrs. Ramirez. But rest assured, we're just doing our job."

Juan's hand found mine under the table, his grip reassuring. "Don't worry, amor. We'll get through this."

The words offered little comfort, the unease gnawing at my insides, but I nodded, forcing a strained smile. "I know, Jui. But why are they doing this?"

The officer's face tightened, her eyes narrowing. "Because we need to ensure everything is in order, Mrs. Ramirez. It's standard procedure."

"Done?" Juan looked at the officer and she raised an eyebrow.

The tension in the room was interrupted by the arrival of District Attorney Cecil Alexander Walrus. He entered with an air of authority, his eyes immediately locking onto the officer questioning Juan.

"With whose permission have you detained him?" Walrus demanded, his tone sharp and unyielding. Juan's lips curled into a subtle smirk.

"Sir—" The officer began to explain, but Walrus cut him off with a wave of his hand.

"Don't 'Sir' me! With whose authority did you detain Lieutenant Ramirez? He's a decorated officer, a Medal of Valor recipient! Answer me, goddamn it! If Sheriff Merci is unaware, if I'm unaware, who the hell is running this circus behind our backs? There will be an investigation into this, Ezekiel. It seems like you're driven by personal agendas these days."

Ezekiel, the officer who had been questioning Juan, turned pale. "Personal agendas, sir? Why would I—"

"You tell me, Lieutenant Commander," Walrus growled. "How dare you handcuff a decorated officer like he's some street thug?"

Juan let out a snort, unable to hide his amusement at the DA's words. Walrus ignored him, his attention still fixed on Ezekiel, who now looked cornered, his authority crumbling.

"Sheriff Merci!" Walrus called, and Rudolf Liam Merci stepped into the room, his posture rigid and his face stern.

"Were you aware of this detainment and interrogation, Sheriff?" Walrus asked sharply.

"No, sir," Rudi responded, his voice steady and clear. "The arrest was made without any information or authorization from the proper authorities. Lieutenant Commander Ezekiel Sanchez is known for working according to his own interests. He has a history of insubordination, even towards me."

The atmosphere in the room was charged with tension. What had once been an interrogation now felt like a courtroom, with everyone awaiting a verdict.

Walrus's eyes narrowed. "Ezekiel, personal agendas have no place in the justice system. Your reckless actions have consequences."

"Sir, sir, there was a request for a welfare check on Lieutenant Ramirez. Sheriff, I assure you, I'd never go against the orders. It was just a routine check. I just—" Ezekiel turned to Rudi, seeking some semblance of support.

"Just what, Ezekiel? You thought you could arrest a decorated officer and bring his wife down to the precinct like he's some kind of Interpol-wanted terrorist? Couldn't you have approached me or Sheriff Merci? Was he fleeing the country, by any chance?" Walrus's words were sharp, and each question hit like a hammer on stone. Juan's coy smirk widened, silently mocking Ezekiel: 'How's that, bitch?'

"I apologize for interrupting, sir," I spoke up, my voice trembling but firm. "However, this is not acceptable. Not anymore."

"Amor, it's okay," Juan said softly, his arm wrapping around me, trying to calm me down. But I shook my head, my fear turning into anger.

"No, let me speak. Why is my husband being targeted? He has taken bullets for this country, has served in Iraq for five years. He holds the Medal of Valor, the NYPD Medal of Honor. How can someone handcuff him, come to my door, and tell me my husband won't be coming home? Why don't they just strip these medals off his chest?" I held Juan tightly, my eyes blazing with a mixture of fear and fury. "It feels like this whole place is against him, planning and waiting for him to slip."

"Ma'am, we are not—" Ezekiel stepped forward, but Rudi stepped in between him and us, his presence imposing and authoritative.

"You've done enough damage for one day, Lieutenant Commander Ezekiel Sanchez," Rudi said coldly. "You are suspended pending further investigation. Consider yourself on administrative leave. Hand me your gun and badge."

Rudolf's tone was final, his eyes never leaving Ezekiel's. "Now!" Rudi repeated, and Ezekiel, his pride bruised and his confidence faltering, nodded. He unholstered his gun and removed his badge, placing them in Rudolf's outstretched hand, his eyes burning with resentment as he looked at Juan and me.

"Thanks for getting me fired!" Ezekiel muttered under his breath, his voice dripping with venom as he turned on his heels and walked out, his phone already in his hand, firing off a message to James Cross.

The tension in the room lingered even after Ezekiel's departure, like a heavy fog that refused to lift. I could feel my heart pounding in my chest, the adrenaline still coursing through my veins. Juan's hand was steady on mine, a quiet anchor in the midst of a storm, but I could see the tightness in his jaw, the barely-contained anger simmering beneath his calm exterior.

District Attorney Cecil Alexander Walrus remained standing, his presence commanding and resolute. His eyes, sharp and assessing, moved from Juan to me, then to Rudi. "Sheriff Merci," he said, his voice still laced with authority, "I want a full report on my desk by the end of the day. I want to know how this... circus was allowed to happen without any of us being informed. I want names, dates, everything. Do you understand?"

Rudi nodded sharply. "Yes, sir," he replied, his tone firm. "I will handle it personally."

Walrus's gaze softened just a fraction as he turned to us. "Lieutenant Ramirez, Mrs. Ramirez," he said, his voice gentler now, almost apologetic. "I deeply regret the inconvenience and distress this situation has caused. It was not sanctioned, and I assure you, there will be consequences for those involved."

"Thank you, sir," Juan replied, his voice calm, but there was a dangerous edge to it. "But I'd like to know who thought it was a good idea to pull a stunt like this. I have enemies, sure, but I didn't expect them to be wearing the same uniform."

Walrus gave a slight nod, acknowledging Juan's frustration. "We'll get to the bottom of it," he promised. "In the meantime, you're free to go. I'll make sure this doesn't happen again."

Juan stood up slowly, his hand still holding mine, and I followed his lead. The air in the room felt lighter, but only just. The storm that had been building seemed to have subsided for the moment, but its threat still loomed on the horizon.

"Come on, amor," Juan said softly, his eyes meeting mine with a reassuring warmth. "Let's get out of here."

I nodded, my hand squeezing his as we made our way toward the door. As we stepped out of the office, I glanced back to see Rudi and Walrus in hushed conversation, their faces serious. The precinct was still buzzing with activity, officers moving about, some stealing curious glances our way.

We moved down the corridor, past the cold fluorescent lights, past the harsh, echoing voices and the metallic hum of machinery. The oppressive weight of the place began to ease as we approached the exit, the fresh air outside a promise of freedom. I hadn't realized I'd been holding my breath until we stepped out into the open, the cool breeze brushing against my skin, the sun dipping lower in the sky, casting long shadows across the pavement.

Juan turned to me, his face softening. "I'm sorry you had to go through that," he murmured, his thumb brushing over my knuckles. "I never wanted you to see this side of things."

I shook my head, trying to push away the lingering fear and frustration. "It's not your fault, Jui," I said, my voice steadier now, though still tinged with unease. "But I need to know what's going on. Why would someone want to target you like this?"

Juan's eyes darkened slightly, a shadow crossing his face. "There are always people looking to make a name for themselves or settle old scores," he replied, his tone careful. "But I have a feeling this runs deeper than that."

I could sense his reluctance, his hesitation to pull me further into whatever web of danger he was caught in, but I needed to understand. "Jui," I said softly, my hand on his cheek, forcing him to meet my eyes, "we're in this together. You need to tell me what you know."

He sighed deeply, his breath a mix of frustration and resignation. "I don't have all the answers yet, Mi Corazon," he confessed. "But I promise you, I'll find out who's behind this. And when I do, they'll regret ever coming after us."

As he spoke, his eyes burned with a fierce determination, and I knew that whatever was coming, whatever shadows were lurking in the corners of our lives, Juan would fight them with everything he had.

And just then Juan's phone chimed, a text incoming from Rudi. "He is closer than we think, drop her home and meet us at our place. Mal and I will be waiting."

Juan glanced down at his phone, his face tightening as he read Rudi's message. His eyes flicked back up to meet mine, his expression a mix of concern and resolve.

"Who is it, Juan?" I asked noticing his change of expression and he quickly began pocketed his phone.

"Just work, Amor." He said, giving a tight smile. "Maybe we should head home? I have a follow up to visit- down town." He said and I found myself nodding.

I nodded, the unease still coiling in my stomach, but I trusted Juan. Whatever was happening, I knew he was trying to protect me from it. We made our way to the car, and the drive home was filled with a tense, heavy silence. I could feel the questions pressing at the edges of my mind, but something in Juan's expression told me that he wasn't ready to share just yet.

As we pulled up to our house, I reached for his hand, squeezing it tightly. "Be careful, Jui," I whispered, my voice laced with worry.

He turned to me, his gaze softening. "I will be. I promise." He leaned over, pressing a gentle kiss to my forehead. "I'll be back soon, Mi Corazon."

I watched him drive away, my heart heavy with a mixture of fear and determination. I couldn't just sit and wait; I needed to understand what was happening. As I entered the house, I grabbed my phone, pacing the living room as I debated my next move. I knew that whatever Juan was dealing with, it was serious. Ever since our paths crossed with James Cross, we were always on the edge. The way he had looked at me, as if he has seen a ghost. My past was still shrouded in mystery, who was I before Juan found me in the river? The questions I had asked a several times. And now, something in my heart screamed, James Cross was the key of unravelling it all.

I had secretly admired is movies, ever since Juan introduced me to him, I mean his films. He had been the one, who had taken me on that premiere. which changed everything. Something about James was familiar, way too familiar... and endearing. As if I adored him way before all this... Perhaps, in a more intimate manner.

Juan tightened his grip on the steering wheel as he drove through the winding streets toward Malcom's house. The city outside his window blurred into a restless swirl of lights and shadows, mirroring the storm of thoughts raging in his mind. Rudi's message had left him uneasy, but he kept his composure for Graxe's sake. Whoever was behind this was playing a dangerous game—one that threatened not just his life, but the life of the woman he loved.

As he approached Malcom's modest two-story house, Juan spotted a familiar black SUV parked out front—Rudi's. His heart thudded in his chest as he stepped out of his car, the cool night air doing little to steady his nerves. This meeting was a pivotal moment; plans would be forged, alliances tested, and truths—bitter and unwelcome—might finally come to light.

Malcom opened the door before Juan had a chance to knock, his face etched with worry but also a grim resolve.

"Juan," he said in a low, tense voice, "come in. Rudi's already here."

Juan gave a curt nod and followed Malcom inside. The living room was dim, illuminated only by the soft glow of a single lamp in the corner. Rudi was seated on the couch, his expression set in a hard line as he looked up to meet Juan's gaze.

"Juan," Rudi greeted him, rising to his feet and extending his hand. Their handshake was firm, a silent vow that they were in this together, no matter where this path might lead them.

Malcom motioned for Juan to take a seat. "We've got a lot to cover," he said, his tone grave. "And not a lot of time to do it."

Juan sat down, his eyes narrowing as he looked between Rudi and Malcom. "What do you know?" he asked, his voice sharp and direct.

Rudi leaned forward, his elbows resting on his knees, his face shadowed in the dim light. "It's worse than we thought, Juan. Ezekiel was just a pawn. There's someone bigger, more powerful, pulling the strings. Whoever it is, they've got influence, and they're using it to come after you. Hard."

Juan's jaw tightened, his voice coming out in a low growl. "Do we know who?"

Rudi exchanged a glance with Malcom before he spoke again. "We have a lead," he said cautiously. "James Cross."

The name landed like a heavy weight in the room, charged with anger and accusation. Juan's hands curled into fists. "James," he muttered, his voice brimming with fury. "He just can't let it go, can he?"

Rudi sighed, shaking his head. "He knows Graxe is Mariyam, Juan. He's obsessed. One way or another, he's going to try to get to her. How long can we keep hiding the truth from her? And what happens if her memories come back on their own?"

The weight of the words pressed down on Juan. He stared at the floor for a moment, his face set with tension, before he spoke. "What do you want me to do?"

Malcom and Rudi exchanged a knowing look, then Malcom spoke up, his voice low and steady. "Maybe it's time, Juan," he said. "Maybe we tell her everything before she finds out on her own. Maybe it's time to reopen her case. Who is Graxe? Is she really Mariyam, James Cross's wife? And what really happened that night on the bridge?"

The room fell silent, each man lost in his thoughts, knowing that whatever came next would change everything.
Malcom's eyes met Juan's; his face lined with the gravity of what he was about to reveal. "Malcom was just...curious," Rudi began, his voice hesitant, "trying to piece things together. When he started looking into the disappearance of James Cross's wife, Mariyam, he found articles saying she jumped from the Brooklyn Bridge. That's just 10 kilometers from where we found Graxe."

Juan's brow furrowed, his mind working through the implications. "And?" he prompted, sensing there was more.

Malcom took a deep breath, his chest rising and falling heavily. "And curiosity got the better of me," he confessed. "I hacked into the private estate cameras near the bridge, even tapped into some of the traffic cams, looking for anything—any clue to tell us whether she jumped or if something else happened." He paused, glancing at Rudi, who gave him a slight nod of encouragement.

"We found something," Malcom continued, his voice barely above a whisper. He leaned in closer, gripping Juan's hand with a sense of urgency. "James Cross, in all his interviews, claimed he was at a party when Mariyam supposedly jumped. But we found unseen footage—footage that shows him leaving the Brooklyn Bridge at 10:05 PM, almost an hour before she 'jumped.'"

For a moment, the world seemed to stop spinning for Juan. His body went rigid, his breath catching in his throat as the weight of Malcom's words settled in. "What are you saying?" he whispered, his voice almost lost in the tension-filled room.

Malcom nodded grimly. "The timeline doesn't add up, Juan. James was there. He was on the bridge that night."

Juan's mind raced, a cold dread pooling in his stomach. He clenched his fists, the realization hitting him like a punch to the gut. If James was there, then he had lied—lied about where he was, lied about what he knew. And if he lied, what else had he done?

Rudi's voice broke through the silence, low and measured. "This changes everything, Juan. If James was there, he could be more involved than we ever thought. This isn't just an obsession—it's a cover-up."

Juan's eyes darkened, his teeth clenching as anger and determination surged through him. "We need more," he said, his voice steady but laced with fury. "If James was there, we need to find out why. We need to know what he was doing and if he's responsible for what happened to Mariyam—or Graxe—whatever the truth is."

Malcom nodded. "We'll need to dig deeper, and it won't be easy. James has resources, connections. If he's been covering his tracks, he's not going to stop now."

Rudi leaned back; his expression resolute. "Then we make a move. We gather every piece of evidence we can find. We push until the truth comes out. But we do this smart. No mistakes."

Juan nodded; his jaw set with determination. "For Graxe," he said quietly, almost to himself. "For Mariyam. Whoever she is, we do this for her."

The three men sat in a moment of heavy silence, their shared purpose binding them together as they prepared for the storm ahead. Whatever the cost, they would uncover the truth, and they would make sure that justice—long overdue—would finally be served.

Malcom nodded; his expression hardened with determination. "Agreed. We'll take this to the precinct tomorrow. I'll get the footage to the right people, people we can trust. Once it's in the system, they can't ignore it."

Juan took a deep breath, his resolve solidifying. "And if James tries to interfere?"

Rudi's eyes flashed with a fierce, unwavering confidence. "Then we handle it. The truth is on our side. We'll make sure he doesn't get a chance to bury it."

Malcom stood; his shoulders squared as he reached for a folder on the nearby table. "I've got more evidence here—interviews, timestamps, discrepancies in his alibis. It's all coming together. We've got enough to convince the higher-ups to reopen Mariyam's case."

Juan felt a sense of grim satisfaction settle over him. "Then let's make it official. No more secrets, no more shadows. We bring everything into the light."

Rudi nodded, a determined smile tugging at the corners of his lips. "Tomorrow, we reopen the case. And this time, we don't stop until we find out what really happened that night on the bridge."

As the three men stood, the weight of their decision hung heavy in the air, but there was also a sense of clarity, a renewed purpose. They knew the path ahead was fraught with danger, but they were ready. For Graxe. For Mariyam. For justice.

Without another word, Juan led them out into the night, the chill of the air biting at their skin. The city stretched out before them, a restless expanse of lights and shadows, but for the first time in a long while, Juan felt a flicker of hope—a hope that the truth was finally within reach.

Tomorrow, they would start a new chapter. The case was being reopened, and nothing would ever be the same again.

As Juan, Malcom, and Rudi exited the house, the night air settled around them with a stillness that seemed almost expectant. They parted ways in the dim light of the streetlamps, each man carrying the weight of the night's revelations with a sobering resolve. The quiet of the neighborhood, usually a comforting blanket, now seemed to echo with the gravity of their decisions, whispering secrets into the wind.

Inside, the room they had left bore the remnants of their gathering—a few scattered papers, a blinking laptop, the lone lamp casting long shadows across the empty chairs. It was a silent witness to the pact they had made, a pact sealed by the promise of justice not just for one, but for all who had been silenced.

As the door clicked shut behind them, the scene was set for the next act in a drama that had been unfolding in the shadows for too long. The stakes were higher now, the players more determined, and the story—Mariyam's story—was about to be told anew.

With the case officially to be reopened, the narrative of that fateful night on the bridge awaited its next, perhaps final, retelling. And as the city slept, the truth, patient and persistent, waited just beneath the surface, ready to break through the calm facade and bring with it the storm of justice long denied.

CHAPTER 7

The hallway was quiet, save for the soft padding of my footsteps on the polished wooden floor. The early morning sun filtered through the curtains, casting gentle, wavering patterns on the walls. I reached the front door and, with a twist of the handle, opened it to the cool, crisp air outside. A delivery man stood there; his cap tilted low over his face. He glanced up and smiled as he handed me an envelope. It was thick, the kind that held cards, and had a faint scent of cologne mixed with something floral.

I thanked him and closed the door, my fingers already peeling away the seal. My heart quickened a little. It was from Juan. Inside, a small card was tucked among fresh rose petals. The delicate scent of roses filled the entryway, and I couldn't help the smile tugging at my lips. I unfolded the card, and his familiar handwriting greeted me.

"Happy Anniversary, Amor. We found you this day, mermaid."

My cheeks warmed as I read the words, my heart swelling with a mixture of joy and a soft blush spreading across my face. I held the card to my chest for a moment, soaking in the affection and warmth radiating from those simple words. Juan had always known how to make me feel cherished, how to turn even the simplest gestures into moments that lingered.

Across town, in a dimly lit hotel room, James Cross sat hunched in a chair by the window, his body hidden in the shadows. His eyes, however, were focused intently through a pair of binoculars, trained on the mansion nestled in the distance. His hands were steady, though his breath came in shallow, uneven bursts. Today had been a good day. He had seen me—laughing, smiling as I played with Tabitha, Juan's niece, in the garden. For a moment, he had allowed himself to believe it was like old times.

A small, almost boyish blush had crept onto his face at the memory. It was a fleeting thing, a soft pink that contrasted sharply with the dark circles under his eyes, the lines etched deep from sleepless nights. But the moment was shattered by a sudden, sharp knock on his hotel room door, pulling him back to his grim reality.

James straightened up, setting the binoculars down on the window sill. He ran a hand through his disheveled hair and took a deep breath. "Yes?" he called out, his voice echoing slightly in the otherwise silent room. He approached the door cautiously, his earlier contentment fading with each step.

He swung the door open to reveal two stern-faced men dressed in plain clothes, their badges flashing briefly in the dim hallway light.

"NYPD, Mr. James Arthur Cross?" one of the officers said, his voice flat and authoritative. James, still riding the strange high from earlier, smiled and nodded, almost too relaxed for what was to come.

"What is it this time? Think I've hidden drugs in my room? Or girls? Or is it tax reports you want? Maybe I've got weaponry stashed somewhere," he chuckled, leaning casually against the doorframe. "Please, come in."

The lead officer's face remained impassive, his eyes scanning James's expression with practiced precision. The stark contrast between James's jolly demeanor and the officers' cold professionalism created an unsettling tension in the narrow corridor.

"Actually, Mr. Cross, we're here for something else," the officer stated, his tone devoid of humor. "You're being detained for questioning."

James's smile wavered, his easygoing facade cracking just slightly. A chill seemed to seep into the room, and his earlier lightheartedness quickly turned to a knot of anxiety. "Questioning? About what?"

The officer's eyes darted to his partner, who reached into his coat and produced a folded piece of paper. He handed it to James with a deliberate, almost mechanical motion. "We're investigating allegations related to a missing person's case. We need to ask you some questions regarding Mariyam Cross."

The name hit James like a punch to the gut. His heart pounded in his chest as he unfolded the paper, his eyes scanning the official language—an order to present himself at the precinct for questioning regarding Mariyam's disappearance.

The echoes of our digital conversation from moments earlier rang in his ears—my laughter, my light-hearted teasing—now twisted into a cruel mockery of the reality staring him in the face. "This... this is absurd," James stuttered, his voice trembling with the strain of suppressed panic. "I've cooperated with every investigation, answered every question. What more do you want?"

"We understand this might come as a shock, Mr. Cross," the second officer spoke, his voice softer but firm. "But we need to address any remaining concerns. The case has been reopened due to new information, and we need to clarify your involvement."

"New information?" James's eyes narrowed into slits, his breath coming faster. "What kind of new information?"

The officers exchanged a glance, their silence stretching uncomfortably long. "That's not something we're at liberty to discuss at this stage, Mr. Cross," the first officer replied finally, his expression unchanged. "But we need you to come with us for questioning. Please cooperate."

The surge of anger that flared within James was white-hot, igniting every nerve in his body. His hands curled into tight fists; his jaw set rigidly. The thought of my name—of my case being dredged up again—was like salt in a wound that had never quite healed. But he knew fighting would only worsen his situation.

"Fine," he muttered through gritted teeth, his voice taut with barely contained fury. "I'll come with you."

The officers nodded curtly, stepping back to allow James room to collect his things. As he shrugged into his coat, his mind raced, churning over the implications of this "new information." What could they possibly have? He had been careful. The hotel room seemed to grow colder, the walls pressing in as he realized that everything could be slipping from his grasp.

The ride to the precinct was heavy with unspoken tension, the city's lights flashing by outside the car windows. James stared straight ahead, his thoughts a chaotic whirl, replaying the earlier moments of joy that now felt tainted. Each passing second seemed to pull him deeper into a darkness he thought he had escaped.

At the precinct, James was led through a labyrinth of hallways, the fluorescent lights buzzing overhead, casting an unforgiving light on the worn, whitewashed walls. The atmosphere was thick with the sterile smell of antiseptic and old coffee. Each step echoed loudly, a reminder of how every move was under scrutiny.

Finally, they stopped at an interrogation room—a small, sterile space with a metal table and two chairs bolted to the floor. The door creaked open with a grating squeal, and James was nudged inside. He sat down, the chair's metal legs scraping harshly against the floor, his hands trembling slightly as he clasped them together on the tabletop.

The room was dimly lit, the single overhead light casting long shadows that stretched across the scuffed linoleum floor. The air was stale and heavy, filled with the sterile scent of disinfectant that seemed to seep into the walls. The clang of the steel door shutting behind James Cross reverberated through the cold, unwelcoming space, sending a chill down his spine. His heart pounded in his chest, a frantic rhythm that matched the intensity of the thoughts racing through his mind.

James took a deep breath and sat down in the cold metal chair, its legs scraping loudly against the floor. The room was designed to intimidate: the two-way mirror on the wall reflected his weary face back at him, adding an eerie sense of observation, a feeling that he was never truly alone. His eyes darted around, taking in the sparse details—the table bolted to the floor, the hard plastic chairs, the dull gray walls with cracks snaking through the paint. It was a far cry from the luxurious hotel suite he had just left, where the curtains were drawn to keep out the prying eyes, where he felt safe. Here, he felt trapped.

James's mind kept replaying the events of the day—seeing me, watching me smile and play in the garden with Tabitha. A smile had formed on his lips, the kind that hadn't touched his face in months. But now, it felt like a distant memory, an illusion shattered by the cold, hard reality of this room. His fingers tapped nervously on the metal table as he waited, each second dragging on like an eternity.

He stared at his reflection in the two-way mirror, trying to gauge if someone was watching him from the other side. His face was tense, the lines around his eyes deeper than he remembered. He hated this—being watched, being judged. His every move, every breath, every twitch of his eye scrutinized as if he were already guilty.

Suddenly, the door creaked open, the noise slicing through the oppressive silence like a blade. Rudolf Liam Merci entered the room with purpose, his steps deliberate, the soles of his boots echoing in the confined space. He was a large man, his presence filling the room. His expression was hard, lips pressed into a thin line, and his eyes carried the weight of someone who had seen too much in his line of work. His uniform was crisp, the Sheriff's badge gleaming under the harsh fluorescent lights, a stark contrast to James's slightly disheveled appearance.

Rudolf didn't sit immediately. Instead, he stood at the edge of the table, studying James like a predator sizing up its prey. The room seemed to grow colder, the walls closing in as the silence stretched between them. James's fingers stopped tapping. His breath was shallow, eyes locked onto

Rudolf's, waiting for the strike. When it came, it wasn't a physical blow, but it cut just as deep.

"Rudolf," James spat, his voice a mix of contempt and barely restrained fury. "What the hell is going on? You bastards are trying to frame me again."

Rudolf's gaze didn't waver. He pulled out the chair across from James and slowly sat down, placing a manila folder on the table with deliberate care. The folder was thick, filled with documents, photos, and notes—a testament to the case that had consumed so many lives. His eyes, however, remained fixed on James.

"James," Rudolf began, his voice steady, almost too calm, "we're reopening the case into Mariyam's disappearance. New evidence has come to light, and we need to clarify some things."

James's jaw tightened, his teeth grinding against each other. His fingers curled into fists so tight his knuckles turned white. He leaned back, trying to mask the boiling anger and fear simmering inside him. "New evidence?" His voice was low, dangerous. "Like what? What kind of sick game is this? We both know she's alive. You sick bastards manipulated her."

Rudolf leaned forward, his face inches from James's. "Cross, for the past two years, you've been repeating the same story: 'I was at the gala, she was at the hotel, I received a call and rushed to the bridge.'" His voice was low, almost a growl, each word heavy with accusation.

"Yes, that's the truth," James countered, his voice rising, his composure beginning to crack under the pressure. "I was at the gala. I have countless alibis, witnesses, pictures, and videos. What more do you want?"

Rudolf leaned back, his chair creaking under his weight. His face was impassive, a stone wall against James's rising tide of frustration. "Fine. Very well then... explain how you were on the bridge at 10.02 p.m. She jumped at 11:32. What did you do, Cross?"

With a deliberate motion, Rudolf reached over and turned off the recording camera, the small red light blinking out. The air seemed to thicken with tension as he pulled a photograph from the folder and slid it across the table toward James. It was a blurry image, grainy but clear enough to recognize his face, his unmistakable profile, standing on the bridge.

A shiver ran down James's spine as he stared at the photograph. The traffic camera's angle caught him perfectly—his stance, his face, his presence undeniable. His eyes shot back up to meet Rudolf's. "What is this? Some doctored photo? This doesn't prove anything," he snarled, but his voice lacked the conviction it had moments ago.

Rudolf didn't move. His eyes bore into James's with a relentless intensity. "Until now, we thought you were just a desperate husband trying to claim his wife back, and we were defending Graxe. But this..." He paused, his voice dropping to a near whisper, "This changes everything. I'll book you for attempted homicide. What did you do, Cross?"

The words hung in the air like a death sentence, cold and final. James felt his heart pound against his ribs, the weight of the accusation threatening to crush him. His mind raced through a thousand scenarios, trying to piece together an explanation, an escape, a way out of the nightmare that was tightening around him like a noose. He took a breath, his voice wavering between rage and desperation. "I didn't do anything. I'm telling you; I didn't do anything."

Rudolf leaned back in his chair, the sound of the metal groaning under his weight echoing in the small room. "Then prove it, James. Because right now, this looks like you're hiding something. And if you don't start talking, you might find yourself in a cell for a very long time."

The room fell silent again, but this time, the silence was deafening. The walls seemed to close in tighter, the dim light overhead casting a sharper glare, and the two-way mirror reflected a man at the edge of his sanity—his world unraveling with every passing second.

Rephrased and Enhanced Scene

"Rudi, this... this is absurd," James stuttered, his voice strained and brittle as he struggled to steady himself. "You're trying to frame me. These are—these are photoshopped!"

Rudolf's gaze remained steely, his eyes narrowing as he leaned forward, the weight of his position palpable. "This isn't about me anymore, Cross. This is about what the evidence suggests. And right now, it suggests you were on the bridge before Mariyam's disappearance. That raises some serious questions."

James's hands curled into fists, his knuckles turning white against the cold steel of the interrogation table. "I was there because I felt something was wrong! I got a call from her. She was... she was spiraling, talking about the Brooklyn Bridge. I rushed there to try and stop her, but she wouldn't listen. I... I left to clear my head."

Rudolf's expression remained unmoved, his eyes fixed on James with a mixture of suspicion and pity. "Yet, the timing of the photos tells a different story, Cross. You were on the bridge, then she jumped. Can you see how this looks?"

James felt a surge of anger, the accusation gnawing at him like a venomous snake sinking its fangs deeper into his soul. "It looks like a coincidence, Rudi. Nothing more. You know how much I loved her. You know I'd never hurt her! Don't stoop this low, Rudolf. Let's keep it decent."

"Coincidence or not, we need to investigate thoroughly," Rudolf retorted, his voice tinged with a cold finality. "The timing is too suspicious to ignore. And this new evidence puts a different light on the case."

James's anger flared, his chest tightening with a mixture of fear and frustration. "New evidence? What kind of evidence?"

Rudolf hesitated, his lips pressing into a thin line, his gaze unwavering. "Let's just say we have reason to believe there's more to the story than what you've been telling us."

James's heart sank, the weight of those words pressing down on him like a crushing blow. The thought of new evidence—of Mariyam's disappearance being twisted into a narrative of deceit and betrayal—sent a chill through his veins.

"I've told you everything," James insisted, his voice taut with desperation. "I loved Mariyam. I still do. I've cooperated with every investigation, answered every question. Why won't you believe me? I am here against everything, fighting for her."

"Stop playing the victim here, damn it! These are your phone records, 11:34 to +52 653 657 8090—Sofia, right? 'It's done!' Your text. What's done, Cross? What did you do?" Rudi shoved another picture into his face, the photograph a damning echo of the past. "Juan, Malcom, and I were all against you, yes, but somewhere, we sympathized. We saved her. We manipulated her, but somewhere, we understood that you're just a man who loved his wife and couldn't move on. But this? Did you push her, James, to be with your fling?"

Another photograph was thrust in front of him—James outside Sofia's hotel at 2 AM, walking inside. "And this? What sort of husband sleeps with a mistress a few hours after his wife supposedly died? You bastard! Did you push her? Say it! She was nagging you; she was an obstacle in your career. Say it, Cross! You were tired. She called you, yelled at you, she wanted a divorce. You were afraid because you didn't have a prenup, and she would have taken the boys. You pushed her!" Rudi's voice thundered, each word a hammer driving a nail into James's chest.

"No, no," James shook his head frantically, his eyes wide with disbelief, but Rudi continued his relentless assault.

"You pushed her. You wanted a free life. You wanted to be with Sofia. Everything could have been settled if she was gone. So you decided to push her?" Rudi's voice was sharp, unforgiving, like a blade cutting through flesh.

Or was it a mistake? Look, I mean, I can talk to the higher-ups. Did you do it by mistake? Were you arguing? You pushed her, and she fell. I understand we can lose our temper sometimes. Tell me, Cross." Rudi changed his tone to be more understanding, though it was just an act. "You wanted someone that matched your status? You were giving hits after hits; she was just a writer, not fitting molds, not good for cameras. I mean, I wouldn't want someone like her next to me either. You left for the gala, then she called. You came back on the bridge. She yelled, called you names, knew about Sofia? She threatened, wanted to take your property. How could she? You weren't thinking straight? You barely pushed her, and she fell? Was it an accident, Cross? Finally, the deed was done. You texted Sofia. You enjoyed in the hotel, a celebration? She was gone. What type of husband does that, Cross? Do your sons know? Should I drag Vercillia here too? I don't care which part of Mexico or the globe she'll hide in. Tell me, Cross, what was it?"

James's blood ran cold as Rudolf's accusations echoed through the sterile room, each word cutting into him like a jagged knife. The images on the table swirled in his vision, a sickening reminder of the night that had unraveled his world. His breath came in ragged gasps, his mind racing to reconcile the new narrative with the truth he knew.

"Rudi, I swear to you, I didn't push her," James's voice cracked, the weight of the situation pressing down on him like a leaden shroud. "It was an accident. I went to the bridge to stop her, to talk to her. She was spiraling, threatening to jump. I tried to reason with her. She grabbed my collar—she was out of control. I walked away, trying to calm her down."

Rudolf's eyes remained cold, his face an impassive mask. "So why did she jump, Cross? What did you say to her?"

James's heart clenched at the memory, the scene replaying in his mind with painful clarity. "She was angry," his voice wavered, his knuckles whitening as he gripped the edge of the table. "She accused me of neglecting her, of putting my career above our family. She knew about Sofia—about the rumors. It broke her, Rudi. I tried to explain, to tell her that none of it mattered, but she didn't believe me. She... she called me a hypocrite, said I cared more about my image than my family."

Rudolf's expression remained unmoved, his eyes narrowing as he leaned forward. "And what did you do, James? What did you do after she said that?"

James's throat tightened, his vision blurring with tears. "I tried to reach for her, but she kept screaming, so I walked away to clear my head!"

Rudolf's eyes bore into him, his lips pressing into a thin line. "You left her there, alone? You didn't stay to help your wife? Instead, you went back to your mistress, back to the gala? The woman you claim to love was threatening to jump, and you thought it was fine to walk away? And now, your mistress is here, right in the adjacent room with Ramirez. Maybe we should put a little pressure on her, see what comes out. The world deserves to know, James Cross, about your role in all this. Your sons deserve to know their father abandoned their mother and ran to another woman. What do you think Graxe—or should I say Mariyam—would say if she remembered what happened on that bridge? Do you feel dirty? Doesn't it weigh on your conscience? You took a mother away from her children for a fling?"

James's face drained of color as Rudolf's relentless accusations hammered down on him, each word a strike against his very soul. The walls of the interrogation room seemed to close in, the stark light casting deep shadows that mirrored the darkness swelling within him.

"No," James's voice was a broken whisper, a plea for understanding amidst the storm. "You've got it all wrong, Rudi. I loved her. I never wanted any of this. That text wasn't what you think—it was about the gala, not Mariyam. I was relieved the event was over, not... not what you're suggesting."

"Ramirez!" Rudolf lifted his head. "Bring her in. And contact LAPD. Get his sons on the line."

James's heart leapt into his throat, panic setting in as he heard Rudolf's command. The thought of involving his children in this twisted narrative sent a chill down his spine.

"Rudi, no! This is insane!" James's voice cracked, desperation lacing his words. "This isn't necessary. You don't need to drag my sons into this."

James's heart raced as Sofia Vercillia was ushered into the room and seated across from him. She avoided his gaze, her eyes darting around the room, betraying her unease. James felt a profound sense of betrayal twist in his gut as he realized the depth of the situation, he was now entangled in.

Rudolf, now more composed, turned to Sofia. "Ms. Vercillia, we need to clarify some details about your interactions with Mr. Cross on the night of Mariyam's disappearance. Specifically, about the text message you received from James saying, 'It's done.' What was he referring to?"

Sofia hesitated, her voice faltering as she replied, "It was about the gala event we both attended. James was confirming that he had left the event, as planned. It had nothing to do with... anything else."

James's gaze hardened as he listened, the simplicity of her explanation clashing with the complex accusations he faced.

Juan Heinrich Ramirez, standing by, raised an eyebrow. "So you were with a married man, and he texts you 'it's done' after his wife jumps into the Hudson, and you expect us to believe it was all innocent? How convenient."

Sofia's eyes flashed with anger. "How dare you accuse me like that."

"Linda!" Juan called out to a female officer, who stepped forward and delivered a sharp slap to Sofia's face.

"Answer the question!" Linda leaned in close, her tone fierce and unyielding. "Were you involved in the attempted murder of Mariyam Cross? What did he promise you? Money? A future? What kind of woman are you, agreeing to harm another woman—a mother of two? Or was it all his idea? Did he manipulate you? Did you just stand by and let it happen, thinking you'd end up with him? Did he promise you some fantasy life together?"

The room crackled with tension as Sofia recoiled from the slap, her cheek stinging with pain. Tears welled in her eyes, but she refused to let them fall, her resolve hardening as she met Linda's accusatory gaze.

"I am not involved in any attempted murder!" Sofia's voice trembled with emotion, her hands balling into fists. "James and I... we had a relationship, yes. But he would never harm his wife. He loved her, despite everything."

Juan scoffed, his expression mocking. "Love? Don't make me laugh. A man who cheats on his wife, who sends texts to his mistress while his wife is missing? That's not love. That's betrayal."

"What was it, Sofia? Were you, his alibi? Because let me tell you, Mariyam is alive." Juan leaned in, his face inches from hers. "Do you want to see?" He pulled out his phone, showing her a Social Media reel of Graxe. Sofia's face went pale as if she'd seen a ghost. Juan withheld the crucial detail that Graxe had lost her memory and didn't remember her past life as Mariyam.

"She'll identify you anyway. She'll remember what happened. So, let's save the trouble—did he push his wife?"

"How is she... alive?" Sofia whispered; her voice barely audible.

"Oh, so you wanted her dead? Did you just confess that on camera?" Linda pressed; her voice sharp as a knife.

James's voice broke through, filled with urgency. "Sofia, tell them I didn't push my wife! Tell them it was just a fling—I made it clear to you, a week before it all happened, we had nothing."

Sofia paused, her face hardening, then pointed a trembling finger at James. "He pushed her. I don't know for sure, but he texted me 'It's done,' and he came back to the hotel. He must have pushed her. He looked disheveled, panicked—yeah, he must have done it."

"You lying—" James erupted, his voice cracking with desperation as officers grabbed him by the arms. "She's lying! She called me after Mariyam jumped. Check my phone records! She said she had contacts with the coast guard, that she'd help me. She's lying, she's setting me up!"

Two officers restrained him as he struggled, his voice growing hoarse. "Listen to me! She drugged me that night, made me drink until I was wasted—I didn't do anything! Why are you doing this to me?"

Sofia's face paled further, the color draining away as James's words hit home, a vivid reminder of that night—the night that haunted her, too.

"What is it, Sofia?" Juan asked, his voicing changing to mock soft and she closed her eyes.

————-

The night air was crisp and cool as Sofia drove across the Brooklyn Bridge, the city lights casting a soft glow over the dark waters below. She was on her way to the gala, her mind buzzing with anticipation and excitement. But as she rounded a bend in the road, her gaze was drawn to a figure standing alone on the bridge's edge then she noticed James's walking away from her, clearly frustrated.

It was Mariyam.

Sofia's heart skipped a beat as she recognized James's wife, her stomach twisting with a mix of guilt and apprehension. She knew she should keep driving; pretend she hadn't seen anything. But something compelled her to stop, to confront the woman whose presence threatened to unravel the fragile web of lies she had woven.

Parking her car in the middle of the bridge, Sofia approached Mariyam cautiously, her footsteps echoing in the stillness of the night. Mariyam turned to face her, her expression drawn and haunted, her eyes shimmering with unshed tears.

"What are you doing here?" Mariyam's voice was barely above a whisper, her words tinged with bitterness and despair.

Sofia's heart ached at the sight of Mariyam's pain, but she pushed aside her sympathy, steeling herself for the confrontation to come.

"I could ask you the same thing," Sofia replied, her tone laced with mockery. "Shouldn't you be at home, playing the dutiful wife? Or is James too busy with his mistress to notice you're gone?"

Mariyam flinched at the mention of James's infidelity, her hands curling into fists at her sides. "You don't know anything about me, Sofia. You don't know what I'm going through."

Sofia scoffed, her facade of indifference crumbling in the face of Mariyam's pain. "Oh, please. Spare me the sob story. You knew what you were getting into when you married him. You knew he'd never be faithful."

The words hung heavy in the air between them, the silence broken only by the distant hum of traffic and the soft lapping of waves against the bridge's supports. Mariyam's eyes searched Sofia's face, a mixture of hurt and anger flashing in their depths.

"You think you know him, but you don't," Mariyam whispered, her voice trembling with emotion. "You don't know the man I fell in love with, the man I thought he was."

Sofia's resolve wavered at the raw honesty in Mariyam's words, her own guilt gnawing at her conscience. But she pushed it aside, focusing instead on her own desires, her own fears.

"I know enough," Sofia retorted, her voice sharp with defiance. "And I know you're not the only one he's been seeing behind closed doors."

Mariyam's eyes widened in shock, her breath catching in her throat. "What do you mean?"

Sofia hesitated, her resolve faltering as she realized the gravity of her words. But it was too late to turn back now.

"I mean, he's been with me," Sofia admitted, her voice barely above a whisper. "For months. And he's never going back to you, Mariyam. You're just holding him back."

The words hung heavy in the air between them, the truth of Sofia's betrayal sinking in with chilling finality. Mariyam recoiled as if struck, her face contorted with a mixture of disbelief and anguish.

"No," she whispered, her voice barely audible over the rush of the wind. "You're lying. James would never—"

But Sofia cut her off, her own desperation driving her to push Mariyam over the edge. "He's moved on, Mariyam. You should too. It's time to let go."

Sofia's lips curled into a cruel smile as she produced a stack of photos from her purse, thrusting them into Mariyam's trembling hands. "Oh, I don't think you want me to leave, darling. Not when you see what I have to show you."

Mariyam's heart sank as she looked down at the photos, her stomach churning with dread. They were pictures of James and Sofia, laughing and smiling together, their faces twisted with a perverse joy.

"What is this?" Mariyam's voice was barely a whisper, her hands shaking as she clutched the photos to her chest.

Sofia laughed, a cold, hollow sound that sent shivers down Mariyam's spine. "Oh, just a little reminder of who your dear husband really is. A cheating bastard who doesn't deserve you."
Tears welled in Mariyam's eyes as the weight of Sofia's words bore down on her. She felt the ground shift beneath her feet, the world spinning out of control. She turned back, intent on leaving, ongoing back to her children, but Sofia continued to follow her.

"Wait, I have more," Sofia taunted, her voice chasing Mariyam as they reached a more secluded part of the shore. "We went on trips. He chose me." Sofia's words echoed in Mariyam's ears, each one like a dagger to her heart. Anger and despair boiled within her, fueling a fire of fury that blazed in her eyes.

"Shut up!" Mariyam's patience finally snapped. "You slut! You whore! You think I'll let you destroy my family?"

"How dare you," Mariyam seethed, her voice laced with venom as she lunged at Sofia, her hands curling into fists as she sought to unleash her rage upon the woman who had betrayed her.

But Sofia was ready, her reflexes honed by years of manipulation and deceit. With a swift movement, she dodged Mariyam's attack, sidestepping her with a grace born of desperation.

"You think you can just waltz in here and ruin my life?" Sofia sneered, her voice dripping with contempt. "I won't let you. I won't let you take him away from me."

Mariyam's vision blurred with tears as she charged at Sofia once more, her fists flying in a blind fury. But Sofia was one step ahead, her movements fluid and calculated as she deflected Mariyam's blows with ease.

"You're nothing but a pathetic excuse for a wife," Sofia spat, her voice cold and cruel. "James deserves someone better than you. Someone like me."

With a cry of rage, Mariyam lunged at Sofia once more, her desperation lending her strength as she tackled the other woman to the ground. They grappled with each other, rolling in the dirt as they fought for dominance.

But Sofia was cunning, her years of manipulation serving her well as she gained the upper hand, pinning Mariyam beneath her with a triumphant smirk.

"You lose, Mariyam," Sofia taunted, her voice a cruel whisper in the darkness. "You lose everything."

With a final surge of strength, Mariyam pushed against Sofia's weight, her breath coming in ragged gasps. But it was too late. With a savage shove, Sofia sent Mariyam sprawling backward, her body tumbling over the edge of the embankment and into the icy waters below.

"Mariyam! Mari!" Sofia screamed, her voice breaking, as she instinctively called for help. She didn't intend to push her—just to scare her. But the horror of what she'd done sank in as she heard the distant splash.

The sound of Mariyam's scream echoed through the night as she plummeted toward the dark depths of the Hudson River, her body colliding with jagged rocks below with a sickening thud.

Sofia stared, breathless and shaking, at the dark water below where Mariyam had vanished. Panic mixed with exhilaration, her breath hitching as she realized what had just occurred. She fumbled with her phone, her hands trembling.

With a final glance at the river, Sofia planted her heel on the ground, pushing back the adrenaline coursing through her veins. She climbed back into her car and sped away, her mind racing.

She dialed James. "Hi, Jamie darling... Are you at the gala yet?" she said, her voice trembling slightly as she forced herself to sound calm, her eyes flicking back to the bridge fading in the distance.

—————————

Sofia opened her eyes and met Juan's gaze, taking a deep breath. She reaffirmed with a calm, calculated voice, "I don't know, Harmano. However, I think... James did it."

"Sofiaaaa! Tell them the truth, I didn't do anything!" James's voice broke as he shouted at the top of his lungs, his desperation cutting through the heavy air of the interrogation room. "Pull my call records! She called me! I called the coast guard that morning! I love my wife—I love my wife! I made mistakes, but I loved her."

James's pleas echoed off the cold, sterile walls, his voice raw and frayed with emotion. Sofia sat rigid in her chair, her face ashen, her eyes darting between James and the officers. Fear flickered across her features, torn between the reality she had created and the truth she had buried deep within herself.

"I am—" Sofia began, her voice wavering as she stood abruptly. "I'm leaving. I need my lawyer." She moved toward the door, her heels clicking sharply on the floor, a staccato beat of her mounting panic.

Juan snorted, shaking his head, amusement gleaming in his eyes. "This'll make a great comedy skit someday," he muttered under his breath, his tone laced with dark humor.

Rudi, standing beside him, gave Juan a mock glare but couldn't help the corner of his mouth from twitching.

James's jaw tightened as Juan's mocking words filled the room, each syllable dripping with contempt. The interrogation room felt like a furnace, the tension thick and stifling, each breath heavy with accusation. James's eyes, normally sharp and clear, were now clouded with a mixture of desperation and fury.

"You think this is funny?" James shot back, his voice cracking with emotion, his eyes blazing with a mixture of fury and grief. "My wife—she was everything to me. And yes, I made mistakes, but that doesn't mean I didn't love her. You don't know what you're talking about."

Before James could continue, the door swung open with a loud bang, and a well-dressed lawyer strode in, his expression severe and no-nonsense. "That's enough," he said firmly, his voice commanding the room's attention. "My client will not be saying another word without proper legal counsel present."

The room fell silent, the atmosphere heavy with a charged tension. The lawyer, a tall man with a steely demeanor, glanced around the room, his eyes narrowing at Juan and Rudi. "And I expect my client to be treated with the respect he deserves. Any further attempts to coerce or mock him will be noted and brought before the court."

Juan's smirk faltered, and he raised his hands in mock surrender. "Alright, alright, Counselor. No need to get your tie in a twist."

The lawyer ignored him, turning his attention to James. "Mr. Cross, sit down," he instructed, his tone softer but firm. "We'll get through this."

James sank back into his chair, his breathing ragged, the adrenaline still coursing through his veins. His eyes flicked to Sofia, who was now standing by the door, her face a mask of conflicting emotions—fear, guilt, and something else, something unreadable.

"Sofia," James's voice softened, almost pleading. "Please. Tell them the truth."

Sofia's lips trembled, but she remained silent, her eyes refusing to meet his. The lawyer stepped in front of James, blocking his view of her, and spoke with authority. "This interrogation is over until we've had a chance to review all evidence and speak with the appropriate parties. My client will not be answering any more questions today."

Rudi exchanged a glance with Juan, a silent conversation passing between them. "Fine," Rudi said, his voice begrudging. "But don't think for a second this is over. We'll be pulling those call records, and if there's anything to back up what he's saying, we'll find it."

The lawyer gave a curt nod. "Do what you have to. Just remember, the burden of proof is on you."

The officers reluctantly backed away, allowing James and his lawyer to leave the room. As they did, James cast one last, imploring look at Sofia. She remained frozen, her face an unreadable mask as he was escorted out.

The door closed behind them with a heavy, echoing thud, leaving Sofia alone with her thoughts and the officers' eyes boring into her, waiting for her next move.

Back at the mansion, I remained unaware of the night's unfolding revelations in the city. I moved through my evening routine with a sense of calm, the house enveloped in a quiet serenity, broken only by the soft hum of distant traffic and the gentle rustle of leaves outside. The peace within these walls was a stark contrast to the storm of emotions and secrets unraveling somewhere beyond.

When Juan finally returned home, it was later than usual. His face was drawn, his steps heavy as he entered the room. His eyes, usually so bright with mischief or warmth, seemed shadowed, weighed down by something unspeakable. I paused, sensing the shift in the air, the invisible burden he carried on his shoulders.

"Jui, what's wrong?" I asked softly, my concern immediate, reaching out to him. "You look like you've seen a ghost."

He managed a small, weary smile as he closed the distance between us, pulling me into a tight embrace. I could feel the tension in his muscles, the quiet storm beneath his calm exterior. "Just a long day at work, amor," he murmured, his voice tinged with a heaviness that belied his words. "Let's just say the past doesn't always stay buried."

I looked up at him, searching his face for answers, but his expression was guarded, his eyes distant. "Whatever it is, we'll face it together, right?" I whispered, pressing myself closer against him, trying to offer whatever comfort I could.

"Right," Juan agreed, his voice stronger this time, as if my presence had given him a reason to believe in the words. "Together."

We stood there for a long moment, wrapped in each other's arms, the world outside our walls continuing to turn. The city, with all its brilliant lights and hidden shadows, remained unaware of the small dramas unfolding within its many lives—lives intertwined by fate, choice, and circumstance.

Meanwhile, across town in a dimly lit hotel room, James Cross sat alone, the weight of the day pressing down on him like an unbearable shroud. The skyline stretched out before him, a sea of lights shimmering against the dark canvas of night. But the beauty of the city offered him no solace. His eyes were fixed, unseeing, as he stared out over the horizon. The room around him was eerily silent, save for the rhythmic ticking of a clock hanging on the wall—a constant reminder of time slipping away, of opportunities lost.

He had no illusions about what the coming days would bring. Challenges lay ahead, perhaps more painful revelations, more of the relentless push and pull between truth and deception. His mind replayed the events of the day over and over, each memory a new wound, each word spoken a blade that cut deeper. Yet, somewhere in the midst of his despair, he felt a spark of something he hadn't felt in a long time: hope. A fragile, flickering hope that maybe, just maybe, there was still a chance for redemption—a chance to make things right, to undo even a small part of the damage that had been done.

As he continued to gaze out at the cityscape, he realized that somewhere, amidst the concrete and steel, beneath the countless windows glowing with life, the truth waited—patient, unyielding, and inevitable. It was out there, ready to be uncovered, ready to bring both light and darkness into full view.

And so, as the night deepened and the city settled into its rhythm, the intertwined stories of James, Sofia, Juan, and myself continued to unfold. Each of us, in our own way, searching for resolution, for understanding, and ultimately, for peace. But the city was relentless, and it demanded its due. Whatever secrets lay buried beneath its bustling surface, it would only be a matter of time before they were unearthed, exposed to the harsh light of day.

"Look at her. She's—" James Cross's voice faltered as he stared at his phone screen, his fingers trembling slightly as they traced over the photo, zooming in and out, as if trying to capture something lost.

"Morris—" he turned abruptly to his manager, his eyes wide with an unsettling mix of longing and hope. "She follows me."

"So?" Morris tilted his head, his brows furrowing as he tried to gauge where James was going with this.

James's hand shook as he held the phone, his gaze locked onto the image of her social media profile. "Morris," he croaked, his voice barely above a whisper, yet laden with a desperation that was impossible to ignore. "She follows me. Look at her account—it's there, on social media. She's following me."

Morris hesitated, his face softening into a look of weary sympathy, tinged with cautious concern. "James, I get it. I really do. But you have to be careful. Don't read too much into this—it's just a follow."

But James couldn't tear his eyes away from the screen. His breath came out in shallow gasps as he scrolled through the reels and posts, her smiling face dancing in front of him, taunting him with a happiness that could have been his. "I can't let this go, Morris," he said, his voice breaking with emotion. "Not when she's right there, living a life that could've been ours. She's there—every day, a reminder."

Morris's hand tightened on James's shoulder, a grounding force against the tide of his rising obsession. "James, I know this hurts. I know it's tearing you apart. But you have to move on—for your own sake. You can't let this consume you."

James's gaze flickered back to the screen, his eyes narrowing with determination. The image of her face—Graxe, no, Mariyam—seemed to taunt him with its impossible familiarity. "I can't, Morris. I can't move on until I know the truth. Until I know if she really remembers nothing."

"James," Morris sighed, his tone softening, "you have to accept—"

"I can't accept anything!" James's voice cracked like a whip in the quiet room, his eyes blazing with a mixture of desperation, anger, and something else—a flicker of hope perhaps. "I need to know if she's out there, if she remembers me, our boys, everything we had! I need to know if any of it still exists in her mind or if it's all been erased like some cruel joke!"

The room fell into a thick, suffocating silence. James's heavy, ragged breaths filled the void, each one laden with an anguish that seemed to echo off the walls. The images on the phone screen blurred together, merging into a painful mosaic of what once was and what could never be again.

"Can I talk to her once? Just like an online friend?" James asked, his voice fragile, teetering on the edge of hope and despair. Morris exhaled deeply, recognizing the futility but also the inevitability of James's need to reach out. He turned his attention to the phone, his fingers flying over the screen as he navigated through social media with the practiced ease of someone accustomed to digital stalking, using a secondary account to search for any link, any shared topic that could serve as an opening.

After about thirty minutes of searching, he found what he was looking for—not on James's official page, but on a fan page. A comment. And he snorted, unable to suppress his reaction.

"What's so funny?" James's eyes narrowed, his cheeks still damp from the tears he had hastily wiped away, clearly irked by Morris's sudden amusement.

In the dim light of the room, shadows danced across Morris's face, his lips pressed into a tight line as he tried, unsuccessfully, to hold back a chuckle. The gravity of their situation seemed momentarily eclipsed by whatever discovery he'd made. "Morris, what did you find? This isn't a joke," James warned, his tone darkening.

Morris attempted to regain his composure, his eyes still glistening with mirth. "Just check it out for yourself, James," he managed to say, stifling a grin as he handed the phone back to him. "Your gaze seems a bit...distracted."

James snatched the phone, his brows knitted in suspicion. He looked down at the screen and his face immediately flushed with color. There it was—a photograph from years ago, showing a younger James Cross standing beside Charlene Vincent, his first wife. She was speaking animatedly to the paparazzi, wearing a low-cut dress that left little to the imagination. And there was James, his gaze unmistakably drawn to her cleavage as she talked.

He swallowed hard, his embarrassment deepening as his eyes moved down to the comments below. There it was, plain as day— 'Men will be men,' signed by Graxe Rehman Ramirez.
James saw the comment, and his face flushed a deeper shade of pink.
"Oiiiii, that was a long time ago when Charlene and I were together," James protested, momentarily forgetting his sorrow, his voice rising in a squeal of both embarrassment and defense.

"Why are you explaining it to me?" Morris burst into laughter, unable to contain himself.

Morris's laughter echoed in the room, his chuckles blending with James's startled outburst. The abrupt shift from James's intense brooding to this sudden, almost ridiculous levity created a peculiar tension that hovered like a cloud, suspended between humor and the lingering shadows of his despair.

James's face burned an even deeper red as he looked again at the comment, his eyes reflecting a confusing blend of indignation and reluctant amusement. "I mean... I wasn't doing anything wrong," he muttered, his voice defensive yet carrying a hint of self-consciousness. "Charlene and I were married then. And besides, it's just a comment, right?"

Morris wiped the tears from his eyes, his grin only widening with each passing second. "Of course, James. But the fact that she remembers this photo—or even cares enough to comment on it—might mean something."

James's expression shifted, the embarrassment slowly giving way to a faint, fragile hope. "You think... you think she might remember more? Or at least that there's a part of her that still connects to me?"

Morris shrugged, his smile softening into something more understanding. "Well, it's not just this. There's more—a whole trail, actually."

James's heart quickened at the prospect, his fingers trembling slightly as he clicked 'view 167 more.'

And there it was—her username: **GraxeRehmanRamirez**. The sight of it struck James like a punch to the gut, a stark reminder of her new identity and the life she had built far away from him. Graxe. Not Mariyam. Not the woman he had married and loved, but someone transformed, someone different—yet still her, somewhere deep down.

His breath caught in his throat as he scrolled through the comments. They were filled with sharp sarcasm and clever wit that felt hauntingly familiar—like whispers from a past life, echoes of the person she once was. The more he read, the more he convinced himself that Graxe, whether consciously or not, still held pieces of Mariyam buried within her.

"Look at this," James whispered, his voice trembling with a mixture of hope and anxiety. "She comments on multiple photos of mine."

"She's just mocking a celebrity," Morris replied, trying to temper James's expectations. But James shook his head, refusing to be deterred. Morris sighed and took the phone, scrolling through the comments until he landed on another one of hers.

It was under a photo of James Cross with a typo in the caption: "James Cross charged 70M for his 2018 blockbuster 'Vigil.'"

Graxe had commented with her signature wit:

"It's not a typo. Indeed, he should be charged for such acting 😄. That's what happens when Napoleon Bonaparte tries playing Romeo... 😄 Please send the invoice to his office."

The comment was posted sixteen weeks ago.

James stared at the screen, his lips parting in a silent gasp. There it was again—the humor, the sharpness, the kind of teasing Mariyam used to throw at him when they were alone, safe in each other's company. A smile tugged at the corners of his mouth despite himself.

"See that? This isn't just some random comment," he said, his voice gaining strength, fueled by a flicker of hope. "This is her. This is Mariyam. She always used to call me Napoleon whenever I got too serious about my roles."

Morris arched an eyebrow. "Or it could just be a fan who's good at roasting celebrities," he countered, but even he couldn't deny the uncanny familiarity of the comment. "I mean, it's not exactly uncommon."

James's eyes were fixed on the screen, his mind racing. "No, Morris. There's more here. She knows things—intimate things about me, my quirks. Look at how she mocks me. It's the same tone, the same voice she used to have."

Morris looked at James, his expression softening. "Okay, let's assume she does remember something—what then? Are you going to confront her? Message her?"

James hesitated, his thoughts swirling in a tumult of longing and fear. "Maybe," he murmured. "I need to see if there's a way to reach her, to break through this... this wall of hers. If she remembers enough to mock me like this, maybe she remembers more. Maybe she remembers us."

Morris watched his friend closely, recognizing the dangerous slope James was on. "You need to be careful, James. If you're wrong, if you push too hard and she shuts down, you might lose whatever little connection there is."

James nodded, but his eyes were still on Graxe's comment. It was like a lifeline tossed to a drowning man, a single thread connecting him to the woman he still loved, even if she was lost in someone else's life. "I'll be careful," he said quietly, more to himself than to Morris. "But I can't just let this go. I need to know if there's a chance, any chance at all."

His fingers hovered over the screen, his heart pounding in his chest. The idea of reaching out, even through a carefully crafted comment or message, felt like stepping onto thin ice—but he had to try. He had to know if, somewhere beneath the surface, Mariyam still existed within Graxe, waiting to be found.

With a deep breath, he typed a reply under her comment using a Smurf account, something light, playful, yet probing, hoping to stir some memory, some recognition:

"Napoleon did his best with what he had. I guess Romeo wasn't his role after all. Care to suggest a better one, Graxe?"

He stared at the screen for a moment, his thumb hovering over the 'post' button. Then, with a quick, decisive tap, he sent it.

The message was out there now, floating in the digital space between them. All James could do was wait and hope that somewhere, somehow, the woman he once loved would respond.

James kept his eyes glued to his phone screen. He knew Mariyam too well—knew her habits, her quirks, the way she could never resist a good comeback. Despite what she might have believed about herself, she was always a social butterfly, never one to let an opportunity for a sharp retort pass her by.

And just as he predicted, after precisely five minutes, his phone chimed with a notification.

"Oh ho, didn't know Cross had fans," came the sharp, witty reply.

James couldn't help the small smile that tugged at his lips. There it was—that familiar bite in her words, the way she always knew how to turn the tables. His heart quickened, his fingers trembling slightly as he typed back, his mind racing to keep up with the flow of their banter.

He knew he had to be careful. If he wanted to get closer, he had to disguise himself as just another random online person—someone neutral. His words needed to be chosen with care.

"What are you planning?" Morris asked, leaning closer to get a better look at the screen.

"To approach her from a neutral angle. As someone else," James replied softly, his smile thoughtful. "I'll try to be her friend, learn her story, find out what she remembers."

Morris frowned; his skepticism evident. "And why would she trust you? She doesn't know who you are."

James's expression grew more serious, his eyes never leaving his phone. "Because she has BPD. She overshares, connects quickly. They can hide her scars, make her disappear from records, but they can't change who she is at her core."

Morris nodded slowly, understanding dawning in his eyes. "You think if you approach her carefully, she might let something slip? Something that shows she remembers more than she admits?"

"Exactly," James replied, his voice filled with quiet determination. "If I can get her to open up, maybe I can piece together what's real. What's left of her past life... of us."

Morris let out a long breath, his gaze still fixed on his friend. "Alright, but you need to tread lightly. She's not just the woman you knew anymore. She's Graxe now, with her own life and her own truths."

James nodded, his fingers moving over the screen, carefully crafting his next response. "I know, Morris. But if there's any part of Mariyam still inside her, I have to try."

He typed his reply under her comment, keeping his tone light but still engaging, still prodding:
"Checked your reel, 'Instead of trying to be someone we are not, what if we are true to ourselves? Messy hairs, acne marks, fat? What if we look in the mirror and confess, It's me?' So, who are you again?" James delivered his curveball.

He could almost see her reaction—the narrowing of her eyes, the tilt of her head as she tried to decipher the intention behind his words. She always did have a way of dissecting comments, breaking them down to their bare bones to find the hidden meaning, the hidden motive. James could only hope she wouldn't see through his ruse too quickly.

Another notification popped up, and he could feel his heart thud heavily in his chest.

"I am... someone who is trying to make sense of it all, aren't we all?"

James stared at the screen, his fingers hovering over the keyboard as he read her response. His jaw tightened. It was a guarded answer, vague and diplomatic, but there was something in it—an echo of the Mariyam he knew. The way she used to talk in circles when she was hiding something, protecting herself.

"Are we?" he typed, his fingers moving quickly. "Or are some of us just running from who we really are? What are you looking for kid?."

He hit send before he could think better of it. He could almost feel the tension in the silence that followed, a thick, oppressive weight pressing down on his chest. James leaned back, rubbing his eyes. He knew he was playing a dangerous game, dancing around the truth without revealing too much. But what choice did he have? The woman who was his wife, the mother of his children, was now living a life where he was nothing more than a stranger—a stranger who might have hurt her.

"James Cross's fans are just like him! Arrogant and creepy." She had replied making James chuckle.

James chuckled softly, his lips curling into a wry smile. The response was biting, almost like a jab she'd throw when she was annoyed, but with an undercurrent of something else—something almost playful. He could imagine her now, staring at the screen, her face a mask of feigned irritation, but her eyes—oh, those eyes—betraying the flicker of a challenge.

He leaned forward, his elbows resting on the desk, his fingers steepled as he considered his next move. He needed to push her just enough to break that mask, to coax out more of the Mariyam he remembered. He typed slowly, deliberately, each word a calculated step on a minefield.

"Someone hates James a lot? What did he ever do to you? Weirdo! Men will always be men, until someone place a collar around their neck, or look deep in their eyes and tell them, 'I am here'." he pressed the paper plane icon to comment then waited.

The seconds ticked by as James waited for her response, his heart pounding in his chest like a drum. He couldn't help but imagine the expression on her face—the way her brows would furrow in concentration as she crafted her reply, the slight purse of her lips as she considered her words carefully. She always had a way with words, using them as both a shield and a weapon.

The notification pinged, pulling him out of his thoughts. He inhaled deeply, steadying himself before opening her message.

"I don't hate, James. He is a good actor— an average, I guess, why will I hate him? However, his Casanova image does precede him."

James's eyes narrowed slightly as he read her response. A good actor, average at best, with a reputation that precedes him—her words stung, but not in the way she might have intended. There was something else beneath the surface, a subtle dig disguised as indifference. Either She was playing her cards close to her chest, careful not to reveal too much. It was like watching her in a game of poker, her face a mask of calm while her eyes betrayed the inner workings of her mind or she genuinely didn't remember anything.

James's fingers moved slowly over the keys, each keystroke deliberate and measured, like a general plotting a battle strategy. "Funny how people think they know someone just from a few headlines. If that were true, I'd be a lot less interesting, wouldn't I?"

The response came swiftly, almost too quickly, like a coiled snake striking out. "Oh, but everyone knows his story, don't they? I read about his wife—how she 'jumped' to her death, though they never found a body, did they? And let's not forget the cheating rumors—how she chose death over the life he gave her. Millions spent to erase every trace of her from the web, as if she'd never existed... Sounds suspicious, doesn't it? What was her crime, I wonder? Was she just too much for him? Maybe she knew too much. He wanted her gone, pushed her into the Hudson, and wiped her name clean from existence, just to silence his own guilty conscience?"

James could almost hear the hiss of accusation in those words, the bite of venom disguised as curiosity. His jaw clenched, the smile fading from his lips as he stared at the screen. Whoever she was now, she wasn't pulling any punches. But beneath that, beneath the barbs and insinuations, there was something more—a dare, a challenge. One that cut deeper than he'd anticipated.

"James, you are pushing her buttons, she is defending herself even if subconsciously!" Morris spoke his voice a mere whisper but James raised his hand, gesturing Morris to stop.

James felt the sting of her words settle deep into his chest, a slow-burning ache that twisted like a knife. He wasn't sure if it was anger, pain, or a twisted mix of both. Maybe it was frustration—the kind that gnawed at the edges of his sanity, the kind that whispered in his ear that she was still there, buried somewhere beneath the surface of this new persona.

"Morris, you don't get it," James muttered, his gaze fixed on the screen, where her words glared back at him like a provocation. "She's not defending herself. She's testing me. Testing him—James Cross." He clenched jaw, He knew how to play her down, she had narcissistic streak in her, and he had mastered the art, over years, in their marriage, how to crumble her defenses.

"You seem quite informed for someone who claims not to know much. Conspiracy theorist or what?"

"I might be, you got a problem with that?" Her reply was instant.

James felt the adrenaline surge through him, his mind racing as he crafted his next response. This was the Mariyam he knew, the one who wouldn't back down from a fight, who would stand her ground even when the odds were stacked against her. He could almost hear her voice, sharp and confident, daring him to challenge her further.

"Do you have any personal vendetta against him or what?" He pressed, he was breaking her defenses, challenging her to step out from the fortress of her mind, to stir the memories his mind was trying to protect her from.

And to his surprise someone else did it for him as another comment popped up from someone called Jim.

"How rude of you! James loved his wife! I am glad you found space to make light of such a terrible situation, she was no saint either, crazy witch always trying to pull him back! You are just some sick coward hiding behind the facade of indifference. All what you can do is, make fun of people, their vocabulary, disrespect them and use slangs when you cannot defend what you preach, you need Jesus and perhaps a good psychiatrist."

James read the comment from "Jim" with a mixture of irritation and amusement. His instinct was to defend Mariyam, to lash out at the stranger who dared to speak ill of her. Even after everything, after all the pain and confusion, there was still a part of him that wanted to shield her from the world's cruelty. But he couldn't afford to be impulsive, not now. Not when he was so close.

He waited, his eyes flicking back and forth between the comments, searching for her reply. He knew she wouldn't let that slide; Mariyam never did. Even in this new life, there had to be remnants of the woman who wouldn't back down, who wouldn't be silenced. The seconds felt like minutes, and James's patience began to wane.

Then, the notification dinged, and his breath hitched.

"If it isn't the righteous defender—Jim, is it? Tell me, Jim, how much does blind devotion pay these days? Enough to buy yourself a conscience?" she had written, her words dripping with sarcasm. "I'm not interested in your half-baked psychoanalysis or your attempts at playing the moral high ground. James Cross provoked his wife! He pushed her to the edge, and he's responsible for her jump! If I were in her shoes, I might have done the same. Why should she share what was meant to be hers? The one person who was supposed to be hers? And, by the way, are you okay? Praising James in one breath and then cursing his late wife in the next. I'm sure he'd absolutely love you for it, wouldn't he?"

James could almost see her now—her eyes narrowed; her lips curled into that familiar smirk of disdain. She was provoking, challenging, drawing blood with her words just as she always had.

But Jim wasn't as forgiving as James.

"You know what?" Jim's reply came swift and brutal. "I won't waste my time on an ugly hag like you. You're probably some 70-year-old grandma with no life. And yes, James Cross is better off without Mariyam! Change my mind. Didn't he give three blockbusters after she was gone? Maybe you're right—maybe he did push her off that bridge. Smart choice. I'll pay a thousand bucks to anyone who does the same to you."

James's hands tightened into fists. His blood boiled at the venomous words. He'd seen plenty of cruelty in his time, but something about this—about this stranger so casually dismissing Mariyam's life, her worth—dug deep under his skin. And then, almost instinctively, his eyes flicked to her response. He didn't know what he expected, but he knew she wouldn't let it lie.

"You're overstepping a boundary; you shouldn't," James finally typed and hit 'send,' pausing the heated exchange for a moment.

"Courtesy is rare these days. And who are you, Mr. Panda? Another James supporter?" she shot back, referencing his profile picture. The comment made James grin.

"No, but I know one thing. He loved her—a lot... maybe he still does," James replied boldly, sending his message before Morris could snatch the phone from his hand.

Morris thought she might block James or his alternate account under the name 'Lee.' But she didn't.

Instead, she responded with a simple question, more curious than confrontational: "And why do you think that?" James read the words aloud.

James stared at her reply, feeling the cold weight of anticipation settle over him. He could feel his heartbeat drumming in his ears, the words on the screen blurring slightly as he read them again. And why do you think so? It was a question that cut deeper than she likely intended, a direct probe into the heart of his truth—the one he couldn't bear to admit even to himself.

He took a deep breath, his fingers trembling slightly as he hovered over the keyboard. He was walking a tightrope, balancing between revealing too much and saying just enough to keep her engaged. The trick was to make her feel without knowing why, to tug at the strings of a memory that wasn't fully hers anymore.

"Because love doesn't disappear that easily," he typed slowly, his brow furrowing with concentration. "It doesn't just vanish into thin air, even when everything else does. It lingers in the small things, in the spaces between what we say and what we mean. James Cross may have his flaws—many of them—but he isn't the monster everyone paints him to be. He's just... human. Flawed. Hurt. And maybe, just maybe, still searching for something he lost, do you think we can unlove someone."

He hit send, feeling the tension coil tighter in his chest as he waited. He wasn't sure if he'd said too much or too little, but he knew he was close—so close to something he couldn't quite grasp.

Minutes ticked by like hours. James's eyes stayed glued to the screen, every nerve on edge as he imagined her reaction. Would she see through the facade? Would she remember the James she once knew—the one who would whisper sweet nothings in her ear just to make her laugh, who would hold her close when the world outside was too much to bear? Or would she see only the stranger she believed him to be?

The notification dinged, snapping him out of his thoughts. He opened her reply with a mixture of dread and hope.
"To be honest, I have no idea," she began, and James could almost hear her voice, tinged with that familiar blend of irony and vulnerability. "But if theory holds any truth, maybe we never truly unlove someone. We just start loving someone else more, enough to overshadow the love that came before. The heart's a foolish muscle, isn't it? It remembers all its owners. How do you reclaim a piece of your soul from someone else? The void remains, as do the flutters."

She was drawing a line between them, a line that wavered and blurred but was undeniably there. Then she pivoted, her words shifting from introspection to a razor-sharp critique. "As for James Cross," she continued, "he sure loves to play the victim. 'My wife jumped into the Hudson; my wife is missing! What will I do? I'm so lost.' Yes, it's tragic, heartbreaking even—we get it, James. But where was he when she was crying backstage, when she was breaking down at events? When he was basking in the limelight with his leading ladies?"

James's jaw tightened, each sentence like a lash. She wasn't just speaking from some detached perspective; this was personal, raw, as if it came from a place of deep-seated understanding. She went on, relentless. "He can spend millions to erase her photos and name from the internet, but how does he erase the stories? How does he wipe his own conscience?"

James stared at her reply, the words cutting through him like shards of glass. It was like she had reached into his chest, grabbed hold of the truth he kept buried deep, and pulled it out for the world to see. She had struck a nerve, and the pain of it reverberated through him, sharp and unrelenting. He could almost hear her voice, laced with that familiar edge of frustration and sadness that he had ignored for far too long.

Her words echoed in his mind—heart is a stupid muscle; it knows all its owners. How could she say that so casually, as if it were a universal truth that everyone understood? Maybe it was. Maybe that was the part that hurt the most— that she was right, that the heart never truly forgets, no matter how hard you try to erase the past.

James clenched his jaw, feeling the weight of his guilt settling heavier on his shoulders. She had laid it all out there— his failures, his selfishness, the way he had reveled in the spotlight while she crumbled behind the scenes. And now, even with her memories fractured, she could still see through him, still recognize the man who had let her down. It was as if the pieces of her past were slowly coming together, forming a picture that he could no longer control.

He inhaled deeply, trying to steady himself before responding. He had to be careful—one wrong move, one misstep, and he could lose her all over again. But he also knew he couldn't keep hiding from the truth, couldn't keep pretending that what happened to Mariyam was something he could just sweep under the rug.

His fingers hovered over the keyboard; each word weighed carefully before he typed it out.

"You speak from place of hurt, who did you lost?"

And the answer was obvious, but he wasn't expecting it, not now, not ever, as the new comment read.

'Myself!'

James's breath hitched, his eyes widening at the stark simplicity of her response. "Myself!" It echoed in his mind, louder and louder, as if her confession had been whispered into a megaphone. For a moment, he could hardly breathe. She had cut through the layers, the masks, and the games with a single word. She had spoken the truth that had been buried under years of deceit, neglect, and half-hearted attempts to mend what was irreparably broken.

He stared at the screen, his mind reeling. Was this it? Was this the crack he'd been waiting for—the moment when Mariyam, or whatever part of her was left in this woman named Graxe, began to surface? He could almost see her there, in that word, standing at the precipice, caught between who she was and who she might become. It was an admission, an acknowledgment of loss, and for James, it felt like both a victory and a defeat.

He leaned back in his chair, rubbing a hand over his face. "Myself," he whispered, as if saying it aloud would make it feel less real. But it only sank deeper, like an anchor dragging him down into a sea of regrets and unresolved emotions. She was lost, not just to him but to herself, too. And maybe, just maybe, he was responsible for that.

"James," Morris's voice cut through the silence, a low, cautious murmur, "you can't keep doing this. She's already…"

"Lost herself," James finished for him, his voice flat, devoid of its usual charm or bravado. His eyes remained glued to the screen, his mind racing. "She's saying she's lost herself. Do you know what that means, Morris?" His tone sharpened, a mix of frustration and desperation, as if he was searching for some sort of validation or understanding in his friend.

Morris sighed, glancing at James's tense form. "I know you're trying to reach her, but there's a fine line between bringing someone back and pushing them away for good."

James knew Morris was right, but he couldn't let go. Not now. He had spent years basking in the limelight, chasing his dreams while his wife had slipped through his fingers like sand. He'd let her fall apart, become a ghost of herself, and now, all that was left of Mariyam was this—this woman with no memory, who only had fragments of who she used to be. But even in those fragments, there was still that sharp edge, that fire that had drawn him to her in the first place.

He inhaled deeply, his chest tightening as he began to type again. Each word was a step forward on a tightrope, and he couldn't afford to misstep.

But before James could type a response to Graxe, a text popped up on his phone, stealing his attention away.

"Did you kill her—? Did you have an affair? You were with Sofia hours after she died, weren't you, Dad?" Aamon's message blared across the screen, the words like jagged shards of glass slicing through James's already fragile state of mind.

"Just yes or no! Don't BS with me." Another text followed almost immediately.

James's heart clenched at Aamon's relentless barrage of accusations, each word a stark reminder of the widening chasm between them. He couldn't dodge the truth anymore; there was no room for half-truths or deflections now. His son deserved answers, even if they were painful.

With a heavy breath, he began typing, his fingers trembling as they danced over the keys, burdened by the weight of what he needed to say.

"No, Aamon, I didn't kill her. And no, I didn't have an affair. I was with Sofia, but not for the reasons you think. Please, let me explain. I love you, Champ."

There was a pause, a tense, suffocating silence as James waited. Then Aamon's reply came through, each word hitting him like a sledgehammer.

"I saw the news, Dad. Sofia confessed! How could you? How could you do this to us! Aaron was 14—freakin' 14 years old! You killed her with your mistress? Then you told us she committed suicide? We used to blame her! We called Mum a coward! You know what? I'm moving out, and I'm taking Aaron with me. You're dead to us. We'll be fine. We survived without her; we'll survive without you. Don't ever try to contact us again. I don't even want your last name. And don't bother contacting Aaron either. I'll explain to him—we're orphans now!"

James's phone slipped from his hand, crashing against the hardwood floor of his dimly lit study. The sound of the impact was like a gunshot in the stillness of the room, but he barely noticed. His son's words echoed endlessly in his mind, a merciless litany of pain and betrayal. His hands shook as he bent down to pick up the phone, the screen now shattered into a web of jagged lines, a perfect mirror of his broken life.

He stared at the message; his vision blurred with tears. The weight of his sons' rejection pressed down on him like a physical force, threatening to crush him. It was as if the ground had been ripped out from under him, leaving him plummeting into a chasm of regret and despair.

"I have to fix this," he muttered to himself, a desperate resolve forming in the storm of his emotions. He couldn't let things end like this, not with his boys thinking he was a monster. They had to know the truth; they had to hear it from him.

James quickly wiped his eyes and typed a response, his fingers fumbling as he fought against the rising tide of panic.

"Aamon, please. I know you're angry, and you have every right to be. But you've got it all wrong. I never hurt your mother. I loved her more than anything. Sofia's confession was twisted, manipulated. I was used, set up. Please, just hear me out. Meet me, just once. For the sake of our family, for the sake of the truth."

He pressed send and stared at the screen, his breath shallow, his heart pounding like a drumbeat of desperation. He could only hope that Aamon would give him that one chance—to explain, to make things right before it was too late.

His troubled thoughts were abruptly interrupted by another notification. A comment from GraxeRehmanRamirez flashed on his screen, pulling him away from the turmoil with Aamon. He clicked on it, his breath still uneven, and read her words:

"It was nice talking to you, Panda. I'm heading out now. Goodbye. Feel free to send a message request!"

A simple message, but it felt like a door slamming shut in his face. James's heart sank as he stared at her words. It was almost as if she was slipping away, just like everyone else in his life. A closing note, a finality that he wasn't ready to accept. He needed more time, another chance to connect with her, to reach that part of Mariyam that he believed was still inside her, buried under layers of new identity and lost memories.

For a moment, James's hands hovered over the keyboard, caught between the desperation to keep her talking and the fear of pushing too hard. Every interaction with her felt like walking a tightrope—one wrong word, and she'd be gone, and he'd be left grasping at air. His mind raced with possibilities, each one more fragile than the last. He couldn't let this opportunity slip away, not after all he had been through to find her again.

With a determined breath, he made a decision. Opening her profile, he clicked 'send message' and began typing, trying to strike a casual tone.

"Where are you heading to, Miss Adventures? Isn't it 8?"

He hit send, his eyes fixed on the screen, waiting for a response. Moments later, her reply appeared, quick and to the point.

"It's 6 PM. Where are you from?"

James felt a small surge of relief at her quick response. She was still engaged, still willing to talk. He needed to keep this going, to find a way to break through that casual exterior without coming on too strong.

"Ah, time zones. I'm a night owl on this side of the world," he replied. "Guess I lose track of time easily. What's got you heading out at 6? Must be something exciting."
There was a brief pause, and then her reply came through, and his blood ran cold.

"Thinking about visiting the Brooklyn Bridge. I feel drawn to it," she wrote.

James's vision blurred with unshed tears. Those words—the very same words she had said to him all those years ago, on the night everything had fallen apart. They had been in New York for a charity gala. Tension had been thick between them; they'd just had a vicious argument about the kids. He had blamed her for neglecting Aaron, who had fainted at school. She was busy, she hadn't noticed he wasn't eating for two days. And the rumors about him and Sofia were already deafening, weighing heavily between them. That night was the first time he had raised his hand—not on her, but the shattered lamp in the corner of the bedroom had seemed to laugh mockingly at his rage.

"You sure you're not coming?" he had asked that day, adjusting his cuffs with an air of forced indifference.

She stood by the window, staring out at the city skyline, her posture rigid, her silence heavy with unspoken hurt.

"What will you do here all alone? I might get late," he had added, his pride preventing him from offering an apology.

"Thinking about visiting the Brooklyn Bridge," she had said softly, without looking back. "Will write or paint. I feel drawn to it. It must be peaceful there."

He had left without another word, without the customary kiss goodbye, without even turning back. Later that night, his phone kept buzzing incessantly, but he was too caught up in the glitz and noise of the gala to notice. It wasn't until 2 AM that he finally checked it, his blood turning to ice at the sight of 57 missed calls from different numbers and a flurry of Messaging App notifications, one of which bore the headline: "James Cross's Wife Jumps from Brooklyn Bridge? Witnesses Claim Suicide... Read More."

The words echoed in his mind, each one a dagger twisting deeper into his gut. James's hands began to tremble as he read Graxe's message. The image of the Brooklyn Bridge, forever burned into his memory, its steel arches towering over the dark waters below, a place of serene beauty turned into a monument of loss. His mind was thrown back to that fateful night, the last time he had spoken to her, the last time he had the chance to turn things around and didn't.

"I feel drawn to it." The same words, that chilling sense of familiarity. His vision blurred as tears threatened to spill over. His fingers hovered over the keyboard, his breathing ragged, heart hammering wildly in his chest.

He remembered how he had run out that night, hoping against hope that it wasn't her, that the reports were wrong. He'd raced to the bridge, his lungs burning, his mind frantic, only to be met with a convoy of police cruisers casting red and blue reflections over the choppy water. In that moment, all the noise had faded away, replaced by a deafening silence as he stumbled to the ground. A police officer had stepped forward, his expression grim, placing a single heel and a phone in front of him on the cold pavement.

"Where is my... Where is... my wife?" James had choked out, his voice breaking.

He paused now, the memory overwhelming him, almost choking him. The heel, the phone—it was like a cruel joke, a mocking twist of fate. The officers had tried to console him, assuring him they were still searching the waters, but he knew. Deep down, he had known the truth from the moment he saw them.

The days and weeks that followed were a blur of anguish and unanswered questions. "We're still searching. Have patience, Mr. Cross," they'd told him again and again. But patience was a luxury he couldn't afford as the world turned against him.

"He was attending parties! He didn't even care! Freak psycho womanizer!"

"Actor! Trying to act worried for the cameras."

"He pushed her!"

"Maybe he was getting a divorce, and she spiraled?"

"You pushed her way before she actually jumped, Dad!"

"He was in Sofia's bed when she jumped!"

The accusations and rumors were relentless, a tidal wave of blame and suspicion that he could never outrun. James's mind was flooded with all the what-ifs that haunted him to this day. Why hadn't he turned back that night? Why hadn't he kissed her goodbye like he always did? Why did he let her stay alone? Why hadn't he noticed she was spiraling? They fought, yes, but they always made up. Always.

But not this time.

James's grip on the phone tightened, his emotions churning like a storm inside him. The chaos of those days replayed vividly in his mind; each moment sharp enough to cut. The confrontation with Sofia, the rage and confusion that drove him to seek answers where there were none, the way she had screamed at him, her voice a razor slicing through his grief-stricken state. He had been so desperate, so blinded by his anguish, that he had lashed out, hoping to find some shred of truth in the mess of his life.

His heart ached with the weight of the memories, the unsolved questions, the wounds that had never healed. He stared at the screen, her words about visiting the Brooklyn Bridge staring back at him, like a ghost from his past calling him back to that place of pain. He could feel it—a pull, a magnetic force dragging him back to that moment, that night when everything had changed.

With trembling fingers, James began to type a response, his mind racing with the implications of reopening old wounds, of stepping back into that darkness.

"Are you sure it's the bridge you're drawn to?" he wrote, his hands shaking. "Or is it something else... or someone?"

He sent the message, his breath hitching in his throat. He didn't know if he was ready to face whatever came next, but he knew he couldn't turn away now. Not when he was so close to the truth—so close to finding the part of her he'd lost so long ago.

While waiting for Graxe's response, James reluctantly opened his social media feed, his eyes scanning the screen filled with a torrent of posts and trending hashtags spiraling out of control. His name was everywhere, tied to accusations and biting commentary that felt like an unending assault.

#JamesCrossIsAMurderer #SofiaAndJamesGuilty #JusticeForHer!

The tags and mentions kept coming, each more venomous than the last.

@Jenna_89: "You don't have any shame, do you? Why don't you take a dive into the river too, you freak? Ugh, same pattern with every woman—no wonder the ones before her ran. They dodged a bullet; she took the fall. @JamesCross You're a disgrace!"

@cityking: "@JamesCross Absolute scum! She deserved better. No wonder your sons walked out on you. Just go to prison with Sofia already. You both belong at the bottom of the river. Look at him—what a joke. Is that what fame does to you?"

James's jaw tightened, his eyes scanning the barrage of hateful comments, each one like a whip against his already frayed nerves. The vitriol was relentless, and the weight of the accusations bore down on him like a physical burden. It wasn't just the words—they were twisting the knife in wounds that had never properly healed. The world had already made up its mind, casting him as a murderer, a liar, a monster who had driven his wife to her death and betrayed his family.

He let out a shaky breath, his eyes lingering on the hashtags, the bile rising in his throat. The weight of it all was suffocating, but there was something else—something that caught his eye amidst the chaos of notifications. A message, one he hadn't noticed in the deluge of hate.

It was from Aamon.

"I am sorry about earlier. I am coming to NYC with Junior, Dad. I want to trust you... Even if my brain and the whole world says you did it, let's talk. Saw your pictures—are you taking your meds or not? You looked pale. Your blood pressure's going to spike again." —Aamon.

James stared at the message, his chest tightening with a mix of relief and anxiety. His son was reaching out, extending a fragile olive branch, even if it was shrouded in doubt and suspicion. Aamon wanted to believe him, even when everything seemed to point to his guilt. He felt a flicker of hope ignite in the darkness that had settled around him. Maybe this was a chance—his last chance—to make things right, to explain his side of the story, to hold onto the frayed threads of his family before they snapped completely.

But that same hope was laced with dread. What if he couldn't convince Aamon? What if the world's narrative had poisoned his son's faith beyond repair?

He typed a quick response, his hands steady but his heart thudding heavily in his chest.

"Aamon, I'm glad you're coming. I want to talk, to explain everything. I promise I'll answer any questions you have. And yes, I'm taking my meds—don't worry about that. Just come safe. I love you, son."

He hit send and stared at the screen, his thoughts racing. He needed to prepare himself for this conversation, to be ready for anything. Aamon deserved the truth, no matter how messy or painful it was. But right now, another truth was hanging in the balance—the truth about Graxe, about Mariyam.

He glanced back at the message screen, hoping Graxe would reply soon. He needed to keep this fragile connection alive, to pull her closer to the memories she'd lost, to remind her of the life they once shared.

A new notification popped up—a message from GraxeRehmanRamirez. His breath caught as he clicked it open, his heart pounding with a mix of anticipation and fear.

James stared at the screen, his eyes burning from the relentless scrolling and the strain of holding back tears. His mind was a battlefield, each thought colliding with another, his emotions swinging wildly between hope and despair. The digital world had turned into a courtroom where he was both the accused and the condemned, and the jury—faceless, nameless masses—had already reached their verdict. Guilty. Guilty of betrayal, of neglect, of something darker that he hadn't even fully reconciled with himself.

The weight of the past bore down on him like a thousand bricks—every mistake, every regret, every moment he could have done something differently but didn't. And now, those choices seemed to have all gathered, conspired even, to choke the life out of him. His breath hitched as he scanned Aamon's message again. There was a crack in the wall his son had built, a small window of opportunity to reach him. But what would he see when he looked through that window? Would it be his son's understanding and forgiveness—or a reflection of his own failures staring back at him?

The irony wasn't lost on him. All his life, he had played roles, crafted personas for the world to see—a loving husband, a devoted father, a celebrated man who seemed to have it all. But those were just roles. Behind closed doors, there was a different story, one written in arguments, broken glass, unspoken apologies, and a love that seemed to fray at the edges with every passing year. Now, the roles had reversed. He was no longer the one in control of the narrative. The world had taken over, rewriting his story in headlines and hashtags, leaving him to wrestle with a version of himself he barely recognized.

And then there was Graxe—or Mariyam, as he still stubbornly thought of her. The woman he had loved and lost, the woman he still believed was out there, hidden beneath the layers of a new identity and shattered memories. Her words lingered in his mind like a ghost: "Thinking about visiting the Brooklyn Bridge. I feel drawn to it." A cruel echo from their past, pulling him back to that night—the night—when everything had changed forever. Was this a coincidence? Was it fate's twisted sense of humor? Or was there something deeper at play, a connection he hadn't yet grasped?

James didn't know. But he did know one thing: he couldn't let her slip away again. Not this time. He had already lost her once—no, he had let her go, driven by pride, anger, and his own blinding ambition. He'd walked out that night, and by the time he wanted to turn back, it was too late. The world had already started spinning out of control, and he had been caught in its dizzying whirlwind ever since.

And now, as he sat there, his screen aglow with the possibility of a new message from her, his heart pounded in a familiar rhythm—a rhythm of fear, of hope, of desperation. His fingers hovered over the screen, not daring to click yet, savoring the moment before everything shifted again. In this small bubble of time, there was still a chance—one last chance—to rewrite the ending of his own story. Or perhaps, to understand that some endings are just new beginnings in disguise.

But he knew better than anyone that hope was a dangerous thing. It could lift you up to the stars or bury you beneath the weight of its own promise. And as he stared at the blinking cursor, waiting for him to make his move, he understood that whatever happened next, he had to be ready for it. Ready for the truth, ready for the fallout, ready to face the person he had become in the wake of all his choices.

Would she remember him, if only for a fleeting moment? Would she see past the mask he had worn for so long to the man who still loved her, even when the world said she was gone? And what of Aamon? Would his son see a father trying to make things right, or would he only see the monster everyone else believed him to be?

The answers, for now, remained elusive. But there was one thing James knew with a clarity that cut through the haze of his thoughts: he couldn't afford to let fear be the one writing the next chapter of his life.

And so, with a deep breath, he prepared himself for whatever would come. The page hadn't turned yet, but he could feel it, right on the edge, waiting to be flipped. And in that brief, uncertain moment, James Cross stood on the precipice of his own redemption—or his own undoing.

CHAPTER 8

James stared at the blinking notification from GraxeRehmanRamirez, his heart hammering in his chest as if trying to pound its way out. He could almost feel the weight of the decision pressing down on his shoulders—click and open it, or let it sit there, an unopened Pandora's box containing either hope or another descent into despair. He swallowed hard, his throat dry, and closed his eyes, trying to center himself. The seconds ticked by, heavy and elongated, stretching into a silence that was almost unbearable.

He thought back to the last time he stood at a crossroads like this, when he chose to leave instead of turning back. That decision had cost him everything—his wife, his family, his reputation. It was a choice he had made out of pride and anger, a choice that haunted him every day. Now, the universe seemed to be offering him another chance. But was it a chance to make things right, or merely another opportunity to falter?

His phone vibrated again, this time a message from Aamon confirming their arrival details. The words were curt but filled with a thread of cautious hope, like someone tiptoeing on a cracked sheet of ice. James could almost hear the apprehension in his son's voice—the uncertainty, the fear, the need for answers. He couldn't lose him, not after losing Mariyam. Aamon was his last anchor to a life that felt real, a tether to a reality that hadn't yet fully abandoned him.

But there was also Mariyam—Graxe, he reminded himself. She was a different person now, living a different life, perhaps with different dreams and desires. The mystery of her resurfacing in his world was like a sudden gust of wind stirring old ashes, reigniting embers he thought had long since died. And here he was, waiting, hoping for those embers to burst into flame once more. He needed to know if this was a sign, a hint of the woman he once loved still buried beneath her new reality. Or was it just his own desperation twisting shadows into shapes he wanted to see?

With a sharp intake of breath, James opened the message.

There was no sudden rush of revelation, no earth-shattering declaration. Just a few lines of text, simple and unassuming:

"I don't know why I feel like I should go there. Maybe I'm looking for something. Or maybe I'm just trying to find a place where I can feel... anything. I know it sounds strange, but it's like the water will wash everything away. Maybe then I'll know what's missing."

James's breath hitched, the words hitting him with the force of a wave crashing against a fragile shore. It wasn't just what she said—it was how she said it. The confusion, the sense of being lost, the subtle call for something she couldn't quite name. This wasn't just a coincidence. This was Mariyam speaking, in her own way, reaching out from the shadows of her new life. She was grappling with something deep inside her, something that felt unfinished, unresolved.

He wanted to tell her everything in that moment—to pour out his heart, to confess all the mistakes, all the regrets, all the things he wished he had done differently. But he knew he couldn't overwhelm her. She was on a knife's edge, caught between two worlds, and the wrong move could push her further away. He needed to tread carefully, to draw her in without frightening her off.

He typed, his fingers deliberate, steady:

"I get it. Sometimes the water has a way of calling to us. Maybe it's not about finding what's missing, but about remembering what's already there. Sometimes, it's just about standing on that bridge, feeling the wind, and knowing that there's a reason you're there."

He hit send and waited, his heart beating in a slow, heavy rhythm. He hoped his words would resonate, that they would find their way to the part of her that still remembered, still felt, still yearned for the truth. He could almost picture her on the other side of the screen, her brow furrowed in thought, her eyes scanning his message as she tried to make sense of it all.

Minutes ticked by, and with each passing second, James's nerves frayed a little more. He glanced out the window, the city's skyline sprawling out beneath the twilight sky. Somewhere out there, she was searching for something—just as he was. He could feel it in his bones, a strange synchronicity that was too profound to ignore.

Then, another message popped up.

"Maybe. Or maybe it's just a fool's errand," she wrote. "But sometimes, fools find what they're looking for, don't they?"

A smile tugged at the corner of James's lips. It was a small crack in her armor, a hint of that sharp wit that had once been so characteristic of Mariyam. She was still there, somewhere, beneath the surface. He had to keep her talking, keep that connection alive.

"Maybe they do," he replied. "And sometimes, they find things they didn't even know they were looking for."

He knew he was pushing his luck, walking that fine line between curiosity and desperation. But what else could he do? He had to believe that this conversation could lead somewhere—that it could help him find her again, and maybe, just maybe, help her find herself.

Another message came through.

"And what about you, Panda? What are you looking for?"

James felt his pulse quicken. She was turning the question back on him, probing, searching for his truth. For a moment, he hesitated. Should he be honest? Should he lay it all out there and risk everything, or play it safe and keep the walls up?

"Perhaps something or someone, only time will tell. For now, Let's go get some sleep, kid. Maybe dreams will make more sense than reality." He sighed then pressed 'send'.

As soon as he hit 'send,' James leaned back in his chair, exhaling a long, weary breath. The tension in his shoulders began to unwind, but his mind remained on edge, teetering between hope and apprehension. He had left the conversation on a neutral note—careful, vague, yet open-ended. Maybe it was enough to keep her thinking, to keep her wondering. Maybe it would draw her back to him when she was ready to confront whatever lay buried in her subconscious.

He closed his eyes, imagining her reading his last message. Would she understand the weight of his words? The subtle plea hidden beneath the layers of casual banter? He could only hope. If she went to sleep tonight with even the smallest thought of him lingering in her mind, then he had a chance. A chance to keep her tethered to a past she didn't fully remember, but one he was desperate for her to reclaim.

James opened his eyes, the dim light of his phone screen casting shadows across his face. The city outside had settled into the quiet hum of late evening, its skyline twinkling with a thousand tiny lights. The world felt heavy, almost too heavy to bear alone. His gaze drifted to his phone, where another notification from social media buzzed to life. He ignored it, his mind too tired to wade through more venomous comments, more hateful words from strangers who knew nothing about his real life, his real pain.

His thoughts circled back to Aamon. His son was coming. The thought filled him with both dread and anticipation. Would Aamon arrive with an open mind, or with the judgment already written in his eyes? Would he listen, really listen, to the story James had to tell? Or would he see only the twisted version of events spun by the media, by those who had always delighted in watching James fall from grace?

He couldn't blame his son for his doubts. The world had turned against James, and he had few allies left. Even those who had once stood by him had grown distant, wary of the scandal that seemed to cling to him like a shadow. He was a pariah, a man stained by loss and suspicion. But Aamon's message, despite its guarded tone, carried a glimmer of something else—hope, maybe. Or at least a willingness to hear his father out.

"Tomorrow," James muttered to himself, feeling the weight of the coming day settle over him like a heavy blanket. Tomorrow, he would face his son and lay bare the truth, however painful it might be. And maybe, just maybe, that truth would be enough to begin rebuilding what had been shattered.

His phone buzzed again, and his heart jumped, thinking it might be another message from Graxe. But when he glanced at the screen, it wasn't her. It was another social media notification, more strangers throwing stones, their words filled with spite. He swiped the notification away, his patience fraying at the edges.

He had to clear his mind. He needed rest, a reprieve from the noise in his head. But sleep was an elusive thing, always just out of reach. He stood up, moving to the window to look out at the city, the lights stretching out like a sea of stars. Somewhere out there, Graxe—Mariyam—was navigating her own labyrinth of thoughts and emotions. And Aamon was on his way, carrying the weight of his own questions, his own doubts.

James knew he wasn't the only one haunted by ghosts.

He pressed his forehead against the cool glass, his breath fogging the surface. In moments like these, when the silence was loud and the darkness pressed in, he felt the full gravity of his choices. The guilt of that night, of every night that followed. The things he'd said and hadn't said, the kisses he hadn't given, the love he'd let slip away. He was a man filled with regrets, but regrets were nothing without the will to change, to make amends.

"Tomorrow," he whispered again, his voice barely audible. "One step at a time."

Aamon. Graxe. The world outside and the demons within. He would face them all. He had to.

With a final glance at his phone, he turned away from the window. Tonight, he'd try to find the peace he'd been searching for, even if only for a few hours. And when morning came, he'd be ready—ready to fight for his son, for his love, for whatever chance he still had at redemption.

He switched off the lamp and sank onto the bed, staring up at the ceiling, his mind a jumble of thoughts, his heart a restless drumbeat. The city outside continued its endless pulse, a reminder that life moved forward, no matter how broken it seemed. And as James closed his eyes, he held onto the fragile hope that maybe, just maybe, tomorrow would bring a little lighter.

James awoke to the soft glow of dawn filtering through the curtains, the world outside stirring to life with the first hints of morning. His body felt heavy, weighed down by a restless sleep that had been more of a battle than a respite. His mind, however, was already racing, snapping into focus on the day ahead—the day that could very well decide everything.

He rolled over, reaching for his phone with a sense of urgency that almost bordered on desperation. Aamon would be arriving soon, and James needed to be prepared, not just with answers but with a calm that he hadn't felt in years. He unlocked the screen, his heart skipping a beat as he saw a new message from Aamon, sent just minutes ago:

"We're on our way, should be there in an hour. Don't make me regret this, Dad."

James stared at the message, his chest tightening. There was hope in those words, but there was also a warning, a reminder that Aamon's trust was fragile, hanging by a thread. He had to handle this carefully, with honesty but also with empathy. His son wasn't looking for a polished story—he was looking for the raw, unfiltered truth, and James had to be ready to give it to him.

He quickly typed a response, his fingers moving with an urgency that matched his thoughts.

"I won't. I promise. Just get here safe. We'll talk, just like you wanted."

He hit send and sat up, swinging his legs over the side of the bed. His head was pounding slightly, a dull ache that came from a night of fragmented sleep and the weight of everything that lay ahead. He needed coffee, something to clear the fog from his mind and steady his nerves. He pushed himself up and headed to the kitchen, each step feeling like a march toward an uncertain fate.

James Cross paced around his New York penthouse, his mind a storm of emotions as he prepared for Aamon's visit. He hadn't seen his son in years, not since everything had fallen apart. This meeting was a chance to clear his name, to tell his side of the story, and maybe—just maybe—begin to bridge the chasm that had formed between them. He longed to show his sons that he had never stopped loving their mother, that he too had been ensnared in a web of lies and manipulation.

When the flight came, James waited at the airport, his eyes darting through the crowd for a glimpse of Aamon. Anxiety gnawed at him, but when he finally spotted his son, his heart leapt. Aamon looked older, more mature than the boy James remembered, but he still had that familiar expression—a blend of Mariyam's calm and his own intensity.

"Dad," Aamon greeted, his voice stiff, a wall between them.

James opened his arms, an uncertain invitation. Aamon hesitated, his body tensing, but after a moment, he stepped into the embrace. James felt his son's resistance, the hurt and anger coiled beneath the surface, but he also felt a slight softening—an acknowledgment of their shared blood.

"Let's go home," James said, his voice thick with emotion. "Let's start fixing this."

Back at the Penthouse, they sat across from each other in the living room, the silence heavy and uncomfortable. James took a deep breath, steadying himself. "Aamon, I know how it looks—the media, Sofia's accusations—it's been a nightmare. But I need you to hear me out. I loved your mother. I did not harm her. Sofia... she was manipulated, and in turn, she manipulated the situation to destroy me, to hurt us all."

Aamon's face remained unreadable, his eyes searching James for any hint of sincerity or deceit. James continued, recounting the misunderstandings, the fights, the relentless pressure of fame and the media, and his own shortcomings as a husband and father. He could see the skepticism in Aamon's gaze, but he also saw a flicker of something else— maybe a desire to believe him, to believe that his father wasn't the monster the world painted him to be.

After a moment, James suggested, "Let's take a walk. Aaron must be here soon." Aamon nodded silently.

The crisp autumn air of New York was a stark contrast to the suffocating tension inside. James led the way through the busy streets, his footsteps echoing on the cobblestone path. Each step felt heavy, laden with the weight of the battles he had faced—both public and private. When they reached a small park, they sat on a bench by a fountain, the sound of water providing a soothing backdrop.

Aamon broke the silence, his jaw tight. "Dad, we need to know the truth," he said, his voice tinged with both desperation and determination. "Did you push Mom? Did you have an affair with Sofia?"

James was about to respond when he saw Aaron approaching. His second son had come straight from the airport, his face twisted with anguish, his hands clenched into fists at his sides. He stood there silently for a moment, his chest heaving with emotion, before he spoke.

"How could you lie to us, Dad? How could you betray Mom like that?" Aaron's voice was raw, cutting into James like a knife.

James felt his heart shatter at the pain in his sons' voices. He knew this conversation was long overdue, a reckoning that would test the fragile threads of their relationship. "I didn't push your mother," James said, his voice steady but strained. "And I didn't have an affair with Sofia. I know what it looks like. I know the rumors, the lies... they've twisted everything. But I never betrayed your mother. I loved her. I still do."

Aamon's expression was tense, his eyes boring into James's as if searching for any sign of a lie. "Then why did Sofia confess?" he demanded; his voice filled with frustration. "Why did she say you were involved? You didn't come back to the hotel that night—where were you?"

James's breath came in ragged gasps, the weight of the accusations bearing down on him. "I don't know, Aamon," he replied, his voice trembling with desperation. "But I'll find out. I'll clear my name. Just give me a chance."

Aaron's face contorted with anger; his eyes blazing. "But she confessed, Dad! How can we trust you?"

James's hands trembled, the accusations tearing at his very core. "I know it's hard to believe," he said, his voice breaking. "But I swear to you, I didn't harm your mother. Sofia's confession... it's a lie. I'll prove it. I promise."

The silence that followed was agonizing, each second dragging on like an eternity. Finally, Aamon spoke, his voice tinged with exhaustion. "I don't know if I can trust you, Dad," he said, his tone heavy with the weight of all the years of uncertainty and pain. "But for Mom's sake, I'll listen. We'll listen. Let's talk more."

James's heart surged with a fragile hope. "Okay, Aamon," he said, his voice earnest. "I'll tell you everything. Ask me anything you need to."

Aaron's face was a mask of conflict, his hands trembling as he spoke. "I don't even know what to ask you, sir. I don't recognize you anymore—as if—was she not enough for you?

You could have divorced her. Why did you—why did you both push her? We could have stayed with Mom; you could have lived your life if we were such a burden."

His voice cracked, and tears streamed down his cheeks as Aamon wrapped an arm around him, trying to comfort his brother. Aaron pulled off his glasses to wipe his eyes, his voice choked with emotion.

James felt a lump in his throat, his own eyes misting over. He wanted to reach out, to pull them both close, but he knew that right now, words mattered more than actions.
"I never stopped loving her," James whispered, his gaze fixed in oblivion. The three of them sat there by the fountain, their breaths visible in the cold air, bound together by blood and broken promises, and the hope that maybe, just maybe, the truth could still set them free.
James felt a heaviness settle in his chest as he looked at his sons, Aamon and Aaron. The weight of the truth he was about to reveal was almost unbearable, and he knew there was no easy way to say it. He had kept it from them for too long, hoping he could find a way to make it right first. But now, with their questions pressing him from all sides, he had no choice.

"I miss Mom," Aaron said again, his voice breaking, his eyes red-rimmed. Aamon put a comforting arm around his brother's shoulders, but his gaze remained fixed on James, waiting for answers.

James took a deep breath, trying to steady himself. "She's alive," he said, his voice barely above a whisper. Both boys froze, their eyes widening in shock. They looked at him, unsure if they had heard correctly.

James nodded, confirming their unspoken questions. "She's alive. A group of three friends found her the day after she fell from the bridge. She was unconscious, pulled from the canal with a severe head injury. They took her to a hospital, but she was in a coma for some time. When she woke up... she didn't remember anything. Not her name, not her past, not us."

Aaron's mouth opened and closed as he processed the information. "But... but why didn't anyone tell us? Why didn't she come back?"

James's eyes filled with tears. "They tried. They posted ads, reached out, but no one connected the dots. I didn't know. No one did. And when no one came forward, one of those friends—he took her in. He helped her rebuild her life. She... she stayed with him, and eventually, they got married."

"Married?" Aamon's voice was incredulous, his face a mixture of confusion and hurt. "Why would Mom marry someone else?"

"Because she doesn't remember us," James said, his voice raw with emotion. "To her, we're just shadows of a life she no longer knows. The people who saved her... they're powerful men. Her new husband is a Lieutenant, his best friend is a Sheriff, and another is a SWAT officer. They've built a life around her, protecting her in their own way. They're not trying to hurt her or us; they're just keeping her safe in the world she now knows."

A cold wind swept through the park, sending leaves skittering across the cobblestone path. Aaron's eyes were wide with disbelief, his hands trembling. "So that's why you're here? To get her back?"

James nodded, his throat tightening. "I came to New York to find her. I've been watching, trying to understand what happened, how she ended up there. I spoke to her husband... he told me she's happy. Told me to move on. But I've seen her... from a distance. She seems content, even without her memories. Maybe... maybe she's even better off not knowing what she lost."

James hesitated for a moment, then pulled out his phone. His hands shook as he opened social media. "I've been following her under a different name, trying to see a glimpse of her life. This is her profile," he said, showing them screen.

A picture of their mother appeared, smiling in a candid shot. Her eyes, while different, held a familiar glimmer, a spark of the person she used to be. Aaron and Aamon stared at the image, their expressions a mix of shock, hope, and profound sadness.

"She looks... happy," Aamon whispered, almost to himself.

James nodded, swallowing the lump in his throat. "She does. But she doesn't remember anything about us, about her life before. It's like she's had to rebuild herself from the ground up."

Aaron's voice trembled, tears threatening to spill. "So, what does this mean for us? Do we just... leave her with them? Pretend she doesn't exist?"

James shook his head, his voice barely steady. "No. I don't know what it means yet. But I do know I owe it to you, to your mother, to figure it out. I'm not giving up on her... on us. But I need time. We all do."

The three of them sat there in the park, the noise of the city around them, yet feeling as if they were in a world apart—caught between the past they had lost and the future that was uncertain, yet painfully real.

James felt a warmth in his chest as he heard his sons laugh—a sound that had been absent for far too long. Aamon, scrolling through his mother's photos, chuckled, "Did this woman forget to age? She looks 20 to me."

"Yeah, she always did say she'd find the Fountain of Youth," he replied, his eyes misty as he remembered her playful declarations from years past.

"Maybe they both are vampires. He forgot to age too. He's two months from 62, and he climbed the Hollywood sign three weeks ago," Aaron added, laughing along with his brother.

James felt a warmth in his chest that he hadn't felt in years. For a moment, they weren't talking about tragedy or loss;

they were just a father and his sons, sharing a light-hearted moment.

Aaron's laughter faded as he studied the screen more closely. "Wait, you're actually talking to her?" he asked, looking up with an expression that danced between hope and hesitation. "What do you say to her? Does she ever... I don't know, does anything ever seem familiar to her about you?"

James sighed, his fingers drumming lightly on the table. "I keep it light, just trying to see if anything sparks a memory. She talks about things, things that are too specific to our past. It's like deep down, some part of her knows, or at least, wants to remember."

Aamon's face turned serious. "And her husband, this Lieutenant—he doesn't know you're the one talking to her?"

"Nope," James said with a slight smirk, standing up. "And let's keep it that way for now."

Aaron's stomach growled audibly, breaking the tension. "Okay, enough of this. I'm starving. Last one to the car drives!" With that, Aamon bolted towards the parking, Aaron hot on his heels.

James followed more slowly, a smile tugging at his lips as he watched his sons race ahead. It had been a long time since he'd felt this kind of warmth. A genuine laugh bubbled up from his chest, surprising him with its intensity.

Aamon, always the more competitive of the two, reached the car first and swung open the driver's side door with a triumphant flourish.

Aaron rolled his eyes but climbed into the back seat without complaint. James donned his hat and sunglasses, his casual disguise, as he slid into the passenger seat.

Aamon drove with the reckless enthusiasm of youth, weaving through traffic with a confidence that bordered on arrogance. It wasn't long before they heard the crunch of metal—a sound that made James wince. Aamon had bumped into the rear of a sleek black Luxury Car.

"Are you fucking stupid?" the driver of the Luxury Car stormed out, his face red with anger. James quickly exited the car, raising his hands in an attempt to diffuse the situation.

"I'm sorry, I'll pay for the damage," James said calmly, trying to placate the furious driver.

The man was too caught up in his rage to recognize James. "Really? You're going to pay? Are you blind, or just an idiot? Who even drives like that?"

Before James could respond, Aamon jumped out of the car and stormed over to the man, grabbing him by the collar and pinning him against the car door. "Do you have any manners? He's your dad's age!" Aamon spat, his protective instincts kicking in.

A sharp voice cut through the commotion. "Ayi!" A woman climbed out of the back of the Luxury Car her presence commanding immediate attention. Aamon's grip on the driver's collar slackened.

The woman, with long hair cascading down her back and an undeniable fire in her eyes, took a step forward. "First, you bump into us while the light was red, and now you're intimidating him?" She threw her hair back, her expression a mix of irritation and bemusement.

The woman, with long hair cascading down her back and an undeniable fire in her eyes, took a step forward. "First, you bump into us while the light was red, and now you're intimidating him?" She threw her hair back, her expression a mix of irritation and bemusement, as another younger man emerged from their car, perhaps their younger son.
All of them seeming to share a strange look of surprise, or perhaps... recognition.

"Leave him. Now," she commanded. "You're what, eighteen? Why are you driving? And you—" she pointed at

James; her tone sharp. "You must be the dad. Your kids are hitting people on the road, and you're just watching? How wonderful! Must have learned from you. And no, we don't need your money."

She turned back to the car. "Tabby, baby, come on. We'll take a taxi," she called, and a small girl with wide, curious eyes peeked out from the back seat.

James stood frozen, his mind reeling. The woman's face, her voice—it was her. Mariyam. The years had not touched her the way they had him; she still had that youthful intensity, the same fire that had drawn him to her all those years ago. And now, here she was, standing right in front of him, without a single spark of recognition in her eyes.

His breath caught in his throat as he watched her turn away, taking the hand of the young girl she called "Tabby." Aamon and Aaron stared, wide-eyed, their earlier banter forgotten in an instant. For a moment, the world seemed to stand still, and James could only watch as the woman he'd lost, the woman who'd forgotten him, walked away once more.
"Mom—" the young lad, likely the youngest of the two brothers, began, taking a tentative step toward me. But his older brother quickly pulled him back.

"Ma'am, he meant Ma'am," he corrected hastily. The younger boy nodded, trying to hide his tears, and I nodded back, not wanting to press the matter further.

"Because of you, my niece will be late for her recital," I glared at who I assumed was their father. "Eduardo, call Señor, take it to the garage and get it fixed, or he'll have a heart attack thinking his precious baby died—" I glanced at the car; it looked pretty bad. "I'll take a taxi," I decided, turning to Eduardo as I picked Tabitha up in my arms, trying to gather her too many bags.

"Tíaaa, my mam will scold meeeee—don't squeeze me, my wings will wrinkleeee—and also take Mr. Flopsy." She threw a fit in my arms, already overflowing with bags, and now she wanted her soft toy too. Huh! Kids—she's just four, so... understandable.

As I struggled to manage Tabitha and her cascade of belongings, the tension in the air was palpable. James, still reeling from the sudden collision and the unexpected confrontation, watched me juggle with my niece and her toys. Recognizing the moment for what it was—a chaotic, yet strangely tender family scene—he stepped forward, instinctively offering his help.

"Let me help you with those," James said, reaching for some of the bags in my arms.

I hesitated for a split second, my eyes locking with his. There was a flicker of something—recognition? Or just a shared understanding of the absurdity of the moment? Reluctantly, I handed him a couple of bags. "Thank you," I murmured, my focus shifting back to Tabitha, who was now fretting about being late.

"Of course," James replied, his voice gentle. The weight of the bags in his hands somehow felt symbolic, as if he were sharing the burden of a past that was both heavy and fragile.

Aamon, observing the interaction, whispered to Aaron, "Do you think she recognizes him?"

Aaron shook his head slightly, his gaze fixed on me. "I don't know. It's hard to tell. But there's something there, don't you think?"

Aamon nodded, his thoughts racing with possibilities. Meanwhile, James, balancing the bags, looked back at Eduardo, who was still assessing the damage to the car. "We'll take care of the repairs," James reassured him, his tone assertive yet apologetic.

hesitated, my eyes flickering between gratitude and wariness. "Thank you," I said, my voice steady yet uncertain as I accepted his help. Turning my attention back to Tabitha, I mustered a smile. "Come on, sweetie, let's go find that taxi."

As we moved away, Tabitha, still cradled in my arms, twisted around and looked back over my shoulder. With a cheerful wave of her tiny hand, she called out, "Bye-bye, nice men!"

A sleek car pulled up beside us just then, the window rolling down to reveal a young man with a cocky smile. "Hey, shawty, you need a ride?" he drawled, his eyes lingering a bit too long.

Watching this unfold from a distance, Aamon nudged his father, James Cross, a mischievous grin spreading across his face. "She still knows how to draw a crowd, huh?" he teased, rolling up his sleeves like he was getting ready for a show.

The driver, a blonde with a lazy grin, leaned closer, catching sight of Tabitha. "Little one, is that your mom?" he asked with a friendly curiosity.

Tabitha, ever the imaginative child, giggled and replied with absolute conviction, "No, Tía is a mermaid!" Her innocent proclamation brought a laugh from the blonde guy, clearly amused.

He turned his attention back to me, unfazed by my earlier cold shoulder. "Hey, Mermaid! It's a strike today. How 'bout I give you a lift? Maybe we could chat—?"

Annoyance flared within me. Tabitha was fidgeting in my arms, her impatience growing, and now this guy thought he could flirt his way into my good graces? I gave him a hard look, my lips curling into a wry smile. "How about you schedule a chat with your dentist first? Those teeth need more attention than I do."

The man's confident expression faltered for a moment, his grin turning into an awkward chuckle. "Ouch, that one cuts deeper than a cavity," he muttered, clearly trying to play it cool, but the humor fell flat. I didn't spare him another glance, pushing forward in my search for a taxi.

Back near their car, Aamon watched the scene unfold with an almost childlike excitement. He turned to his father, nudging him again. "Go save her, Dad! I mean, aren't you James Cross? The James Cross?"

James shot him a stern look but couldn't completely hide the flicker of emotion in his eyes. "She's married, Aamon," he replied, his voice low but firm. "She has a life. A husband."

Aamon, ever the bold one, wasn't deterred. "Yeah, well, that someone is you! She's your wife! Since she never died, your marriage was never annulled. Her marriage is the invalid one. Screw the Lieutenant—go get your girl, champ!"

Aaron, who had been silently observing, finally chimed in, his voice softer but no less intense. "He's right, Dad. You always taught us that the truth matters. And the truth is, she's still your wife. Somewhere deep down, she might still be Mariyam. You owe it to both of you to try."

James stared at his sons, their words striking a chord that resonated deep within him. He had spent years haunted by the past, torn between the woman she was and the woman she had become. For so long, he'd been caught in that purgatory of loss and longing, but maybe, just maybe, they were right.

His gaze shifted back to me, watching as I held Tabitha close, moving further away, my silhouette outlined against the busy city backdrop. A wave of determination flooded through him—an emotion he hadn't felt this strongly in years.

With a deep breath, James took a step forward, ready to bridge the gap that time and tragedy had built between them.

"Tíaaaaaaa, I'm going to be laaaate! Mamá y Papá must be there already—do some mermaid magic, Tíaaa! My wings are wrinkling, I'll be laaate, Tíaaa Graxeee, Tía, Tía!" Tabitha continued to wail, her voice growing more frantic with every word. "You promised you'd dress meee, and now we're lateee! Aaaaaah!"

Aaron nudged James; his eyes filled with amusement. "Dad, she might need rescuing from that kid."

James shook his head, a hint of a smile tugging at his lips. "I think it's the kid who needs rescuing from her. She's on the verge of snapping."

Aamon winced, recalling memories from long ago. "And when she does—ouch! Remember how she used to slap us around?"

Aaron nodded, smirking. "And you'd hide in your study. What kind of father leaves his sons to fend for themselves like that? You should have protected us, James. Almost forgot how badly she used to whoop us."

"A smart father," James replied with a sly smile, but Aamon let out a snort.

"What's so smart about letting your crazy wife smack your precious kids?" Aaron shot back, mock glaring at his father.

Aamon leaned in closer to Aaron, whispering with a grin, "She would've smacked him too if she had the chance."

They both burst into laughter, their voices mingling with the noise of the city around them.

"Hey, she never smacked me," James protested, trying to suppress his amusement, though his eyes betrayed a hint of fondness.

"They think he's an action star," Aamon continued, mock-whispering to Aaron, "but little do they know, he learned all those dodging skills avoiding flying objects at home."

Aaron looked back at James, a mischievous glint in his eyes, as if imagining his father navigating their chaotic household like an action scene from one of his movies.

James chuckled, a deep, genuine sound that had been absent from his life for too long. He couldn't help but marvel at how his sons could lighten even the most tangled moments with their humor. His eyes drifted back to me—Mariyam, or Graxe, as she called herself now—struggling to hail a taxi with her hands full of bags and a squirming, impatient child. She was still fierce, still the woman who could command attention and handle herself, but there was a softness there too, a maternal protectiveness that struck him.

"Alright, boys, enough jokes," James said, his smile fading into a more serious expression. "Stay here and don't cause any more accidents."

He didn't wait for a reply. With a decisive stride, he made his way toward me, weaving through the crowd and dodging cars as if it were second nature to him. As he approached, he could hear Tabitha's continued whining about her wings, her recital, and something about a missing teddy bear, her small voice climbing in pitch.

I was about two seconds from losing my patience when James stepped in, his calm presence immediately catching my attention. "Hey," he said softly, his voice carrying an odd familiarity that made me pause. "I know this is a bit... unorthodox, but maybe I could help you get to where you need to be?"

I glanced at him, my expression a mix of annoyance and curiosity. "And why would you do that?"

James shrugged, flashing a charming yet earnest smile. "Because it seems like you could use a hand. And I'm not exactly in a hurry. Besides, she's starting to sound like she could use a break too," he nodded toward Tabitha, who was now tugging on my sleeve, her small face scrunched up in frustration.

For a moment, I weighed his offer. There was something oddly reassuring about him. Despite the chaos of the day, he remained calm and collected—a stark contrast to the hot-tempered man yelling at my driver moments earlier. I let out a sigh, my shoulders relaxing slightly. "Alright, fine. But if you pull any funny business, I'll—"

James raised his hands in mock surrender. "No funny business, I promise. Just trying to help."

He turned to Tabitha with a gentle smile. "Hey there, little mermaid fan, how about we get you to your recital on time? Would that make you happy?"

Tabitha, caught off guard by the sudden attention from a stranger, blinked up at him with wide eyes. Then, as if deciding he was trustworthy, she nodded enthusiastically. "Yes, yes! Let's go! Tía, can we go with the nice man?"

I glanced at Tabitha, then back at James, and sighed. "Alright. Fine. But make it quick."

James nodded and signaled to Aamon to pull the car around. The boys, who had been watching intently, didn't waste any time. They maneuvered the car with a bit more care this time and pulled up beside us. James opened the back door, and I helped Tabitha climb in, her excitement bubbling over as she continued to ramble about her recital and the "mermaid magic" I was supposed to perform.
"Give her back to the boys. You need to put on your seatbelt," James instructed, his voice calm yet authoritative. I nodded, carefully passing Tabitha back to his sons in the rear seat while fumbling with the seatbelt, trying to get it to click into place.

"Here, let me," James offered, leaning over to help buckle me in. As he did, the subtle blend of his cologne wafted past my nose—a scent that stirred something deep within me. It was familiar, like a whisper from a distant memory that I couldn't quite grasp.

"Your cologne... it's... it's..." I struggled to place it, my brows furrowing in concentration. "I don't know. It reminds me of someone. Maybe Rudi? Or Juan?" I glanced at him, searching for some kind of confirmation. James's jaw tightened for a moment, but he forced a smile. This wasn't just any fragrance; it was his own unique blend—three different colognes mixed meticulously to create a scent unmistakably his. A scent that was undeniably James Cross.

"Can I smell it again?" I asked, an almost childlike curiosity in my voice. James nodded, leaning closer. I inhaled deeply, trying to latch onto the elusive familiarity. "I know this smell—I just can't remember."

James turned to look at me, his eyes soft yet probing. "Do you tend to forget things often?" he asked, his voice carrying a hint of genuine concern.

I sighed, a small chuckle escaping me. "Yeah, a lot. I—"

Before I could finish, Tabitha's excited voice cut through, her tone filled with absolute conviction. "She's a mermaid! Uncle Juan found her in the river! A real mermaid!" she exclaimed; her eyes wide with wonder.

The words hung in the air, and for a moment, everything seemed to pause. James's gaze shifted to me, his expression a mix of amusement and a deeper, more searching intensity. He was trying to connect the dots, to see if there was any glimmer of recognition in my eyes. But all I could do was laugh softly, the echo of Tabitha's innocent declaration still ringing in my ears.

James chuckled, a warm sound that momentarily lightened the atmosphere. "A mermaid, huh?" he mused, glancing at me with a twinkle in his eye. "Is that what you are?"

I shook my head, smiling despite the uneasy feeling settling in my chest. " No— It's just, my now husband saved me from the river— so she just thinks I am a mermaid." I chuckled awkwardly and James probed

"Saved you?" James repeated, his tone deceptively light, but I could hear the edge beneath it. I sighed, choosing my words carefully.

"Yeah—maybe I jumped into the Hudson," I said, my voice soft as I stared out the window, watching the city blur past.

"I don't really remember much, but he found me. I had lost my memory... and, well, he took me in."

The car fell silent, except for the hum of the engine and the soft, steady breaths of his sons in the backseat. I could feel James's eyes on me, weighing my every word, as if searching for the truth hidden between the lines.

"You're a mermaid, right? You came from the ocean!" Tabitha squealed; her voice filled with unrestrained excitement. I couldn't help but laugh, her enthusiasm infectious.

"Yes, I am," I whispered conspiratorially, turning toward her with a playful glint in my eyes. "But it's a secret! We can't tell anyone. Shhh..." I brought a finger to my lips, then dramatically tossed some of the sparkle I had been sprinkling on her hair for the recital into the air, making a grand show of it. Tabitha gasped, her eyes wide with delight, and clapped her hands together.

James watched, his expression softening as he saw the exchange. For a moment, I caught a glimpse of something in his eyes—nostalgia, perhaps, or a longing for something that once was. The tension seemed to ease, but only slightly, like a taut string pulled back, waiting to snap.

"Memory loss can be a tricky thing," he said finally, his voice steady, but I could hear the cracks beneath it. "Do you ever wonder what you left behind? What you might be missing?"

I turned back to him, my smile fading. "Every day," I admitted, a raw honesty breaking through. "Sometimes it feels like there's a whole life out there that I should know, but... it's like trying to catch smoke with your hands. It's there, but I can't quite grasp it."

James nodded slowly, his fingers tightening around the steering wheel. "And Juan... he helps you forget?"

"Not forget," I corrected gently. "He helps me live with the pieces I have."

For a moment, James's expression was unreadable, a storm of emotions I couldn't quite decipher. Then, he glanced in the rearview mirror at his sons, a flicker of pain passing through his eyes.

"I've never met anyone with memory loss before," his elder son Aamon, piped up from the back seat, his voice filled with a mix of curiosity and innocence. "What's it like? I don't mean to be rude, but do you remember anything? Like, flashes? Or maybe dreams, like in the movies?"

I turned slightly in my seat to face him, a soft smile tugging at my lips. His eagerness was endearing. "No flashes like in the movies," I said, my voice gentle, understanding the weight behind his question. "But I do dream. Sometimes, I get these small snippets—fragments, really—of things that feel familiar.

"Snippets?" James turned to me, his eyes searching mine, and I nodded.

"Yeah... certain places feel oddly familiar, like a big white mansion with those blue, hut-like roofs—whatever they're called. Sometimes, it's a garden filled with sunlight, laughter, and roses." I explained, and Aamon's eyes darted to James, recognizing the description of what was once their home—the Beverly Hills mansion James and Mariyam shared.

"And?" James gently urged, his voice laced with a mix of hope and apprehension. I tapped my chin thoughtfully, piecing together the vague fragments in my mind.

"A baby... a chubby baby sitting on the grass, laughing," I said with a soft chuckle, the memory slipping through like sand. Aamon lowered his gaze, his eyes fixed on the floor, the weight of realization settling heavily on him.

James chuckled, a warm sound that momentarily lightened the atmosphere. "A mermaid, huh?" he mused, glancing at me with a twinkle in his eye. "Is that what you are?"

I shook my head, smiling despite the uneasy feeling settling in my chest. " No— It's just, my now husband saved me from the river— so she just thinks I am a mermaid." I chuckled awkwardly and James probed

"Saved you?" James repeated, his tone deceptively light, but I could hear the edge beneath it. I sighed, choosing my words carefully.

"Yeah—maybe I jumped into the Hudson," I said, my voice soft as I stared out the window, watching the city blur past. "I don't really remember much, but he found me. I had lost my memory... and, well, he took me in."

The car fell silent, except for the hum of the engine and the soft, steady breaths of his sons in the backseat. I could feel James's eyes on me, weighing my every word, as if searching for the truth hidden between the lines.

"You're a mermaid, right? You came from the ocean!" Tabitha squealed; her voice filled with unrestrained excitement. I couldn't help but laugh, her enthusiasm infectious.

"Yes, I am," I whispered conspiratorially, turning toward her with a playful glint in my eyes. "But it's a secret! We can't tell anyone. Shhh..." I brought a finger to my lips, then dramatically tossed some of the sparkle I had been sprinkling on her hair for the recital into the air, making a grand show of it. Tabitha gasped, her eyes wide with delight, and clapped her hands together.

James watched, his expression softening as he saw the exchange. For a moment, I caught a glimpse of something in his eyes—nostalgia, perhaps, or a longing for something that once was. The tension seemed to ease, but only slightly, like a taut string pulled back, waiting to snap.

"Memory loss can be a tricky thing," he said finally, his voice steady, but I could hear the cracks beneath it. "Do you ever wonder what you left behind? What you might be missing?"

I turned back to him, my smile fading. "Every day," I admitted, a raw honesty breaking through. "Sometimes it feels like there's a whole life out there that I should know, but... it's like trying to catch smoke with your hands. It's there, but I can't quite grasp it."

James nodded slowly, his fingers tightening around the steering wheel. "And Juan... he helps you forget?"

"Not forget," I corrected gently. "He helps me live with the pieces I have."

For a moment, James's expression was unreadable, a storm of emotions I couldn't quite decipher. Then, he glanced in the rearview mirror at his sons, a flicker of pain passing through his eyes.

"I've never met anyone with memory loss before," his elder son Aamon, piped up from the back seat, his voice filled with a mix of curiosity and innocence. "What's it like? I don't mean to be rude, but do you remember anything? Like, flashes? Or maybe dreams, like in the movies?"

I turned slightly in my seat to face him, a soft smile tugging at my lips. His eagerness was endearing. "No flashes like in the movies," I said, my voice gentle, understanding the weight behind his question. "But I do dream. Sometimes, I get these small snippets—fragments, really—of things that feel familiar.

"Snippets?" James turned to me, his eyes searching mine, and I nodded.

"Yeah... certain places feel oddly familiar, like a big white mansion with those blue, hut-like roofs—whatever they're called. Sometimes, it's a garden filled with sunlight, laughter, and roses." I explained, and Aamon's eyes darted to James, recognizing the description of what was once their home—the Beverly Hills mansion James and Mariyam shared.

"And?" James gently urged, his voice laced with a mix of hope and apprehension. I tapped my chin thoughtfully, piecing together the vague fragments in my mind.

"A baby... a chubby baby sitting on the grass, laughing," I said with a soft chuckle, the memory slipping through like sand. Aamon lowered his gaze, his eyes fixed on the floor, the weight of realization settling heavily on him.

James chuckled softly, shaking his head. "No need to apologize. It's been a... strange day for all of us, I think."

Aaron nodded in agreement from the back seat, a small smile playing on his lips. "Yeah, I mean, how often do you meet someone who thinks they're living in Season 8 of their life?"

Tabitha, sensing the lighter mood, giggled again, her small laugh filling the car with a sense of warmth. "Tía, you're funny!" she said, her eyes twinkling with innocence.

I turned back to her, smiling. "Am I, sweetheart? Maybe I should become a comedian."

"I don't even know your name, but you look familiar," I said, turning to James, a hint of curiosity in my eyes. His face lit up with a small smile, a flicker of hope sparking in his chest. But before he could say anything, Tabitha chimed in.

"He's Tetan, Tía—Tetan!" she announced confidently, drawing my attention back to her.

"Tetan?" I repeated, eyebrows furrowing in confusion. Tabitha nodded enthusiastically.

"Yes, Tetan! He drives the bike—vroom vroom!" she exclaimed, mimicking the sound of a revving motorcycle with her little hands.

I glanced back at James, piecing it together. And then, like a bolt of clarity, it hit me. He wasn't just some stranger—he was James Cross, the James Cross. The actor who played Ethan in the popular action movie series, 'Beyond'.

My eyes widened in recognition, and James could see the realization dawn on my face. "You're... James Cross," I said slowly, almost as if testing the words on my tongue. "The actor from Beyond."

James's smile grew, but there was a hint of something deeper in his eyes—relief, perhaps, or maybe a trace of sadness. "Yeah, that's me," he admitted, a soft chuckle escaping his lips. "I guess I should've expected Tetan to be more famous than I am."

Tabitha beamed proudly, as if she had just identified a superhero. "See, Tía? I told you he was Tetan!"

I laughed lightly, the tension easing just a bit. "I can't believe I didn't recognize you sooner. You look... different in real life."

"Less makeup, fewer explosions," James quipped with a grin. "And a lot grayer hair than in the movies."

Aamon chimed in from the back seat, unable to resist. "Don't forget the stunt doubles, Dad."
James rolled his eyes playfully. "Thanks for the reminder, son."

For a moment, the atmosphere in the car felt almost normal, like a family sharing a lighthearted conversation. But beneath the surface, the reality of the situation remained—heavy and unresolved.

I studied James for a moment longer, my curiosity piqued. "So, what brings a big Hollywood star to New York? Looking for a new role or something?"

James hesitated, his smile fading just a bit. "Something like that," he said softly, his gaze flicking to his sons in the rearview mirror. "I guess you could say I'm trying to find my way back to a role I lost a long time ago."

I nodded, sensing there was more to his words than he let on, but I didn't press further. Instead, I offered a small smile. "Well, whatever it is, I hope you find it."

James nodded, appreciating the sentiment. "Thank you," he replied, his voice sincere. "I hope so too."

Just then, the car pulled up in front of a small theater, where a bustling crowd of parents and children were already gathered. Tabitha's face lit up; her earlier worries forgotten as she bounced excitedly in her seat.

"We're here!" she squealed, her little hands clapping together. "We made it, Tía! We made it!"

I turned to James and his sons, a genuine smile spreading across my face. "Thank you for the ride. Really. It means a lot."

James nodded; his expression warm. "Anytime," he said, his voice steady but with a hint of emotion. "Take care, Graxe."

I hesitated for a moment, then nodded. "You too, James. And... it was nice meeting you, Aaron, Aamon."

The boys both smiled, waving from the back seat. "Nice meeting you too," Aaron said. "And good luck with everything."

Aamon added with a playful grin, "Yeah, and keep an eye out for more 'Season 8' episodes."

I laughed, shaking my head. "I will."

With that, I helped Tabitha out of the car, gathering her bags and holding her hand as we made our way toward the theater entrance.

"Hey—wait a second," James called out from his car, lowering the window. I turned around, surprised by the sudden call.

"Yes?" I asked, a bit cautiously. His lips curled into a small, knowing smile.

"Ever thought about why my cologne felt familiar to you?" he asked, his voice calm but with a hint of something deeper. His words hung in the air, and I found myself pausing.

"I... I don't know. Maybe," I replied, unsure. "But why does that matter? Why are you even bringing it up?" I questioned; a bit more defensively than I intended.

He smiled again, but this time it was different—genuine, almost tender. "That's for you to figure out, hon. Why don't you tell me who I am?"

And with that, he rolled up the window and drove off, leaving me standing there, rooted to the spot.

What did he mean by that?

I stood there, the crowd around me moving like a rushing river, while I was stuck in place, trying to make sense of his words. There was something there, just out of reach—a connection that felt both tantalizingly close and impossibly far.

I turned back toward the theater, Tabitha tugging on my hand, eager to get inside. "Tía, come on! We're gonna be late!" she insisted, her voice cutting through the haze of my thoughts. I nodded, shaking myself out of my daze.

"Right, right... I'm coming," I mumbled, forcing a smile for her sake. But my mind was elsewhere, still turning over James's words like a puzzle I couldn't quite solve.

I didn't know what to make of it—why a scent could stir something so deep within me, something that felt like a whisper from a life I couldn't fully remember. And why did he call me "hon"? It wasn't just the familiarity of it; there was a weight to his tone, like he was speaking from somewhere far beyond the present moment.

I followed Tabitha inside, her excitement bubbling over as she rushed ahead, and I tried to focus on the task at hand—getting her ready for her recital. But even as I helped her with her costume, adjusted her tiny wings, and listened to her ramble about her performance, my thoughts kept drifting back to that moment.

Who was James Cross to me? And why did it feel like my heart knew the answer, even if my mind couldn't quite grasp it?

The scene at the theater became a blur—parents talking, children running around, the distant sound of music starting up—but I felt strangely detached, caught in a web of half-formed memories and elusive emotions.

Maybe I didn't have all the pieces, not yet. Maybe I was still living in "Season 8" of my life, trying to catch up to a story that had started long before I could remember. But there was something in James's eyes, in his words, that made me feel like this wasn't the end—just another beginning.

I took a deep breath and let the thought settle. Whatever the truth was, it would come in its own time. For now, I had a little girl who needed her "mermaid" Tía by her side, and that was enough.

I smiled down at Tabitha, who was now spinning in her tiny ballerina shoes, completely absorbed in her own world. "Alright, little mermaid fan," I said, gently touching her cheek, "let's go show them what magic looks like."

And as I led her toward the stage, I couldn't help but glance back one last time, wondering if somewhere, James was doing the same.

Maybe, just maybe, the answers weren't as far away as I thought. Maybe... There was closer, closer than I thought.

CHAPTER 9

The sky above New York was a deep indigo, dotted with faint stars that struggled to outshine the city's glow. Graxe stood on the balcony of her apartment, the crisp night air brushing against her skin. Below, the city pulsed with life—cars honking, people talking, the distant hum of music drifting up from the streets. It was a night like any other, and yet, something felt different. Something felt... unsettled.

She couldn't shake the feeling that had taken root in her chest after the encounter earlier that day. Meeting James Cross—the James Cross—had been surprising enough, but there was something else, something about the way he looked at her, as if he was searching for someone he'd lost long ago.

She took a deep breath, trying to calm the whirlwind of thoughts spinning through her mind. She should have been preparing for bed, getting ready for another day at the clinic, another day of living the life she had rebuilt from the ashes of her forgotten past. But instead, she found herself caught in the web of memories that felt just out of reach.

"That's for you to figure out, hon. Why don't you tell me who I am?"

His words echoed in her mind, replaying over and over like a song stuck on repeat. There was a familiarity to him, beyond just the fame, beyond the cologne. It was in the way he spoke to her, the way he looked at her—as if he knew her in a way that no one else did. But how could that be? She was certain she'd never met him before today. Certain... yet not entirely.

Graxe wrapped her arms around herself, leaning against the railing, her eyes scanning the city skyline. The bustling metropolis that had become her home was suddenly foreign, filled with shadows and whispers of a life she couldn't quite remember. Her thoughts wandered to the fragments of dreams that haunted her sleep—the white mansion, the laughing baby, the roses.

Why did it feel like those dreams weren't just figments of her imagination but pieces of something real? Something she had lost?

She heard the door behind her slide open, and she turned to see Juan stepping out onto the balcony, his face softening when he saw her. He was still in his uniform, the badge on his chest catching the light from the living room.

"Hey, amor," he said, his voice gentle. "What are you doing out here? It's late."

She offered him a small smile, though it didn't reach her eyes. "Just needed some fresh air. I couldn't sleep."

Juan came closer, wrapping his arms around her from behind, pulling her into his warmth. She leaned back into him, closing her eyes as she inhaled his familiar scent—so different from the one that had clung to James earlier.

"Are you okay?" he asked, pressing a kiss to the top of her head.

Graxe hesitated, unsure how to put her feelings into words. "I'm just... thinking," she finally said, her voice barely more than a whisper.

"About what?"

"Today, when I met that actor... James Cross." She felt Juan's body tense slightly, but he said nothing, waiting for her to continue. "He said something that's been bothering me. Something about why his cologne felt familiar to me, why it stirred something in me that I can't quite place."

Juan was silent for a moment, his hold on her tightening protectively. "Do you think you knew him before?" he asked, his voice cautious, as if he was afraid of the answer.

"I don't know," Graxe admitted, shaking her head. "But it feels like... maybe I did. Or at least, like he's connected to something I used to know. Something important."

Juan turned her around gently, so she was facing him, his dark eyes searching hers. "Graxe, it's okay to be curious, but remember—you have a life now, with me, with us. Whatever happened before, whatever you lost, we've built something new together. Don't let this... stranger pull you away from that."

His words were meant to comfort her, but they only deepened the sense of unease growing inside her. Graxe looked up at him, wanting to believe him, to let go of the questions gnawing at her mind. But she couldn't. Not entirely.

"I know, Juan," she said softly, resting her head against his chest. "And I'm not trying to let go of that. I just... I need to understand. I need to know why this is happening, why these memories, or whatever they are, keep coming back."

Juan stroked her hair, his voice low and soothing. "Then we'll figure it out together. But remember, no matter what you find out, you're my Graxe now. And nothing will change that."

She nodded, closing her eyes as she let the steady rhythm of his heartbeat calm her. But even as she clung to him, the questions lingered in the back of her mind, like shadows refusing to be banished by the light.

As the night stretched on, Graxe found herself staring at the city once more, her thoughts drifting back to James's words, to the strange sense of familiarity she couldn't explain. She didn't know what the future held, but one thing was certain: she couldn't ignore the echoes of the past any longer. They were calling to her, pulling her toward something she had lost, something she needed to find—before it was too late.

The sky above New York was a deep indigo, dotted with faint stars that struggled to outshine the city's glow. Graxe stood on the balcony of her apartment, the crisp night air brushing against her skin. Below, the city pulsed with life—cars honking, people talking, the distant hum of music drifting up from the streets. It was a night like any other, and yet, something felt different. Something felt... unsettled.

She couldn't shake the feeling that had taken root in her chest after the encounter earlier that day. Meeting James Cross—the James Cross—had been surprising enough, but there was something else, something about the way he looked at her, as if he was searching for someone he'd lost long ago.

She took a deep breath, trying to calm the whirlwind of thoughts spinning through her mind. She should have been preparing for bed, getting ready for another day at the clinic, another day of living the life she had rebuilt from the ashes of her forgotten past. But instead, she found herself caught in the web of memories that felt just out of reach.

"That's for you to figure out, hon. Why don't you tell me who I am?"

His words echoed in her mind, replaying over and over like a song stuck on repeat. There was a familiarity to him, beyond just the fame, beyond the cologne. It was in the way he spoke to her, the way he looked at her—as if he knew her in a way that no one else did. But how could that be? She was certain she'd never met him before today. Certain... yet not entirely.

Graxe wrapped her arms around herself, leaning against the railing, her eyes scanning the city skyline. The bustling metropolis that had become her home was suddenly foreign, filled with shadows and whispers of a life she couldn't quite remember. Her thoughts wandered to the fragments of dreams that haunted her sleep—the white mansion, the laughing baby, the roses.

Why did it feel like those dreams weren't just figments of her imagination but pieces of something real? Something she had lost?

She heard the door behind her slide open, and she turned to see Juan stepping out onto the balcony, his face softening when he saw her. He was still in his uniform, the badge on his chest catching the light from the living room.

"Hey, amor," he said, his voice gentle. "What are you doing out here? It's late."

She offered him a small smile, though it didn't reach her eyes. "Just needed some fresh air. I couldn't sleep."

Juan came closer, wrapping his arms around her from behind, pulling her into his warmth. She leaned back into him, closing her eyes as she inhaled his familiar scent—so different from the one that had clung to James earlier.

"Are you okay?" he asked, pressing a kiss to the top of her head.

Graxe hesitated, unsure how to put her feelings into words. "I'm just... thinking," she finally said, her voice barely more than a whisper.

"About what?"

"Today, when I met that actor... James Cross." She felt Juan's body tense slightly, but he said nothing, waiting for her to continue. "He said something that's been bothering me. Something about why his cologne felt familiar to me, why it stirred something in me that I can't quite place."

Juan was silent for a moment, his hold on her tightening protectively. "Do you think you knew him before?" he asked, his voice cautious, as if he was afraid of the answer.

"I don't know," Graxe admitted, shaking her head. "But it feels like... maybe I did. Or at least, like he's connected to something I used to know. Something important."

Juan turned her around gently, so she was facing him, his dark eyes searching hers. "Graxe, it's okay to be curious, but remember—you have a life now, with me, with us. Whatever happened before, whatever you lost, we've built something new together. Don't let this... stranger pull you away from that."

His words were meant to comfort her, but they only deepened the sense of unease growing inside her. Graxe looked up at him, wanting to believe him, to let go of the questions gnawing at her mind. But she couldn't. Not entirely.

"I know, Juan," she said softly, resting her head against his chest. "And I'm not trying to let go of that. I just... I need to understand. I need to know why this is happening, why these memories, or whatever they are, keep coming back."

Juan stroked her hair, his voice low and soothing. "Then we'll figure it out together. But remember, no matter what you find out, you're my Graxe now. And nothing will change that."

She nodded, closing her eyes as she let the steady rhythm of his heartbeat calm her. But even as she clung to him, the questions lingered in the back of her mind, like shadows refusing to be banished by the light.

As the night stretched on, Graxe found herself staring at the city once more, her thoughts drifting back to James's words, to the strange sense of familiarity she couldn't explain. She didn't know what the future held, but one thing was certain: she couldn't ignore the echoes of the past any longer. They were calling to her, pulling her toward something she had lost, something she needed to find—before it was too late.

Next morning, in James's penthouse, the sun barely peeked through the curtains, casting soft shadows across the room. The weight of the previous night still hung heavily in the air, and a sense of unease seemed to settle over everything. James, deep in thought, stared out the window at the cityscape below. His phone buzzed, jolting him from his reverie.

"Excuse me," James muttered, stepping away to answer the call.

"Mr. Cross," a voice greeted him on the other end.

"Yes?" James replied, his voice tense.

"Please come to the precinct. We have some new leads on the case," the officer informed him. James's heart skipped a beat at the mention of new leads. This could be the break he had been waiting for—the opportunity to finally uncover the truth and clear his name. He quickly relayed the news to his sons, their expressions mirroring his mix of anticipation and apprehension.

With a sense of urgency, they made their way to the precinct. The streets were quieting down as the night deepened, the city slowly surrendering to the darkness. The air was charged with anticipation, each step bringing them closer to potential answers.

As they entered the precinct, James couldn't shake a sense of déjà vu—the sterile white walls, the echoing footsteps, the faint scent of stale coffee lingering in the air. But this time, there was a flicker of hope burning within him—a belief that maybe, just maybe, they were on the verge of a breakthrough.

They were ushered into a small conference room where a weary-looking detective greeted them, a file folder clutched in his hand.

"Rudi," James gave a curt nod and glanced sideways at Sofia.

"Cross." Sheriff Rudolf Liam Merci leaned forward, his hands clasped in front of him, and Lieutenant Juan Ramirez stood by his side.

"We tried to validate the version of events you gave us last time, and we found some loopholes. Let me read out your statement to you and Miss Vercillia, okay?" Rudi said, and James nodded.

Rudi began, "So, you said: 'We were at the hotel. She was yelling at me, nagging. I threw a lamp at her feet, and she snapped. She had this terrible temper. She knew about Sofia; I had ended it all a week earlier, but she wouldn't believe me. I got ready, and she said she didn't want to come. I was frustrated. We are in show business; we have to act for the camera, and she was not willing to join me. So, I left. I asked her before leaving what she would do here alone. She said she'd probably write or go to Brooklyn Bridge to paint. She paints. She had canvas and all—I was at the gala, and she kept calling me. She said she'd jump, and I rushed to the bridge. She wasn't planning to jump; she acts childish sometimes. She has BPD. I thought it was just her impulsivity, empty threats. I walked away when she grabbed my collar. I didn't want to lose my temper on her—so I left—and then I texted Sofia 'It's done.' 'Done' as in we were done; I didn't want to hurt my wife anymore. Sofia confessed; she spotted me leaving around 10:34 PM. I had to go back to the gala! We were planning to use it for publicity, too. I... activated Do Not Disturb when my phone kept buzzing. She kept calling me, and I ignored it until 2 AM or so when I received a call from Vasquez—yes, Sergeant Vasquez was the name. I rushed to the bridge, and they handed me a heel and a phone. How could I have gone to my kids? What would I have told them? I stayed there for God knows how long. They said it's a high tide and flash flood. They'd update me, and I should go home, but Sofia called me again. She said she heard what happened. She has some contacts in the coastal guard, and she'll help me. I rushed to her—to find Mariyam. Aamon and Aaron were waiting at the hotel, but she kept saying someone was coming; she had called them. I drank. She kept serving, and then I woke up at 11 AM the next day. I didn't lay a finger on her. It's just that I didn't connect the dots until today. I rushed to the coastal guard person she gave me the number of—I've been searching for her since then.' Right?" Rudi asked, his eyes locked on James.

James nodded, his face unreadable, but his mind was racing, processing every word.

"Very well, then. You never called anyone after 3:37 a.m., Cross," Sheriff Rudolf Liam Merci straightened his posture, his eyes fixed intently on the man before him. "Your call records prove it. And you, Miss Vercillia—" He turned his sharp gaze toward Sofia, who sat fidgeting beside James. "You claimed it was a mistake. But here's your Messaging App chat with Mrs. Harold: 'The bitch is finally out of the picture! I can finally live in peace. Hard work pays off.' Am I reading that correctly? Why don't you read it once yourself, just in case I got it wrong." Rudi shoved a hard copy of the chat transcript and the call records across the table toward them.

"How would he have called if he was drunk?" Aamon, James and Mariyam's eldest son, spoke up defensively from the corner of the room. His tone was edged with frustration, his eyes filled with defiance.

"Kid, don't obstruct the interrogation," Rudi warned with a firm voice, his gaze narrowing on Aamon. "This is a serious investigation."

"Mr. James Cross," Rudi continued, his face impassive and unyielding, "I'll ask you one last time: were you involved in the attempted murder of Mariyam Cross?"

"He didn't, okay?" Aamon interjected again, his voice rising. "He said he didn't! Are these the same Sheriff and Lieutenant who supposedly saved her, right?" He turned to James, his eyes pleading. "You think you can keep our Maa away from us?"

"Kid, I'm warning you for the last time," Rudi shot back, his voice now carrying the commanding authority of a sheriff who had interrogated countless suspects over the years. "I'll charge you with obstructing justice. And by the way, aren't you 20 now? Which means you were 18 when your mother fell from that bridge—not exactly a 'kid.' Where were you, Aamon Cross? Didn't feel like coming to the bridge? Didn't feel like looking for your mother? Or were you involved in this too?"

Aamon's face flushed red with anger at the accusation. "I was with Aaron, trying to make sense of everything!" he shot back, his voice trembling with emotion. "We trusted him—" he gestured furiously at James, "to handle things while we protected each other from the chaos. We were just kids who had found out their mom might be dead!"

Aaron, usually the quieter of the two brothers, stepped forward then, his demeanor calm but his voice tinged with a deep-seated pain. "We stayed back because we were in shock," he said slowly, his gaze steady. "We were trying to keep each other together. That's what she would have wanted us to do—look out for each other."

James placed a calming hand on Aamon's shoulder, his expression a mixture of exhaustion and sorrow. "Sheriff, my sons were not involved," he said firmly. "None of us were. We're here to find the truth, not to cover it up."

Rudi's eyes remained skeptical as he shifted his attention back to Sofia. "And you, Ms. Vercillia," he said, his voice dripping with suspicion, "it seems your 'accident' was rather convenient for your plans. Last time, I recall you yelling at Mr. Cross, 'Don't try to play the victim card; you're no saint.' What did you mean by that? He's clearly stating he has nothing to do with you, that he loved his wife. He didn't even lay a finger on you that night, yet you manipulated him, delayed him, so he couldn't find her. Are you taking a fall for someone who doesn't care?"

"He's a liar!" Sofia spat, frustration lining her features. "I'm telling you; he must have said something to her before he left. He wasn't even sad—he was happy she was gone. Arrest him!" Her voice rose, almost hysterical. "If he loved her so much, why was he cheating? Why was he with me? Then suddenly, he wanted to leave me as if I was a piece of trash! She was a piece of trash!"

"Can't we broadcast this?" Juan Heinrich Ramirez muttered from his corner, shaking his head and pinching the bridge of his nose in frustration. "And by the way, Yes, I am the same Lieutenant who saved whoever she was," Juan continued, his voice dripping with sarcasm. "Now she is my wife, and no, you cannot meet her. We have doctors' notes stating she is not in a state to be dragged into this or reminded of what happened, so no, you are not going to speak with her. If necessary, I'll get restraining orders against all of you." His tone turned stern as he turned back to Sofia. "Now, Sofia, I hope you remember Linda from the last time?" He nodded toward a female officer, whose expression was as stern as Juan's.

Sofia visibly stiffened, clearly recalling the sharp slap Linda had delivered during the last interrogation. "This is neither a talk show nor a place for fans to feel sympathy about your heartbreak. Speak coherently before Linda warms up."

"Hi, Sofia," Linda said with a cold wave.

"JAMES DID IT!" Sofia screamed, her voice shrill with desperation. Juan turned to James.

"No," James said firmly, his eyes filled with a mix of indignation and pain. "I didn't have anything to do with this. I loved Mariyam. I never wanted her hurt. Sofia, you're lying!"

"You did it! You pushed your wife!" Sofia accused; her face twisted with fury.

Juan seized upon her words, his voice rising as he hammered his accusations. "You struck her, Cross! You wanted her dead. You struck her, didn't you? You hit her from behind, she stumbled back, then you hit her on the forehead and kicked her into the river! That's what you did, right? That's what you did! Why does Sofia say you did it? Because you did it! DIDN'T YOU, JAMES CROSS? You tried to kill your wife!"

James's face fell into his hands, his body shaking with silent sobs, his shoulders heaving under the weight of the accusations. "No..." he muttered; his voice choked with anguish.

"He said no!" Aamon shouted, pushing Juan back with a force that caught everyone by surprise. Within seconds, an officer had Aamon pinned to the table, tension thick in the room.

"Step back! He's just a kid," Juan huffed, his eyes catching the fierce gaze of Aamon. His eyes—an awe-striking mix of green and blue, so different from their usual brown—glared back at him with a fire he was all too familiar with at home. The same rage, temper, and fierce independence he knew too well.

"Please, sir," Aaron intervened, his hand resting gently on James's shoulder as he looked imploringly at Sheriff Rudi. "His blood pressure will spike."

Aamon shrugged off the officer who was holding him down, his glare still locked on Juan and Rudi.

"Go have some water, Lieutenant," Rudi suggested, his voice softening ever so slightly. Juan sighed, nodding as he stepped outside for a moment to collect himself.

Under the harsh glare of the fluorescent lights, the tension in the room seemed almost palpable. The stark white of the precinct walls felt oppressive, pressing in on everyone seated around the table. The dim hum of an overhead fan was barely audible over the charged silence. A metal filing cabinet in the corner rattled occasionally with the vibration of passing traffic, adding to the uneasy atmosphere.

James sat back in his chair, his posture rigid, his knuckles white as he gripped the edge of the table. The flickering lights above cast a cold, clinical glow on his face, highlighting the deep lines of stress etched into his skin. His eyes were red-rimmed, not just from exhaustion but from the deep, haunting weight of the accusations that had been thrown at him.

Across from him, Rudi leaned forward, his elbows resting on the table, his face partially shadowed under the unyielding lights. His eyes were hard and piercing, locked onto James with a focus that was unrelenting. Every word he spoke cut through the room like a blade, measured and deliberate, as he read through the details of James's last statement. The only thing more cutting than his gaze was the sharp tone in his voice.

Sofia shifted uncomfortably in her chair, her gaze darting between James and Rudi. She couldn't seem to find a comfortable position, the chair's hard plastic digging into her back. The flickering of the lights overhead seemed to match her own erratic, nervous energy. Her fingers fidgeted incessantly with the corner of her sleeve, and every so often, she'd cast a wary glance at Linda, who stood in the corner, arms crossed, her expression one of cold, silent vigilance.

Juan's exit from the room had done little to alleviate the tension. The door creaked shut behind him, leaving a faint echo that hung in the sterile air. The moment stretched long, the fluorescent lights buzzing faintly, casting an unforgiving light that seemed to amplify every crease, every nervous twitch.

Rudi took a slow breath, his eyes narrowing as he studied James. "Let's shift gears for a moment," he repeated, his voice softer now, almost as if he were coaxing a confession from James. He flipped through another file, its pages rustling like dry leaves in the otherwise still room. The sound seemed to scrape against the nerves of everyone present, a small but constant irritation.

He continued, "We've been cross-referencing all your statements, your timelines, and your actions that night." He glanced up, his eyes like a hawk's. "And some things just don't add up, Mr. Cross."

James swallowed hard, his Adam's apple bobbing visibly in his throat. The fluorescent lights cast deep shadows under his eyes, giving him the look of a man haunted by more than just the events of one fateful night. He opened his mouth to speak, but his voice caught in his throat, dry and raspy from hours of tension.

Aaron leaned in slightly from his position beside his father, his youthful face pale and drawn under the unforgiving lighting. "He's told you everything," he said, his voice steady but low. "What else do you want to hear? What's not adding up?"

Rudi didn't even glance at Aaron. Instead, he kept his eyes firmly on James, as if he could extract the truth through sheer force of will. "The timeline, Aaron," he replied, his voice deceptively calm. "The way things happened. The exact sequence. Something isn't sitting right."

The oppressive lights flickered again, casting momentary shadows that seemed to dance across the walls, playing tricks on tired eyes. Sofia's fidgeting grew more pronounced, her breathing shallower. Her eyes were wild, darting around as if searching for an escape route. She seemed like a caged animal, cornered and desperate.

James finally found his voice, though it was strained. "I told you everything that happened," he said, his voice trembling. "I left the hotel, I went to the bridge, and I left when things got out of hand. I didn't push her. I didn't hurt her."

Rudi's lips twitched slightly, almost as if he wanted to smile but was too tired to bother. "And yet," he said slowly, "everything points to you being the last person who saw her alive before she fell. And your dear Sofia here seems awfully sure of your guilt. Makes one wonder, doesn't it?"

Sofia's head snapped up at the mention of her name. "I told you what happened!" she hissed, her voice high-pitched and strained, like a taut wire about to snap. "He's the one who did it! I saw him leave—"

"Yeah, we heard you," Linda cut in, her voice ice-cold from the corner of the room. "You're the one who's been screaming it from the rooftops, Sofia. But it's not adding up either."

Aamon, simmering with a quiet fury, couldn't hold back any longer. "What do you mean, 'not adding up'? Are you saying my dad and Sofia are lying? Are you saying we're all in on this?" His voice was almost a growl, each word spoken through gritted teeth.

The fluorescent lights hummed louder, as if mirroring the tension in the room. Rudi glanced at Aamon; his expression unyielding. "I'm saying," he replied slowly, "that maybe not everyone in this room knows what really happened that night. Or maybe some of you know more than you're letting on."

Silence descended over the room again, thick and suffocating. James felt a cold sweat break out on his forehead, the fluorescent lights making everything feel more stark, more real. His gaze flicked over to Sofia, whose eyes were wide with panic, then to his sons, who were both staring back at him with a mix of defiance and fear.

"Please, just... let's get to the truth," James said finally, his voice almost a whisper, the weight of the situation pressing down on him like a thousand bricks. "I can't live like this anymore."

Linda moved from her corner, her boots clicking on the cold linoleum floor. "Then let's start peeling back the layers," she said, her tone almost predatory. "One by one. Until there's nothing left but the truth."

Rudi nodded, the fluorescent lights casting a stark shadow across his face. "Let's see how deep this rabbit hole goes, Mr. Cross. Because something tells me, we've only scratched the surface."

"These are vague circumstantial evidences, Sheriff. My father is not well—we would like to leave," Aamon interjected, his voice firm but steady, standing up from his chair. His tall frame cast a long shadow under the unforgiving fluorescent lights. His eyes, a striking green-blue mix that stood out starkly against the sterile white walls, bore into Rudi with a fierce determination.

Rudi's eyes narrowed slightly; his calm demeanor unwavering. "Sit down, Aamon," he said in a measured tone, though his voice held a note of warning. "We're not done here. Not by a long shot."

Aaron stepped closer to his brother, his hand resting on Aamon's shoulder. "He's right, Sheriff," Aaron added, his voice quieter but equally resolute. "Our father isn't in the right state of mind for this. We've been here for hours. If you don't have anything more concrete, we're leaving."

James, seated between his sons, looked up at them both with weary eyes. He was proud of their strength, but he could feel the tension rising again, the room's oppressive atmosphere closing in on them. His head was throbbing, the fluorescent lights above making everything seem hazy, distorted. "Boys, it's okay..." he started, but Aamon quickly cut him off.

"No, Dad, it's not okay," Aamon snapped, his frustration bubbling over. "They've been dragging this on, hoping to get something out of you that isn't there. They're playing games, and I'm not going to sit here and let them break you down."

Rudi leaned back in his chair, his gaze now on the two young men standing protectively over their father. "This isn't a game, Aamon. Your mother's life—her jump—whatever happened to her, it's not a game. You might want to rethink your approach here."

Aamon's eyes flashed with anger. "Don't you dare talk to me about approach, Sheriff. We've been cooperative from the start, but this—this is a witch hunt. You have nothing solid, just a bunch of theories and some shady footage that doesn't prove a damn thing."

The room grew colder, if that was even possible, under the cold, buzzing fluorescent lights. The tension between Aamon and Rudi thickened, and everyone could feel it—a battle of wills, one born out of love and desperation, the other out of a relentless pursuit of the truth, however elusive it might be.

Juan, who had been silently watching from the back of the room, finally stepped forward, his expression neutral but his presence commanding. "Aamon," he began, his voice firm but not unkind, "we understand this is hard. No one is denying that. But you need to understand something—there's more going on here than just your father's word."

Aamon turned sharply to face Juan, his fists clenched at his sides. "I know what's going on," he said through gritted teeth. "You're trying to pin this on him because you want to protect your own sweet home, you want to keep your 'Graxe' to you, but you know what? She is not Graxe! She is my mom! I want my mom!"

Juan's eyes darkened, his patience thinning. "Watch it, kid," he warned, his tone losing its earlier calmness.

The room seemed to pulse with the intensity of emotions, every word spoken like a match to gasoline. Aamon's face was red with fury, his eyes burning with a mix of defiance and desperation. Juan's gaze, equally fierce, bore down on him, the tension between them a thick, almost tangible force in the air.

"Watch what? That you and your friends are hiding my mother from us? Because you found her!" Aamon shouted, his voice breaking with raw emotion. "You think you can just keep her from us like she's some prize you won? She has a family—real people who care about her, who deserve to know her, to see her!"

"She is my wife!" Juan roared back, his own composure fraying at the edges. "And where was your father all this time? Where were you? She is happy now, she is content, and she will never go down that sinkhole again. I will get restraining orders against all of you if I have to. Do you understand me, kid? She's not some trophy for you to reclaim!"

Aamon's fists clenched and unclenched at his sides, his chest heaving with each breath as he struggled to rein in his anger. "You don't get to decide that for her!" he shot back. "You found her, great. You gave her a new life, but that doesn't erase everything that came before! You don't get to just rewrite her history and cut out the people who love her!"

Juan's expression darkened further, his jaw tightening. "I'm not rewriting anything," he said through gritted teeth. "I'm protecting her—from all of you, from anyone who thinks they have a right to drag her back into the chaos that nearly killed her! Do you even know what she's been through? Have you seen the way she wakes up screaming some nights, clutching at her head like it's splitting apart? You want her back in that nightmare?"

Aamon took a step forward, his voice dropping to a low, dangerous tone. "She's my mother," he said, his words trembling with intensity. "And we deserve to know her. To help her. Not you, not your friend over there," he gestured to Rudi, "not any of you get to decide that for her. She's not a child. She's not your property."

Rudi leaned back in his chair, his eyes narrowing thoughtfully as he observed the heated exchange between Juan and Aamon. The tension in the room was almost palpable, a thick cloud of emotions and accusations swirling around them. He could see how deeply both sides were entrenched in their beliefs, how much they were willing to fight for the woman they each considered their own in different ways. But something had to give.

"Lieutenant Ramirez," Rudi began, his voice calm but firm, cutting through the thick atmosphere like a knife. "I think it's time for you to step down from this case."

Juan's head whipped around to face Rudi, his eyes widening in shock. "What?" he spat out; his voice filled with disbelief. "Rudi, you can't be serious."

"I'm very serious, Juan," Rudi continued, his tone unyielding. "Your personal feelings for Graxe—or Mariyam, as she's known to these boys—are clouding your judgment. This investigation needs to remain impartial, and right now, you're too close to it. Too involved."

Juan's face flushed with anger, his fists clenching by his sides. "I'm doing my job, Rudi," he argued, his voice rising. "I'm protecting her from people who could hurt her, who've already hurt her. You think this is about me? This is about keeping her safe!"

"Safe from what?" Aamon interjected heatedly. "From us? Her family? The people who've been looking for her, grieving for her?"

"Enough!" Rudi's voice boomed, silencing the room instantly. He turned his steely gaze back to Juan. "I'm not questioning your intentions, Juan, but your emotions are running high. You've just threatened to get restraining orders against her sons, her blood, and you're escalating a situation that doesn't need it. That's not impartial. That's personal."

Juan glared back at Rudi, his chest heaving, but he didn't say anything. He knew, deep down, that Rudi was right. He was too close to this, and it was getting harder to separate his role as an officer from his feelings as a husband.

Aamon, sensing a shift in the room, stepped forward, his voice more controlled but still charged with emotion. "All we want is a chance to see her," he said, his eyes locked on Juan. "To help her heal, to let her know she's not alone. You can't just keep her from us because you're afraid of what might happen."

Rudi nodded slowly, appreciating Aamon's calm but firm demeanor. "And that's exactly why this needs to be handled carefully," he said, turning his gaze back to Juan. "You're too close, Lieutenant. I'm taking you off this case effective immediately. I'll handle things from here."

Juan looked like he was about to protest, his mouth opening as if to argue, but then he stopped. He took a deep breath, his shoulders slumping slightly. "Fine," he muttered through gritted teeth. "But you better make sure she stays safe, Rudi. Because if anything happens to her—"

"Nothing's going to happen to her, Juan," Rudi interrupted, his tone softening but still firm. "I promise you that."

There was a moment of tense silence as Juan stood there, his eyes boring into Rudi's, before he finally turned on his heel and stormed out of the room, slamming the door behind him.

Aamon and Aaron watched him go, a mix of relief and uncertainty crossing their faces. They knew this was far from over, but at least now, they felt they had a fighting chance.

Rudi sighed heavily, running a hand through his hair, he took a deep breath, his eyes scanning the room. "Alright," he said, his voice heavy with the fatigue of the long night. "We're done here for today. We'll continue this on Friday. I expect everyone to come back prepared, and I mean it—leave your emotions at the door."

The room began to clear out, the tension still hanging in the air but with a slight sense of release, like a pressure valve had been opened just a little. James remained seated, his head in his hands, the weight of everything pressing down on him. His sons stayed close by his side, ready to support him through whatever came next.

The investigation was far from over, and the battle for Mariyam—Graxe—was only just beginning.

James lay on his back, staring at the ceiling of his penthouse, feeling the weight of the silence pressing down on him. The room was dimly lit, only a sliver of moonlight seeping through the partially drawn curtains, casting long shadows that seemed to stretch and bend like restless spirits. The city outside was alive, the hum of distant traffic and the occasional siren breaking through the thick glass, but in here, it felt like a world apart—isolated, cold, and suffocating.

He hadn't bothered to turn on any lights. Darkness suited his mood, shrouding the room in a veil that kept his thoughts hidden, even from himself. His eyes traced the patterns on the ceiling, but his mind was far away, drifting through a sea of regret and uncertainty. The events of the last few weeks had left him feeling untethered, as if he were floating in a void with nothing solid to hold on to.

The clock on the nightstand ticked softly, its sound almost drowned out by the rhythmic beating of his heart. He turned his head slightly, glancing at it—2 AM. He knew sleep would be elusive tonight, as it had been for many nights now. The weight of his choices, the tangled mess of his life, pressed down on him, making his chest feel heavy and his mind feel foggy.

The moonlight shifted slightly as a cloud passed over the sky, casting a softer, more muted glow around the room. It illuminated the edges of the furniture, the sleek lines of the penthouse decor that once felt luxurious but now seemed sterile and unwelcoming. He turned his gaze back to the ceiling, his eyes unfocused, lost in thought.

His mind drifted back to Mariyam—to her smile, to the way she used to look at him like he was her whole world. There was a time when he believed they were unbreakable, that their love could withstand anything. But now, that belief felt distant, like a fading echo of a song he could barely remember.

He could still see her eyes, filled with questions and hurt, the last time they were together—the way she had looked at him as if searching for answers he couldn't give. He had tried to make things right, but it always felt like he was one step behind, stumbling through a maze with no way out.

The moonlight panned across the room, landing on the framed photos on the dresser—their wedding day, their sons, moments frozen in time that felt like they belonged to another life. His gaze lingered on a picture of the four of them, smiling at a park. It felt like a lifetime ago, and yet the ache in his chest was fresh, raw.

He ran a hand over his face, feeling the roughness of his stubble. What had gone wrong? When had things started to slip away from him? He had always been in control, always had a plan. But now, everything was unraveling, and he was powerless to stop it.

A deep sigh escaped his lips as he closed his eyes, trying to push away the thoughts that clawed at him. But the more he tried to escape them, the more they seemed to pull him under, dragging him back to that night—to the last time he had truly seen her, the last time he had held her in his arms.

The memory washed over him, unbidden, pulling him under like a riptide...

————————

"James..." I whispered in the darkened room, feeling his body press close to mine.

"Hmm?" he responded, his lips brushing against the curve of my neck, sending a familiar shiver down my spine.

"Do you love me?" I asked quietly, my voice filled with a mix of longing and doubt. His hands slid beneath the fabric of my dress; his touch warm against my skin.

For a moment, he paused, his breath lingering near my ear. "Of course I do," he murmured, his lips moving softly against my neck. "We're married."

James's hands moved with a deliberate slowness, lifting the hem of my dress. I arched my back slightly, helping him, feeling the cool air touch my skin. The moonlight spilled through the curtains, casting a soft, pale glow around us. I could sense his eyes on me, searching and intense, and it made my heart race.

His fingers traced familiar paths along my side, their touch both tender and insistent. I leaned into him, craving the closeness, feeling a familiar heat build between us. "James..." I breathed, my voice trembling with unspoken questions. "Shouldn't we... talk about this?"

He kissed me deeply, his lips pressing against mine, and I felt his grip tighten. "Aamon and Aaron would love a little sister," he said softly, his voice teasing, but there was an edge to it, a tension just beneath the surface.

I let out a soft laugh, though it was tinged with nervousness. "Aaron's fourteen. He might not be thrilled about a new baby," I replied, trying to keep the mood light, to keep things from spiraling into the unspoken tension that hung between us.

He chuckled low in his throat, his breath warm against my ear. "Maybe not right away," he admitted, "but he'd come around. They both would."

I smiled at the thought of our sons, imagining their reactions, but a knot of anxiety settled in my chest. "You've been drinking," I whispered, my voice barely audible, pulling him closer. His movements were swift, his touch almost impatient, and I gasped at the suddenness of it.

Our bodies moved together, finding a rhythm that was both familiar and yet strained. The room filled with the soft sounds of our breaths, the rustle of sheets, the quiet urgency of our need for each other. For a few moments, it felt like we were alone in the world, like nothing else mattered but this.

But the words I had been holding back finally slipped out. "James," I whispered, feeling the weight of my confession in every syllable. "I know about Sofia."

He didn't stop; he didn't even flinch. His lips continued their path along my neck. "I come home to you," he murmured, his voice steady, almost too calm. "Every night, it's you I come home to."

I closed my eyes, feeling a sting of tears. "I'm not like you, James," I said softly, the words tumbling out. "I'm not from your world—your world of flashing cameras and glamorous parties. I can't live like this... sharing you with everyone else."

His hands tightened around me, and I could feel the tension in his grip. "You don't have to be like me," he said, his tone more serious now, almost pleading. "I'm trying to fix things. You can't leave me because of this—because of her."

I looked up at him, my vision blurred with unshed tears. "I don't recognize you anymore," I whispered, my voice breaking. A tear slipped down my cheek, and he leaned down, kissing me again, more forcefully this time, his actions filled with a desperation I hadn't felt before.

The room felt smaller, the air heavier. Each movement was laden with a mix of love, anger, and fear of what was happening to us. I clung to him, feeling the turmoil bubbling beneath the surface, wrapping my legs around his waist as if I could somehow hold us together.

"I want a baby," he said suddenly, his voice rough, his eyes searching mine for some kind of reassurance.

I reached up, brushing my fingers against his cheek, feeling the warmth of his skin under my touch. "You can't keep me with a baby, James," I said gently, my heart aching. "A baby won't fix what's broken between us."

His expression shifted, something raw flashing in his eyes—an urgency, a plea. He moved with a renewed intensity, his breath coming faster. "Don't do this, Mariyam," he whispered, his voice breaking. "For the kids, for us… it was just a mistake."

His words hit me like a wave, and I could feel the tears burn behind my eyes, the weight of everything pressing down on me. The room seemed to close in around us, filled with the scent of him, the warmth of our tangled bodies, and the sound of our ragged breaths.

"James, you need to stop lying," I whispered, my voice barely a breath above the chaos of my emotions.

We moved together, caught in a moment that felt like it could shatter at any second. There was love there, I could feel it—but there was also something darker, a desperation that scared me. I knew we couldn't stay like this, caught between what was and what could never be again.

His breath was hot against my neck, his body trembling slightly with the weight of what he wasn't saying. "We have a flight in three hours and a gala tomorrow," he said quietly, his lips brushing my ear. "Please… don't do anything reckless."

I lay there, staring up at the ceiling, his words settling over me like a heavy fog. As he drifted off beside me, his breathing steadying, I stayed awake, the reality of our situation settling in. I couldn't help but wonder if we'd already reached the point of no return.

James blinked back to the present; his eyes misty with unshed tears. He could still feel the weight of that night, heavy and unresolved. The clock on the nightstand read 2:30AM, and he knew sleep would not come easy.

James decided to open his gallery, scrolling through his phone until he found that one video—taken before he and Mariyam were married, before he even knew her. It was the video that had captured his attention years ago and led him to search for the woman behind that lively, unforgettable voice.

He tapped on the screen, and the video began to play. It opened with a shot of a white Persian kitten sitting elegantly on the floor, its fur dusted with glitter. Sunlight streamed through colored glass in a nearby window, casting small, vibrant rainbows around the room. The camera seemed to be held by someone lying on a bed, capturing the kitten's wide-eyed stare as it looked up.

"Jack!" Mariyam's voice called out playfully, off-screen. "Make me marry James Cross, Jack! Why aren't you making it happen? I want to marry James Cross!" Her tone was half-serious, half-mocking, filled with the kind of unrestrained joy that can only come from a private joke.

From somewhere nearby, a deep, exaggerated voice replied, pretending to be Jack, the kitten. "I can't misuse my powers, you know," the voice said, imitating a serious tone.

Mariyam giggled, her laughter filling the small room and the recording. "But you're a magical cat, Jack. You can do it," she coaxed, her words dripping with dramatic flair.

"I could, but he has to agree too, right?" the voice continued, still pretending to be the cat. "I told him, 'Marry my Mumma, or else I'll get rid of your family.' And he said, 'Do it. Get rid of me too while you're at it.'"

Mariyam burst into a fit of laughter, her joy so infectious it made the camera shake slightly. The kitten, seemingly oblivious to the conversation, blinked up at the camera, its whiskers twitching.

"Why can't you make me marry James Cross, then?" she demanded, her voice louder, filled with mock frustration.

"Where do these crazy people come from?" the voice replied as Jack, sighing dramatically. "Even at gunpoint, he wouldn't marry you. You want James Cross? Isn't the milkman James interested in you?"

Mariyam laughed even harder, her squeals of amusement shaking the camera as she struggled to keep it steady.

"Fine, I won't talk to you anymore, Jack. You couldn't make me marry James Cross," she said, feigning indignation but breaking into another giggle. "Do it! Make me marry him!"

"Okay, fine... I'll arrange it in 2060," the voice pretending to be Jack conceded.

"Why 2060?" she asked, tapping the kitten's nose gently.

"Because... either you'll be dead, or he will be by then. Problem solved." The voice delivered the line with a dry, comedic finality that sent Mariyam into another bout of laughter. She fell back, still chuckling, and the camera jostled before dropping to the floor with a soft thud, catching a brief glimpse of her still laughing before the screen went dark.

James stared at his phone, the echo of her laughter still playing in his mind. The video had ended, but the warmth and energy of that moment lingered, filling his chest with a bittersweet ache for a time when things were simpler—when the biggest concern was the imaginary whims of a glitter-covered kitten and the playful dreams of a young woman who hadn't yet known the pain of what was to come. James's hand trembled as he held his phone, his eyes lingering on the last frame of the video where Mariyam's laughter still seemed to echo. He remembered how carefree she was back then, her spirit unburdened by the weight of betrayals, secrets, and lies that now suffocated them both. A lump formed in his throat as he recalled her warmth, her laughter, and her fierce determination—the things that had drawn him to her in the first place.

He tapped the screen again, letting the video play once more, her voice and laughter filling the empty room. It was almost painful to hear it now, knowing how far they had drifted from those innocent dreams. His chest tightened as he thought about how he had failed her—how his mistakes, his weaknesses, had led them to this point.

James put the phone down and turned onto his side, the video continuing to play in the background. His mind was a whirlwind of memories, accusations, and lingering doubts. Sofia's words from the interrogation room replayed in his head: "If he loved her so much, why was he cheating? Why was he with me?" Her words were like needles, pricking at his conscience, forcing him to confront the ugliness he had tried to bury deep within.

He had been so sure of his love for Mariyam—convinced that he could protect her, even from himself. But every decision he'd made seemed to have driven her further away. And now, she was with someone else—someone who had found her when he couldn't, someone who was trying to keep her safe from the chaos James had created.

He clenched his eyes shut, willing away the images of Juan standing protectively beside Graxe—Mariyam, as he still wanted to call her—claiming her as his wife. He had to believe that she was still in there somewhere, that she remembered something about them, even if it was buried deep within her fractured mind.

The thought of her being truly lost to him—of her living a new life, being loved by another man—gnawed at him like a relentless ache. She was his. She had always been his. And yet, in his desperation to keep her close, he had lost her.

The video ended, the room falling silent once more. James stared into the darkness, feeling the oppressive weight of his solitude. His phone buzzed again, a message lighting up the screen. It was from Morris, his manager:

"James, don't do anything rash. We're working on getting things back under control. Call me when you can."

James stared at the message, his jaw tightening. Control. Wasn't that what this was all about? Control over his life, his family, his career? But it all felt like sand slipping through his fingers. He tossed the phone aside, letting it slide across the bed and onto the floor with a soft thud.

He needed to clear his head. He needed to see her. Not the version of her that Juan painted or the one the officers were digging for, but his Mariyam. The woman who laughed with him, who loved him fiercely, who looked at him as if he were her world. He needed to remind her of that life, to bring her back from whatever spell she was under.

James stared at the darkened screen of his phone, the lingering sound of Mariyam's laughter still echoing in his mind. It was a sound he hadn't heard in so long—pure, unrestrained, filled with a joy that seemed so distant now. The weight of the silence that followed felt almost unbearable, a stark contrast to the warmth and light of the memory he had just revisited.

He sighed deeply, setting his phone down on the nightstand, his hands trembling slightly. It felt like every part of him was unraveling, like he was trying to hold on to something that was slipping through his fingers. The past few weeks had been an endless cycle of hope and despair, each new revelation pulling him deeper into a labyrinth of guilt, fear, and uncertainty.

The penthouse felt suffocating, the walls closing in on him. He couldn't stay here, not now, not after reliving that memory. He needed air, space to think, to clear his mind. Without bothering to grab a coat, he rose from the bed and walked to the large glass doors that led to the balcony.

The night air was cool, a welcome contrast to the stifling atmosphere inside. James stepped out onto the balcony, leaning heavily on the railing as he gazed out at the city. The lights stretched out endlessly before him, a sea of distant stars twinkling against the dark sky. It was a beautiful view, one he had often admired, but tonight, it felt cold, empty—like the world was moving on without him.

He closed his eyes, taking in deep, steadying breaths, trying to calm the storm raging inside him. But the images wouldn't stop—Mariyam's smile, her laughter, the look in her eyes that last night they were together. He could still feel the warmth of her body against his, the way she had clung to him, as if trying to hold on to something she knew was slipping away.

The guilt gnawed at him, an insidious voice whispering that this was all his fault. That if he had been a better husband, if he hadn't let his career and the temptations that came with it drive a wedge between them, maybe things would have been different. Maybe she wouldn't have been standing on that bridge, looking down at the water below, contemplating the unthinkable.

James gripped the railing tighter, the cool metal digging into his palms. He had thought he was doing the right thing, giving her space, trying to fix things in his own way. But now, with everything falling apart, he realized how much he had failed her—how much he had failed their family.

A soft breeze rustled through the city, carrying with it the faint sounds of distant traffic and the occasional siren. It was a familiar symphony, one that usually brought him comfort, but tonight, it felt like a reminder of how far he had fallen, how disconnected he had become from the life he once knew.

His thoughts drifted back to Aamon and Aaron, to the way they had stood by his side at the precinct, their loyalty unwavering despite everything. They were his sons, a living testament to the life he had built with Mariyam—a life that now seemed fractured, broken beyond repair. He had always tried to protect them, to shield them from the worst of the world, but now they were being dragged into the chaos he had helped create.

James swallowed hard, a lump forming in his throat. He had to find a way to make this right, to piece together the fragments of their lives and somehow mend the broken bonds. But how could he do that when he could barely keep himself together?

He opened his eyes, staring out at the city once more, a single tear escaping down his cheek. He hadn't cried since the night Mariyam disappeared, hadn't allowed himself to show that kind of vulnerability. But now, alone on the balcony with only the city lights for company, the tears came unbidden, a silent release of the pain he had been holding inside for so long.

He wiped at his face with the back of his hand, angry at himself for breaking down. He needed to be strong, needed to find a way to fight for his family, for the truth. But the truth was elusive, tangled in a web of lies, secrets, and half-remembered moments that seemed to blur together in his mind.

What are we going to do, Dad?" Aamon's voice broke the stillness, emerging from the shadows as if he had been one with them all along.

James didn't turn around; his gaze remained fixed on the distant skyline, the city lights flickering like stars in a vast sea of darkness. "It's time, Aamon," he said, his voice low but resolute. "Time to reach out to her."

Aamon shifted his weight, his eyes dropping to the ground as he searched for the right words. "But... Juan said the doctors think she shouldn't be reminded," he said cautiously, his voice filled with uncertainty. "They think it could hurt her."

James finally looked at his son, his expression a mix of determination and pain. "She deserves the truth," he replied, his eyes never wavering from the city that sprawled before them. "We owe her that much."

Aamon nodded slowly, his mind churning with the weight of what his father was suggesting. "And if she doesn't remember us? Or if it hurts her even more?" he asked, his voice barely above a whisper. "What if we're pushing her into something she's not ready for?"

James sighed deeply, running a hand through his hair as he leaned on the balcony railing. "There's no easy answer, son," he admitted, his voice heavy with emotion. "But hiding her past from her, pretending it doesn't exist—it's not fair to her. She has a right to know who she was, who we were... who we are."

Aamon's brow furrowed in thought as he looked up at his father, the city lights reflecting in his eyes. "You think she'll want to remember?" he asked, his voice softer now, almost vulnerable. "After everything? After what happened?"

James turned his gaze back to the skyline, his jaw tightening. "I don't know," he said honestly. "But I'd rather give her the choice than let someone else decide for her. She's stronger than they think. She always has been."

Silence settled between them again, punctuated only by the distant sounds of the city below. Aamon took a deep breath, steeling himself for what lay ahead. "Then we go to her," he said finally, his voice firm with newfound resolve. "And we tell her everything. No more hiding, no more waiting."

"Not like this," James murmured, shaking his head as if clearing away the thought. "I still have my old alias in her social media friends list—my Smurf account. We can use that to send her a message... something compelling enough that she can't ignore it. An unknown person who claims to know who she is," he suggested, his voice filled with cautious hope. Aaron nodded in agreement, his mind already working through the possibilities.

"But what if she doesn't show up?" Aaron asked, turning to face James, concern etched on his face.

James sighed, the weight of uncertainty hanging heavily in the air. "That's where you come in, Champ," he said, placing a hand on Aaron's shoulder. "I need you to fly back to L.A. and bring some things—our photo albums, her wedding dress, maybe some fresh photos of the mansion, the lawn, the garden. She mentioned seeing snippets of memories before... maybe some baby pictures of you and Aamon, too. I'm done chasing ghosts."

Aaron's expression hardened with determination. "If there's a chance this could help her remember, I'll do it," he replied, his voice steady. "I'll get everything together and be back as soon as I can."

James nodded, a small smile of gratitude crossing his lips. "Good. We'll need every bit of help we can get. And if she shows up... we have to be ready. She deserves to see the pieces of the life she's forgotten."

Aamon chimed in, his brow furrowed with thought. "And if she doesn't come? If this doesn't work?"

James looked between his sons; his eyes tired but resolute. "Then we try something else," he said firmly. "We don't give up. Not on her, not on us."

Aaron gave a sharp nod and pulled out his phone, already booking the first available flight to L.A. Aamon stared out over the city, his jaw clenched. "We're going to bring her back, Dad," he said quietly, almost to himself. "No matter what."

James gazed at his sons with a mixture of pride and sadness. "We will, Aamon," he agreed softly. "We have to believe that."

As Aaron confirmed his flight details, Aamon turned to his father, his voice suddenly softer. "What are you going to say to her? When she finally meets us?"

James took a deep breath, the question hitting him harder than he expected. "I don't know," he admitted. "I suppose I'll start with... 'I'm sorry.' And then I'll tell her everything—everything she deserves to know. After that, it's up to her."

Aamon nodded, understanding the weight of what was to come. "We've got a lot to make up for."

"Yes, we do," James replied, his voice tinged with regret and determination. "But it starts with giving her the choice."

Aaron looked up from his phone. "Flight leaves in three hours. I'll head out now and get started."

James pulled him in for a quick hug. "Be careful, Aaron. And hurry back. We might need you sooner than you think."

Aaron nodded, grabbing his coat and heading for the door. "I'll be quick," he promised. "We'll get her back, Dad."

As the door closed behind him, Aamon and James stood in the dim light of the penthouse, the gravity of their plan sinking in. They were on the brink of a new chapter—one that could either mend their broken family or push them further apart.

"Let's get to work," James said, his voice filled with a new determination. "We have a message to craft."

James stared at the dark screen of his phone, his fingers hovering just above the keys, searching for the right words to pull her back into their lives without pushing her away. His mind raced through the possibilities—how much to reveal, how much to hold back. Every choice felt like walking a tightrope over a chasm of uncertainty.

"So, what do we write?" Aamon's voice was steady, but there was a slight tremor of apprehension in it. "It has to be something that grabs her attention... but doesn't scare her off."

James nodded, his brow furrowing in concentration. "Vague... but riddled," he murmured, as if testing the words on his tongue. His eyes flashed with a sudden idea, and he began typing slowly, deliberately, each word a carefully chosen piece of a larger puzzle.

He typed:
"Those flashes haunt you, don't they? Chubby baby on grass... Garden filled with roses... A cologne, a laughter... The sound of a song you can't quite remember? If you want

to know more, if you want to know who you are... come to this address."

He stopped, staring at the screen, a small line forming between his brows as he considered the impact of each word. "It has to feel like a whisper from the past," he said quietly, almost to himself, "something that stirs those memories without overwhelming her."

Aamon peered over his shoulder, reading the message. "This could work," he admitted, though his voice was tinged with doubt. "But what address do we give her?"

"This- "James handed him a card and Aamon looked up.

"What place is this?"

James handed Aamon a small, white card with embossed letters that read: "Chateau Rosewood, 143 West Riverview Lane." It was an address that only James and a few others knew about—a secluded estate outside the city, far from prying eyes and the noise of the world.

"It's an old property we used to own, back when things were different," James explained, his voice quiet but firm. "It's private enough, away from everything... but familiar. Maybe familiar enough to her, too."

Aamon nodded slowly, turning the card over in his hands. "Are you sure this is the right place, Dad? What if she doesn't recognize it, or it doesn't mean anything to her?"

James stared out at the skyline, his eyes narrowing as he considered his son's question. "It might not mean anything at first," he said after a moment, his tone thoughtful. "But it's not just the place; it's the feeling. The rose gardens, the old stone paths... that's where we used to go when we needed to talk, really talk. When we needed to be honest with each other. If anything could bring her back, it might be that."

Aamon nodded, understanding the weight of his father's words. "It's worth a shot," he agreed, his voice steadying with determination. "And if it doesn't work, we'll find another way."

James took a deep breath, feeling the weight of the decision they were making. This wasn't just about reaching out to Graxe, or Mariyam, as he still thought of her. It was about breaking down the barriers that had kept them apart for so long—barriers built on fear, on regret, on the choices they had made and the consequences that followed.

He hit "send," watching as the message disappeared into the digital ether, carrying with it a piece of his heart, a fragile hope that maybe, just maybe, they could find their way back to each other. "It's done," he said quietly, more to himself than to Aamon. "Now we wait."

Aamon shifted beside him, the silence stretching between them like a taut wire. "Do you think she'll come?" he asked finally, his voice laced with a mix of hope and anxiety.

James didn't answer right away. Instead, he stared at the city lights, his mind replaying every memory he had of Mariyam—the way her eyes would light up when she laughed, the way she used to hum softly when she thought no one was listening. He missed her more than he could ever put into words, and the thought of never truly reaching her again twisted his heart into a knot.

"I don't know," he said at last, his voice barely a whisper. "But if there's even a chance... we have to try."

Aamon nodded, sensing the gravity of his father's words. "We're in this together, Dad. No matter what happens, we'll face it as a family."

James glanced at his son, a faint smile touching his lips. "Yeah," he said softly, "as a family."

James and Aamon stood side by side, the weight of their shared decision settling heavily between them. The city continued its restless hum below, indifferent to the silent turmoil in their hearts. A faint breeze rustled the leaves of a nearby tree, whispering secrets that only the wind could carry. James's grip tightened on the railing, his knuckles whitening as he stared into the horizon, where the city lights bled into the distant dark.

"Chateau Rosewood," he murmured, almost to himself. The name carried a weight—a mixture of nostalgia and longing, wrapped in the delicate threads of a past that seemed to stretch across an unbridgeable chasm. It wasn't just a place; it was a memory, a piece of their history, a gamble that felt like their last.

Aamon glanced at his father, sensing the storm of emotions swirling within him. He wanted to say something reassuring, to tell him it would be okay, but he knew better. James was a man who had faced more than his fair share of battles—both on-screen and in life. This one, though, felt different. This one wasn't about fighting; it was about letting go.

"Dad," Aamon began softly, but James cut him off with a gentle nod.

"Go get some rest, Aamon," James said, his voice steady despite the turmoil within. "We'll need to be ready for whatever comes next."

Aamon hesitated, but then he nodded, understanding that his father needed a moment alone. "Goodnight, Dad," he said quietly, squeezing his father's shoulder before turning to leave.

James didn't respond. He watched his son disappear down the hallway, his footsteps fading away until the only sound left was the distant hum of the city. He closed his eyes, feeling the cool night air brush against his skin, and he allowed himself a moment—a single, fragile moment—to hope.

Would she come? Would she remember? Would the rose gardens and the stone paths stir something within her—a flicker of recognition, a tug on the threads of her lost memories?

The questions were endless, each one heavier than the last, but James clung to the idea that somewhere, deep inside, Mariyam—his Mariyam—was still there. That she was waiting to be found.

His phone buzzed in his pocket, snapping him back to the present. A text from Morris: "Be careful, James. Don't push too hard. Sometimes the past is best left buried."

James stared at the message for a long time before typing a response: "Some things are worth digging up."

He hit send and pocketed the phone, his eyes drifting back to the skyline. The meeting was set, and now there was nothing left to do but wait.

Chateau Rosewood stood silent and still in the moonlight, a relic of a love that once was—a love that could be again. And somewhere in the distance, a figure stood at the crossroads of fate and memory, deciding which path to take.

As the night deepened and the city lights flickered like stars scattered across the earth, James took a deep breath. The stage was set. The next move wasn't his to make.

Would she come? Would the place mean anything to her? Only time would tell. But whatever the outcome, he was ready to face it. Ready to confront the past, to find the truth, to hold on or let go.

"Come back to me, Mariyam," he whispered to the night, his voice lost in the wind.

And with that, he turned away from the balcony, leaving the city to its restless dreams and the stars to keep their silent vigil over Chateau Rosewood, where everything could change with the dawn.

CHAPTER 10

The night was dark, the kind of inky blackness that seemed to swallow the world whole. The moon, a sliver of silver barely peeking through the thick blanket of clouds, offered little comfort to Graxe as she lay awake in bed, her eyes tracing the ceiling's uneven patterns. She could feel the weight of the silence pressing in from all sides, like a dense fog wrapping around her, pulling her deeper into her thoughts.

Juan lay beside her, his breathing deep and steady, a rhythm that should have calmed her. But tonight, his presence felt distant, almost foreign. He'd been so preoccupied lately—late nights at the precinct, cryptic conversations that trailed off whenever she entered the room. She hadn't pressed him on it, hadn't wanted to seem paranoid or insecure. Yet now, as she stared into the darkness, she wondered if she should have.

She turned her head slightly, watching the outline of his face in the dim light. He looked peaceful, his brow unfurrowed, his lips slightly parted. She envied that peace. She hadn't known true peace in what felt like an eternity—since that night on the bridge. Or rather, since she woke up from it, drenched and cold, with no memory of how she'd ended up in that river, clutching an emerald necklace that felt both alien and intimate. Since then, she'd been living a borrowed life, piecing together fragments of a puzzle that never quite fit.

Tonight, however, something felt different. Her phone, tucked away in the bedside drawer, seemed to pulse with an invisible energy. She could still feel the phantom vibration of the message she'd received yesterday, the one with the address: "Chateau Rosewood, 143 West Riverview Lane." No name, no explanation, just an address. But it was enough.

She didn't know why it felt so familiar, but it did. Like a whisper from a forgotten dream, the name echoed in her mind, stirring something deep within—a memory buried so deep that it was almost beyond her reach. She had stared at the message for what felt like hours, turning her phone over in her hands, trying to decide what to do.

Juan would never approve. He'd been adamant about keeping her away from anything that might trigger her past, anything that could bring her back to that life she'd left behind. And for a while, she'd agreed. She'd embraced her new life, her new identity as Graxe. She'd tried to forget that she had once been someone else—Mariyam. Someone who had a husband named James Cross, someone who had a life filled with glitz and shadows, secrets and lies.

But something about that message wouldn't let her rest.

She sat up slowly, careful not to disturb Juan, and swung her legs over the side of the bed. The wooden floor was cold against her bare feet, sending a small shiver up her spine. She stood up, moving like a ghost across the room, and slipped into the bathroom. She closed the door quietly, the soft click of the latch echoing in the silence.

In the dim light, she caught her reflection in the mirror. Her face looked pale, her eyes wide and searching. Who are you? The question hung in the air, a specter she could never quite shake. She leaned in closer, tracing the outline of her own lips with her finger, as if trying to remember a kiss that no longer existed.

"Chateau Rosewood," she whispered to herself, testing the name on her tongue. It felt strange, yet familiar, like a word in a foreign language she used to know. She couldn't shake the feeling that this place held some kind of answer, some key to unlocking the door to her past.

Decision made; she turned back to the bedroom. She moved carefully, grabbing a pair of jeans and a sweater from the closet, along with a pair of sturdy boots. She hesitated for a moment, her eyes drifting to Juan's sleeping form. She wished she could tell him, wished he'd understand. But this wasn't something he could be a part of—not yet, at least.

She slipped out of the bedroom and down the narrow hallway, each step feeling like a betrayal, a crack in the foundation they'd built together. But she couldn't ignore it. Not anymore.

The night air was cool as she stepped outside, the crisp autumn chill biting at her skin. The streets were empty, save for the occasional car passing by, its headlights slicing through the darkness like a knife. She kept her head down, moving quickly, the address replaying in her mind like a mantra.

The drive to Chateau Rosewood felt longer than it should have, the roads winding and narrowing as she left the city behind. The trees grew taller, thicker, forming a canopy that blocked out what little moonlight there was. She gripped the steering wheel tightly, her eyes darting between the road ahead and the rearview mirror, half expecting to see someone following her. But the road remained empty, a ribbon of asphalt cutting through the woods.

As she approached the estate, a sense of unease settled in her stomach. She slowed the car, her headlights catching the weathered iron gates that marked the entrance to Chateau Rosewood. They were slightly ajar, as if someone had left them open for her, inviting her into the shadows beyond.

Graxe took a deep breath, feeling her heart rate quicken. She turned off the engine and sat there for a moment, staring at the gates, the address still etched in her mind. "Chateau Rosewood, 143 West Riverview Lane." What was she hoping to find here? She wasn't sure. Maybe a clue, maybe a memory, maybe nothing at all. But she had to know.

She pushed the car door open and stepped out, the gravel crunching under her boots. The air was thick with the scent of damp earth and decaying leaves, and somewhere in the distance, she could hear the faint trickle of a stream. The path ahead was lined with towering oaks, their gnarled branches twisting together like skeletal fingers reaching for the sky.

She made her way up the gravel path, her eyes scanning her surroundings, taking in every detail—the ivy-covered stone walls, the faded wooden benches, the rose bushes that looked like they hadn't been tended to in years. The place had a haunting beauty to it, like a forgotten painting covered in dust. It was old, timeless, holding onto secrets that time itself had forgotten.

As she walked, a sense of familiarity began to wash over her, like déjà vu but stronger, deeper. The crunch of the gravel beneath her feet, the smell of the roses mingling with the crisp night air—it all felt like she'd been here before, like she'd walked this path a thousand times in another life.

She reached the end of the path and stopped, her breath catching in her throat. Before her stood the chateau, its stone façade bathed in the soft, eerie glow of moonlight. It was grand but worn, like a mansion pulled from a gothic novel. The windows were dark, the curtains drawn, giving the house a hollow, lifeless look. Yet, there was something undeniably inviting about it, like it was waiting for her, like it had always been waiting for her.

Her heart pounded in her chest as she stepped closer, her eyes drawn to the grand wooden door with its intricate carvings. She reached out, her hand trembling slightly, and pushed it open. It creaked loudly, the sound echoing through the empty halls like a ghost's whisper.

Inside, the air was colder, the kind of chill that seeped into your bones. The foyer was vast, with a grand staircase spiraling up into the darkness above. Dust covered every surface, and cobwebs hung like delicate curtains from the chandelier. She took a step forward, her breath coming out in shallow puffs as she moved deeper into the house.

And then, she saw it—a single light flickering in the far corner of the room, a small table lamp casting a soft, warm glow. Her heart leaped into her throat. Someone was here. She wasn't alone.

Graxe moved toward the light, her steps slow and deliberate, her eyes scanning the shadows for any sign of movement. The house creaked and groaned with every step she took, as if it, too, were waking up from a long slumber. She could feel her pulse in her ears, her nerves stretched taut like a wire ready to snap.

And then she heard it—a faint rustling, the sound of someone shifting in their seat. She froze, her breath hitching, her eyes locking onto the source of the noise. A figure sat in the corner, cloaked in shadows, their face obscured by the dim light. Her heart pounded in her chest, her mind racing with a thousand possibilities.

"Who's there?" she called out, her voice steady despite the tremor in her hands.

For a moment, there was nothing but silence, thick and oppressive, filling the room like a tangible thing. And then, the figure leaned forward, into the light, revealing a face she knew all too well.

James Cross.

"Hello, Mariyam," he said softly, his voice carrying a weight that hung heavy in the air. "I knew you'd come."

Graxe felt a shiver run down her spine. The tension in the room was palpable, a living, breathing entity that seemed to press down on her from all sides. She didn't know what she had been expecting, but it wasn't this. Not the man who claimed to know her, who called her by a name that no longer felt like her own.

And as she stared into his eyes, searching for answers, she couldn't help but wonder—had she made a mistake in coming here? Or was this exactly where she was meant to be?

I stared at him as he extended his hand. For reasons I couldn't comprehend, I placed my hand in his. He gently guided me to the center of the room, and suddenly, it was as if I had stepped into the dream that had haunted me for so long. But this time, the face of the person dancing with me wasn't a blur—it was his.

He wore a timeless black tuxedo, the bow tie slightly askew, his face softened by a hint of a blush and a wistful smile. We swayed together, moving in time to a rhythm that wasn't really there, a haunting melody that only we seemed to hear.

"You remember this, don't you?" he murmured, his voice barely above a whisper. I looked down at our entwined hands, my mind spinning with confusion and a strange sense of familiarity. Why did this feel like I'd been here before? Why did this feel so much like... déjà vu?

"I don't..." I started to deny, my voice trembling, but the words felt hollow. Deep down, my heart whispered a different truth. I did know this. Somehow, somewhere in the hidden depths of my memory, this moment was real.

James's gaze softened, and he leaned in closer, his eyes searching mine. "You were wearing a blue dress that night," he continued, his words carrying a weight that felt both tender and unbearably heavy. "And your hair was pinned up, just like this." His hand reached up, gently brushing back a loose strand of hair, and I felt a shiver run down my spine. "You laughed when I stumbled over my own feet. You always laughed when I did that."

A flicker of a memory—brief, like a spark in the dark—flashed before my eyes. A swirl of blue fabric, a soft, golden light, and a warm laugh that bubbled up from deep within me. I blinked, and it was gone, like smoke dissipating into the night air. My breath hitched. How could I see something I didn't remember?

"Stop," I whispered, my voice breaking. I tried to pull away, but his grip on my hand tightened, not painfully, but firmly, as if he were afraid, I might vanish. "I don't want to remember," I insisted, my eyes welling with tears.

"But you do, Mariyam," he pressed, his voice filled with a mix of desperation and hope. "You're just scared to face it. To face... us."

I shook my head, the room around us seeming to spin. "Graxe," I corrected. "My name is Graxe! I am Graxe!" I protested but he smiled instead.

"Are you?"

His question lingered in the air, a soft challenge that reverberated through me like the distant toll of a bell. My heart pounded in my chest, each beat echoing in my ears. I wanted to scream at him, to push him away, to tell him he was wrong—but the words wouldn't come. His eyes, deep and unyielding, held mine in place, searching for the truth I was desperately trying to bury.

"Are you really Graxe?" he asked again, his voice steady, almost gentle. "Or is that just the name you've been hiding behind because it's easier than facing what happened?"

I felt my throat tighten. "I don't know what you're talking about," I lied, my voice barely a whisper. But even as I spoke, I could feel the fragile walls I'd built around my new life starting to crack. Images began to flash before my eyes—quick and disjointed, like old film reels spinning out of control. A bridge. A fall. A cold, rushing river. A pair of blue-green eyes staring back at me, filled with something I couldn't quite grasp. Love? Fear? Desperation?

"You jumped that night," James continued softly, his gaze never wavering. "You were running—from me, from everything. And I wasn't fast enough to catch you." His voice broke on the last word, a tremor of pain rippling through it. "I tried, Mariyam. God, I tried."

The weight of his words pressed down on me, squeezing the breath from my lungs. I wanted to deny it all, to scream that he was lying. But deep down, beneath the layers of confusion and fear, I felt the faint tug of truth. The darkness of that night, the icy chill of the water, the sensation of falling—it all felt too real to dismiss.

"You are lying! Let me go, Juan says you are delusional, desperate— trying to manipulate me." I screamed, trying to push him away.

James flinched at the mention of Juan's name, a flash of pain and anger crossing his features before he regained control. His grip on my hand loosened slightly, enough for me to feel the tension but not enough to break free. His eyes, however, never left mine, burning with an intensity that made it impossible to look away.

"Juan," he said, his voice tight with barely suppressed emotion, "is a good man. He loves you, Mariyam, or Graxe, or whatever name you've chosen to hide behind. But he wasn't there that night. He doesn't know what happened on that bridge, what led you to that moment. I do."

His words cut through the air, sharp and unforgiving. I wanted to reject them, to cling to the life I'd built with Juan, to the safety of not knowing. But the weight of James's words hung between us, heavy with a truth I couldn't ignore.

"Gulnaz, your mother's name was Gulnaz." He smiled resting his forehead against mine. "You always wonder what she looked like, no? She looked just like you, she was almost your twin." He said and I paused, my breaths coming ragged, as I echoed the name, like a sacred chant.

"Gulnaz...."

The name slipped from my lips, soft and hesitant, as if uttering it too loudly might break whatever fragile connection I'd just felt. A warmth spread through my chest, a feeling so unfamiliar, yet so profoundly intimate, it nearly brought me to my knees. I didn't remember my mother, not really. But the name, the sound of it, resonated within me, like a key turning in a long-forgotten lock.

James's eyes shimmered with a blend of sorrow and a flicker of hope, his breath warm against my skin. "You used to tell me stories about her," he murmured, his voice steady but weighted with emotion. "About how she sang you to sleep when you were a child, and how her voice made you feel safe even on the stormiest nights. Do you remember?"

A sudden, sharp ache pierced my chest, like a knife cutting through the fog in my mind. I didn't remember those things, not exactly—but I wanted to. I wanted to feel the comfort of that lullaby, to picture her face, to know her again. Tears blurred my vision, spilling over as I shook my head, my throat constricting painfully.

"I don't know," I whispered, my voice breaking. "I don't know what's real anymore." My hands trembled in his, and I tried to pull them away, to retreat back into the safety of ignorance. But James held on, his grip firm yet gentle, his thumbs brushing soothing circles against my skin.

"Mariyam," he said softly, "I know you're scared. I know it's easier to forget, to let this new life shield you from the pain. But I'm begging you, don't shut me out. Don't shut out who you were... who you are."

His words struck a chord deep within me, resonating with a truth I didn't want to face. I wasn't just Graxe. I wasn't just this new person Juan had come to love. There was a whole world of memories, of pain and love and loss, locked away inside me. And they were fighting to be set free.

"But what if I don't want to be her?" I choked out, tears streaming down my face. "What if I don't want to be Mariyam? What if I can't... be her again?"

For a moment, James was silent, his expression softening. Then he leaned in, his lips brushing against my forehead in a gentle kiss. "You don't have to be her," he whispered against my skin. "You don't have to be anyone you don't want to be. But you deserve to remember, to know the truth. Not for me, not for anyone else, but for yourself."

I closed my eyes, letting his words wash over me, my breath coming in shallow, shaky gasps. The room around us seemed to blur and spin, the walls closing in as if they were alive, pressing in on all sides. I was caught between two worlds—one of safety and familiarity with Juan, and another of chaos and uncertainty with James. But it wasn't just about them. It was about me, about reclaiming the pieces of myself that had been lost.

"You see a chubby baby in your dreams, don't you?" James asked, his voice tinged with a fragile vulnerability. I nodded, my eyes still closed, bracing myself for what was to come. "What does he look like?"

I hesitated, my mind racing to bring forth the image that had haunted my dreams for so long. It was always the same—a chubby baby with wide, innocent eyes, reaching out to me with tiny hands. His face was round and soft, his cheeks flushed with a rosy hue and marked by a small dimple when he smiled. But there was something more, something about him that I could never quite place. Now, with James standing so close, the memories began to sharpen, coming into focus like a picture emerging from the mist.

"He has... dark, curly hair," I whispered, my voice trembling. "And his eyes... they're blue, but not just any blue. They're like... green-blue, like the ocean at dusk—deep and endless. And when he smiles, it's like the whole world lights up."

James nodded, his expression a mix of pride and sorrow. "Does he look like him?" He gestured toward something behind me, stepping back slightly. I opened my eyes.

There, on a small table, was a framed photograph of two young boys, their faces beaming with joy. One had dark, curly hair, and the other a lighter shade, but both shared the same striking blue-green eyes, like the ocean at dusk. The image was slightly blurred at the edges, as if captured in a moment of spontaneous happiness, but the smiles on their faces were unmistakable.

My heart tightened as I stared at the photograph, my breath catching in my throat. Those boys... I knew them. A flicker of recognition passed through me, followed by a surge of emotions so powerful it nearly overwhelmed me. The chubby baby in my dreams—he wasn't just a figment of my imagination. He was real. And he was one of these boys.

"But how...?" I began, looking up at James, who leaned casually against the desk, a soft smile playing on his lips.

"Do you want to meet him?" he asked, his tone gentle, as I glanced back and forth between him and the photograph.

"This baby... he's here? He's real?" I asked, my voice wavering with disbelief.

"Just as real as you and me," James said with a wink. "Though he's not quite as cute anymore—he's 20 now."

I tilted my head, confusion knitting my brows.

James chuckled softly at my reaction, his smile taking on a wistful edge. "Hi... Mom," a voice suddenly chimed in, catching me off guard. I turned toward the source, my heart skipping a beat. "Long time no see?" The young man winked; his eyes gleaming with familiarity. I instinctively stepped back, retreating a little.

"You're all playing games with me! He's your son! And he has a younger brother—they were in the car that day when you offered me a ride!" I shouted at James, my voice trembling with accusation. My eyes darted between him and the young man standing before me.

James's smile faltered, replaced by a look of deep concern, the weight of his words hanging in the air. His face reflected the burden he had carried for so long, the truth he was about to reveal. "No, Mariyam," he said gently, his voice steady but filled with quiet intensity. "They aren't just my sons. They're ours—yours and mine. Aamon and Aaron."

Aamon stepped forward, his frustration clear. "Stop hiding behind those walls your mind has built, Mom!" he interrupted, his voice rising with emotion. "You know me. Deep down, you know who I am. Don't let your brain keep protecting you—you don't need to be protected from our memories." His words cut through the air like a knife, each one closer, sharper.

"Do you have any idea what it was like for us, Mom?" Aamon continued, his voice trembling with a mix of pain and anger. "You know all too well, don't you? Your own mom died when you were 19—you always told us you'd be there for us. You promised. But you didn't keep that promise. You abandoned us. You jumped into that river and left Aaron and me to face everything alone. And now, is your mind protecting you from the trauma, or is it the guilt?"

He leaned closer, his breath ragged, and I shook my head, tears streaming down my face as I covered it with my hands, trying to block out his words.

"Aaron was just 14, Mom!" Aamon continued, his voice breaking. "I was 18. You left us! Look at me! Look at me and tell me you don't know who I am." His voice cracked with raw emotion. "Aaron doesn't paint anymore. He left art school. And I... I became just like Dad, the very thing you told me never to be. Ask yourself—do you really not remember? Do you really not know the truth?"

His words pierced through me, each one a painful reminder of the life I might have forgotten, a life filled with promises, with love and loss. My body trembled, torn between the fear of remembering and the fear of losing something—someone—irreplaceable.

"Mumaaaaaaaa." I cried, I finally cried my body shaking with sobs, the pain of loss and grief, enveloped my heart anew as I sank on the floor. "Mumma, Ammi— Mumma." I sobbed, I sobbed inconsolably, because, I remembered for the first time, I remembered my Mumma's face and the fact... she was gone.

James sank down beside me, his arm slowly wrapping around my shoulders, his touch warm and steady. "It's okay, Mariyam," he whispered, his voice gentle, a balm against the open wound my heart had become. "Let it out. It's all right to feel this... it's all right to remember."

I buried my face in my hands, my body trembling with each sob that wracked my chest. Memories—so many memories—flooded my mind now, crashing against one another in a chaotic, overwhelming tide. I could see her—my mother, Gulnaz—her face lit up with laughter as she twirled me around in our small kitchen, her voice softly singing a lullaby I'd thought I'd forgotten. I could hear her comforting words when I scraped my knee or failed a test, her scent lingering in the air like jasmine and cardamom. She was gone. She'd been gone for so long, and yet, in this moment, she was here with me.

And there were other memories too, equally sharp and painful. Aamon's first steps, Aaron's first laugh, the way James looked at me the first time he said he loved me. The way I had fallen out of love with him. The fights, the nights spent wondering if things would ever be the same. The growing distance that turned into a chasm, wide and deep, until that night on the bridge.

Aamon knelt down on my other side, his expression still tense but softening with concern. "Mom," he murmured, his voice now quieter, gentler. "I'm sorry. I didn't mean to... to be so harsh. But we've been waiting for you to come back to us for so long. Aaron's waiting too. He just... he couldn't be here today. It was too much for him."

I lifted my head, my eyes bloodshot and swollen from crying, and looked at him—really looked at him. This was my son, my boy who I'd watched grow up, who'd inherited his father's stubbornness and my fire. He was right. Deep down, I did know him. And it broke my heart to see the pain I'd caused etched so deeply into his face,

Perhaps it was finally time to confront the truth—my truth. The truth of what really happened that night on the bridge.

"I didn't jump," I said, the weight of the words settling heavily on my conscience, grounding me in a reality I had tried so hard to forget. "I didn't jump," I repeated, my gaze fixed on Aamon's eyes, pleading for him to believe me. "He chose his own life over ours, Ammu. He walked away that night, left me standing on that bridge. He didn't turn back, didn't pause, didn't hesitate. It was like he didn't care if I lived or died. I fought for him, against everyone who warned me he was a cheater, a womanizer, but I trusted him... only him. And he treated me like a doormat, stepping all over me again and again. He betrayed us, Ammu."

My body trembled with sobs, and Aamon nodded, his own tears falling into my hair as he pulled me into a tight embrace.

"I didn't jump," I whispered again, the words surer this time. "Sofia pushed me. I was heading home after he left when she stopped me. She threw pictures at my face—pictures of them together, from all their trips. He was betraying us, Ammu—you and me. Betraying our family, breaking the vows we made. I was furious, but I didn't jump. I confronted Sofia, and things got physical. She kicked me, and I almost slipped over the edge, but I managed to hold on. Then she struck me on the head with an iron rod, and I fell backward into the Hudson. I was conscious for hours, lying on those rocks, bleeding and unable to move... terrified I might die there. And then a flash flood swept me away like I was nothing."

"They saved me," I continued, my voice hoarse but steady as I thought of Juan. "Juan and his friends—they cared for me, gave me everything when I had nothing. He isn't a bad man. You have to understand that, Ammu. The bad guy was your father. He destroyed his own family."

Aamon held me tighter, his body shaking with silent sobs as he tried to process the truth of my words.

"Dad," he finally whispered, his voice breaking, "he said he was sorry. He said he didn't mean to... that he was lost..." He whispered, looking up at James, who's hand hovered in air above my shoulder, unsure, if He was late, perhaps too late for redemption.

James's hand hovered above my shoulder, trembling slightly as his eyes searched my face—seeking understanding, forgiveness, perhaps even the faintest spark of hope. The weight of his remorse seemed to fill the room, thickening the air between us.

"Don't you dare," Juan's voice cut through the tense silence like a blade, his tone cold and sharp as James recoiled. Unbeknownst to us, Juan had arrived moments earlier, tracking my car's GPS when he realized I was no longer in the bedroom. He had witnessed everything, his heart breaking anew as he heard the truth spill from my lips. He had always known the woman he saved was troubled, perhaps lost, but he never imagined the depth of the hell I had endured.

"I said, don't you dare touch her again," Juan repeated, his voice low and threatening. His steps were firm as he crossed the room, He gently helped me to my feet, and as I buried my face in his chest, his strong arms encircled me, offering the comfort I so desperately needed.

"You, okay?" he asked softly, looking down at me with concern etched in his features. I shook my head, unable to find the words to explain the turmoil inside me.

"It's okay, amor," he murmured, pressing a tender kiss to my temple. His voice was a soothing balm, grounding me in the midst of the emotional storm raging within.

"You cannot—" James started, but Juan raised a hand, cutting him off mid-sentence. "Not now, James. You've done enough," he said firmly, then turned to Aamon. "Grab your things, Aamon. You're coming home with us."

"You can't just take my kids!" James protested, his voice rising in panic. Juan turned to him, his expression fierce, like a lion ready to defend his pride.

"They're *her* kids too," Juan countered, his voice unwavering. "She has every right to be with them."

"I..." Aamon began, his voice wavering with uncertainty, but James interrupted with a weary shake of his head, silently pleading for him to stay.

Meanwhile, Aaron, who had been listening from the top of the stairs, ran down, his school bag bouncing against his back. He rushed past James and Aamon and flung himself into my arms, burying his face against my shoulder.

"I'll go with you," he declared, his voice muffled by my embrace. Aamon's eyes widened in shock at his brother's choice.

"Aaron! Dad needs—" Aamon began, but I gently cut him off, shaking my head.

"He'll be okay, Ammu," I reassured him softly. "I just need a few days... We'll meet again, I promise. But for now, I need to rest." I pulled him close, ruffling his hair affectionately as I hugged him tight.

"You've always been your father's son, haven't you, my little traitor?" I teased, a shaky chuckle escaping through my tears as I shook Aamon playfully. He shook his head, but I could see the hint of a smile tugging at his lips.

"I know you won't come with me, my love," I continued, my tone more serious now. "But will you do something for me?" I asked gently, meeting his gaze.

Aamon nodded, his eyes searching mine for whatever came next. "Can you take care of your Papa while Aaron stays with me? Don't let him smoke too much, and make sure he takes his blood pressure meds on time, okay? I'll call you both soon, maybe in a week or two, once I've cleared my head."

Aamon's expression softened as he considered my words. He nodded, though his eyes were still clouded with concern. "Okay, Mom," he finally agreed, his voice barely above a whisper. "I'll look after him. Just... promise you'll come back."

I cupped his cheek and smiled, my thumb brushing away a tear that had escaped down his face. "I promise, Ammu. I just need to sort things out. For myself, for you, for Aaron... for all of us."

With a heavy sigh, Aamon turned to James, his eyes filled with a mixture of love and disappointment. "Come on, Dad. Let's get you home," he said, gently taking his father's arm.

James looked at me, his eyes filled with a painful mix of regret and longing. "Mariyam..." he began, but his voice faltered, unable to find the right words.

"Please, James," I whispered, my voice trembling but firm. "Let me go... just for now."

James nodded, his shoulders sagging under the weight of everything unsaid. "Alright," he murmured, his voice almost inaudible. "But I'm not giving up on us."

As James and Aamon slowly made their way to the door, Juan placed a protective arm around me and Aaron. I leaned into him, feeling the warmth of his strength, while Aaron hugged me tighter, his small frame trembling with the enormity of everything happening around him.

Once they were gone, Juan turned to me, his expression gentle but serious. "You did the right thing," he said softly. "Taking this time. We'll get through this together."

I nodded, feeling a sense of calm slowly begin to settle over me. "Thank you," I whispered, leaning into his embrace, grateful for his steady presence. "For everything."

Juan pressed a kiss to the top of my head, his hand stroking Aaron's back soothingly. "Always, amor," he replied, his voice a promise. "We're in this together, no matter what."

For the first time in what felt like forever, I felt a glimmer of hope. It wouldn't be easy—there was so much to face, so much to remember, so much to heal—but with Aaron by my side, Juan's unwavering support, and Aamon looking after his father, maybe, just maybe, we could find a way forward.

Juan sat quietly beside me as he drove, his presence steady and reassuring. Every so often, he'd glance my way, a soft, silent question in his eyes, asking if I was okay. His hand reached over, gently squeezing mine. "We're almost home," he whispered, his voice low and comforting.

Aaron, on my other side, leaned his head against the window, watching the world go by. His quiet presence was like a soothing balm to the wounds still raw in my heart. "It's going to be okay, Mom," he murmured softly, as if he could sense the storm of emotions churning within me.

I caught his gaze in the rearview mirror and smiled, trying to ease the tension that clung to the air. "Why did you leave art school, Aaru?" I asked gently, my voice tinged with a playful lightness. "Did Daddy forget to buy you those fancy paints and canvases again?" I teased, hoping to bring a smile to his face.

But Aaron's response took me by surprise, his words veering into the heart of the matter with a directness that cut through the thin veil of normalcy I was trying to maintain. "Is Juan our new dad? Where have you been all this time?"

The question hung in the air, heavy and unspoken for so long. I felt my breath catch in my throat, the weight of everything—the lost years, the buried memories, the pain—pressing down on me all over again. I took a slow, deep breath, my eyes meeting Aaron's in the mirror, and then I turned to face him.

"No, sweetheart," I said softly, choosing my words carefully. "Juan isn't replacing your dad. He's... he's just someone who took care of me when I didn't know who I was, when I was lost." I glanced at Juan, who kept his eyes on the road but gave me a reassuring nod, encouraging me to continue.

"I was gone for a long time, Aaru, and I wish I could explain it all to you in a way that makes sense," I said, my voice trembling slightly. "I lost my memory, and I didn't remember who I was, where I came from... or even who you and Aamon were. I thought I was someone else entirely—Graxe. But I'm starting to remember now."

Aaron's eyes stayed on me, a mixture of curiosity and hurt lingering there. "So, you forgot us?" he asked, his voice small and a little broken.

I nodded, feeling my heart ache at the sadness in his tone. "I didn't mean to, Aaru. I didn't want to forget you or your brother. But I'm trying to make up for it now. I want us to have a chance to be a family again, even if it's a little different than before."

Aaron shifted in his seat, his gaze dropping to his hands. "It's just... a lot," he whispered. "I just couldn't paint anymore. No colors came to my mind, I didn't feel like doing it." He said without realizing his innocent words, shattered my heart to pieces.

"How old is he?" Juan mouthed to me and I sighed.

"15 years 8 months." I mouthed him back.

The air in the car seemed to thicken with unspoken words, a palpable tension that clung to us all as we drove toward a place, I once called home but now felt like foreign territory. Aaron's words echoed in my mind, each one cutting deeper than the last. My heart ached, not just for myself, but for my son—for everything he'd lost, everything he'd been forced to endure without me. And now, to hear him say he couldn't paint anymore, that the colors that once brought him joy had faded into nothingness—it was almost too much to bear.

"I'm sorry," I whispered, the words barely audible over the hum of the engine. "I'm so sorry, Aaru."

Aaron didn't respond immediately, his gaze fixed on the passing scenery outside the window. He looked so much older than his years, the innocence that should have been his shield now replaced by a quiet resignation, a maturity forged in the crucible of pain and abandonment. It was a maturity he should never have had to develop, not at his age.

"I missed you," he finally said, his voice so soft I almost didn't catch it. "I missed you so much, Mom."

A sob caught in my throat, and I squeezed his hand, trying to convey all the love and regret I felt in that single touch. "I missed you too, sweetheart. More than you'll ever know."

Juan remained silent, his hand still resting on mine, grounding me, letting me know he was there without needing to say a word. I was grateful for that—grateful that he understood this moment was about Aaron and me, about the fragile bond between mother and son that had been stretched to its breaking point but was somehow, miraculously, still holding on.

"Aaru... can I call you that?" Juan broke the silence gently, and Aaron nodded, his expression guarded.

"How about we stop by a store I know, pick up some paint and canvases? It's open 24/7," Juan suggested with a hopeful smile, but Aaron shook his head.

"My dad will get them for me," Aaron replied with a firmness that made me smile a little at his loyalty.

"Hmm..." Juan hummed thoughtfully, then his smile widened a bit. "You know, Aaru, when I was your age, I had a pet hamster. I'd spend hours painting his portrait, just him—no crazy stuff like painting rabbits' bright colors or anything."

Aaron finally looked at him, a faint spark of interest in his eyes. "And then?" he asked, leaning forward slightly.

"Well," Juan continued, "he was my little muse, my only friend for a while. I'd draw him all the time. But one day... he just disappeared."

Aaron's eyes widened; his curiosity piqued. "Where did he go?"

Juan leaned closer, his voice lowering as if sharing a great secret. "That's the thing—I never found out. One moment he was there, and the next, he was gone. I looked everywhere. I even drew posters to put up around the neighborhood."

Aaron chuckled softly. "Posters? For a hamster?"

Juan grinned. "Yep. With a reward and everything. I thought maybe he'd come back if he saw his face plastered all over the town. But you know what? It wasn't just about finding him. It was about not giving up on something that mattered to me. Drawing those posters helped me feel like I was still connected to him, like he was still around somehow."

Aaron was quiet for a moment, mulling over Juan's story. "And did you keep drawing after that?" he finally asked.

Juan nodded. "I did. I kept drawing. Different things, different places. It wasn't the same, but it helped. And sometimes, when I'd draw, I'd remember him. The way he'd twitch his nose or how his fur looked under the sunlight. It brought some of the color back."

Aaron looked down, his fingers toying with the hem of his sleeve. "Maybe... maybe I could try that," he said softly. "Not the posters, but... drawing again."

A warmth spread through me at his words, and I squeezed his hand once more. "I'd like that, Aaru," I whispered. "I think you'd find it helps."

Aaron glanced at me, and for the first time in what felt like forever, there was a glimmer of something hopeful in his eyes. "Yeah. Maybe it will."

"Maybe I should call Dad and ask him to send me some paint," Aaron said, quickly pulling out his Tablet. He dialed James, and within moments, the call connected.

"Hey, Dad," he greeted, his voice a mix of determination and affection. I exhaled softly, a small smile forming on my lips as I glanced at Juan. There was so much ahead of us to work through, but this felt like the beginning—a small step toward something that resembled happiness.

"Can't go even 30 minutes without missing Dad, huh?" Aamon's voice came through the speaker instead, laced with a teasing tone. Aaron's eyebrows knitted together, a hint of sibling rivalry flaring up.

"It's not like that—I want to talk to Dad!" Aaron shot back, his lips forming a slight pout while Aamon's smug laugh came through, clearly enjoying getting a rise out of his younger brother.

"But Dad said he doesn't want to talk to traitors, Aaron," Aamon continued, his tone dripping with mockery.

"Daaad!" Aaron shouted, frustration creeping into his voice as he tried to get James to intervene. But Aamon kept up his act, now mimicking a deep, authoritative voice.

"Hi, Aaron, this is Dad. I don't want to speak with you!" he imitated, clearly enjoying his brother's exasperation.

Aaron's face flushed, torn between annoyance and disbelief. "Stop it, Aamon! Just let me talk to him!" he insisted, his fingers tightening around the Tablet.

"Alright, alright, I'm just messing with you," Aamon finally relented, though his laughter still lingered. A few moments later, James's voice came through the line.

"Alright, alright, hold on," Aamon chuckled, the sound of footsteps and muffled conversation filling the line before James's voice broke through.

"Aaron? What's up, buddy?" James's tone softened immediately, his affection for his son evident even through the call.

Aaron's expression softened too, though a hint of frustration lingered. "Dad, can you send me some paint and canvases? I want to try painting again." His voice wavered just a bit, the vulnerability of the request hanging in the air.

There was a brief silence on the other end, and I could almost picture James's face—probably stunned and relieved all at once. "Of course, Aaru," he said gently. "I'll get them to you as soon as I can. I'm glad you want to start painting again."

Aaron's eyes flickered with a mix of emotions—relief, perhaps a bit of pride. "Thanks, Dad," he murmured, and I felt a swell of warmth in my chest, watching him take this first step toward reclaiming something he loved.

Juan leaned in slightly, his voice low and encouraging. "See, Aaru? Everyone's ready to help you find your colors again."

Aaron gave a small nod, a hint of a smile playing at his lips. "Yeah, maybe they're not as lost as I thought."

CHAPTER 11

I found myself in the familiar corner of the café, a place that had become my sanctuary ever since that fateful confrontation with James, and the flood of memories that had come rushing back. Picking up music had been an unexpected solace in the aftermath, a way to pour out everything that words couldn't capture.

Three months had slipped by since that pivotal night—since everything changed, since everything came back to me. I remembered it all now: the bridge, the fall, and the life I had tried to piece together as Graxe. And with the memories, a flood of emotions I had long buried surfaced, overwhelming me, leaving me breathless, and driving me into something unexpected—music.

It was a slow evening, the kind where time seemed to stretch languidly, melting into the golden glow of the café lights. The familiar scent of freshly brewed coffee mingled with the faint notes of vanilla and cinnamon that always hung in the air. I was seated on the modest little stage at the back, a warm, inviting spot tucked between worn bookshelves and cozy armchairs, where I had started performing weekly. The stage had become my own small world—a place where I could be vulnerable, bare my soul without fear of judgment.

My guitar rested comfortably on my lap, my fingers lightly tapping the wood as I waited for the right moment to begin. The strings felt alive beneath my fingertips, vibrating with a quiet energy, waiting for me to breathe life into them. The crowd was a mix tonight: regulars who had become familiar faces over the past months, and newcomers drawn in by the café's reputation for live music and its intimate atmosphere. I could see a few heads nodding to the background music, a couple whispering softly to each other, and some solo patrons with their eyes fixed on books but ears tuned to whatever might come next.

I played the first few chords, letting the soft, melodic notes float through the air. A gentle hush fell over the crowd, their attention drawn to the stage. Then, a ripple of applause started from one corner, spreading like a wave throughout the room. I looked up, smiling in appreciation, my heart swelling a little at the response. This was what I needed—connection, even if only for a fleeting moment. I caught the eye of a young woman in the front row who gave me a thumbs-up, her face lit with anticipation. I couldn't help but smile back.

"What's on the setlist tonight?" a voice called out from somewhere in the middle of the room, light and playful, breaking the silence. I leaned closer to the microphone, feeling the warmth of the crowd's attention on me.

With a playful grin, I let my eyes sweep over the audience, searching for familiar faces and new ones alike. "Well," I started, my voice carrying a teasing lilt, "I was thinking of something a bit closer to the heart tonight. A Hindi song, perhaps." I paused, gauging the crowd's reaction, then continued with a mischievous glint in my eye, "Any Indians in the house? Pakistanis? Bangladeshis? How about our friends from beautiful South Asia? Let's see some hands—or better yet, let me hear a big 'Oh ho!' if you're out there!"

There was a moment of silence, and then, as if a switch had been flipped, the room burst into a cheerful chorus of "Oh ho!" accompanied by a few playful whistles and claps. I laughed softly, my heart lifting with the sound. There was something magical about these moments—a sense of belonging, of unity in a room full of strangers. It felt like an embrace, warm and welcoming, a reminder that even in a foreign land, there were threads that connected us, bound us together in shared stories and melodies.

I adjusted the strap of my guitar and leaned back into my chair, my fingers finding their place on the strings. The buzz of excitement rippled through me as I prepared to dive into a song that spoke of love, loss, and everything in between—a song that mirrored my own journey, one that had brought me here, to this café, to this stage, on this very night.

"Okay, Okay, let's not get carried away, No Hindi songs, okay?" I announced chuckling , then strummed the first chords of the son, My song. The melody filled the cafe, weaving through the air like a familiar friend. As I sang, memories of home, of family, and of resilience flooded my mind.

"To be or not to be,

To see or not to see,

You hear what you fear the most,

You believe in sheer unseen,

To ask, what no one would,

To dare to take that fateful leap,

To stand apart and alone,

And say, it's me, I am me,

In all my gloom and glee,

I am me..."

As the last notes of the song faded into the cozy atmosphere of the cafe, there was a moment of stillness, as if the music had cast a spell over the audience. Then, a wave of applause erupted, mingled with cheers and whistles.

I couldn't help but smile at the enthusiastic response, feeling a rush of gratitude for the opportunity to share my music with such an appreciative crowd. As I took a bow, the warmth of their applause washed over me like a comforting embrace.

Stepping off the small stage, I made my way through the cafe, pausing to exchange a few words and smiles with the patrons who had come to listen. Their kind words and encouragement filled me with a sense of fulfillment, reminding me why I had chosen to pursue music in the first place.

At a corner table, a group of friends waved me over, offering me a seat among them. I gladly accepted, grateful for the chance to unwind after the performance.

"Great set, Graxe!" one of them exclaimed, raising their glass in a toast. "You always know how to lift our spirits with your music."

I chuckled, feeling a warmth spread through me at the compliment. "Thanks, I'm glad you enjoyed it. It's always a pleasure to play for such a wonderful audience."

As we chatted and laughed, I couldn't help but feel a sense of contentment settle over me. These moments, surrounded by friends and fellow music lovers, were precious reminders of the joy to be found in simple pleasures and human connection.

"Did you like it?" I asked without turning around, sensing the familiar presence behind me.

"I did," James smiled.

"But did you understand it?" I continued, my back still to him, a small smile tugging at my lips.

James's voice carried a note of melancholy. "I may not understand all the words, but I understand the emotion. It's beautiful," he admitted, pulling up a chair to sit beside me. His presence was both unexpected and, surprisingly, not unwelcome; our interactions had gradually become less tense.

I turned to face him, raising an eyebrow. "Learning Hindi on the sly, are you?"

"Maybe a little," he confessed, a sheepish grin spreading across his face. "I've been trying. Music, movies... anything to get a bit closer to your world."

"You're serious?" I asked, a mix of disbelief and admiration in my voice.

"Yeah, well, it's about being connected, isn't it?" James replied, his gaze steady and sincere. "If music can bridge gaps, why not let it?"

The conversation eased into a comfortable pause as the café patrons around us began to chime in, sharing their experiences with music and how it had connected them to others. The soft clinking of glasses and low murmurs of conversation in the background added an intimate layer to our little gathering.

"So, how are the boys? Aaron and Aamon?" James inquired, steering the conversation to safer, familiar territory.

"They're doing well. Aaron is applying for art school, and Aamon's been a great support to him. They both miss you; you know. They talk a lot about the summers with you."

James's face softened at the mention of our sons. "I miss them too. How about we go? We have a reservation," he said, smiling as he extended his hand.

"Reservation?" I asked, my curiosity piqued.

"Yes," he replied, his smile broadening. "With the stars and the night sky, Central Park, and our little picnic basket is waiting."

As James's words sank in, I was momentarily taken aback by the unexpected invitation. Central Park, with its vast greenery and quiet corners, held a special place in our family's memories. It was where we had shared picnics, played games, and simply enjoyed being together.

A flicker of hesitation passed through me, memories of past hurts and unresolved feelings pulling at my heart. But then I looked into James's eyes, and within them, I saw sincerity and a genuine desire to reconnect.

"Central Park sounds lovely," I finally said, a tentative smile forming on my lips. "I'd like that."

With a nod of agreement, James offered his hand again, and together we stepped out of the café, leaving behind the warmth of laughter and music for the cool embrace of the night.

As we walked through the streets of New York, the city lights cast a soft glow around us, illuminating our path ahead. The air was crisp and invigorating, carrying the promise of a new beginning.

We soon arrived at Central Park, its sprawling green landscape a comforting sight amid the city's urban chaos. James guided me to a secluded spot beneath a canopy of trees, where a picnic blanket was spread out, adorned with an array of delicious treats.

"Surprise," he said with a grin, gesturing to the spread before us. "I thought we could indulge in a little nostalgia."

I couldn't help but laugh at his thoughtfulness, a wave of gratitude washing over me. Settling down on the blanket, we began unpacking the picnic basket, sharing memories and laughter as we enjoyed each other's company.

"You look tired," I said, looking up at him as he arranged our little picnic. The fine lines on his face seemed deeper than before. "You're getting old, Mr. Cross. I guess those rumors about the fountain of youth are just that, huh?" I teased.

James chuckled at the playful jab, his eyes crinkling at the corners. "Ah, you caught me. Maybe I need to plan a trip to that fountain sooner rather than later," he quipped, his tone light and playful.

As we settled into our impromptu picnic, surrounded by the serene beauty of Central Park, the tension that had once loomed between us seemed to melt away, replaced by a sense of ease and familiarity. It was almost as if time had rewound, and for a fleeting moment, we were the young couple who had fallen in love in this very park.

"So, tell me," James began, pouring a glass of wine for each of us, "what's been on your mind lately? You seem lost in thought. Is everything okay with Juan?"
I took a sip of the wine, savoring its deep, velvety flavor as I mulled over James's question. My mind was a whirlwind of thoughts, each vying for attention, a storm of emotions that had been building up for some time.

"It's been... a lot," I confessed, setting my glass down carefully on the blanket. "After everything that happened with us, and then the boys—" My words were cut short by a sudden, unexpected sensation—a cool droplet of water landing squarely on my cheek. Then another, and another, until the soft patter turned into a heavy downpour.

"Seriously, what's up with Manhattan?" I chuckled, half amused, half exasperated, as James quickly took my hand, guiding me toward the shelter of a nearby gazebo.

We made a run for it, laughter bubbling up between us despite the rain soaking through our clothes. The park, just moments ago bathed in the soft glow of twilight, had transformed into a shimmering, rain-swept landscape. The leaves on the trees glistened under the relentless onslaught of raindrops, and puddles began to form along the winding pathways, reflecting the city lights like little mirrors on the ground.

By the time we reached the gazebo, we were breathless and drenched, our hair and clothes clinging to our skin. The structure was a small, wooden refuge with a peaked roof, nestled among a cluster of trees. It was just large enough to provide us with shelter, the wooden slats creaking beneath our feet as we stepped inside. The rhythmic drumming of the rain against the roof filled the air, an oddly comforting sound that seemed to cocoon us from the rest of the world.

"Looks like Mother Nature had a different plan for us," James remarked, a grin spreading across his face as he shook the water from his hair, droplets flying in every direction.

I laughed, feeling a lightness I hadn't felt in a while, the absurdity of the situation making it even more surreal. We found a seat on the gazebo's weathered wooden bench, our shoulders almost touching. Outside, the rain grew heavier, pouring down like a shimmering curtain that transformed Central Park into a glistening wonderland. The trees, now weighed down with water, swayed gently, their branches dipping low as if bowing to the sudden downpour.

I watched the rain for a moment, feeling its strange pull, then sighed, breaking the tranquil silence. "What are we doing, James? Chasing shadows?" I asked, my gaze drifting around the misty park before settling back on him. "I'm practically cheating on Juan by meeting you like this, you know." My words held a heavy truth, even though we both knew that, deep down, neither of us wanted to stop meeting, even if we tried.

James leaned forward slightly, his expression caught somewhere between a smirk and a frown. "Maybe we're just trying to coexist for the kids," he suggested vaguely, though his tone betrayed the real complexity of his feelings—feelings we both knew ran far deeper than just co-parenting.

A lull fell between us, thick with the things left unsaid. Seeking a way out of the tension, I decided to steer the conversation elsewhere. "So, tell me, Mr. Versatile," I began with a teasing lilt, "what are the new projects? I heard you're collaborating with that big animation universe now."

James's expression softened, and a spark of excitement flickered in his eyes as he leaned back against the bench, looking more relaxed. "Yeah, I've been working on a few interesting projects," he said, his voice taking on a more animated tone. "Collaborating with them has been a dream come true, honestly. We're putting together a new adventure film set in this fantastical world, full of magic, mythical creatures, and wonder."

As he spoke, his face lit up with genuine enthusiasm, the passion for his craft evident in every word. "It's been such a refreshing change of pace from all those action-packed roles. This one's more whimsical, imaginative—like stepping into a whole new world. It's really brought out the kid in me," he added, his smile broadening.

"Let me guess," I interrupted with a mock-serious tone, a grin tugging at my lips, "you're going to be a dashing prince?"

James turned his head to me, eyes narrowing playfully. "Really?" he scoffed, a playful glint in his eyes.

I couldn't help but snort. "You're more like the frog, waiting for someone to come along and break that spell," I teased.

His laughter rang out, rich and genuine, mingling with the steady rhythm of the rain. The moment felt timeless, suspended in a bubble of nostalgia, humor, and a strange sense of comfort—a fleeting yet meaningful pause in the chaos of our lives.

The rain continued to dance around us, turning the world outside into a blurred masterpiece, but within that little gazebo, everything felt strangely clear.

"Frog! Frog, you are a frog." I chuckled, wagging a finger at him. "Go jump in puddles." I pointed toward the grass.

I teased, but James grabbed my finger, and suddenly the playful moment shifted to a more intimate one. He gently pulled me closer by the finger, and I found myself pausing, our breaths mingling as we stared into each other's eyes.

"I—" he began, his voice soft, our hearts beating so loudly that they were nearly audible. He leaned in, cautiously, as if unsure how I would react. And I, almost instinctively, leaned in too. It was like a rubber band stretched to its limit—snapping back with a force neither of us expected. Without thinking, I grabbed his collar and pulled him in for a kiss.

Our lips met in a tender yet passionate embrace, and the world around us seemed to fade into the background, leaving only the sound of rain and the pounding of our hearts. The kiss was filled with a longing that spoke of years of separation and countless unspoken words finally finding release.

The kiss deepened, fueled by a mix of desire and nostalgia, as though we were trying to make up for all the lost time in this single, charged moment. Our hands found each other, fingers intertwining as if seeking reassurance that this was real—that we were here, together, right now.

But just as suddenly as it had begun, the kiss ended. We pulled away slightly, our breaths heavy, and our eyes met in a silent understanding of the gravity of what had just happened.

"I'm sorry," James whispered, his voice barely audible. "I shouldn't have—"

Before he could finish, I pulled him in again, wrapping my arms around his neck. He responded by holding me tighter, drawing me in as our lips met once more, this time with an urgency and hunger that left no room for doubt.

The rain continued to pour outside the gazebo, creating a rhythmic backdrop to the raw emotion swirling between us. In that moment, there were no words—no explanations needed. Just the undeniable pull of two hearts finding solace in each other's embrace.

As our kiss deepened, the world around us dissolved, leaving only the sensation of his lips on mine, igniting a fire that had been smoldering beneath the surface for far too long. Time seemed to stop as we became lost in the intensity of our shared desire, each touch and caress speaking volumes without the need for words.

But eventually, the need for air forced us to pull away, though the electricity of our connection still crackled in the space between us. For a moment, we simply gazed at each other, breathless and captivated by the intensity of what we had just shared.

James tangled his fingers in my hair and gently pulled my face closer, our foreheads resting against each other.

"I still want that baby girl," he murmured with a smirk on his lips, both of us breathing heavily.

"I don't... think..." I took a deep breath, and James looked momentarily taken aback. "Aaron would be thrilled with a sibling sixteen years younger," I chuckled, catching my breath.

James's laughter mingled with the sound of the rain, a joyful, resonant sound that filled the gazebo. "Maybe not," he agreed, his eyes twinkling as he brushed a strand of hair from my face. "But it was worth a shot, right?"

I nodded, unable to suppress the smile pulling at my lips. In that moment, the weight of the past few months seemed to lift slightly, swept away by our laughter and the surreal beauty of the rain-soaked park around us.

Our conversation shifted as we reminisced about the past, recalling moments of joy, challenges we'd faced, and the wild journey that had led us to this point. As we spoke, I realized how much I had missed this—talking with James, sharing stories, and reconnecting on a level that once felt lost forever.

"Remember that trip to the Hamptons?" James asked, a nostalgic smile spreading across his face. "When Aaron tried to catch crabs at the beach and ended up falling into the water?"

I laughed; the memory vivid in my mind. "How could I forget? He was so determined to catch those crabs, and you were just as determined to save him from turning into a popsicle."

James's laughter mingled with mine, filling the gazebo with warmth. "He's always been so adventurous, hasn't he? Just like his mother."

The affection in his voice was undeniable, stirring something inside me—a mix of fondness and sadness for the moments we'd missed. But as we continued to talk, the sadness began to fade, replaced by a cautious hope that maybe, just maybe, we could find a way to move forward together.

As the rain started to lighten, James glanced outside and then back at me. "Looks like it's clearing up. Want to come back to my place?" he asked, his tone casual.

I raised an eyebrow, a playful glint in my eyes. "Oh? And why would I do that?" I replied, my voice teasing.

James's cheeks flushed slightly, a hint of embarrassment coloring his demeanor as he fumbled to find the right words. "I just thought... maybe we could continue our conversation somewhere more... private. Plus, I've got a breathtaking view of the city from up there."

I chuckled at his flustered response, unable to resist teasing him further. "Oh, so you just want to show off your fancy penthouse view, huh? Well, I suppose I could be convinced," I said, feigning reluctance as I took a step closer to him, my lips curling into a playful smile.

His face brightened with a mix of relief and delight, clearly grateful for my lighthearted response. "Great! It's not far from here, just a short walk," he said, gesturing for me to follow him.

We walked side by side, enveloped in a comfortable silence, the tension from earlier slowly unraveling with each step. The sun dipped lower on the horizon, casting long shadows across the park as evening settled in. The air was alive with the sounds of birds chirping and leaves rustling in a gentle breeze, creating a serene backdrop that seemed to smooth the edges of our earlier conversation.

When we reached his building, James held the door open for me with a subtle, gentlemanly flourish. I couldn't help but take in the grandeur of the lobby—the polished marble floors, the refined, understated elegance of the furnishings. It was clear that James had done well for himself in the years since we'd last seen each other.

As the elevator ascended to his penthouse, a quiet anticipation built within me. I found myself wondering what awaited us at the top. Would this be the beginning of something new, or just a fleeting moment of connection amidst the chaos of our lives?

The doors slid open to reveal a spacious, beautifully appointed penthouse. Floor-to-ceiling windows stretched across the room, offering a sweeping, breathtaking view of the city skyline. The sight was so stunning that, for a moment, I could only stand there, speechless.

"This place is—" I began, but before I could finish, James took my hand, his grip firm yet tender.

Without another word, James tugged me gently towards the bedroom, and I couldn't help but laugh at his eagerness. His enthusiasm was contagious, and despite my initial surprise, I felt a rush of excitement coursing through me as I followed him, anticipation thrumming in my veins.

Upon entering the bedroom, I was struck by the luxury and intimacy of the space. Soft, ambient lighting bathed the room in a warm, golden glow, illuminating the elegant furnishings and the plush bedding. The subtle, enticing scent of expensive candles filled the air, adding to the intimate atmosphere.

James turned to face me; his eyes darkened with a deep, smoldering desire. He reached out, his fingers gently brushing against my cheek. "I've imagined this moment for so long," he murmured, his voice husky with emotion. "Having you here with me, in this place... it feels like a dream come true."

His words sent a shiver of anticipation down my spine, and I instinctively leaned into his touch, craving the closeness and connection that only he could offer. Without another word, he closed the space between us, capturing my lips in a searing kiss that left me breathless, yearning for more.

The kiss deepened, our bodies pressing together in a deliciously intimate embrace as we lost ourselves in the heat of the moment. It was as if the world outside vanished, leaving only the two of us and the raw intensity of our shared desire.

When we finally pulled apart, breathless and flushed with a heady mix of emotions, I couldn't help but smile. Despite everything that had come between us, the spark hadn't faded. If anything, it had only grown stronger with time, fueled by the unspoken longing that had simmered beneath the surface.

James's hands roamed over my body with a reverence that left me trembling, his touch igniting a fire within me. With each caress, each whispered word of affection, I felt myself surrendering to the moment, to the overwhelming tide of emotions that threatened to sweep me away.

"James..." I whispered as he trailed kisses down my neck.

His lips continued their descent, leaving a trail of heat along my skin, and I felt a surge of desire coursing through me. His touch was like a balm to my soul, soothing old wounds and filling me with a sense of belonging I had longed for.

His hands moved with a practiced, tender skill, exploring every curve and contour of my body as if committing each detail to memory. I gasped softly as his fingers traced my spine, sending shivers of pleasure cascading through me.

"James," I breathed, my voice barely a whisper as I arched into his touch, craving more of the exquisite sensations only he could evoke.

He lifted his head, his gaze meeting mine, his eyes dark with desire. "Mariyam," he murmured, his voice thick with emotion. "You are so beautiful, so perfect... I've missed you more than words can express."

His words were like music to my ears, filling me with warmth and affection, washing away any lingering doubts or fears. In that moment, there was only us—two souls bound together by an unbreakable bond.

Without a word, he lifted me into his arms and carried me to the bed with a gentleness that contrasted with the passion burning in his eyes. As he laid me down on the soft sheets, I looked up at him with eyes full of love and longing, silently inviting him to continue this journey of rediscovery and desire.

With a hunger that matched my own, he leaned down to claim my lips in a fervent kiss, his body pressing against mine in a deliciously intimate embrace. The world around us faded into nothingness as we lost ourselves in the heat of the moment, each touch, each caress a testament to the depth of our connection.

With a whispered plea, James lowered himself onto me, our bodies moving together in a rhythm as old as time itself. I gasped as he filled me, the sensation sending waves of pleasure crashing over me.

Our movements were instinctive, driven by a primal need that transcended words. In that moment, there was no past, no future—only the intoxicating present, where we surrendered ourselves completely to the consuming fire of our desire.

The room seemed to pulse with energy, the air thick with the heady scent of passion as we climbed higher together. With every touch, every caress, I felt myself teetering on the brink of oblivion, lost in a haze of ecstasy.

James's hands roamed over my skin, igniting a trail of fire wherever they touched, his lips finding mine in a searing kiss that left me breathless. I clung to him, my nails digging into his skin as I gave myself over to the pleasure that threatened to consume me.

There was no room for doubt or hesitation—only the raw, unrestrained passion that bound us together. With every heartbeat, every shared breath, we became one, lost in a blissful oblivion.

As the intensity of our passion reached its crescendo, I felt myself hovering on the edge, teetering on the brink of release as pleasure washed over me in relentless waves. With a soft cry, I let go, surrendering completely to the overwhelming sensation that swept me away.

And as I tumbled over the edge into the abyss of pleasure, I felt James's own release shudder through him, our bodies entwined in a symphony of passion. In that moment, there was no past, no future—only the sweet, consuming present, where love and desire collided in a breathtaking crescendo.

As we lay entwined in each other's arms, our bodies bathed in the warm afterglow, I knew this was just the beginning of our journey. In each other's arms, we had found not just solace, but a renewed sense of purpose and belonging.

"Our hearing is tomorrow, James..." My voice was barely more than a whisper.

"I know..." he replied, nodding as our bodies pressed closer together.

"I told the police everything... how you left me on that bridge." My voice caught in my throat, and James nodded, pressing a kiss to the nape of my neck.

"And what if you get pregnant while I'm in jail?" he asked, a hint of humor in his tone that made me chuckle. I playfully smacked his hand, shaking my head at his attempt to lighten the moment.

"Aren't you 62?" I teased, pressing closer against him, my voice a low murmur filled with playful challenge.

James chuckled, his breath warm against my skin as his arms tightened around me, pulling me nearer. "Age is just a number, darling," he whispered, his tone a blend of humor and tenderness that melted the tension between us. "And if I'm 62, well, that just means I've had 62 years to perfect the art of loving you."

A soft laugh escaped my lips despite the weight of the moment. It was always like this with James—his uncanny ability to find light in the darkest corners, to make me smile when my heart felt heavy. It was that charm, that unyielding spirit, that reminded me why I had fallen so deeply for him all those years ago.

"Always the charmer," I whispered, reaching up to brush a stray lock of hair from his face. His eyes, dark and intense, met mine, filled with an emotion that both soothed and unsettled me.

His expression softened, the teasing giving way to something deeper as he cupped my face in his hands, his thumbs gently tracing the contours of my cheeks. "I'm serious, Mariyam," he said softly, his voice low and steady. "Whatever happens tomorrow, I need you to know... loving you has been the greatest privilege of my life."

His words settled over me like a warm embrace, pulling a tight knot of emotion to my throat. Tears pricked at the corners of my eyes, and I placed my hands over his, feeling the strength and warmth of his touch grounding me. "James..." I began, but the words tangled in my mouth, caught in the web of everything we'd been through—the love, the heartbreak, the regrets that shadowed our past.

He leaned in, his lips brushing my forehead with a feather-light kiss. "Shh," he murmured against my skin. "You don't have to say anything. Just... let me hold you, just a little longer."

I nodded, my heart heavy yet somehow full, as I rested my head against his chest. The steady rhythm of his heartbeat thrummed in my ear; a sound I once took for granted. Now, each beat felt like a fragile, precious reminder of the life we had shared, the love we had lost and found, and the uncertainty that lay ahead.

In that moment, with his arms around me, the looming shadow of tomorrow's hearing seemed to recede, if only for a while. I chose to stay there, wrapped in his warmth, finding solace in his presence—the man who had been both my greatest joy and deepest wound.

"I'll be there by your side tomorrow," he whispered, his voice firm yet gentle. "You deserve justice, Mariyam." His words hung in the air like a vow, and I nodded, pressing a kiss to his hands, a silent agreement between us.

Before I could respond or fully absorb the depth of his words, a sudden, sharp knock echoed through the room, slicing through our fragile moment of solitude.

"DAD!" Aamon's voice boomed from the other side of the door, thick with frustration and urgency.

I pulled back, glancing at James with a raised brow. "What did you do?" I asked, suspicion creeping into my tone.

He shrugged, genuinely clueless, his eyes wide with surprise. "I have no idea," he muttered, a mixture of worry and exasperation flickering across his face as he glanced towards the door.

"Yes! Hi, champ," James greeted with a sheepish smile as he cracked the door open, revealing Aaron and Aamon standing there, both looking slightly annoyed.

"Hi, Dad," Aamon said, his jaw clenched and his expression a mix of curiosity and suspicion.

"Umm... yes?" James chuckled nervously, sensing the tension. Aamon lifted a stiletto heel, holding it up like it was evidence in a courtroom.

"We found this heel! Are you cheating?" Aaron blurted out, his eyes narrowing.

"On Mom! You said you were going to try to win her back—" Aamon cut in, his words overlapping with Aaron's as they both tried to voice their outrage.

Before things could escalate further, I stepped forward and placed a hand on James's shoulder. Aaron and Aamon's jaws dropped simultaneously, eyes widening as they finally noticed me standing behind their father.

"Ohhh..." they both murmured, their voices harmonizing in a stunned realization.

I glanced down at the heel in Aamon's hand and sighed. "That's mine," I clarified, raising an eyebrow at their startled expressions.

The brothers exchanged a look, a mix of embarrassment and relief washing over their faces. "Umm... yeah, we thought... never mind," Aamon mumbled, turning on his heel and dragging Aaron along with him. As soon as they reached the kitchen, I could hear them burst into a fit of laughter, their tension dissolving into humor.

"Your kids are weird," I remarked, turning back to James, who was doing his best to stifle a laugh.

"Yours," he countered, pointing at me with a playful grin.

"Oh, no," I shot back. "They are your buns! I just baked them for you." We exchanged a moment of incredulity before bursting into laughter.

James could barely contain his laughter, his shoulders shaking as he leaned against the doorframe for support. "Buns? Really, Mariyam?" he managed to gasp out between fits of laughter, his eyes sparkling with amusement. "What kind of bakery are you running down there?"

"Only the finest bakery in town," I shot back, trying to keep a straight face but failing miserably. "Freshly baked buns, made with love and a dash of chaos."

James laughed, a deep, hearty sound that echoed through the room and filled it with a warmth I hadn't felt in a long time. It was infectious, and soon, I found myself giggling along with him. It was a strange, almost surreal moment—standing in his penthouse, laughing about 'buns' after all the tension and the heaviness that had hung between us just minutes earlier.

"Well, I suppose I should be grateful for that," James finally said, wiping a tear of laughter from his eye. "After all, where else would I get such... exquisite craftsmanship?"

"Exquisite craftsmanship?" I repeated, shaking my head as I bit back a smile. "Now who's the one running a bakery metaphor into the ground?"

James chuckled, his eyes twinkling with mischief. "Touché," he conceded, raising his hands in mock surrender. "But hey, it's good to see you smile like that, even if it's over something ridiculous."

I nodded, feeling a genuine warmth spread through me. "Yeah," I agreed softly, my smile lingering. "It is."

For a moment, we simply stood there, holding hands and gazing at each other, the world outside the room fading into the background. It was as if time had stopped, allowing us a brief respite from the chaos and uncertainty that awaited us.

But the sound of Aaron and Aamon's continued laughter from the kitchen brought us back to reality, and I couldn't help but smile at the absurdity of the situation. "We should probably go see what those two are up to before they start causing any real trouble," I suggested, giving James's hand a gentle tug.

He nodded, a grin tugging at the corners of his lips as he followed me toward the kitchen. "Yeah, let's go check on our little buns," he teased, earning an exasperated eye roll from me.

As we walked into the kitchen, we found Aaron and Aamon sitting at the table, their laughter subsiding into amused chuckles as they saw us enter. They exchanged a quick glance, and I could see the mischief dancing in their eyes.

"Hey, Mom, Dad," Aaron greeted, trying to sound nonchalant but failing miserably as a grin broke across his face. "We were just... you know, making sure everything's... under control."

"Uh-huh," I replied, raising an eyebrow as I crossed my arms over my chest. "And what exactly did you think needed 'controlling'?"

""Listen to the first wonky pancake talking!" Aaron shot back, and this time I couldn't hold it in—I sprayed water on James as I burst into laughter. I gasped as the water splashed onto James, his expression shifting from surprise to amused acceptance in an instant. He wiped his face with the back of his hand, a grin spreading across his lips. "Well, that's one way to cool things down," he quipped, grabbing a towel from the counter to dry off. "Aren't you getting a bit too comfortable around here, Mrs. James Arthur Cross?" he teased, his tone playful.

I rolled my eyes affectionately. "It's Mrs. Juan Heinrich Ramirez, thank you very much," I shot back. But before I could step away, James pulled me back against his chest, my back pressing into him as his arms encircled me. My breath hitched, heart racing at the unexpected closeness.

"Well, I gotta say, he's still got his prime," Aamon remarked to Aaron with a knowing nod, his tone half-serious, half-mocking.

Aaron snorted. "Yeah, he's definitely not lost his touch," he added, his eyes gleaming with mischief as he leaned back against the kitchen counter, arms crossed.

I turned slightly to catch a glimpse of James's face, his expression a mix of amusement and that familiar smirk that always made my heart skip a beat. His hold on me tightened, his lips hovering near my ear. "See? Even the kids agree," he murmured, his voice low, sending a shiver down my spine. "I've still got it."

I lingered in his embrace for just a moment longer, savoring the warmth of his body against mine, the steady rise and fall of his chest as he breathed. It was a sensation I had missed, a connection that felt like a lifeline in the midst of the storm that had become our lives. But as much as I wanted to stay lost in this moment, reality beckoned, tugging at the edges of my consciousness.

James must have sensed my hesitation because he loosened his grip just enough to let me turn around and face him. His dark eyes searched mine, a silent question lingering there—one I wasn't ready to answer. Not yet.

"We should probably focus on dinner," I said, my voice soft but steady. It was a gentle reminder that life went on, that despite the gravity of what lay ahead, the mundane still demanded our attention.

He nodded, a faint smile tugging at his lips, though I could see the flicker of disappointment in his eyes. "Right," he agreed, releasing me with a tender squeeze of my hand. "But this conversation isn't over."

I offered a small nod in return, a silent promise that we would revisit this, even if the timing wasn't quite right. The truth was, there were too many unresolved feelings between us—emotions that couldn't simply be tucked away or ignored. But for now, we both needed a moment of normalcy, a reprieve from the emotional intensity that had been brewing between us.

As we moved into the kitchen, the boys were still grinning, their earlier tension replaced by the easy camaraderie that often defined their relationship. Aaron was leaning against the counter, a smirk playing on his lips as he watched Aamon rummage through the refrigerator.

"So, what's for dinner?" Aaron asked, glancing between James and me with a mischievous glint in his eyes. It was clear he wasn't just asking about food; there was an unspoken curiosity about what had transpired between us in the other room.

James chuckled, moving to stand beside Aaron and ruffling his hair affectionately. "How about we whip up something together?" he suggested, his tone light. "A team effort."

Aamon, who had pulled out a pack of chicken from the fridge, raised an eyebrow at his father. "You cooking, Dad? This I've got to see."

I couldn't help but laugh at Aamon's skepticism. "Don't worry, Aamon," I chimed in, "I'll supervise. We won't let your dad burn anything."

"Hey!" James protested, feigning offense as he grabbed an apron from a nearby hook and tossed it over his head. "I'll have you know I'm perfectly capable in the kitchen."

"Sure, you are," Aaron teased, crossing his arms over his chest. "Just don't burn the buns."

That last comment earned him a playful swat from James, who was clearly enjoying the banter. There was something comforting about this, about the way the four of us could slip into this easy rhythm despite everything that had happened. It was a reminder that, no matter how complicated our lives had become, there were still moments of laughter and lightness to be found.

We fell into a comfortable routine as we prepared dinner. James took charge of the chicken, seasoning it with a blend of spices that had me raising an impressed eyebrow. Aamon and Aaron worked on the side dishes, while I floated between them, offering advice and stepping in when needed. The kitchen buzzed with activity, the air filled with the mouthwatering aroma of sizzling food and the sound of clinking utensils.

At one point, James caught my eye across the kitchen, a small smile playing on his lips as he mouthed, *"Thank you."* It was a simple gesture, but it carried the weight of all the unspoken emotions between us. I returned his smile with one of my own, feeling a warmth spread through my chest that I hadn't felt in a long time.

As the sun dipped below the horizon, casting a soft, golden glow through the windows, we finally gathered around the dining table. The boys were still teasing each other, their laughter filling the room as we dug into the meal we had prepared together. It was a moment of peace, a brief respite from the storm that loomed just beyond the walls of James's penthouse.

But as much as I wanted to stay lost in this moment, I knew that tomorrow would come all too soon, bringing with it the weight of the past and the uncertainty of the future. For now, though, I allowed myself to enjoy this slice of normalcy, to cherish the sound of Aaron and Aamon's laughter, the warmth of James's presence beside me, and the simple joy of sharing a meal with the people who mattered most.

As we finished dinner and the boys began to clear the table, James reached out to take my hand, his touch gentle but firm. He didn't say anything, but the look in his eyes spoke volumes. It was a look that promised we would face whatever came next together, no matter how difficult it might be.

And as I squeezed his hand in return, I knew that, despite the uncertainty of the future, I wasn't alone. Not anymore.

Later that evening, we lay in bed, the room bathed in the soft, dim glow of a bedside lamp. The remnants of our earlier passion still hung in the air, a mix of warmth and exhaustion wrapping around us like a heavy, comforting blanket. James pressed a tender kiss to my forehead, his lips lingering for just a moment longer than usual, as if sealing an unspoken promise between us.

"James... what are we going to do?" I murmured, my voice barely above a whisper, as I rested my head against his chest. His heartbeat thudded steadily beneath my ear, a rhythm that felt both familiar and foreign after so many years apart.

His expression shifted, his brows knitting together in thought, a shadow crossing his features. "I know I have no right to ask you to leave him," he began, his voice low, laced with a mix of regret and sincerity. "Not after everything that's happened. But if it comes to that, if you choose this path with me, I'll be here. I'll be waiting, Mariyam. Always. But you don't have to decide anything right now. We can take it slow... keep meeting, spending time together." He tried to offer a smile, a tentative attempt to lighten the weight of his words, and I felt a pang of tenderness for him. I moved closer, wrapping my arms around him, my face buried in the curve of his neck.

"So, you're telling me to cheat on my husband with my ex-husband?" I teased softly; my breath warm against his skin. "How very scandalous of you, Cross."

He chuckled, a deep, rumbling sound that vibrated through his chest. "I'm just suggesting you spend some time with a guy who managed to give you two incredibly handsome kids," he countered, leaning down to kiss the top of my head.

I snorted, pulling back just enough to meet his gaze, my eyes narrowing playfully. "Oh please, they're just copies of you. I carried them for nine months, went through all the labor, and they come out looking exactly like you. How is that fair? You're terrible." I shook my head in mock frustration, then snuggled back into him, feeling his body relax beneath mine. "And I never even got a girl to dress up in cute frocks."

James's laughter filled the room again, the sound rich and genuine, dissolving the tension that had built between us. "Well, we could always try for that girl, you know," he suggested, his tone playful but with a glimmer of hope behind it. "Third time's the charm."

I drew back, giving him a mock glare, my lips twitching with amusement. "James Cross, are you seriously proposing we add to this already tangled family mess?" I asked, though my eyes betrayed the laughter I was holding back. "Remember, you promised me no more half measures."

His expression softened, his hand reaching up to tuck a loose strand of hair behind my ear. His touch was gentle, his fingers lingering for a moment longer than necessary. "I'm just saying, anything is possible when we're together," he murmured, his voice softening with sincerity. "But for now, let's focus on us—on healing, on finding our way back to each other. No pressure for anything more."

His words, spoken with such earnestness and understanding, resonated deeply within me. I felt a sense of calm settle over me, like the first rays of dawn breaking through a long, dark night. "That sounds perfect," I agreed quietly, my voice steady. "Let's take our time, find our rhythm again. Whatever happens, happens."

The room seemed to breathe with us, the soft hum of the city outside providing a distant, comforting soundtrack. The last light of the day had faded, replaced by the soft glow of twilight filtering through the sheer curtains, painting the walls with a delicate, muted palette of blues and purples.

"Come on," James said after a moment, his tone lighter as he slid out of bed and offered me his arm with that familiar, charming smile that had always made my heart flutter. "Let me walk you out. It's the least I can do after keeping you here so long."

I took his arm, and together we moved toward the door, the plush carpet soft under our bare feet. The hallway was dimly lit, shadows dancing along the walls as we walked, the silence between us filled with unspoken words and shared history. When we reached the door, he opened it for me, the cool evening breeze immediately brushing against my skin, a stark contrast to the warmth we'd left behind.

"Thank you, James," I said, standing on the threshold, the city lights beginning to twinkle beneath the darkening sky. "For everything today. It's given me a lot to think about."

His face softened, his eyes locking onto mine with a depth that made my heart ache. "Anything you need, anytime, just call me," he replied, his voice carrying an earnest weight. "And remember, I'm always here for you, Mariyam."

I nodded, touched by his unwavering commitment. "I know. And... I'll see you soon?"

"Soon," he echoed, his voice tinged with a mixture of hope and longing. "Take care, Mariyam."

I hesitated for a second, then added with a faint smile, "See you in court." It was a small attempt at levity, a reminder of the legal battle that loomed ahead of us.

James chuckled, though his smile didn't quite reach his eyes. "Court it is," he replied, a hint of seriousness creeping into his tone. "But let's hope it's the last place we have to reconnect."

As I stepped out into the cool night air, I felt the world shift back into focus, the reality of the situation settling around me like a heavy cloak. I paused on the sidewalk, glancing back one last time to see James standing there, framed in the doorway, his silhouette outlined by the warm glow from inside.

"Goodbye, James," I said softly, my voice barely audible over the distant hum of the city.

He nodded, his expression filled with a blend of sorrow and determination. "Goodbye, Mariyam."

And with that, I turned away, the cool night breeze carrying the scent of the city—exhaust, rain-soaked pavement, and a hint of something blooming somewhere far off. The path ahead was uncertain, but for the first time in a long while, I felt the stirrings of hope, fragile and new, but undeniably there.

The drive back home was steeped in silence, a heavy quiet that offered space for introspection. The streets of Manhattan flowed past in a haze of lights and shadows, each block mirroring the complexities entwining my life—twisting and turning like the labyrinthine grid of the city itself. As I neared the familiar building of our apartment, the weight of my dual existence pressed down on me. Here I was, returning to Juan—my husband and the man who had built a life with me—after a deeply emotional encounter with James, my ex-husband and the first man I ever truly loved.

When I entered the apartment, Juan was there, waiting, his posture tense but his expression warm with a mixture of concern and cautious inquiry. "Everything alright?" he asked, his eyes scanning mine, searching for any sign of what might be lying beneath the surface.

I managed a small smile, finding a strange comfort in his steady presence. "Yes, just a long day," I replied, my tone light, trying to keep the evening free from any unnecessary drama. We moved through our routine almost like actors on a stage—sharing a quiet dinner, discussing everyday things: work updates, snippets from the news, amusing little stories from our day. But underneath the casual conversation, a different layer existed—a quiet tension, an unspoken awareness of the unresolved issues that lingered between us, a shadowy presence in the room.

Later, as we settled in the living room, each nursing a glass of wine, I could feel Juan's gaze lingering on me with an intensity that caused me to pause. His eyes held a steady, piercing look, and I knew he could sense the turmoil within me. "Mariyam," he began softly, his voice carrying a calm strength, "if there's something you need to tell me, you can. Whatever it is, we'll face it together."

A pang of guilt tugged at me. I leaned against his chest, my heart heavy with conflicting emotions. "It's nothing, Jui," I lied, my voice almost a whisper. How could I possibly confess to him that I had spent the day with James, let alone that we had shared a moment that went beyond what should have been allowed? After everything Juan and I had been through, after all the efforts to rebuild what we had... I closed my eyes, choosing to stay silent, remembering James's words about taking things slowly, about seeing where things could go. I pressed closer to Juan, feeling the steady rise and fall of his breathing beneath me, and let myself drift into the fragile comfort of his embrace.

The next morning, the first rays of sunlight filtered through the curtains, casting a warm, golden glow over the room, illuminating the day ahead. As I prepared for the court hearing, I felt a subtle shift within—a sense of clarity and purpose emerging amidst the turmoil. Today's court date was more than just another legal formality regarding the custody arrangements for Aaron and Aamon. It was a pivotal moment, an opportunity to redefine the boundaries that had grown blurred and to make decisions that would carve the path forward.

Arriving at the courthouse, I spotted James already there, standing tall and composed, though his expression held a somber note. When our eyes met, there was no need for words; a silent exchange of understanding passed between us, a quiet promise of mutual support amidst the chaos. I glanced around to see Juan and Rudolf seated at the designated police desks, their expressions focused and ready. Across the room, James and Sofia's lawyers were positioned, preparing for the proceedings. My own attorney stood beside me, giving my hand a firm, reassuring squeeze as we waited for the judge to arrive.

The air was thick with anticipation, the tension almost palpable. Each person in the room was playing their part in a story far more complex than any of us had ever imagined, a story that had brought us all here today to seek some semblance of resolution—or perhaps, just a moment of clarity in the midst of so much uncertainty.

The courtroom was charged with an almost suffocating tension as everyone settled into their seats. The weight of the day's proceedings bore down on us all, filling the air with a palpable sense of anticipation. The room was a blend of muted colors—dark wood paneling, deep green leather seats, and the soft but unwavering glow of overhead lights that gave the space a heavy, almost oppressive atmosphere. My gaze drifted over to James, who sat a few rows away, his face set with a calm but resolute expression. When our eyes met, he offered a small, supportive nod, a silent gesture that steadied my nerves, even if only a little.

Juan sat a short distance from me, his posture upright, his eyes never leaving mine. His lips curved into a subtle, reassuring smile that seemed to say, "We're in this together." I wanted to draw comfort from that look, to let it soothe the storm of emotions within me, but the complexity of everything that had happened made it difficult to fully grasp the solace he was trying to offer.

The heavy oak doors swung open, and the judge entered with a measured stride, his robes flowing behind him like the dark shadow of justice itself. Instinctively, everyone rose, the sound of chairs scraping against the polished floor breaking the silence. "Please be seated," the judge commanded, his voice deep and authoritative. The room filled with a collective rustle as we all settled back into our seats, and the proceedings began without delay.

"Ms. Murphy, please approach the bench," the judge requested, his sharp gaze now fixed on my attorney. His tone suggested he had questions—likely about my unexpected presence today. The case before us involved the attempted homicide of none other than myself, stemming from the day I took that fateful fall from the Brooklyn Bridge. Until now, four months since the last hearing, I had been absent from court due to the amnesia that had clouded my memories and identity. My psychiatrist had advised against my involvement, warning that forcing memories to resurface could be harmful. But today was different. Over these past months, fragments of my past had returned to me, and with them, my reconnection with James had taken on a deeper, more urgent significance. Both James Cross and Sofia were here, their fates intertwined with mine, both facing charges under conditional evidence.

As Ms. Murphy made her way to the bench, the tension in the room thickened. She moved with a purposeful stride, a thick folder of documents in her hands, her face a mask of focus and determination. After a respectful nod to the judge, she began her argument for my presence.

"Your Honor," Ms. Murphy began, her voice strong and unwavering, "my client, Mrs. Mariyam Cross, has recently regained full recollection of the events surrounding the incident on the Brooklyn Bridge. In light of this, she is not only fit to participate in these proceedings, but her testimony is also essential to uncovering the truth and achieving a fair resolution."

The judge, a seasoned figure with silver hair and an unyielding gaze, leaned back slightly in his chair, listening intently. His eyes, sharp and discerning, flicked to me as Ms. Murphy spoke, nodding occasionally as he took meticulous notes. "I see," he said thoughtfully when she finished. His voice was deep and resonant, a calm yet commanding presence in the room. "Mrs. Cross, would you please stand?"

I rose slowly, feeling every eye in the courtroom turn toward me. The air felt heavy, the weight of expectation pressing down on me. My heart pounded, but I kept my chin up, my gaze steady. Across the room, I could feel James's eyes on me—his expression a mix of concern, encouragement, and something else I couldn't quite define. "Yes, Your Honor," I responded, my voice surprisingly firm despite the anxious fluttering in my chest.

"Do you understand the nature of today's proceedings, and are you prepared to participate fully?" the judge asked, his tone both stern and unexpectedly kind, as if trying to gauge my readiness for the ordeal ahead.

"Yes, Your Honor. I understand, and I am prepared," I replied, my voice carrying a new sense of resolve. A quiet determination began to settle over me, solidifying my decision to be here, to face whatever came next.

"Very well," the judge acknowledged with a measured nod. He then shifted his attention to the attorneys. "We will proceed with the testimonies. Mr. Cross, you are called first to the stand."

James stood slowly, his demeanor calm but serious. His lawyer gave him a reassuring pat on the back, a silent boost of confidence as he made his way to the witness stand. The room seemed to hold its breath, every creak of the wooden floorboards beneath his steps echoing in the silence. Once sworn in, James began his testimony.

His voice was steady, but there was an unmistakable tremor beneath the surface—a hint of the deep emotion simmering just beneath his composed exterior. He spoke with a careful, deliberate cadence, recounting the events of that day—the day that had shattered so many lives. His words were vivid and precise, painting a clear picture of the moments leading up to the incident. Yet, there was a weight to his account, each sentence carrying the burden of his pain, his regrets, and his hope for redemption.

"I left her on the bridge that night, thinking she was just upset and needed some time alone," James confessed, his voice steady but tinged with regret. His eyes flicked to mine for a brief moment, searching for something—understanding, forgiveness—before shifting back to the judge. "I never imagined she would jump. I never wanted any harm to come to her."

James's lawyer guided him through the sequence of events that followed that night, emphasizing the panic and desperation that gripped him when he realized I was missing. His words painted a picture of frantic phone calls, sleepless nights, and a relentless search—actions I knew all too well, having lived through the aftermath of that terrifying, confusing night myself.

When it was my turn to testify, a hush fell over the room, the kind of silence that stretched and amplified the pounding of my heart. The weight of the moment settled heavily on my shoulders as I took a deep breath, rising to face not only the judge but my past.

"Mrs. Mariyam James Cross, now Graxe Juan Ramirez, please recall the events from the beginning," my attorney, Caileen Murphy, prompted gently, giving me a small, encouraging smile. I nodded, my eyes shifting momentarily to my sons, Aamon and Aaron, who sat close by. They were watching me intently; their expressions calm yet supportive. Their reassuring smiles gave me the strength I needed, and I smiled back.

"Your Honor," I began, my voice initially uncertain but gaining strength as I spoke, "my husband and I faced challenges like any other couple. He's a great father, and I thought we were... fine, or so I believed, until the night of July 11, 2021. I was at our home in Beverly Hills when it came to my attention through a trusted source that James was seeing Sofia Vercillia. We had been married for 18 years, Your Honor, with two children—an 18-year-old and a 14-year-old. It was earth-shattering for me. But the source was credible. That night, when he returned home, I was already on edge. He mentioned we'd be leaving for New York for a charity gala scheduled for the evening of July 13th. I didn't want to go, but he insisted."

The courtroom seemed to shrink around me as I continued, the rows of seats, the heavy wooden benches, and the gallery blurred at the edges of my vision. All I could see was James, his jaw clenched tightly, his gaze locked on the judge as I spoke.

"On the night of the 13th, when we were in New York City at the Hotel Elysian Crown, we had a fight. It got ugly, but with the event looming and the kids excited, we kept things civil. The next day, while I was getting ready for the gala, we argued again. I told him I didn't want to attend because Miss Vercillia would be there, and that if he truly cared about us, he shouldn't attend either. But he wouldn't agree. He had a promotional campaign for his upcoming movie. After another heated argument, he left for the event around 8:30 PM. I had told him I would be heading to the Brooklyn Bridge to clear my head before he left, but he seemed... indifferent."

I glanced at James as I said this, watching the way his jaw tightened, his eyes narrowing slightly. The room felt like it was holding its breath, the tension thick enough to touch. I continued, my voice steady, though my hands trembled slightly at my sides.

"I sat on the Brooklyn Bridge until about 9 PM, lost in my thoughts—thinking about everything. Aamon and Aaron were back at the hotel, unaware of what was happening. I was spiraling, angry, hurt, and frustrated. Finally, I called him. I threatened to jump and said I'd post on social media, that I was doing it because of him, to destroy his career. We argued over the phone, and he eventually showed up on the bridge around 10 PM. We argued again. I was furious. I called him names, accused him of destroying our marriage, of not caring about our kids. I may have gone too far. I grabbed his collar and slapped him. He kept repeating that he'd ended things with Sofia, that it was all lies, but I wasn't thinking clearly. I was not planning to jump; I was trying to get his attention... or perhaps I wasn't even sure myself. We kept arguing, and then James left. He said he needed some air and had to get back to the gala because Morris Clark was calling him. He turned his back on me and walked away without a second glance. I shouted after him, but he didn't stop. I stood there for a few minutes and then decided to return to the hotel to be with our children."

I paused, taking a deep breath, feeling the weight of the memories press down on me like a heavy, damp blanket. I could see the judge's eyes fixed on me; his expression inscrutable yet focused.

"But before I could leave the bridge, I was confronted by Miss Vercillia. She was in an evening gown, probably for the gala. She approached me, but I had no interest in talking. After a few minutes, she started mocking me about her relationship with Mr. Cross, bragging about it, telling me to leave him—that it's what he wanted. She tossed pictures at me—photos of them on trips, some personal, some professional, I assume. I didn't want to see them. ward the forested shore of the Hudson, but she followed, taunting me. I snapped—I admit it. I turned back and pushed her first, slammed her face against a tree. She kept laughing, and I was losing control. Things became physical, and then she shoved me. I was right on the edge when she did. I stumbled back, lost my balance."

I could feel the courtroom holding its breath as I continued, my voice thick with emotion. "But that's not how I fell. I managed to steady myself just before I would have gone over. But as soon as I looked up, Miss Vercillia struck me on the forehead with an iron rod. I lost my footing and fell. I hit the rocks below. I was conscious for a while—I could see the cruiser lights from below, but I couldn't move or scream. I was bleeding. I was there for what felt like hours, and then, just before dawn, a flash flood came, and I was washed away... I don't remember much after that."

I glanced at Juan and his friends, pointing them out. "My husband, Lt. Juan Ramirez, along with Sheriff Rudolf Liam Merci and SWAT officer Malcolm Damon Wyatt, found me washed up in a canal later that day, around 3 PM. I was unconscious and was rushed to the ER. I was in a coma for six weeks, followed by nearly two years of amnesia. But, Alhamdulillah, I've made a full recovery... And that is the truth, Your Honor."

The courtroom was eerily silent as my testimony came to an end, my words hanging heavily in the air like a fog that refused to lift. The expressions on the faces of those present—judges, attorneys, onlookers—ranged from shock to sympathy, each one processing the gravity of what had been shared.

Judge Martinson, who had been jotting down notes throughout my testimony, finally looked up, his gaze piercing and thoughtful. "Thank you, Mrs. Ramirez, for your honesty and for sharing what must have been an incredibly painful and traumatic experience," he said, his voice carrying both respect and a quiet compassion that resonated through the room.

There was a brief pause as Judge Martinson reviewed his notes, his brow furrowed in concentration. Then, turning his attention to Sofia Vercillia's attorney, he gestured for him to speak. The attorney rose quickly, a sense of urgency in his movements. "Your Honor, my client, Ms. Vercillia, vehemently denies these allegations. She maintains that she was never at the Brooklyn Bridge that night and asserts she has witnesses to verify her presence at the gala continuously until midnight."

The attorney's statement sent a murmur rippling through the courtroom, a palpable wave of tension passing over the gathered crowd. Sofia sat motionless at the defense table; her face composed in a mask of neutrality. But her tightly clasped hands, white-knuckled in her lap, betrayed the anxiety simmering beneath her calm exterior.

"Very well," Judge Martinson acknowledged, nodding to Sofia's attorney. "We will hear from your witnesses shortly. However, first, we will allow Mr. Cross to respond to the testimony given by his former wife."

James, who had been listening closely, his face a complex mix of emotions, rose from his seat. His lawyer leaned in, whispering something to him while passing a document into his hand. James glanced at it, his expression solemn, and then gave a slight nod.

"Your Honor," James began, his voice steady, though a strain of emotion ran just beneath the surface, "I want to reiterate my deep regret for the events that led to the incident involving Mrs. Ramirez. While it is true that our marriage was under immense pressure from various misunderstandings and external factors, I want to make it clear that my relationship with Ms. Vercillia was strictly professional."

He paused, taking a slow breath to compose himself, his eyes briefly closing as if to push back a wave of conflicting emotions. "Regarding the night in question, I admit I left the bridge in a state of frustration and despair. However, I was unaware of any confrontation between Mariyam and Ms. Vercillia that might have taken place afterward. Learning about this now deeply troubles me, and I am horrified at the extent of the suffering Mariyam endured."

"That's a lie!" I burst out, unable to contain myself, my voice echoing in the hushed courtroom. Judge Martinson turned his stern gaze on me.

"Please wait for your turn, Mrs. Ramirez," he said firmly, his eyes locking with mine for a moment. I nodded, swallowing my frustration as I sat back down.

James's lawyer then proceeded to present a series of time-stamped photos from the gala, showing James present at various moments throughout the evening, clearly attempting to establish an alibi for the time I had claimed he had returned to the bridge.

Judge Martinson nodded thoughtfully, taking in the evidence. "Thank you, Mr. Cross. We'll now proceed with the witnesses. However, let's hear from Mrs. Ramirez again."

"Thank you, Your Honor," I began, rising to my feet again. "I apologize for my earlier outburst. I would like to present photographic evidence concerning the so-called 'professional relationship' between Mr. Cross and Ms. Vercillia. My old social media account, is still active, although I don't have access to it anymore. However, if I am permitted to use Mr. Cross's phone, which is a recognized device, I could log in and show the court the pictures. We can then discuss what sort of 'professional' relationship looks like this, because clearly either some are blind, or we're missing out." I rolled my eyes, and a few chuckles broke out in the courtroom.

"The pictures were shared with me by someone close to both of them," I continued. "That person prefers not to be dragged into this situation, but I can certainly show you the chat history between us."

The judge considered my request, his face impassive and unreadable. After a few moments, he nodded. "Proceed, but ensure that the proceedings remain respectful and focused on the facts," he instructed, his gaze sweeping across the room, immediately silencing the remaining murmurs.

I nodded in understanding and approached James, who handed over his phone with visible reluctance. I could feel his eyes on me as I logged into my old account, aware that the entire courtroom was watching, the tension so thick it was almost stifling. As I scrolled through the account, I located the incriminating photos that had been sent to me. I held up the phone so the judge could see, flipping through several images that showed James and Sofia in various intimate settings—pictures that were far from what would be expected of a strictly professional relationship.

"These photos were taken at times when both claimed to be on business trips or attending industry events," I explained, my voice steady even as the emotions roiled within me. "As you can see, the nature of their interactions suggests something much more personal."

James's lawyer tried to interject, but the judge waved him off, signaling for me to continue.

"I also have chat logs," I said, pulling up the messages that had come with the photos. I read aloud, "'You need to be careful, M. This isn't just a simple affair. They're serious.' This was sent by the person who took these photos—someone concerned about what was happening and the impact it would have on my family. And before Mr. Cross's or Ms. Vercillia's lawyers claim it's from some movie..." I added mockingly, "Was it from a movie that never got released? A director's cut that's still in editing?" Laughter broke out in the courtroom, and even Aaron snorted beside me, prompting me to bow my head slightly, suppressing a small, reluctant grin.

Judge Martinson raised his hand, and the laughter quickly faded under his stern gaze. "Thank you, Mrs. Ramirez. Please submit the phone to the clerk so the evidence can be officially recorded and examined," he instructed, his tone firm but fair.

I nodded, stepping forward to hand the phone over to the clerk, feeling a mix of vindication and nervous anticipation settling in my chest. The room seemed to breathe collectively, the tension rising once more as the judge prepared to move forward with the next phase of this complex and deeply personal trial.

My attorney rose, her presence commanding as she addressed the court with a voice that was both clear and resolute. "Your Honor, as evidenced by the testimonies and documentation presented, this case extends beyond a mere tragic accident. It reveals a pattern of deceit, emotional manipulation, and gross negligence that culminated in a series of events causing substantial harm to my client, Mrs. Graxe Ramirez."

She turned to face the courtroom, her eyes sweeping across the audience before locking onto the judge. "I request that Mr. James Arthur Cross be called to the witness stand for cross-examination," she continued. The judge nodded in assent, and James stood, adjusting his coat with a visible tension in his shoulders, before making his way to the witness box.

"Good morning, Mr. Cross," Caileen greeted him with a composed smile. James returned the greeting with a polite nod, his expression serious.

"Mr. Cross, let's begin with the basics of what happened on the night in question," Caileen said, her tone calm but with an undercurrent of sharp intent. She then tilted her head slightly, her gaze unwavering. "But actually, before that, let me ask you something more fundamental: Do you love your wife? You have repeatedly asserted in your statements, 'I love my wife, I ended things with Sofia, but she wouldn't believe me. I loved her, never wanted to hurt her.' So, Mr. Cross, do you love Mrs. Ramirez?"

James hesitated for a moment, his expression growing more somber as he gathered his thoughts, aware of the intensity with which the courtroom was watching him. "Yes, I do love her. I always have. The difficulties in our marriage never changed my feelings for Mariyam," he replied, his voice steady but carrying the weight of sincerity.

Caileen gave a small nod, her face remaining composed as she moved on with her line of questioning. "In your statement, you mentioned that you were at the gala and only left after receiving repeated calls from Mrs. Ramirez, which you initially ignored. Can you clarify why you chose to ignore these calls, especially considering the distressed state Mrs. Ramirez was in at that time?"

James exhaled deeply, a look of regret passing over his features. "It was a critical moment for my career, and I was under substantial pressure to remain at the event. Looking back, it was a grievous error in judgment. Mariyam was clearly upset, and I should have attended to her calls immediately. By the time I grasped the seriousness of the situation, it was too late."

Caileen's tone sharpened slightly, her gaze narrowing as she continued. "And when you finally arrived at the bridge after Mrs. Ramirez had threatened to jump, why did you decide to leave the scene without ensuring her safety?"

James's eyes dropped momentarily, his face tightening with the strain of recalling that night. "I was overwhelmed and, to be honest, frustrated by the continuous conflicts between us. I thought giving her some space might help diffuse the situation. It was a decision I deeply regret," he admitted, his voice low, laden with remorse.

Caileen leaned forward, her next question precise and cutting. "Mr. Cross, were you aware of Ms. Vercillia's actions after you left the bridge? Specifically, her confrontation with Mrs. Ramirez?"

James's face paled slightly at the mention of Sofia's actions. He hesitated, his eyes searching the room as if weighing the consequences of his answer. "No," he said finally, his voice tense. "I had no idea that Sofia would confront Mariyam, let alone that it would escalate in such a dangerous way."

Caileen didn't let up, her expression growing more intense. "But you were aware of Sofia's interest in you, were you not? And of the potential volatility of the situation, given the state of your marriage and Mrs. Ramirez's emotional state?"

James's lawyer shifted uncomfortably, sensing the mounting pressure, but James spoke up. "Yes, I was aware of Sofia's interest," he admitted reluctantly, "but I did not anticipate she would take it this far. I never wanted any of this to happen."

The room seemed to tighten around his words, every eye fixed on him. The tension was almost palpable, a courtroom full of people caught in the gravity of the unfolding revelations. Judge Martinson looked up from his notes, his expression stern but contemplative, assessing the weight of

James's statements against the evidence and testimonies already on record.

Caileen nodded thoughtfully, then pivoted her line of questioning, adopting a more assertive stance. "Mr. Cross, you claim you still love your wife and that you care deeply for your children. Yet, here you stand, denying that Ms. Vercillia had any motive to harm Mrs. Mariyam Cross—denying that she was upset about you ending your relationship with her in an attempt to save your marriage. You insist you love your wife, but your actions suggest otherwise. You're trying to paint her as a delusional, unstable person who imagined it all. So, Mr. Cross, do you truly love your wife, or—"

"Objection, Your Honor!" Sofia's attorney interjected, rising to his feet with urgency. "Ms. Murphy is badgering the witness and attempting to manipulate his testimony!"

"Overruled," Judge Martinson declared without hesitation, his gaze steady. "Ms. Murphy, you may proceed."

Caileen continued, her voice rising in intensity, her words charged with emotion. "Your wife and children deserve the truth, Mr. Cross. The mother of your children was pushed from a twenty-foot-high, forested shore of the Hudson River, landing on jagged rocks! Picture that—her spine fractured, partially paralyzed, unable to move or cry out, bleeding profusely, lying there terrified, wondering if she would die alone. No one to comfort her, to hold her hand. She was left to the elements, left for dead. She remained on those rocks for hours, clinging to life until a flash flood swept her into a canal where she was eventually found. This isn't some dramatic scene from a film, Mr. Cross; this was her reality. And where were you? The man she loved was nowhere to be seen. She deserves justice, James. You owe her the truth. How can you stand here, in this court, claiming she was delusional?"

As Caileen's voice escalated, she slammed her hand down on the wooden lectern for emphasis. The sharp crack echoed through the courtroom, and James visibly winced. She pressed on, relentless. "Did you, or did you not, have an extramarital affair with Ms. Vercillia?"

"Prove that you love your wife, Mr. Cross! Tell the truth!" Caileen leaned in, her words piercing through the silence like a blade.

"Your Honor, this is—" Sofia's lawyer tried to interject again, standing up in protest.

"I did," James said abruptly, cutting through the tension in the room. His voice was low but clear, and the courtroom seemed to freeze in that moment, every eye turning toward him.

Caileen allowed a small, knowing smile to cross her lips. "What did you say, Mr. Cross?" she asked, her tone firm but calm, pushing him to repeat his admission.

"I had an extramarital affair with Ms. Vercillia," James confirmed, his voice carrying a mixture of defeat and reluctant honesty.

With a satisfied nod, Caileen turned to the judge. "Your Honor, the witness has admitted to the affair. The defense may proceed with cross-examination if they wish." She then returned to her seat, her demeanor composed, leaving the courtroom buzzing with murmurs and shifting unease as the weight of the confession settled over everyone present.

"Your Honor, based on recent developments, it is evident that Mr. and Mrs. Cross have been seen together on multiple occasions. Clearly, they are reconnecting and now presenting a united front against my client, altering the narrative to fit their version of events!" Sofia's attorney, visibly rattled, spoke with his face flushed, struggling to maintain his composure.

Judge Martinson raised a hand, calling for order as the courtroom buzzed with murmurs following James's startling admission. His gaze fixed firmly on Sofia's attorney, his expression stern. "Counselor, please keep your arguments focused on the evidence and the charges at hand. Mrs. Ramirez's current relationship with Mr. Cross is not the subject of this trial. We are here to address the events of July 13th, 2021."

"Your Honor, this is clearly influencing the trial; they are clearly togeth—" he attempted to argue further.

"Overruled," Judge Martinson declared, striking his gavel firmly to silence the room.

Turning his attention back to Sofia's attorney, Judge Martinson's face hardened. "Continue with your defense, Counselor, but keep it relevant to the charges at hand."

Sofia's attorney, though visibly frustrated by the judge's rebuke, took a deep breath to regain his composure. After a quick, whispered exchange with Sofia, he addressed the courtroom. "Your Honor, my client, Ms. Vercillia, maintains her innocence. To substantiate this, I would like to call Mr. Aamon Cross to the stand."

I felt a jolt of anxiety as I realized the implications of what was happening.

"Objection, Your Honor," Caileen immediately stood up, her voice firm. "He is not on the witness list—"

"The evidence presented by the opposing counsel was not on the list either, Your Honor," Sofia's attorney countered, his voice rising in frustration.

"I object, Your Honor," James's attorney, Goldstein, chimed in, "Aamon Cross was not an adult at the time of these events—"

"He was only two months shy of 18, Your Honor!" Sofia's attorney shouted back, his tone growing more insistent.

"Overruled," Judge Martinson sighed, striking his gavel again to quiet the room. The tension was palpable as Aamon stood up, his expression a mix of nervousness and determination. He walked toward the witness stand, glancing briefly at me with a reassuring nod before being sworn in.

His presence added another layer of tension to the already charged atmosphere.

Sofia's attorney approached Aamon with a deliberate calmness, his eyes narrowing slightly. "Mr. Cross, can you please tell the court where you were on the night of July 13th, 2021?"

Aamon cleared his throat, his voice steady but his nerves visible in the slight tremble of his hands. "I was at the Hotel Elysian Crown with my brother, Aaron. We were waiting for our parents to return from the gala."

"And did you see your mother that night before she went to the bridge?" the attorney pressed further.

"No, I did not," Aamon replied, his tone firm. "The last time I saw my mom was before she and my dad supposedly left for the gala earlier that evening."

The attorney nodded, then shifted tactics. "Mr. Cross, were you aware of any difficulties in your parents' marriage around that time?"

Aamon hesitated, his discomfort evident in the way he fidgeted with his hands. "Yes, I was aware there were some tensions, but I didn't know the details. They tried to keep that from us."

"However, you overheard them fighting the night before, didn't you?" The attorney leaned in closer, pressing him, and Aamon nodded slowly.

"Mr. Cross, please recall what your father was yelling at your mother during that argument." The attorney's voice dripped with a smug confidence.

Aamon swallowed hard. "He said—" Aamon paused, his face tightening as if reliving the moment. "He said she was delusional, crazy, that he had nothing to do with Sofia, and that she should take her meds and stay out of his business." Aamon closed his eyes, his face reflecting the pain of the memory.

"What medication does she take, Mr. Cross?" the attorney pressed further, leaning in closer, sensing a moment of advantage.

"She has BPD," Aamon answered quietly, keeping his eyes shut, his voice filled with both reluctance and resignation.

"Thank you, Mr. Cross." The attorney turned back to the judge, seizing the moment. "Your Honor, it is clear—Mrs. Ramirez is delusional and unstable. Mr. Cross knows it. He is now changing his narrative to reconcile with his wife, aligning against my client to gain her favor. This is a charade, pure and simple!" Henkins, Sofia's attorney, argued passionately, his voice rising with each word, while Caileen and Goldstein exchanged tense, knowing glances, preparing for the next steps.

The courtroom crackled with tension in the wake of Henkins's allegations. A wave of murmurs swept through the audience—a mixture of disbelief and skepticism at the insinuations cast on Mariyam's mental stability.

Judge Martinson, sensing the mounting commotion, brought his gavel down with a sharp rap. "Order!" he commanded, his voice cutting through the noise like a blade. The room gradually fell into a begrudging silence, eyes flicking back to the judge. He fixed Henkins with a stern glare. "Counselor, be mindful of your accusations. This court is convened to uncover the truth, not to cast aspersions or inflame emotions with baseless conjecture."

"Your Honor," Henkins retorted, his face flushed with a mix of frustration and defiance, "I stand by my assertion. This is a farce. The opposing side is manipulating the court!"

Judge Martinson's patience was thinning, and he waved off the attorney with a firm hand. "We will proceed with the testimonies. Ms. Murphy, you may cross-examine the witness."

Caileen Murphy rose from her seat with measured composure. Her steps were confident as she approached Aamon, who sat rigidly, his eyes betraying a mixture of nerves and resolve. "Mr. Cross," she began, her voice steady yet probing, "you mentioned your mother has BPD. Are you aware of what that entails regarding her behavior and how it is managed?"

Aamon shifted slightly, squaring his shoulders. "Yes," he replied, his voice more assertive now. "She has borderline personality disorder. It means she can have intense emotions and fears of abandonment, but she's been in therapy for it as long as I can remember. It's well-managed with medication and therapy. She's not delusional or detached from reality."

Caileen nodded thoughtfully, her gaze sweeping over the jury and the audience. "Your Honor," she said, directing her words to Judge Martinson, "having BPD does not mean one is delusional or incapable of distinguishing truth from fiction. It is a recognized mental health condition, and many live productive lives with it, especially with appropriate treatment, as is the case with Mrs. Ramirez."

She returned her focus to Aamon, her expression sympathetic but firm. "Mr. Cross, on the night of the incident, did your mother appear particularly unstable or unable to grasp reality?"

Aamon's face tightened with determination. "No, not at all," he answered, his voice unwavering. "She was upset, yes—about the issues with Dad—but she was fully aware of what was happening. She wanted to clear her head, which is why she went to the bridge, not to jump."

"Thank you, Mr. Cross. No further questions." Caileen concluded, casting a satisfied glance toward her table as she returned to her seat.

Judge Martinson's gaze then shifted to Sofia's attorney. "Your witness, Counselor."

Henkins stood; his earlier bravado now slightly dampened by the exchange. "No further questions for this witness,

Your Honor," he said tersely, before adding, "We would like to call Ms. Sofia Vercillia to the stand."

All eyes turned to Sofia, who had been a silent observer until now. As she rose, her movements were deliberate, her face a mask of calm control, though her eyes flickered with an undercurrent of anxiety. She made her way to the witness stand, her composure seemingly unbreakable, yet those who looked closely might notice the slight tremor in her hands.

After being sworn in, Henkins wasted no time. "Ms. Vercillia, can you tell the court where you were on the night of July 13th, 2021?"

"I was at the gala the entire night," Sofia replied clearly, her voice steady but with an edge of rehearsed precision. "I did not leave until it ended, well after midnight."

"And did you have any interaction with Mrs. Ramirez that night or afterward?" Henkins continued; his tone almost coaxing.

"Absolutely not," Sofia responded sharply, her eyes narrowing slightly. "The accusations that I followed her to the bridge and then attacked her are entirely fabricated."

Henkins nodded, as if to lend weight to her words. "Your Honor, we have several witnesses from the gala who can attest to Ms. Vercillia's presence there throughout the evening. We submit their sworn affidavits to the court."

Judge Martinson accepted the documents with a nod. "These affidavits will be reviewed. Ms. Murphy, you may cross-examine."

Caileen stood, her steps slow and deliberate, a lioness preparing to circle her prey. "Ms. Vercillia," she began, her voice smooth but with an unmistakable undertone of challenge, "you claim to have been at the gala all night. How do you explain the photos and messages that suggest a relationship with Mr. Cross far closer than mere colleagues—a relationship that might motivate you to confront Mrs. Ramirez?"

A fleeting crack appeared in Sofia's carefully constructed facade. She stiffened, her eyes darting toward Henkins briefly before refocusing on Caileen. "Those photos were taken out of context," she said, her voice now edged with defensiveness. "James and I were friends, colleagues. Nothing more."

"But isn't it true," Caileen continued, her tone relentless, "that you and Mr. Cross traveled together, stayed in the same hotels, often without Mrs. Ramirez?" She held up copies of travel records and hotel bookings, letting them hang in the air like damning evidence.

Sofia hesitated, the color in her cheeks rising. "We were working on a project together. That's common in our industry."

"Yet," Caileen pressed on, "the messages between you two suggest a familiarity that extends well beyond professional boundaries. How do you explain that?"

"It was... flirtatious, I admit," Sofia conceded, her face now flushed with a mix of anger and embarrassment. "But it never crossed into anything physical."

Turning back to Judge Martinson, Caileen spoke with conviction. "Your Honor, the evidence suggests a pattern of behavior that corroborates Mrs. Ramirez's account. We ask that this be taken into consideration regarding Ms. Vercillia's credibility."

Judge Martinson nodded, making a notation in his ledger. "It will be. Anything further, Ms. Murphy?"

"Just one more question," Caileen said, her gaze piercing into Sofia. "If you were innocent of these allegations, why then, according to these messages, did you express concern about 'things going too far' and needing to 'fix' the situation?"

Sofia's composure finally began to crack. Her eyes darted nervously around the courtroom, and her breathing became shallow. "I was worried about the scandal," she stammered, "about how it might affect our careers. It was a moment of panic."

"Thank you, Ms. Vercillia. No further questions," Caileen concluded, her steps measured and her expression one of quiet triumph as she returned to her seat, leaving Sofia visibly shaken in her wake.

Judge Martinson, his face a canvas of impartial authority, leaned forward slightly. "Very well," he said, his voice steady but carrying a weight that pressed upon the room. "We will recess for today. Court will reconvene tomorrow morning at nine o'clock to continue with testimonies. Until then, you are all reminded of the sanctity of this courtroom and the seriousness of the matters at hand."

The gavel struck down once more, and the tension that had gripped the courtroom began to ease, though it lingered like a fog unwilling to lift. People began to stir—lawyers whispering urgently to their clients, spectators muttering amongst themselves, and reporters scribbling furiously in their notepads, eager to capture the day's revelations.

Caileen leaned back in her chair, her eyes still fixed on Sofia Vercillia, who had retreated to her seat, visibly rattled. A quiet sense of accomplishment settled over her. She knew she had cracked a fault line in Sofia's story, and now it was only a matter of widening it, of letting the truth spill forth for all to see. She exchanged a quick glance with James Cross, who sat rigid at the defense table, his face a mask of conflicting emotions—anger, fear, hope—all wrestling beneath the surface.

James's mind was a whirlwind. His thoughts were pulled in a thousand directions: Mariyam's face, Aamon's steady voice defending his mother, Aaron's quiet resolve as he watched from the gallery, and Sofia's faltering composure. He could feel the walls closing in, the once-clear lines of right and wrong now blurred in a haze of mistakes, regrets, and buried truths.

As the courtroom slowly emptied, Aamon approached his father. His expression was a mixture of fatigue and determination, his eyes searching James's for some semblance of reassurance. "Dad, we're getting closer," he said quietly, his voice firm despite the exhaustion lacing it.

James nodded, a tight, weary smile pulling at his lips. "I know. We just have to hold on a little longer."

Juan Heinrich Ramirez watched from across the room, his eyes never leaving James. A storm of emotions churned within him—his love for Mariyam, his hatred for the man who had held her heart before him, and his desperate need to protect her at any cost. He caught James's eye, and for a moment, there was a flicker of unspoken understanding between them—a truce born not of peace, but of necessity.

Across the courtroom, Sofia Vercillia remained seated, her hands clenched tightly in her lap. The carefully constructed facade she had worn throughout the trial was crumbling. She could feel the weight of every gaze, every whisper, as though they were daggers aimed at the truth she had buried deep inside. The truth that now clawed its way to the surface, threatening to tear apart everything she had fought to preserve.

Judge Martinson rose, signaling the final end to the day's proceedings. The bailiff called out, "All rise," and the crowd stood, the shuffle of feet and the murmur of voices filling the air as people began to file out.

As the heavy wooden doors of the courtroom swung shut, a palpable sense of anticipation hung in the air—a sense that the next day would bring them closer to the truth, closer to the final unraveling of the night on the bridge, and the secrets that still lingered in the shadows.

And in the midst of it all, Mariyam—Graxe—remained the unseen anchor to the storm, a woman caught between the life she lost and the life she had rebuilt, her fate hanging delicately in the balance of justice, truth, and the love of two men who could not let her go.

As the heavy wooden doors of the courtroom swung shut, the room seemed to exhale a collective breath, releasing the day's tension but not its weight. Conversations broke out in hushed tones, footsteps shuffled toward the exits, and the scent of sweat and stale coffee mingled in the confined air. Yet, beneath the surface of routine, an electric undercurrent pulsed—a sense that this was the calm before the storm, that tomorrow would be different.

There was no mistaking it. They were on the cusp of something final. This was the last act of a long, twisting play, where the curtains were set to be drawn one last time. One last time before everything laid bare. The final pieces were being moved into place, each testimony a stroke in a larger picture that was beginning to take shape, though its full meaning remained elusive, just out of reach.

The courtroom itself felt like a stage now, with its cast of characters—each playing their parts, each driven by their desires, fears, and unspoken truths. It was a stage where emotions ran high and the stakes even higher. Tomorrow, the final act would unfold. Tomorrow, the masks would drop, and what was hidden in shadows would be thrust into the unforgiving light.

James Cross stood by his sons, his heart pounding against his ribcage like a drum, a desperate rhythm underscoring his thoughts. He could feel the tension like a knot in his chest, a mixture of dread and longing—longing for answers, for absolution, for a future that felt increasingly out of his grasp. He glanced at Aamon and Aaron, seeing the determination in their eyes, a reflection of his own. Tomorrow, everything could change. Tomorrow, they would either find closure or face a deeper abyss.

Across the room, Juan Heinrich Ramirez watched James with eyes that burned with his own mix of emotions—anger, love, and a relentless drive to protect the woman he now called his wife. He understood that the final moment was approaching, that soon the truth would either destroy or vindicate them all. His hand tightened on the back of a chair; his knuckles white with tension. Tomorrow, they would all face the music.

And Sofia Vercillia, still seated at the witness stand, felt her carefully constructed world beginning to collapse. She knew that with the next sunrise, she would be forced to step back onto this stage, to stand under the harsh scrutiny of justice and reveal the truths she had tried so hard to bury. Her breath was shallow, her mind racing through possibilities, through strategies, through fears. Tomorrow would be the end—one way or another.

It was as if the courtroom itself held its breath, waiting for the final act to begin. The curtains would rise, and there would be no more rehearsals, no more lies. One last time, the truth would be performed in all its raw, untamed form. One last time before the world would finally learn what happened on that dark, stormy night.

That night when everything changed.

That Night On The Bridge.

CHAPTER 12

The morning sun broke over the courthouse, casting long, creeping shadows across its stone facade. The world outside was already awake and buzzing—reporters lining the steps, microphones poised, cameras flashing, all waiting to capture the final moments of a drama that had captivated everyone far beyond this small city. Inside, however, there was a different energy—a tense, almost suffocating stillness, as if the air itself knew the weight of what was about to unfold.

The courtroom filled quickly. Spectators filed into the benches with a mix of eagerness and apprehension, whispering among themselves as they settled in. The jury, too, took their seats with a solemn awareness. Some had dark circles under their eyes, betraying sleepless nights spent replaying testimonies and evidence in their minds. They had witnessed enough of human frailty, deceit, and desperation to last a lifetime, and yet, here they were—one last day, one last verdict.

James Cross sat at the defense table; his hands clasped tightly together. He looked around the room, taking in every face, every detail, every slight movement. The walls seemed closer today, the room smaller. Beside him, Aamon and Aaron sat with a united front, a silent, supportive presence that bolstered him. The weight of the past, of every choice, every regret, pressed down on him, and his heart hammered in his chest like a prisoner rattling his cage.

Aamon leaned over, his voice low but steady. "Stay calm, Dad. Whatever happens today, we face it together."

James nodded, though his jaw was tight. "Together," he echoed, his eyes shifting to the empty seat where Mariyam—Graxe—might have sat. The memory of her, the real her, was a ghost that haunted this room, and today, he needed to see that ghost laid to rest.

Across the room, Juan Heinrich Ramirez stood by his attorney, his face a mask of determination. His eyes never left James, never wavered. He was a man in love, but also a man ready to fight, ready to protect his wife and the life they had built from the ashes of a past neither had asked for. His heart was a battlefield, torn between the woman who had once been Mariyam and the woman he now knew as Graxe. Whatever truth came out today, he had already made his choice—he would stand by her, no matter what.

As Judge Martinson entered, the room rose in unison, the murmurs dying down to a hushed silence. The bailiff's voice echoed, "All rise," and the gravity of the moment settled in like a dense fog.

"Be seated," Judge Martinson instructed, his voice carrying the authority of someone who had presided over countless trials but sensed that this one was different. "We are here today to conclude the testimonies and reach a verdict. This is the final day of this trial, and I expect full decorum from everyone present."

He turned to the prosecution. "Ms. Murphy, are you ready to proceed?"

"Your Honor," Caileen began, her voice resonating with authority and precision, "while the case has moved beyond initial deliberations, I must draw the court's attention to a crucial piece of evidence. This evidence not only places Ms. Vercillia at the scene but also directly implicates her in a physical altercation with my client, Mrs. Ramirez."

The room fell into a hush as Caileen took a few steps toward the center of the courtroom. She held the gaze of each juror, her expression one of earnest determination. "Ladies and gentlemen of the jury," she continued, her tone measured and deliberate, "we have witnessed a series of compelling testimonies throughout this trial. We have reviewed evidence that, piece by piece, has begun to form a comprehensive narrative of the events that took place on the night of July 13th, 2021."

She paused, allowing her words to sink in, letting the gravity of the moment settle over the room. "However, there remains a single piece of evidence that has yet to receive the attention it warrants—a piece that is pivotal, one that unequivocally connects Ms. Sofia Vercillia to the events of that night and to the violent encounter involving my client."

With a deliberate motion, Caileen gestured toward the large screen behind her, where the courtroom lights dimmed and a video flickered to life. The grainy footage from the night in question began to play, capturing the audience's full attention.

"Direct your attention to the surveillance footage," Caileen instructed, her voice clear as she narrated the sequence of events unfolding on the screen. "You will observe Ms. Vercillia wearing a distinctive emerald droplet-shaped pendant on the red carpet at the gala—this is undisputed. Now, follow closely." She paused and zoomed in, enhancing the images on the screen to emphasize the pendant's unmistakable glimmer under the event's lights.

The atmosphere grew tense; the air was thick with anticipation as the courtroom focused on the screen, the seconds ticking by like a slow drumbeat.

"Notice," Caileen continued, her voice cutting through the silence with a sharp, unyielding edge, "Ms. Vercillia is seen wearing this same pendant throughout the event, verifying her presence at the gala that night."

The jury leaned forward, eyes narrowing with increased interest, their attention caught by the significance of this visual detail.

"But now," Caileen pressed, her voice rising with an undercurrent of intensity, "observe the footage after the alleged altercation between Ms. Vercillia and Mrs. Ramirez. You will note that the pendant, so visible before, is now conspicuously absent. It has vanished—just as Ms. Vercillia's claims of innocence seem to do under closer scrutiny."

A ripple of gasps spread through the courtroom, the sound like a wave cresting over rocks, as the realization began to dawn on those present. A palpable shift occurred; eyes darted between the screen and Ms. Vercillia, who sat rigid at the defense table, her expression tightening. From across the room, James's hands gripped the edge of the table, his knuckles white with the force of his grip, his breath held in anticipation.

"Where is the pendant now, Ms. Vercillia?" Caileen asked, a slight smile curling at the corner of her lips. "Did you perhaps lose it? Was it misplaced in the chaos of the evening?"

The silence that followed was thick enough to cut. Sofia's carefully maintained facade slipped for a brief moment—a flicker of doubt flashed across her eyes before she quickly recovered, sitting straighter, her expression stiffening.

"Objection, Your Honor," Henkins interjected, rising to his feet, a slight quiver of urgency in his voice. "Speculation. There is no concrete evidence linking the missing pendant to the alleged assault, nor any proof that my client had any involvement in its disappearance."

Judge Martinson held up a hand, his gaze firm, commanding silence. "Overruled," he said evenly. "The line of questioning is relevant. Ms. Murphy, you may proceed."

Caileen did not miss a beat. "Ms. Vercillia," she continued, her eyes locked onto Sofia's, "I ask you again: did you lose the pendant, or is there something you'd like to clarify about its disappearance?"

All eyes were on Sofia now—every gaze, every breath in the room seemed to converge on her, waiting for her next move. Judge Martinson leaned forward slightly, his stare penetrating, his patience thinning as the seconds stretched on.

The courtroom seemed to hold its breath, the tension mounting as Sofia's eyes dropped to the table. A heartbeat passed, then another, as if time itself had paused in anticipation.

Finally, Sofia lifted her head, her expression hardened, her voice steady despite the mounting pressure. "I did not lose the pendant," she stated, her tone holding firm. "It's possible it fell off during the chaos of the evening, but I had no part in its disappearance."

The courtroom remained silent, suspended in the weight of her words. Caileen's eyes never left Sofia, her lips pressing into a thin line, sensing the cracks beginning to form. She knew the stage was set for the final blow, for the truth that had been buried to surface at last.

"Objection, Your Honor," Henkins practically shouted, his voice rising with a mix of urgency and exasperation. "Similar jewelry items are common and not exclusive. This necklace could belong to anyone."

Caileen remained unfazed, her expression cool and collected as she turned toward the jury. "Of course, counsel," she replied smoothly, her tone almost patronizing. "But what the authorities failed to recognize that day was the uniqueness of this piece. This is not just any pendant; it's a photo locket with a distinctive emerald flap and an embedded photograph inside." She carefully opened the locket, revealing a small photograph of James Cross and Sofia Vercillia together. "This locket serves as a crucial link to Ms. Vercillia and Mr. Cross. Fingerprint analysis from forensic reports confirms its ownership. This was not a mere coincidence; it was a deliberate, calculated attempt on Mrs. Cross's life."

Henkins shifted uneasily, his fingers drumming against the table, his jaw clenched tightly. The courtroom was deathly silent, save for the rustle of someone shifting in their seat or the faint scribbling of a reporter's pen. Eyes darted between the evidence, Caileen, and Sofia, who was now visibly rattled, her face paling as her lips pressed into a tight line.

"Objection, Your Honor," Goldstein, James Cross's attorney, intervened, his tone more measured but strained under the pressure. "My client has expressed remorse and was manipulated by Ms. Vercillia. He admits negligence on his part regarding his responsibilities toward Mrs. Cross and their children. However, my client had no involvement in the attempted manslaughter, whether involuntary or premeditated."

James Cross sat rigid in his chair, his hands gripping the armrests tightly. His face, usually so composed, was etched with a mix of frustration and a flicker of guilt. He knew his lawyer was doing his best to distance him from the accusations, but he could feel the weight of every eye in the room on him, judging, accusing. His chest rose and fell in uneven breaths, his eyes darting briefly to his sons sitting in the gallery, their faces a mix of confusion and hurt.

Henkins, still visibly agitated, rolled his eyes and tugged at his tie, loosening it with an irritated sigh. "Your Honor, Mr. Cross is sixty-one, not sixteen," he muttered under his breath, the tension in the room palpable.

The air in the courtroom was thick with anticipation, a mix of anger, disbelief, and a thirst for truth. As the judge prepared to respond, the crowd seemed to lean in collectively, waiting for the next revelation that would either condemn or absolve the man who sat before them. The fate of James Cross—and perhaps Sofia Vercillia—hung delicately in the balance, the scales tipping precariously with each new piece of evidence.

Judge Martinson, his brow furrowed and eyes sharp, tapped his gavel gently but firmly, calling the courtroom back to order. The tension in the air was nearly suffocating, the crowd shifting restlessly in their seats. The gallery was filled with hushed murmurs, the collective breath of those who knew they were about to witness the climax of a case that had gripped everyone from the press to the casual observer.

"Order, please," Judge Martinson commanded, his voice cutting through the rising noise. He turned his attention to Caileen. "Ms. Murphy, you may proceed, but ensure your arguments remain tightly bound to the evidence presented."

Caileen nodded; her gaze unyielding. She stepped away from the evidence table, her heels clicking with a measured cadence against the polished wooden floor. Her eyes bore into Sofia Vercillia, who sat rigid, her posture unnaturally straight, her fingers twisting the hem of her sleeve as if she could unravel the fabric to escape. James Cross was beside her, his face a mask of stern concentration, yet the faint sheen of sweat on his brow betrayed the storm raging inside him.

"Ladies and gentlemen of the jury," Caileen began, her voice resonating with conviction, "the truth often comes in fragments, scattered pieces that, when put together, reveal a clear and damning picture. We've heard how this locket was cherished by Ms. Vercillia, how it suddenly vanished on a night fraught with chaos and violence. We've also seen the photographs—the ones that show Mrs. Cross holding this very locket when she was found unconscious, near death."

Caileen continued, stepping closer to the jury box. "This was not an act of randomness, but of intent. Mrs. Cross was a threat to Ms. Vercillia, a woman who saw an opportunity to eliminate that threat—one who believed she could manipulate Mr. Cross and twist the narrative to her advantage." She pointed toward the locket, still in the evidence bag, catching the light. "The locket is a key—a key to unraveling the lies and bringing justice to Mrs. Cross."

Sofia's composure finally cracked. Her lips quivered, and tears welled up in her eyes, but she bit down hard, refusing to let them fall. She had been so careful, so calculated, but now it felt as if everything was crumbling around her, the walls closing in with every word Caileen spoke.

The jury watched with rapt attention as Caileen turned back to them for her final statement. "You have seen the evidence. You have heard the testimonies. And now, it is up to you to decide. Decide whether this was a case of unfortunate negligence or a cold, calculated attempt to destroy lives. The truth has been laid before you. It is up to you to deliver justice."

With that, Caileen stepped back, her gaze unwavering, her expression resolute. The silence that followed was almost deafening as the judge turned to the jury. "The jury will now deliberate," Judge Martinson declared, his voice somber.

The jurors rose and filed out of the room, leaving behind an atmosphere thick with anticipation. The courtroom buzzed with hushed conversations, but James could hear nothing, his world narrowing down to the thundering beat of his heart. His eyes flicked to his sons again—Aaron's face pale, Aamon's stoic expression masking the turmoil beneath. The weight of his actions, the choices that had led them all here, pressed down on him like a crushing force.

Sofia's eyes were locked on the locket, her mind racing with a thousand thoughts, each one a desperate attempt to find a way out, to somehow undo the inevitable. But deep down, she knew the truth—she had gone too far, and now there was no turning back.

Judge Martinson, his brow furrowed and eyes sharp, tapped his gavel gently but firmly, calling the courtroom back to order. The tension in the air was nearly suffocating, the crowd shifting restlessly in their seats. The gallery was filled with hushed murmurs, the collective breath of those who knew they were about to witness the climax of a case that had gripped everyone from the press to the casual observer.

"Order, please," Judge Martinson commanded, his voice cutting through the rising noise. He turned his attention to Caileen. "Ms. Murphy, you may proceed, but ensure your arguments remain tightly bound to the evidence presented."

Caileen nodded; her gaze unyielding. She stepped away from the evidence table, her heels clicking with a measured cadence against the polished wooden floor. Her eyes bore into Sofia Vercillia, who sat rigid, her posture unnaturally straight, her fingers twisting the hem of her sleeve as if she could unravel the fabric to escape. James Cross was beside her, his face a mask of stern concentration, yet the faint sheen of sweat on his brow betrayed the storm raging inside him.

"Ladies and gentlemen of the jury," Caileen began, her voice resonating with conviction, "the truth often comes in fragments, scattered pieces that, when put together, reveal a clear and damning picture. We've heard how this locket was cherished by Ms. Vercillia, how it suddenly vanished on a night fraught with chaos and violence. We've also seen the photographs—the ones that show Mrs. Cross holding this very locket when she was found unconscious, near death."

Caileen continued, stepping closer to the jury box. "This was not an act of randomness, but of intent. Mrs. Cross was a threat to Ms. Vercillia, a woman who saw an opportunity to eliminate that threat—one who believed she could manipulate Mr. Cross and twist the narrative to her advantage." She pointed toward the locket, still in the evidence bag, catching the light. "The locket is a key—a key to unraveling the lies and bringing justice to Mrs. Cross."

Sofia's composure finally cracked. Her lips quivered, and tears welled up in her eyes, but she bit down hard, refusing to let them fall. She had been so careful, so calculated, but now it felt as if everything was crumbling around her, the walls closing in with every word Caileen spoke.

The jury watched with rapt attention as Caileen turned back to them for her final statement. "You have seen the evidence. You have heard the testimonies. And now, it is up to you to decide. Decide whether this was a case of unfortunate negligence or a cold, calculated attempt to destroy lives. The truth has been laid before you. It is up to you to deliver justice."

With that, Caileen stepped back, her gaze unwavering, her expression resolute. The silence that followed was almost deafening as the judge turned to the jury. "The jury will now deliberate," Judge Martinson declared, his voice somber.

The jurors rose and filed out of the room, leaving behind an atmosphere thick with anticipation. The courtroom buzzed with hushed conversations, but James could hear nothing, his world narrowing down to the thundering beat of his heart. His eyes flicked to his sons again—Aaron's face pale, Aamon's stoic expression masking the turmoil beneath. The weight of his actions, the choices that had led them all here, pressed down on him like a crushing force.

Sofia's eyes were locked on the locket, her mind racing with a thousand thoughts, each one a desperate attempt to find a way out, to somehow undo the inevitable. But deep down, she knew the truth—she had gone too far, and now there was no turning back.

As the jurors filed out, the courtroom remained in a tense standstill, every breath a whisper, every movement a tremor in the charged air. The gallery, filled with both strangers and those who had long been invested in the lives intertwined by this trial, waited with bated breath. James Cross sat unmoving, his eyes distant and unfocused, his mind playing back each second of the past few months, every mistake, every regret, and every fleeting moment of hope.

Across from him, Graxe—Mariyam—watched quietly, her face a study in calmness. She had fought her own battles to reclaim her identity, to reconcile the fractured pieces of her memory, and now, here she was, standing on the precipice of closure. She glanced at Aaron, who stood beside her, clutching his Tablet, his eyes darting between his father and his mother. Aamon, in contrast, sat beside James, his hand resting on his father's arm, as if anchoring him to reality.

Judge Martinson glanced at the clock on the wall, its ticking the only sound cutting through the silence. "The court is in recess until the jury returns with a verdict," he announced, striking the gavel. The sound reverberated like a final, somber note, underscoring the gravity of the moment.

The courtroom began to stir. Reporters and spectators leaned in to exchange whispers, while others stretched their legs or made their way to the hallway. Sofia remained rooted in her seat, her eyes hollow, staring ahead but seeing nothing. Her world had shrunk to a single, unbearable moment—the waiting, the uncertainty, the fear that the jury would see through her carefully constructed facade.

James felt Aamon's hand tighten on his arm. His son's touch was grounding, yet it felt like a tether to everything that had gone wrong. He hadn't intended for any of this to happen—at least, that's what he kept telling himself. But the choices, the alliances, and the secrets had created a web so tangled that even his best intentions had become lost in it.

Aaron, on the other hand, seemed to be in constant motion, his fingers dancing nervously over his Tablet's screen. Graxe noticed his restlessness and placed a gentle hand on his shoulder, her presence steadying him. "It's going to be okay," she whispered, her voice carrying a calm that belied the storm swirling in her mind. Aaron nodded, but his eyes betrayed the anxiety gripping him.

Juan stood on the opposite side of the room; his eyes fixed on Graxe. His heart ached with a mixture of love and worry. She was so close, yet a world away, surrounded by the people she once knew but who now felt like strangers. He hadn't imagined his life becoming so complicated when he found her that day by the river. He had just wanted to help a lost soul, to give her a new beginning. He had never expected to find himself in the middle of such a twisted saga.

Rudi and Malcom lingered near the back of the room, their eyes constantly scanning for any signs of trouble. They had been drawn into this drama through their friendship with Juan, and now they were as invested in the outcome as anyone else. Both men exchanged a glance; the weight of everything that had transpired was written clearly on their faces.

"Jui?" I called softly to Juan, who crossed the room in a few quick strides to stand beside me.

"Sí, amor," he responded, trying to read the reason behind my call. I just shook my head and rested my face against his chest.

"I want to sleep," I murmured, though I wasn't entirely sure why.

"Sleep?" he echoed with a light chuckle at my unexpected request, and I nodded.

"I'm sorry, Juan... Lo siento, Por favor," I whispered, my voice trembling with the weight of my words. "I've caused you so much trouble, haven't I? You thought you were saving someone from the river, but did you ever consider that perhaps I was the one who pulled you into its depths instead?"

Juan's expression softened, his dark eyes searching mine as he cupped my face gently in his hands. "Mi Corazón," he murmured, his voice tender and filled with emotion, "I would dive into that river a thousand times if it meant finding you. You haven't pulled me into anything I didn't choose. You've given me more than I ever thought possible."

Tears welled up in my eyes, but they were not just tears of sadness. They were tears of gratitude, of love, of an overwhelming realization that this man had willingly become a part of my turmoil, not out of obligation, but out of genuine care.

"I don't deserve you," I whispered, the words almost lost in the space between us.

He shook his head, a soft smile playing on his lips. "Deserve has nothing to do with it, mi Corazón. We're in this together, no matter what comes."

I leaned into him, feeling the steady beat of his heart against my cheek. It was a sound that brought comfort in the midst of chaos. For a moment, the world outside faded away, leaving just the two of us in a cocoon of quiet understanding.

"I'm so tired, Juan," I confessed, my voice barely more than a breath.

"Then rest, amor," he whispered back, pressing a gentle kiss to the top of my head. "I'll be right here when you wake."

"Why did you do it, Sofia?" I asked her, softly as she was staring at me. "I know it was not entirely you, I know how it feels to lose someone you love..., the feeling that they are slipping away, it makes you desperate... You loved James, don't you?" I smiled softly.

Sofia's eyes flickered, the mask of indifference wavering for a moment before slipping back into place. She tilted her head slightly, considering the question, her lips pressed into a thin line. The silence between us stretched thin like a thread about to snap. When she finally spoke, her voice was strained, almost brittle, as if carrying the weight of her own guilt and regret.

"Love?" she scoffed softly, though there was no real conviction in her tone. "Maybe once, in some twisted, misguided way. But it wasn't enough, was it? Nothing ever is."

I felt a pang of empathy, unexpected but undeniable. There was something in her eyes—a deep, hollow ache that mirrored the desperation I once felt standing on that bridge, on the brink of losing everything. "He didn't love you the way you needed, did he?" I asked gently, my words like a soft breeze that could either soothe or unsettle.

Sofia's jaw clenched, and for a moment, I thought she might lash out. Instead, her shoulders sagged slightly, and she looked away, her gaze distant, lost somewhere in the tangle of her own memories. "No," she murmured, almost inaudible, her voice carrying a tremor. "Not like he loved you."

A murmur swept through the courtroom, drawing the attention of the onlookers who had been watching our exchange with rapt attention. The air was thick with anticipation, like the charged stillness before a storm. James's face, lined with tension, softened just a fraction. His eyes, always so guarded, held a flicker of something akin to regret, or perhaps understanding.

"He was my everything," Sofia continued, her voice steadier now, but no less pained. "And I was his distraction. I knew that. I knew it from the beginning. But I thought if I could just... if I could just make him see me, really see me, then maybe he'd—"

"Choose you?" I finished for her, my voice soft, a mirror to the sadness in her eyes.

She nodded, her throat working as she swallowed back the tears threatening to spill. "But he never did. Even when you were gone, you were still there. In his thoughts, in his every word, his every action. And I—" Her voice broke, and she let out a shaky breath. "I couldn't stand it. I couldn't stand being second, being nothing."

"Sofia," I said, feeling the weight of the moment pressing down on us both. "We're all just trying to find someone who sees us, truly sees us. And sometimes, that search makes us do things we never imagined we were capable of."

Her eyes darted to mine, and for the first time, I saw something fragile there, something almost like a plea. "I didn't mean for any of this to happen," she confessed, her voice breaking into a whisper. "I just wanted him to see me. I didn't think—"

"That it would end like this?" I asked softly, my heart tightening in my chest. She shook her head, a tear slipping down her cheek.

I took a step closer, feeling Juan's steady presence behind me. "Maybe it's not too late," I continued gently. "Maybe this is your chance to make things right, to show that you're more than what's happened here. It's not just about what we've done, Sofia. It's about what we choose to do next."

For a moment, Sofia seemed to consider my words, her eyes searching mine as if trying to find an answer hidden there. Then, slowly, she nodded. "I... I don't know if I can undo what I've done," she said, her voice trembling with the weight of the truth. "But I don't want to hide anymore."

There was a pause, a fragile moment suspended in time, and then Judge Martinson re-entered the courtroom. The bailiff announced the jury's return, and the room fell into a hushed, tense silence once more. Sofia took a deep breath, straightening in her chair, her gaze steady but resigned. James, standing beside Aamon, gave her a long, inscrutable look. I felt Juan's hand slip into mine, a silent promise that no matter what came next, we would face it together.

The foreperson of the jury stood; a small white card held in her hand. "We, the jury, find the defendant..."

The rest of her words seemed to stretch out endlessly, a blur of sound and emotion. And in that heartbeat between judgment and fate, between the past we could not change and the future we could still shape, all I could think of was the life that lay ahead—the life that Juan and I, Aaron, Aamon, and perhaps even Sofia, could still choose to make, even in the shadow of everything that had been lost.

Whatever the verdict, this was not the end. It was, instead, another beginning.

The courtroom felt like the center of a gathering storm. The air was thick with tension, the kind that clung to the skin and made it difficult to breathe. Every face in the room was taut with anticipation, eyes fixed on the jury as they filed back in, their expressions carefully blank, revealing nothing of the decision they carried with them. Judge Martinson sat upright, his gaze steady and commanding as he took his place on the bench, waiting for the formality that would end this chapter of uncertainty.

"Will the defendant, Sofia Vercillia, please rise," the bailiff's voice rang out, firm yet almost reverent, as though he were announcing the arrival of fate itself. Sofia stood, her face drained of color, but her chin lifted, a small act of defiance against the enormity of the moment. James stood beside her, his face a mask of steely resolve, though his hands betrayed a slight tremor.

The foreperson of the jury—a woman in her fifties with a no-nonsense demeanor—took a breath and unfolded the small white card in her hands. The room seemed to hold its collective breath. "In the matter of The People vs. Sofia Vercillia," she began, her voice clear, steady, and carrying the weight of the decision that had been reached. "We, the jury, find the defendant, Sofia Vercillia, guilty of grave harm, attempted murder, and conspiracy to commit murder."

A ripple of sound spread through the courtroom—gasps, murmurs, and the shuffling of feet as some spectators leaned forward, drawn by the gravity of the words. Graxe felt her own breath hitch, her heart pounding in her chest. She squeezed Juan's hand, feeling his warmth and steadiness beside her. For all the chaos that had brought them here, there was something grounding about this moment—something almost final.

The judge nodded, his expression grave, his eyes like twin pools of shadow. "Ms. Vercillia," he addressed her directly, his tone heavy with authority and a hint of sorrow, "You have been found guilty of multiple charges. This court acknowledges the pain caused by your actions, and while the law must be served, there is a recognition here of the complexities and the human element involved in these events."

Sofia remained silent, her face stoic, but her eyes were glassy, filled with a mix of resignation and regret. She stood alone in that moment, despite being surrounded by so many. For the first time, her composure seemed to crack, and a single tear slipped down her cheek.

"Will the defendant, James Cross, please rise," the bailiff announced, shifting the weight of the room's attention. James took a deep breath and stood, his face tightened with a mixture of defiance and dread.

The foreperson continued, her voice steady, "In the matter of The People vs. James Cross, we, the jury, find the defendant, James Cross, guilty of neglect and obstruction of justice."

There was a murmur of surprise from the crowd, a few gasps breaking the otherwise tense silence. James's shoulders sagged just slightly, a small but telling sign of the weight that had settled on him. Aamon, standing beside him, clung tighter to his father's arm, his young face trying to grasp the enormity of the verdict. Aaron watched from across the room, his Tablet held limply in his hands, the screen dimming as his focus shifted entirely to the unfolding drama.

Judge Martinson leaned forward, his gaze encompassing both Sofia and James. "Ms. Vercillia, Mr. Cross," he began, his voice calm yet firm, "the law demands accountability for the actions that have led to this moment. Sofia Vercillia, for the charges of grave harm, attempted murder, and conspiracy to commit murder, this court sentences you to life imprisonment without the possibility of parole. You will be remanded to a maximum-security facility where you will serve your sentence."

Sofia's face seemed to drain of its last remnants of color. Her lips parted, but no words came out, only a shuddering breath. She closed her eyes for a moment, as if trying to absorb the weight of the words that had sealed her fate.

The judge then turned his attention to James. "Mr. Cross," he continued, "for the charges of neglect and obstruction of justice, this court sentences you to five years of incarceration, followed by two years of probation. It is the court's belief that, while your actions did not directly cause the events leading to Ms. Mariyam's fall, your failure to act in accordance with the law and your obstruction of the subsequent investigation have contributed significantly to the pain and confusion experienced by all parties involved."

James swallowed hard, his face a mask of conflicting emotions—relief mixed with a deep, pervasive guilt. His eyes flicked toward Graxe, and for a moment, their gazes met. His expression softened, a glimpse of the man who had once loved her so deeply, yet his eyes were clouded with the weight of his own culpability.

The judge's voice rang out one final time. "This court is adjourned," he announced, the gavel striking down with a finality that resonated through the room like the end of an era.

The courtroom erupted into movement. Reporters rushed to the doors, eager to relay the verdict to the waiting world outside. Spectators stood, talking amongst themselves in hushed, urgent tones. The tension that had bound the room seemed to break all at once, releasing a flood of emotions that had been held back for too long.

Graxe turned to Juan, her eyes still glistening with unshed tears. "It's over," she whispered, though she knew deep down that it was never truly over. This was merely a conclusion to one chapter, and the beginning of whatever came next. Juan nodded, pulling her closer, his embrace warm and reassuring.

"We're free, mi Corazón," he murmured softly, his lips brushing her forehead. "Free to start again, to live without these shadows hanging over us."

As Sofia was led away in handcuffs, she cast one last look back at Graxe. There was no malice in her gaze, only a tired acceptance, perhaps even a hint of gratitude for the opportunity to finally face her truth. For her, the prison walls might soon become a reality, but she had already been living in a different kind of confinement for far too long—a confinement of her own making.

James, on the other hand, lingered for a moment, his hand resting on Aamon's shoulder. Aaron approached cautiously, his eyes flicking between his father and brother, a silent question hanging in the air. "We'll be okay," James whispered, more to himself than to his sons. He reached out, tentatively placing a hand on Aaron's shoulder. The three of them stood there, bound by a fragile thread of what once was and what could still be.

As the crowd began to disperse, Morris, James's manager, approached quietly. He looked at James with a mixture of pity and resolve. "You're going to need a lot of help getting through this," he said, his tone more compassionate than before. James nodded, acknowledging the truth in his words.

"Yeah," James replied, his voice barely audible over the din of the courtroom. "But maybe it's time I start fixing things on my own."

Outside the courthouse, the sun had begun to set, casting long shadows across the ground. The air was thick with the smell of rain, the first drops beginning to fall, a prelude to a storm that seemed almost fitting. Graxe and Juan walked out hand in hand, their future uncertain, but for the first time in a long while, filled with hope.

Aaron and Aamon followed, their steps tentative but in sync. James trailed behind, his gaze fixed on the horizon, where the last light of the day was fading. Sofia was already gone, her path now separates, yet irrevocably intertwined with theirs in ways that would linger like ghosts in the years to come.

And as the rain began to fall in earnest, washing over the steps of the courthouse, it felt like a cleansing—a new beginning for all of them, forged in the aftermath of what had been lost and found on that night on the bridge.

The rain fell in torrents, each drop a tear from the heavens, soaking the ground and washing away the last remnants of the day. The courthouse loomed behind them, a monolith of judgment and consequence, yet as they stepped away from its shadow, it began to shrink in their minds, just another piece of the past that had shaped them but no longer defined them.

Graxe looked up at the sky, her face tilted to the storm as if she could absorb its fury, its cleansing power. The rain mingled with the tears she had held back for so long, and she felt something within her begin to crack, to shatter, and then, finally, to heal. She squeezed Juan's hand, the warmth of his touch grounding her even as the world seemed to dissolve into a blur of gray and water.

Juan turned to her, his eyes soft with a mixture of love and pain. "Mi Corazón," he whispered, his voice barely audible over the rain, "we made it. We're still here."

She nodded, but her voice caught in her throat. "We lost so much," she murmured, her words carried away on the wind. "But maybe... maybe we found something too."

He pulled her close, his arms wrapping around her as if he could shield her from everything that had ever hurt her. And in that moment, she realized he already had. He had been her anchor, her lifeline in a world that had tried to drown her, and she had clung to him, not because she was weak, but because he had given her the strength to survive.

The boys stood a few steps behind, their eyes wide as they watched their parents. Aaron, always the more sensitive of the two, wiped at his eyes with the back of his hand, the Tablet forgotten in the crook of his arm. Aamon, still too young to fully grasp the enormity of what had happened, but old enough to understand that something had shifted, reached out and took his brother's hand. They stood together, united in the way only brothers could be, a silent promise that they would face whatever came next as one.

James lingered on the steps, his heart heavy with the weight of all that had transpired. The rain soaked through his clothes, but he barely noticed. He was lost in thought, in memory, in the realization that he had been both the architect and the victim of his own downfall. He had loved Mariyam—Graxe—so fiercely, so desperately, that he had destroyed everything in his path to try and keep her. And in the end, he had lost her anyway.

He watched as Graxe leaned into Juan, her eyes closing as if she could shut out the world and just exist in this moment, in his arms. James felt a pang of something deep and raw in his chest, a sadness so profound it almost brought him to his knees. But beneath that sadness, there was a flicker of something else—something like hope. Not for a future with her, but for a future at all.

The rain pounded against the pavement, a relentless rhythm that seemed to echo the beat of his heart. And in that moment, James understood that this was his penance, his path to redemption. Not in the courtroom, not in the judgment passed down by others, but in the quiet, solitary journey he would now undertake to rebuild what he had torn apart.

Sofia was gone, taken away in a blur of sirens and flashing lights, her fate sealed by the choices she had made in the darkness of her own soul. James didn't know if he could forgive her—not yet, maybe not ever—but he understood her. And in understanding, there was the beginning of forgiveness.

The rain began to ease, the storm passing as quickly as it had arrived. The air was cool, fresh, carrying the scent of wet earth and new beginnings. Graxe opened her eyes, looking around at the world that had changed so much in the span of a few hours, a few days, a lifetime. She felt different, lighter, as if the storm had washed away the last of the fear, the doubt, the pain that had clung to her for so long.

She turned to Juan; her voice soft but steady. "Let's go home," she said, the words simple yet profound. And he nodded, understanding that home wasn't a place, but a feeling, a presence, the people you chose to stand by when everything else fell apart.

They began to walk, the four of them, side by side, through the rain-soaked streets that glistened like glass beneath the fading light. James watched them go, his heart aching with the knowledge that he would not follow, not now. But maybe, someday, he could find his own path, his own way back to something that resembled peace.

And as the night began to close in around them, the last vestiges of the storm giving way to the calm, there was a sense of something new in the air—a sense that, despite everything, there was still a future to be found, a future to be made.

For Graxe, for Juan, for the boys, and even for James, the journey was not over. But for now, they had weathered the storm. And in the quiet that followed, there was something almost like hope.

The bridge, the river, the courthouse—they were all behind them now, mere markers on the road they had traveled. Ahead lay something different, something unknown, but they would face it together. And that was enough.

And so, they walked, into the night, into the future, their steps sure, their hearts full, and their spirits unbroken. Whatever came next, they would meet it with open arms and a willingness to believe that even in the darkest moments, there was always the possibility of light.

The end.

THE LAST NOTE

Hello readers,

Confused? I thought you might be.

I know, I know—the last chapter felt like a conclusion. The perfect ending. But let's be honest—life isn't a fairytale, is it?

First and foremost, if you've reached this point, it means you've completed my novel.

Congratulations!

This story is incredibly close to my heart—perhaps more than you could imagine. My journey as a writer began in 2021, but to truly understand my path, let me take you back to the beginning of my struggles.

I was just like many of you—a bit of a brat, a teenager, a young adult with plenty of attitude and a carefree belief that nothing could possibly go wrong.

But life has a peculiar sense of humor, doesn't it? It knocks us down when we least expect it, and I was no exception. I crumbled, too. My mother was my rock, my only support system, and losing her to COVID was a devastating nightmare.

But it would be a lie to say that's when I started writing, or that grief alone sparked my interest. I've always been a storyteller at heart. In fact, my school labeled me 'Miss Storyteller' during my farewell—a title I found more than a bit embarrassing at the time.

Maybe losing Mum was the turning point. It was then that I truly found solace in my writing, and this novel became the result—a combination of my creativity and a therapeutic journal that kept me going, helping me find the strength to face just one more day.

The ending you just read in the previous chapter—that's the one everyone wanted, right? (Chuckles)

If only life were that simple.

But do you want to know what really happened?

I'll ask you again: do you?

Hmm... always the stubborn, fine, here...

"The courtroom felt like the center of a gathering storm. The air was thick with tension, the kind that clung to the skin and made it difficult to breathe. Every face in the room was taut with anticipation, eyes fixed on the jury as they filed back in, their expressions carefully blank, revealing nothing of the decision they carried with them. Judge Martinson sat upright, his gaze steady and commanding as he took his place on the bench, waiting for the formality that would end this chapter of uncertainty.

"Will the defendant, Sofia Vercillia, please rise," the bailiff's voice rang out, firm yet almost reverent, as though he were announcing the arrival of fate itself. Sofia stood, her face drained of color, but her chin lifted, a small act of defiance against the enormity of the moment. James stood beside her, his face a mask of steely resolve, though his hands betrayed a slight tremor.

The foreperson of the jury—a woman in her fifties with a no-nonsense demeanor—took a breath and unfolded the small white card in her hands. The room seemed to hold its collective breath. "In the matter of The People vs. Sofia Vercillia," she began, her voice clear, steady, and carrying the weight of the decision that had been reached. "We, the jury, find the defendant, Sofia Vercillia, guilty of grave harm, attempted murder, and conspiracy to commit murder."

A ripple of sound spread through the courtroom—gasps, murmurs, and the shuffling of feet as some spectators leaned forward, drawn by the gravity of the words. Graxe felt her own breath hitch, her heart pounding in her chest. She squeezed Juan's hand, feeling his warmth and steadiness beside her. For all the chaos that had brought them here, there was something grounding about this moment—something almost final.

The judge nodded, his expression grave, his eyes like twin pools of shadow. "Ms. Vercillia," he addressed her directly, his tone heavy with authority and a hint of sorrow, "You have been found guilty of multiple charges. This court acknowledges the pain caused by your actions, and while the law must be served, there is a recognition here of the complexities and the human element involved in these events."

Sofia remained silent, her face stoic, but her eyes were glassy, filled with a mix of resignation and regret. She stood alone in that moment, despite being surrounded by so many. For the first time, her composure seemed to crack, and a single tear slipped down her cheek.

"Will the defendant, James Cross, please rise," the bailiff announced, shifting the weight of the room's attention. James took a deep breath and stood, his face tightened with a mixture of defiance and dread.

The foreperson continued, her voice steady, "In the matter of The People vs. James Cross, we, the jury, find the defendant, James Cross, guilty of neglect and obstruction of justice."

There was a murmur of surprise from the crowd, a few gasps breaking the otherwise tense silence. James's shoulders sagged just slightly, a small but telling sign of the weight that had settled on him. Aamon, standing beside him, clung tighter to his father's arm, his young face trying to grasp the enormity of the verdict. Aaron watched from across the room, his Tablet held limply in his hands, the screen dimming as his focus shifted entirely to the unfolding drama.

Judge Martinson leaned forward, his gaze encompassing both Sofia and James. "Ms. Vercillia, Mr. Cross," he began, his voice calm yet firm, "the law demands accountability for the actions that have led to this moment. Sofia Vercillia, for the charges of grave harm, attempted murder, and conspiracy to commit murder, this court sentences you to life imprisonment without the possibility of parole. You will be remanded to a maximum-security facility where you will serve your sentence."

Sofia's face seemed to drain of its last remnants of color. Her lips parted, but no words came out, only a shuddering breath. She closed her eyes for a moment, as if trying to absorb the weight of the words that had sealed her fate.

The judge then turned his attention to James. "Mr. Cross," he continued, "for the charges of neglect and obstruction of justice, this court sentences you to five years of incarceration, followed by two years of probation. It is the court's belief that, while your actions did not directly cause the events leading to Ms. Mariyam's fall, your failure to act in accordance with the law and your obstruction of the subsequent investigation have contributed significantly to the pain and confusion experienced by all parties involved."

James swallowed hard, his face a mask of conflicting emotions—relief mixed with a deep, pervasive guilt. His eyes flicked toward Graxe, and for a moment, their gazes met. His expression softened, a glimpse of the man who had once loved her so deeply, yet his eyes were clouded with the weight of his own culpability.

The judge's voice rang out one final time. "This court is adj— "

"Ah, ah, ah! Hold on, readers. Up to this point, everything was the same... but then...

Right at this moment, something had changed!

Let me take you back.

The judge's voice rang out one final time. "This court is adj— "

"Your honour!" James's attorney interrupted his voice cutting the chaos. "We have a request."

The room froze. The judge's hand hovered over his gavel, eyes narrowing as they fixed on James's attorney. The murmur of the crowd swelled again, a low hum of confusion and curiosity rippling through the spectators. Graxe's heart began to pound anew, her breath catching in her throat. She glanced at Juan, who held her hand tighter, his brows furrowing with concern.

"Mr. Goldstein," Judge Martinson said, his tone laced with caution, "this is highly irregular. What is the nature of your request?"

James's attorney, a sharp, graying man, stepped forward, his movements purposeful yet measured. He knew the gravity of what he was about to say... "Your Honor, we respectfully submit a motion to annul the marriage between Lieutenant Juan Heinrich Ramirez and Mrs. Mariyam James Arthur Cross," Mr. Goldstein declared, his voice resonating through the courtroom. "Mrs. Cross, has been suffering from amnesia for almost the past two years—a period during which she entered into a marriage with Lt. Ramirez. This, however, occurred while she was still legally married to my client, Mr. James Cross. Under New York Domestic Relations Law, Section 6, concerning the prohibition of polygamy, this marriage is legally invalid. Furthermore, under California Family Code, Section 2201, which similarly addresses bigamy, this union must be declared null and void."

Goldstein paused, letting the weight of his words settle before continuing, "Additionally, we contend that Mrs. Cross, due to her compromised mental state and memory loss, was not capable of providing informed consent at the time of her second marriage. Her decision-making was undoubtedly impaired, guided by fragmented or nonexistent memories. As such, my client, Mr. Cross, petitions this court to formally dissolve the aforementioned marriage and to order individual and joint counseling sessions for both Mr. Cross and Mrs. Cross, as well as their children, Aamon and Aaron James Arthur Cross. This is in the best interest of all parties, particularly to ensure the welfare and emotional stability of the minor child involved." The courtroom fell into a stunned silence as Goldstein finished his argument. The atmosphere grew tense, the unexpected plea reverberating off the walls. Graxe felt a sudden jolt of confusion and betrayal. Her gaze flicked between James and Juan, searching for some explanation in their faces, while Juan's grip tightened around her hand, his heart hammering in his chest.

Judge Martinson's brow furrowed deeply as he considered the implications of the request. "Mr. Goldstein, this is a serious accusation and a significant request. I will need to see substantial evidence supporting the claim that Mrs. Cross was not in a sound state of mind when she entered into her marriage with Lieutenant Ramirez."

Goldstein nodded, pulling out a stack of documents. "Your Honor, we have here medical reports and expert testimonies indicating that Mrs. Cross was suffering from significant memory loss and psychological stress which could have impaired her decision-making capabilities."

Juan, who had remained composed until now, stood up. His voice was steady, but there was an undeniable edge of emotion as he addressed the judge. "Your Honor, I can assure you that Mariyam's decision to marry me was made in a moment of clarity and love. We have built a life together based on mutual respect and understanding, not on the vulnerabilities of her condition."

The judge nodded, signaling Juan to continue.

"Furthermore," Juan added, "our marriage has been a key factor in Mariyam's recovery. To dissolve it on these grounds would not only be legally questionable but also morally unjust."

"That's exactly what we demand, Your Honor. Legality. Morals have no place in a court of justice. Mr. Ramirez married Mrs. Cross under the impression she was entirely someone else. Mrs. Cross didn't even know her real name—they named her Graxe. While I understand Mr. Ramirez has provided her with a home and safety, a selfless act of love, we cannot deny the fact she was already married at the time of marrying Lt. Ramirez. Polygamy is prohibited as per the constitution." Goldstein stated, his tone firm and unwavering.

Judge Martinson listened intently to Goldstein's argument; his expression inscrutable. The courtroom held its breath, the air thick with tension as each word weighed heavily on the gathered crowd.

"Mr. Ramirez, do you have legal representation who might speak on your behalf?" Judge Martinson inquired, looking over at Juan.

"Yes, Your Honor. My attorney is here," Juan replied, gesturing towards a woman who stood up from the second row. She approached the bench confidently.

"Your Honor, my name is Eliza Cortez, representing Lieutenant Juan Heinrich Ramirez. While we acknowledge the legality of polygamy laws, it is essential to recognize the unique circumstances under which Lieutenant Ramirez and Mrs. Cross were married. Mrs. Cross, now known as Mrs. Ramirez, was believed to be an orphan at the time due to her presumed death. All legal documents, including a death certificate, were filed based on this belief, initiated by Mr. Cross's own admission that he believed her to be deceased after the incident," Eliza stated, laying out a folder filled with documents for the judge's review.

"That does not change the fact she is not Graxe. She is Mariyam James Arthur Cross, the wife of James Arthur Cross. Is she not? Her fingerprint matches the latter, so does her DNA. We request the honorable judge to uphold the constitution before any moral or emotional beliefs. Once the marriage is dissolved, Mrs. Cross can decide whether she wants to seek a divorce from Mr. Cross. However, as of now, the constitution is paramount."

"Your Honor, why should an innocent man suffer? He gave a home to Mrs. Ramirez. He took care of her expenses, medical and otherwise. He married her unaware of the whole drama. He wanted a simple life, and Mr. Goldstein is asking the court to snatch it away from him based on what—some written rules? A husband who left his wife to die on the bridge is appealing to the court for his rights against a husband who was her only shore when she stumbled, literally and metaphorically."

Judge Martinson raised his hand to still the courtroom, which had become a tumult of whispered discussions and shifting papers. He looked over the documents provided by both parties, his expression reflecting the gravity of the decisions at hand.

After a few moments of contemplation, he spoke, his voice clear and authoritative. "This is indeed a complex case with many emotional and legal intricacies. However, the law must guide our actions and decisions."

The judge paused, allowing his words to resonate in the tense atmosphere of the courtroom.

"Regarding the request for the dissolution of marriage between Lieutenant Ramirez and Mrs. Cross, I find myself in a difficult position. The circumstances under which this marriage occurred were highly unusual and tragic. However, the fact remains that Mrs. Cross was legally presumed dead at the time of her marriage to Lieutenant Ramirez—a marriage entered into under an alias and without full knowledge of her previous life and existing marital status."

He paused again, looking directly at Graxe, then at Juan, his gaze sympathetic yet resolute. "Therefore, regrettably, I must grant the dissolution of the marriage on the grounds of bigamy, despite the benevolent intentions behind it."

A murmur swept through the courtroom, and Graxe felt Juan's hand tighten around hers, a gesture of support and shared disappointment.

"However," Judge Martinson continued, his voice turning firmer, "this court recognizes the extraordinary circumstances that led to this situation. While the marriage between Lieutenant Ramirez and Mrs. Cross must be annulled in accordance with the law, this does not negate the profound emotional bond and life they have built together over the past two years. It is clear to this court that Lieutenant Ramirez acted in good faith and with the utmost care and affection for Mrs. Cross, believing her to be an entirely different person."

James's attorney, Goldstein, opened his mouth to protest, but the judge silenced him with a raised hand.

"Moreover," Judge Martinson said, "Mr. Goldstein, while you argue for the dissolution of this marriage on the grounds of bigamy, you have also requested joint counseling for Mr. Cross and Mrs. Cross along with their children. This request implies an acknowledgment of the complexities and traumas both parties have endured, especially Mrs. Cross, whose life has been upended by an incident she cannot even recall."

He shifted his gaze toward Graxe, whose eyes were wide with a mixture of shock and apprehension. "Mrs. Cross, it is this court's understanding that you were thrust into a life you could not remember, and you have sought to rebuild it in the best way you knew how. This court respects your autonomy and your right to make decisions regarding your future."

Judge Martinson then turned to Juan. "Lieutenant Ramirez, while your marriage to Mrs. Cross must be annulled, it is not a reflection of your commitment to her well-being. This court acknowledges your role in providing her stability, love, and care during an incredibly difficult period. It is also apparent that Mrs. Cross has relied on your support for her recovery."

The room was silent, every word hanging in the air like a suspended breath.

"Therefore, while I am compelled to dissolve the marriage under the law, I will not issue a mandate for joint counseling or any other forced intervention for Mrs. Cross and Mr. Cross at this time. Mrs. Cross shall have the autonomy to decide her next steps, including whether to file for a divorce from Mr. Cross or pursue her relationship with Lieutenant Ramirez. This matter will be entirely in her hands. Additionally, I order an immediate review of the circumstances surrounding her original presumed death to clarify any outstanding legal matters."

A surge of emotion rippled through the room. Graxe felt a rush of both relief and turmoil, a chaotic blend that left her trembling. Juan's grip on her hand remained firm, steadying her amidst the whirlwind of feelings.

James, who had been sitting in tense silence, leaned forward, his expression unreadable. His eyes locked onto Graxe's, searching for some unspoken answer, some hidden clue of what she might decide. For a moment, time seemed to stretch, every second dragging under the weight of anticipation.

The judge's voice broke the tension once more. "Court is adjourned," he said, his gavel coming down with a resounding crack. The decision was made.

The room erupted into a flurry of motion and sound as people stood, whispering to each other, reporters scribbling notes or speaking hurriedly into microphones. Graxe stayed seated, her mind spinning with the implications of the judge's ruling. She glanced at Juan, whose face, though calm, bore the marks of deep contemplation and concern.

"Graxe," he whispered, his voice steady but soft, "whatever happens next, know that my love for you doesn't change. We'll face it together, whatever you decide."

She nodded; her throat tight with unshed tears. She looked over to where James stood, his attorney beside him. He appeared both relieved and anxious, a man caught between victory and uncertainty. He gave her a small nod, an unspoken gesture of hope—or perhaps expectation.

And then there were Aamon and Aaron, her sons, standing on opposite sides of the courtroom, both looking at her with expressions that cut through her heart. They were torn between two worlds, two fathers, and a mother who was still trying to piece herself back together.

As the crowd began to disperse, Graxe realized that the hardest part was yet to come. She would have to choose not just between two men, but between two versions of herself—the woman she was, Mariyam James Arthur Cross, and the woman she had become, Graxe, reborn from the waters of the river with no memory and a heart stitched together anew.

"Let's go," she whispered to Juan, squeezing his hand one last time as they made their way through the throng of people. She needed time, space, and clarity to make a decision that would alter all their lives forever.

But one thing was certain: the bridge she stood on now was just as fragile and uncertain as the one she had fallen from years ago, and she would have to tread carefully to find her way to the other side.

"Mariyam, wait! I didn't mean to hurt you, I just wanted—" James called out, chasing after me as I started to leave. His voice trailed off, but I shook my head, cutting him off. "...a chance, I thought you wanted...."

"You never changed, did you, James?" I asked, my voice breaking. He looked down, then nodded—accepting or maybe just admitting the truth.

"I'll be filing for a divorce, James," I whispered. He nodded again. Today, he wasn't the confident James Arthur Cross. He was a man defeated, for the final time—a man destined to watch me walk away, fully aware he had no right to stop me.

I might still be alive, but his wife had died '*That Night On The Bridge.*'

That's how it ended, dear readers. (Sigh)

I'm sorry—I didn't mean to tug at your heartstrings like that. But, well... life isn't always fair, is it?

But wait, that's not it...

Come on, I am not that bad, there is more to it.

Would you like to hear it?

I knew you would, here...

"Jui..." I leaned against Juan's shoulder, feeling utterly shattered.

"Why do you look so down, amor?" Juan asked, his face unusually serene. He studied me for a moment, then a genuine smile spread across his lips.

"Why are you smiling? They just annulled our marriage, and you're happy about it?" I asked, bewildered, as he chuckled softly.

"Let them say what they want, amor! So, what do you think—Santorini or... Moscow?" he proposed with a mischievous grin. I tilted my head, still lost.

"For what?" I questioned, and he laughed at his own playfulness in such a serious moment.

"Vow renewal, perhaps? Or even better, a wedding?" he said, his eyes sparkling. I stared at him, speechless, before lunging into his arms, sending us both tumbling onto the soft grass in the courthouse garden.

"Will you marry me, Graxe—no, wait—Mariyam? Will you marry me, Mariyam?"

"When?" I laughed, and Juan's laughter followed, rolling us over in our embrace.

"Soon... very soon!" His laughter was warm, infectious—a stark contrast to the gravity that had filled the courtroom just minutes earlier. His arms held me close as we lay there on the grass, and for a moment, the chaos of the world seemed to vanish. It was just us—wrapped in love, relief, and the strange joy of a new beginning born from an ending.

A short distance away, James stood still watching us and then, He smiled—his lips curling in a rueful smile but a genuine smile. He understood what he once had, and he understood what he had lost.

He knew the road ahead was long and fraught.

But he also knew this: Juan would cherish her, protect her with his life, like he always had. And sometimes—just sometimes—love, true love, meant letting go.

And then he hummed, hummed again, the same hymn that had kept him alive....

"Only If I would have known,

Only If.... I would have known......"

You see, Dear, readers.

This was not an ending for them... but a beginning.

A beginning filled with possibilities, possibilities ... of could haves and should haves.

Possibilities that suggest, that maybe, just maybe, this novel won't be my last.

But some answers are better left blank, waiting for time to reveal them.

Until then?

Hasta La Vista.
With love,
Mariyam.

www.ingramcontent.com/pod-product-compliance
Lightning Source LLC
LaVergne TN
LVHW041219080526
838199LV00082B/798